# Copyright

Editor/Proofreader: Script Easer Editing/Shawna Gavas
Cover Design: Cover Me Darling (www.covermedarling.com)
Cover Photo Credit: Shutterstock
Formatting: CP Smith

D0365972

# The One

The cattiness.

The fights.

The shaming.

I don't generally watch reality television, but I definitely don't watch reality dating shows. Besides the fact that it's completely staged, it's a horrible depiction of people—women especially.

Women are pitted against each other to compete for the affection of a man they "fall in love" with after a week or two.

I call B.S.

It is complete crap.

So when my best friend, Koko, was hired as a makeup artist on the set of the most popular reality dating show, *The One*, I teased her mercilessly.

She told me that if I didn't stop teasing her, she would get me back.

And she did...

Which is how I ended up as a contestant on *The One*.

# Chapter 1

"What?" I screeched aloud in the empty room.

I reread the congratulatory letter stapled to the top of the confidentiality agreement and other contractual forms to be a contestant on *The One*. "This has got to be a joke. This has something to do with Koko."

Although I didn't let my best friend forget that she was working for a television program that set women back decades, I was so proud of Koko for following her dreams and landing a big time job on a network TV show.

*But what does that have to do with me?*

Putting my law degree to work, I carefully read each document addressed to me, starting with the one welcoming me to join the "most popular dating show on TV." With each line I read, I became uncomfortable.

*This almost looks real.*

When I finished, I tossed the stack of papers on the wooden coffee table and picked up my cell phone. Standing in the center of the rustic living room of my parents' Virginia home, I tapped my bare foot against the cold hardwood floor as I pushed the call button. With a hand propped on my hip, I waited for my call to be answered.

I glanced at the clock hanging over the crackling fireplace, calculating the time difference between Virginia and California. *It's only four o'clock over there so she should be—*

"Zoe!" My best friend's light airy voice chirped as she answered the phone. "Oh my God!"

"Kumiko Liane Green," I barked her full name, walking toward my childhood bedroom and closing the door behind me. I flipped on the light and the oceanic blue walls lit up. "This bullshit has your name written all over it."

The gasping sound of her laughter was infectious as my suspicions were confirmed.

"You ass!" I exclaimed, my smile taking the bite out of my words.

Koko laughed harder.

"This is not funny," I argued, stifling my own amusement. "I don't even watch reality TV so as soon as I saw *The One* in the first line of the letter, I knew your ass had something to do with it!"

My mass of curly hair flopped around my shoulders with each shake of my head.

"Two months after you are attached to the show, I get this mysterious paperwork in the mail. Tsk tsk. Your pranks are usually a little more elaborate. You have to step your game up, my friend. You're slipping," I teased.

She scoffed, her light voice cackled like an evil villain in a cartoon. "Remember when I first got the offer letter to work with Julia Jones on *The One* and you kept giving me shit?"

I smiled even though my eyes narrowed suspiciously. Standing by my desk, I let my fingers slide across the old leather bound book of poems by Pablo Neruda that I took everywhere.

"Yes," I replied slowly, before making a beeline to the oversized reading chair in the corner of the room. I tucked my legs underneath me as I got comfortable in the chair. "When my best friend gets hired to work with the Makeup Guru, we celebrate. Even if she'll be working with her on a show that highlights the death of the feminist movement."

We both chuckled.

"Do you remember how wasted we were when we celebrated?" Koko asked.

"We?" I laughed, shaking my head at the memory. "Do *you* remember that night at all? You were the one who got drunk."

"I was so drunk," she giggled again. "But do you remember how I kept saying that I was going to get you back once I was sober again?"

"Mm-hm. And the next day you told Ethan that I wanted to hook up with him."

"No..." She stretched the word out longer than necessary. "Well, yes, I did do that. But that wasn't to get you back; that was a favor. You need to keep Ethan interested and on your radar. He's a catch!"

I closed my eyes and groaned. "When are you going to let that go? Ethan is my boss and we are just friends."

Ignoring my protests, she continued, "So anyway, that was a favor, not retaliation. You're welcome."

"Ugh," I grunted in exasperation, throwing my arm up and kicking my legs out. "When I get back to Los Angeles, I'm going to fight you."

"So as I was saying, I knew exactly how to get you back for saying that I would be painting the faces of—."

"Of women who possibly have Stockholm Syndrome," I interrupted, finishing the statement with thinly veiled amusement. Unable to hold back, my head tilted upward and

3

a deep belly laugh erupted out of me. "That was funny. I crack myself up."

"It's still funny... which is why I had to come up with the perfect way to get you back."

I stared at my black tipped fingernails, focusing on a small chip I hadn't seen earlier. "Faking this letter and this paperwork is pretty good," I admitted begrudgingly.

"Wait, I haven't even told you the best part," Koko insisted between giggles.

"The best part? The best part was how good of a job you did with the legal jargon. Maybe you should've attended law school with me."

The line went silent as my words hung in the air.

*Shit. Here it comes.*

"Well...now that you brought it up, are you ready to talk about the bar yet?" Koko's tone shifted abruptly from flighty to serious, catching me off guard.

She wasn't talking about Breakers Bar, the bar in which I worked. She was talking about the California State Bar Exam, the exam in which I skipped.

I frowned, shaking my head even though she couldn't see me. "Nope."

Koko made a grumbling noise from the back of her throat. But it wasn't a judgmental noise. It was the noise she often made when she was struggling to hold her tongue.

I exhaled nosily in defeat as I slumped deeper into the chair. It wasn't that I didn't appreciate her concern, because I did.

"I just couldn't do it. It's—it's hard to explain." I lowered my voice so my mother couldn't hear me if she was walking around. "My mom is here and I haven't told my parents yet. But as soon as I get to the airport, I'll spill."

"Swear?"

"Swear. But you mentioned something about the best part?"

"Oh yes!" Her voice cracked before she broke into her gasping giggles. "The best part is that it's real!"

I felt my brows crease in confusion as a smile pulled at the corner of my lips. "What? I can barely understand you."

No matter what, the loud gasping screeches of Koko's laugh amused me without fail.

*Okay.* I pulled the phone from my ear with a rueful smile. *It's a decent prank, but it's not that funny.* I shook my head.

"Hello?" I called out, hoping to get her back on track. "What are you talking about?" My stomach plummeted when the realization hit me. "Did you steal this from work? Kumiko! I know I gave you shit about it, but this really is a great opportunity for your career. Don't get fired over this."

For whatever reason, my warning just made her gasps turn into a wheezing, choking sound.

I rolled my eyes, trying not to be amused by her. I bit the inside of my cheek to keep from laughing. "Koko."

"No, I didn't steal it. The letter is real!" She explained between pants as she calmed down.

I froze. The word 'real' echoed in my head as I struggled to pull what she meant from it. Part of me knew, but I needed confirmation. "Real? What do you mean it's real?"

"My goal was to submit a packet for you to be a contestant and then post the response letter up at Breakers to get everyone in on the joke. Just being on the set this early, I already know they send out 'thanks but no thanks' letters and confidentiality agreements. I should've waited for you to get back so I could've seen your face! But I had waited too long already for this day so I had the package forwarded to your parents' house as soon as it arrived here."

"So you're saying that the package is real?" I jumped out of the chair and marched out of the bedroom toward the living room. "No, no, no. You're bullshitting me right now. There's no way. The paperwork said that I passed the background check. There's no way it could've gone that far without…"

My sentence trailed off.

Over the course of our seven-year friendship, Koko and I told each other everything. We shared our L.A. apartment and we stored all of our personal information in the same safe. Koko knew almost everything about me. She could've easily filled out the necessary paperwork.

Gripping the thick stack of papers, I returned to the bedroom. The door closed with a louder bang than I anticipated. "You illegally accessed my personal information and forged documents in order to submit an application for me to compete on a show that I don't watch and don't believe in to get me back for joking on you?"

The question was met with immediate silence.

After thirty seconds, Koko cleared her throat. "Too far?"

"Hell yes!"

"Are you mad?"

"I'm mad that I'm now associated with this crappy show and there's a paper trail and electronic proof floating around. I'm mad that if I want to get elected to the Supreme Court, someone is going to pull out the list of applicants to *The One* and I will lose my bid because this clearly displays poor judgment."

"But are you mad?"

"Am I mad that you're a diabolical bitch? No."

I had to hand it to her. She waited two months for her prank to come full circle. That's a hell of a commitment.

"I wish I could've seen your face when you got the letter. I can almost visualize you noticing the title and then climbing on your soapbox about the sexist undertones of the show and then the shock of realizing that you applied to be on it. Are you going to write a strongly worded letter about the selection process?" Koko joked.

"Ha ha," I replied without any inflection in my voice. My eyes kept scanning the paperwork.

"Thousands of women enter and only twelve get selected to participate on the show. Well technically twenty-four but twelve are eliminated before the big cocktail party with the eligible bachelor. And there was less than a one percent chance that you'd get selected because of how many people apply so I felt like you were safe from actually being too attached to the show. They may not even keep it on file. I just wanted a letter or email that had your name and that you applied to be on *The One*."

"Like I said, diabolical." I looked at the congratulatory letter once more before dropping the stack of papers on the desk and pressing my fingertips into my forehead. "But there's just one little problem with your plan though."

"What's that?"

"I'm not going on this bullshit show and I'm going to burn all evidence that could link me to it."

"No!" Koko shouted, making my ear ring. "I've waited two months for this! I earned this Zoe Elise Jordan! And I heard that at the bottom of the letter, they actually say 'Our bachelor is looking for the one Zoe...and it's not you.' Please, please tell me it says that. Please."

I let out a puff of air. "That's not what mine says."

"What does it say?"

"Mine says 'our bachelor is looking for the one Zoe...is it you?' And then a hefty stack of papers asked me to give up my right to privacy and go parade around on this demeaning show so that I can compete against other women for the affection of a man I don't know."

7

"Wait, what?"

"I've been invited to be a contestant on the show," I clarified, running my free hand down my face. "I've been given a week to decide. Well, a week from when they mailed the packet."

"Oh. My. God!"

I pulled my phone away from my ear, but the damage to my eardrum was already done.

Her words became garbled and then she continued, "Are you going to do it? You have to do it! When do you have to get it back to them?"

Glancing down at the paperwork, I skimmed the paragraphs until I found what I was looking for. "Tomorrow. By close of business."

"You have to do it!"

I started pacing from one side of the room to the other. "I most certainly do not. That's a big hell to the no."

"I know you're not a risk taker, but just think about it. If you win, you get prize money. That prize money, depending on when you get sent home, would be more than enough to pay for us to go on a shopping spree or for us to go to every Beyoncé and Rihanna concert on the West Coast."

I stopped in my tracks, trying not to laugh. "So in this scenario, I, alone, whore myself out on TV and we, together, spend the earnings if I win?"

"Or if you don't like those suggestions, it would be more than enough money for you to reapply to take the bar exam."

My lips pursed. I walked right into that.

Before I could respond, she rushed on. "We would get to see each other all the time. I'm going to be there every day except Sundays. We can't go that long without talking! The location is incredible. You'd be staying in a mansion with a pool, a hot tub, a steam room and a relaxing place to read.

And, most importantly, the eligible bachelor is Julian Winters."

We were both quiet for a second. She was likely waiting for a reaction, but I was waiting for clarification.

"Julian Winters?" I asked, starting to pace again.

"Yes!"

My eyebrows came together, perplexed. I threw my hand up in the air. "Who the hell is that?"

"Julian Winters, the music producer."

As a music lover, I was still stumped. "I have no clue who he is or why you thought I'd care."

"Well, he's a song writer and a music producer and he's totally your type. He kind of looks like that Resident Assistant we had a crush on freshman year. And he was caught up in that copyright infringement lawsuit with that socialite, Janna White. I can't think of the song now."

"Ohhhh, yeah," I remembered, familiarity of the case and the names flooding my brain. "'Sweet'. That case ended her music career, didn't it? I loved that song. I vaguely remember that he was the one who wrote it, but they settled out of court, right?"

"Yes. But do you know what he looks like now?"

"No... I just remember being fascinated by the case because—"

"I'm going to go ahead and stop you right there," she interrupted, cutting me off mid-sentence. "We are not going to talk law right now. We are going to talk about you having the chance to bump uglies with Julian Winters. He is the—"

I frowned as I interjected, "The sheer fact that you said 'bump uglies' has disqualified you from giving me advice about anything in general, but sex specifically. You need to—"

A quick knock on the door followed by the sound of it being pushed open forced my sentence to end abruptly.

"Hi," my mother greeted me as she poked her head into the room. Her bronzy skin glowed with a youthfulness most fifty-five year old women didn't have. "Are you ready?"

I smiled and nodded.

"I'll meet you in the car," my mom whispered, closing the door behind her.

"I'm going to call you later. I'm about to head out with Mom before we meet Dad for dinner."

"Okay, but search the internet for pictures of Julian and text me your thoughts."

I chuckled to myself. "Will do."

Slipping my phone into my back pocket, I quickly put on my socks and boots. Grabbing my grey and blue college hoodie, I pulled it over the white t-shirt and checked myself out in the mirror.

Wearing a hoodie that dwarfed my C-cup breasts and a pair of jeans that I remembered looking better when I purchased them, I was a sad, cold version of myself. Although my face and hair were flawless, my outfit was questionable at best. But I pulled on my heavy down coat that I kept in Virginia for my visits home and trotted out to meet my mother. I may not have looked like the fashionista that I was in L.A., but the unpredictable Virginia weather put fashion on the backburner.

On the way to the car, I pulled out my phone and searched Julian Winters. My eyebrows flew up immediately when I saw the piercing, grey eyes, short, sexy beard, and endearing smile. There was even a hint of a tattoo peeking out from the sleeve of his t-shirt.

*That can't be him.*

I was expecting some boring, cookie-cutter, clean-cut guy. But based on the first few pictures, Julian Winters was the exact opposite of boring. Between his looks, his wardrobe, and his career choice, he was interesting. There weren't many photos of him looking directly at the camera. Most of the photos were of him writing or recording.

*Successful. Bearded. Tattooed. With an amazing smile.* I felt like I was checking off the top tier of my wish list. *He's definitely my type.*

"What's with the goofy grin?"

I looked up and my mother had rolled the window down. Opening the door to her BMW, I showed her the picture on my phone as soon as I slid into the seat.

"Nice." She nodded in appreciation. "New boyfriend?"

I made a face. "No. Just some guy."

"Mm hmm. Not the way you were just grinning."

I rolled my eyes and pursed my lips to keep from telling her about Koko's prank.

"Fine," she continued. "I'll leave it alone for now. There are more pressing issues." She gestured to my bundled up state before she backed out of the driveway. "It's a rather warm, early March night and you're dressed like we're going to a football game in the dead of winter. It's not that cold."

I looked at her purple pantsuit, multicolored scarf and black leather jacket. She looked warm, but fashionable.

"I'm a California girl now, Mom. Forty-five degrees might as well be sub-zero."

Mom and I laughed, joked and talked as we ran errands on our way to our favorite Italian restaurant to meet Dad. As she told me about the pro-bono case she took on for a small business, I found myself completely riveted.

"...because giving up is the first step toward failure," she concluded, using her favorite motivational line.

My stomach tied itself in a knot as I nodded in agreement.

*She's talking about her case. She's not talking about me,* I assured myself as she moved on to tell me about the items she ordered from Neiman Marcus.

Sometimes the line blurred where my mother ended and Elise Jordan the attorney began. My mom was a badass in the courtroom and in life. With her short black hair contrasting with her bronze complexion, she was beautiful. She dressed like she was going to a business meeting with a fashion company at all times. And although I was blessed with her skin tone, hair color, and shapely figure, my mother's beauty extended beyond her looks.

My mom was fearless. She was the smartest person I knew and a fantastic storyteller. She was the youngest person to make partner at her firm and the first woman. She did mission trips to change the world. She volunteered her time to feed the homeless. She advocated for women in the workplace. She was well-traveled and entertained me with stories about her adventures before she had my brother and me. I'd spent my entire life wanting to follow in her footsteps.

I felt incredibly relaxed as we pulled into the parking spot. For the first time since I arrived on Friday, she didn't ask me why I came home unexpectedly. She didn't try to pepper me with questions. Everything felt like it was finally back to normal. It was the best conversation we'd had all week.

"There's your father," Mom pointed out as soon as we walked through the front door.

Zachary Jordan II was sitting at a table near the front politely ignoring the flirtatious waitress. Even from across the room, I could tell by the hair flip and arched back that she was flirting.

It wasn't unusual for women to flirt with my father. He was a handsome man with an awesome wardrobe, courtesy of my mother. He regularly got complimented on his light brown eyes and long lashes, in which I was fortunate enough to inherit.

Besides the fact that he was a great father, what always resonated deeply with me was that the successful pharmacist made it clear that he only had eyes for my mother. And as if on cue, he looked up and spotted her. His grin stretched from ear to ear, but his eyes always seemed to hold so much adoration for her. Even after almost thirty years of marriage, when they were apart for any amount of time, he looked at her like she was the only person who existed. Looking at that type of love and devotion caused my heart to swell.

*One day someone will look at me like that. Hopefully.*

Once the hostess led us to his table, Dad stood to kiss his wife before pulling me in for a bear hug.

"Hi Dad." I pulled out of the hug and removed my coat. Once we were all seated, I noticed the table was set for three. "Zach isn't coming?"

My older brother never turned down a free meal.

The look my parents exchanged gave me pause. I shifted my eyes from one to the other. "Is Zach okay?"

"Yes, of course. He's working," my mother answered before the waitress arrived.

We ordered drinks and our favorite dishes without glancing at the menus.

"Okay, what's going on?" I asked cautiously, nervousness coursing through my veins.

"Zoe..." Dad took a sip of water before he leaned forward. "Is everything okay?"

*They know.*

With a deep breath, I nodded slowly, looking between them. "How long have you known?"

My mom clasped her hands in her lap. "It's a two-day exam and you arrived on what would've been the second day. We've known the whole time."

Averting my eyes, I nodded and attempted to get my thoughts together.

"Did something happen?" My father's brows furrowed with concern.

"No. I'm okay. I just..." The words wouldn't form and my sentence just trailed off into the light buzz of people around us.

"This isn't like you. You're impulsive at times, but you don't shirk your responsibilities. And you're not frivolous with money," he sat back in his chair. "I don't understand, Zoe."

*Shit! I didn't even think about the money. Eight hundred dollar exam and five hundred dollar exam prep course...courtesy of my parents' generosity.*

My manicured hand covered my mouth as I realized just how royally I fucked up. "I will pay you back every dime."

Although they always assured me that I didn't need to work while I was in school, I showed up to work almost every night to take care of myself. But they paid for my school expenses—which included everything related to the bar exam.

"It's not about the money, Zoe. Your father and I just want to know what made you decide to skip the biggest exam of your life and immediately come here. Don't get us wrong, we loved having you and seeing you so soon after Christmas. But there has to be an explanation."

I didn't know what to say. I didn't know how to explain it. Fortunately, the waitress dropped off our food and the conversation halted for one full minute. Even after the waitress left, the awkwardness of knowing they were waiting for a response and not knowing what to say only suppressed my appetite.

"I never meant to keep it from you," I started, looking between them. "I just didn't know how to tell you. I'm sorry."

"What is it that you're not telling us?" My mother's exasperated voice filled me with dread because I knew I'd disappointed her. I'd disappointed both of them.

I blinked at her, contemplating my truth.

*I'm freaking out.*

*I'm not ready.*

*I'm overwhelmed.*

*Because taking that exam changes everything.*

"Zoe." My father's baritone pulled me out of my thoughts.

"I've been selected to participate on *The One*." The words flew out of my mouth before I had time to think about it.

"What? What is that?" He looked at Mom who was staring directly at me.

"A reality dating show," she answered without taking her eyes off of me. She tilted her head to the side slightly, assessing me, assessing my answer. "You didn't take the California State Bar Exam because you are going on *The One*? The same show you said, and I quote, 'was setting women back'?"

*She doesn't believe me. She knows me too well.*

I had a choice. I could either admit that I was essentially going through a quarter-life crisis or I could dig in and commit.

"I'm interested in knowing more about Julian Winters..."

*Which is the truth.*

"Filming starts next week..."

*Also the truth.*

"I decided to just sit for the next exam. In July."

*All facts.*

My dad seemed content with my reasoning. "Well that makes sense. You should do something different before beginning your career and take at least one risk. So this makes sense." He nodded. "I get that. We traveled before

15

starting our careers. And you haven't dated anyone since Tate so this should be good for you. Have you heard from him?"

I looked over at my mother for help, but she seemed to still be sizing me up, focusing on the holes in my story. I quickly returned my gaze to my father.

"Dad." I shook my head. "No."

My father loved Tate Lewis. Even though Tate dropped me as soon as he got an NFL offer and broke my heart three years ago, Dad was still in denial that the situation was seriously over.

"Okay, okay." He lifted his hands and gave me an easy smile. "So this is one of those shows where the last woman standing gets to be with the man?"

Just hearing it reduced to that made me ashamed of even pretending to go on the show. I almost balked and told the truth, but I heard my mother's words in my head.

*Giving up is the first step to failure.*

The words played on a loop.

*I took the first step toward failure. Walking away from the test, running home because I got scared, that's a failure.*

I cleared my throat. "Yes. This season the man in question is Julian Winters. He's a songwriter and music producer. On a fundamental level, I don't believe in reality dating shows. But I figure, if I participate and I am myself and stay above the fray, it could actually help the image of women that is being conveyed. And he is very intriguing."

I sold that so smoothly, I almost bought it myself.

My dad nodded in agreement. My mother was a harder sell.

Pulling out my phone, I pulled up the picture of Julian.

"This is him." I showed my father first and then my mother.

She looked at the phone and then me and then the phone

again. A smirk played on her lips. "Ah, I see. Well the look on your face earlier makes a little more sense now. I look forward to watching you on the show, Zoe."

She didn't look completely convinced, but she was dropping the issue.

*Shit, it worked!*

I was surprised, but grateful. But then it hit me.

*Shit! Now that means I have to actually go on the show.*

# Chapter 2

Slipping my oversized black sunglasses onto my face, I thanked the taxi driver one more time. The sun settled onto my skin as I pushed the sleeves of my thin black sweater up my arms. Grey clouds littered the sky and it smelled like rain could be on the horizon.

*I hope it rains.*

The sound of horns squawking, music thumping, and people yelling pulled me out of my daze. It was a typical Saturday in Downtown Los Angeles. The smell of something burning mixed with a sweet fragrance floated through the air. I inhaled deeply.

*Home sweet home.*

I grabbed my weekend bag in one hand and pulled my suitcase with the other as I made my way across the sidewalk and into The Attic Loft Apartments. The five story building was the perfect mix of historic architecture and modern interior design.

My black and white flats carried me up the short staircase

and through the heavy glass doors. The greyish cement floor with its glossy finish complimented the stark white walls of the first floor common area. Readjusting my bags, I took the elevator to the second floor apartment I shared with Koko.

"Hello!" I announced my arrival as the heavy oak door banged against the exposed brick wall.

Koko screamed from somewhere in the back and burst into the living room, thin arms flailing. With long, jet black hair framing the porcelain complexion of her heart-shaped face, she looked like an excited child bounding toward me. Before I had a chance to put my stuff down, she had grabbed me into a hug, knocking the wind out of me. I coughed and then laughed.

Within fifteen minutes, we were sitting on the couch with wine and a laptop as she told me about her week. But a swift internet search changed the course of the conversation abruptly.

"I still can't believe you're actually going to do it," Koko marveled as we stared at the internet images of Julian Winters. She brought her face closer to the computer screen. "He's definitely your type though."

I stared at the picture of him in the studio. The way his arms flexed as he leaned over the soundboard and the look of determination in his eyes as he stared straight ahead was sexy. He was sexy. Physically, he was my type—tall, dark, and strong with a little bit of geekiness on top. But I wouldn't go as far as to say that he was my type since he voluntarily agreed to do a reality TV show.

"Yeah, he is hot. But the fact that he's on this show makes me question his intelligence."

Koko giggled. "I'm sure comments like that will get you kicked off of the show."

"Exactly. Problem solved. Then I'm in and out without

incident." I took a huge gulp of the cheap wine someone gave us as a gift. "My letter said that the interviews are happening on Thursday and those who are selected are expected to be at the house on Friday."

"Interviews are important because that's how you get on the show. So we need to figure out what you're going to wear. But Friday is when filming officially starts and everybody is getting full hair and makeup for that so my work begins." She tapped her cheek contemplatively. "I wonder if Julian will be there for the interviews."

A flutter rippled through my belly and my eyebrows flew up. I didn't want to be on the show, but I did want to meet him. I pushed the thought aside before it had time to settle.

"My goal is to just do enough to get on TV so my parents can see me, but not actually have to spend too much time on the show so no one else will notice me. So, it doesn't even really make sense for me to pack too much."

"Zoe, look at you. If you don't curse anyone out or tell the creators that they are sexist pieces of shit, you're moving on to the next round. I'll more than likely see you on Friday. Wow, I'm still trying to wrap my mind around you being a contestant on *The One*. You, of all people!"

"I know. I'm sure there was a glitch in the system. If they did a background check and did a search of any of my social media posts, I'm sure they saw that I am not a fan."

"Ha! I'm sure!" She hovered over another picture of him before clicking on an article about Julian that I'd read on the flight. "What did your parents say when you told them that you were going?"

I took another sip of wine. "My dad was cool with it. My mom, on the other hand, was suspicious...is suspicious. She didn't press though. But she gave me this look..." I twisted my body so that I was fully facing her. "And said, 'I look forward to seeing you on the show, Zoe' in that tone she uses when she's baiting someone. She didn't press anymore about it, but I could tell that she was calling my bluff."

Koko's eyebrows flew up. "Oh shit."

I nodded. "So I have to at least make it on TV. It's not about trying to compete or getting very far. I just have to have a minute of screen time and then I won't feel like such a liar. Do they film the interviews?"

"Yes, they do. But I'm pretty sure they only show the interviews of the actual contestants. And if your mom has a hunch, she pretty much knows you're full of it. If you don't want to be a liar, you're going to need to get on air."

"You're just saying that because you want me on the show!" I teased. "But you're right. I just need to make it through the interviews and get on the first episode. Episodes air on Tuesdays and Thursdays right? So if I can get on the show and pass the interview part, I'll move in the mansion on Friday. My parents will see me on the show on Tuesday and they'll see me get voted off, then I'll fade away and no one will be the wiser. After that..." I shrugged.

"All to avoid telling your parents you need a break and you need a minute to just enjoy life."

I nodded. There was more to it, but essentially, yes.

"Everyone is going to flip that you're on there."

I laughed, refilling my glass. "I know."

"Me too, please." Koko held up her glass so I could refill it. "Thank you. Have you looked at this stuff?" She clicked on a new webpage. "Twenty-eight year old Julian Winters is the man behind some of your favorite songs. Now he's stepping from behind the scenes and taking his talents in front of the mic," she read before looking at me. "You might need to take this seriously and actually compete. Look at him...he's kind of a nerdy badass."

A flicker of something swirled in my belly. I shrugged in a noncommittal way. "He's also the kind of guy who wants women to compete for him on television in the name of love."

She ignored me. "Did you see this thing about how he likes poetry?"

"Yeah, I saw something about that." I conveniently left out the part about how I'd thoroughly researched Julian Winters before bed and on the flight. "I'm not going to lie. I'm intrigued."

She wiggled her eyebrows. "Because he's your type. And this is a great way to get back out there. You haven't dated anyone since Tate."

I groaned. "My dad said the same thing."

"I think your dad posted a picture of him and Tate online on Father's Day last year."

Laughing, I choked on the sip I'd just taken. "You are ridiculous," I sputtered, tears wetting the corners of my eyes.

"It's true though! Your dad loves Tate. I'm sure if you told him the way he left things with you, he wouldn't be such a fan."

"I can't break my dad's heart like that. You should see his face when a New York Generals game comes on." I rolled my eyes.

"Did Tate even play? He's third string."

"Exactly!" I shook my head. "Tate Lewis is definitely the past."

"And Julian Winters is the future!"

"Come on, Koko. Seriously?" I objected with an undeniable giddiness that caught me off guard.

I put my glass down and pushed it to the other side of the coffee table.

*I've had enough to drink.*

We clicked through a few more pictures and talked about

the apparent physical transformation Julian went through from a cute, nerdy college kid writing songs in his dorm room to a sexy, geek-chic grown ass man writing songs for almost everyone.

"Okay, enough of this," I announced, closing the laptop and removing it from her lap, placing it on the coffee table. "I still need to unpack and nap before work tonight and I have to go to urgent care to see if a doctor can squeeze in a physical and STD testing because I have to have it on record that I am clean as of one week of the show. Oh and I have to mentally prepare myself for Thursday's interview. So lots to do and you're trying to get me drunk."

Koko's small, angular eyes widened. "I didn't know they did that! But it makes sense. The last week before he makes his decision, the bachelors take their top two women to Destination Desire."

"What the hell is that?" My eyebrows seemed to have relocated and established permanent residence in the middle of my forehead.

"You know? Destination Desire? Pound Town? Penetration Station? Knocking boots?"

I looked at her blankly. "What the hell happened? Who are you? I leave for a week and you sound like a middle school boy!"

She laughed. "I've been trying to take a crash course in *The One* and things are blurring together. But the point is, during the last week, when he has two women left to choose from, he fucks them to see which one he likes best."

"What? At the same time? Over the same weekend?"

"No..." Koko made a face. "I don't think so. Okay, I don't know for sure, but I think it's two separate trips. He takes a couple of days to deliberate and then he makes his selection." She must have read my facial expression because she added, "I'm sure it's not as skeevy as it sounds."

"Having sex with two different women hours apart...classy."

"Don't think about that! That's weeks away! You just need to focus on getting on the show and meeting Julian Winters. Are you looking forward to that at least?"

It sounded like a question, but I knew it wasn't. She already decided how I felt. I pursed my lips and cocked my head to the side.

"You're into Julian, aren't you?"

Again I stayed silent. But my pursed lip twitched and I prayed she didn't see it.

"Ah ha! You have a crush!"

The word forced my lips to curl upward. I fought the urge with all I had in me, but failed.

"AH!" She let out a short, but loud yelp. "You do!"

I shook my head profusely, my hands lifting, palms upward, in confusion.

"I knew it! I knew it! This is so cute. When was the last time you had a crush?"

I stood up and walked around the couch. "I don't...I meant to say...ah, I...forget it," I chuckled, stopping near where I'd dropped my bags on the floor. "He's cute and I'm intrigued, but that's just because his lyrics read like poetry. And you know how I am about poets."

She nodded. "Yeah, you've always had a lady boner for poets. It's impressive that you have such a Maya Angelou vibe, but you picked a straight-laced career." She smiled and wiggled her eyebrows. "Which is why falling in love with a musician who you call a poet is exactly what you need to balance you out."

Putting my hands on my hips, I arched an eyebrow. "First of all, I don't know who you've been hanging out with while I've been gone, but if you say 'lady boner' again, I will smother you with a pillow. Second, and most importantly, yes, he's attractive and talented and a poet. But I'm not seriously interested in a man who is trying to sleep with twelve different women as they compete for his affection."

"Okay, I admit the situation is not ideal. But..." She stood up and waved her arms in the air. "Hear me out, you two have a lot in common! Did you read the article about how when he has down time, he goes out with his friends to do karaoke?"

I read the article.

"So we both like karaoke. So do you. So do millions of other people," I argued, fidgeting under her excited gaze. "I feel like you're trying to push this because you feel bad that you kind of forced me into telling my parents that I'm going on this sexist show."

She cackled, her gasping laugh amusing me. "You are not going to put that on me! That was all you." She walked around the couch until she was directly in front of me. "Don't be mad at me because you and Julian would be perfect together."

*Perfect.*

I was more than a little uncomfortable because I didn't believe in perfection in relationships. Perfection was the outfit I wore to meet Tate that night. Perfection was the flawless three karat diamond ring Tate purchased to propose to me after graduation. Perfection was tied to my broken ideas of monogamy, commitment and forever. Perfection was what movies and television shows propagated to make viewers believe in happily ever after. But I knew two things for sure: perfection didn't exist in relationships and happily ever after was a choice.

I sighed. "You and I both know that perfection—."

"Yeah, yeah, yeah." She rolled her eyes. "Well, you and Julian would be amazing together."

I tried not to smile at her antics. "Wait a minute." I cocked my head to the side. "Twenty-four hours ago, you told me I needed to give Ethan a chance."

"Ethan who? We've moved on to a hot, famous guy." Koko pulled her hair back into a messy bun. "Now come on, let's figure out what you're wearing to this interview. Once Julian meets you, you're definitely getting picked to be on the show. After you're at the mansion, fireworks will explode and your lady boner will be at full salute and then you're going to fall in love for all of America to see."

She turned on her heel and skipped away with her middle fingers in the air.

"I kind of hate you right now," I called after her playfully, causing her to laugh.

Grabbing my bags, I trudged in the direction of my bedroom.

# Chapter 3

The leather pleated skirt skated against my thighs as I made my way through the crowd of gorgeous women and headed down the hallway toward the restroom. I didn't think it was an accident that a woman bumped me, causing me to spill a little bit of champagne on my white chiffon shirt. I had to bite the inside of my lip and walk away to keep from saying something that was going to get me kicked out before the interviews even started.

It was supposed to start at six o'clock; however, once we had all arrived, we were informed that the interviews would happen after the cocktail party. I didn't recall rolling my eyes, but the urge was there.

*I just need to get on T.V for one scene and then I can be done with this shit.*

I pushed the bathroom door open and breathed a sigh of relief when I realized it was empty.

*Thank God.*

Making a beeline to the mirror, I smiled at my reflection as I drew closer. From the coarse curls wild and loose around my shoulders to the black spiked heels, I stood out in the crowd. That could be a good thing or a bad thing, but my hope was that it was good.

Women who all generally looked to be between the ages of twenty-one and thirty-four and varied in physical appearance wore dresses that ranged from short and flirty to long and elegant. Most of the women participated in a weird dynamic where they would size each other up and then giggle nervously together whenever a door would open. It was such an odd experience. We were gathered in the L-shaped lounge to wait for a chance to be interviewed for the possibility to compete for a man we may or may not like.

I kept to myself at the bar.

*How did I end up here? Oh that's right. I was too scared to tell my parents that I freaked out. I was too scared to tell my loving, supportive parents that after all of their hard work, I had disappointed them.* I paused. The thought of their disappointment left a bad taste in my mouth. *I do still want to be a lawyer. I just... I don't know. I just need to focus on something else for a second.*

Squaring my shoulders, I let out the breath I was holding.

The door banged against the wall as it swung open. Two blonde women loudly entered the restroom, talking shit about some of the other women. Although I could clearly be seen, they ignored me and continued their pettiness.

That's when it hit me.

*I can't do this. I'm going to tell my parents the truth and get the hell out of here. If they are disappointed, at least I won't see it in their faces. By the time I make it back to Virginia, they will be over it.*

Refreshing my lipstick, I gave myself another once over and smiled at my appearance again. With the knowledge that I was going to leave the cocktail party fresh on my brain,

I was fresh out of fucks to give. Twisting to look at the way my ass made the skirt flare out in the back, I nodded in appreciation.

I moved toward the door, but stopped short.

"Real classy," I called out to the blondes who were still calling other women derogatory names as they drunkenly fixed their makeup. "Calling women you don't know 'whores' says more about you than it does about them."

The one in pink mumbled something I couldn't hear, causing the one in blue to snort with laughter. They walked toward the exit, closing the distance between us. My fists clenched in anticipation.

*California law states that I can't be found guilty of a violent crime that I commit in self-defense if I need to protect myself from these catty bitches.*

I smirked, sizing them up as they drew closer. Although there were two of them, they were petite and I wouldn't go down without a fight...even though, they didn't look like the fighting type. They looked like the type to spread vicious rumors about their enemies and then sleep with their men out of spite.

I stared at them hard as they narrowed their bleary eyes at me and then walked around me. The one in the pink muttered something as they opened the bathroom door.

"What was that?" I asked, following behind them. I stopped, crossing my arms over my chest. "I didn't hear you."

"I said good luck. I'm sure you and your fat ass are exactly what Julian Winters is looking for." The sarcasm dripped from the words that she threw over her shoulder. Both women fell into a fit of giggles as they bumped into a waiter heading away from the party. "Get out of the way!"

I rolled my eyes at their rudeness. The kitchen was around the corner and down the hall from the restrooms. The poor guy was probably on his way to get another tray of crab cakes and they just ran into him like he didn't exist.

With a deep breath, I tried to shake off the entire encounter with those two. I stared daggers into the back of their heads. Rolling my shoulders back, I slowly let go of the desire to find them in the crowd and trip them as I moved in the direction of the party.

"Hi," the waiter greeted me.

He was stopped, leaning up against the wall and staring straight at me. Having his undivided attention threw me off and caused me to freeze mid-step.

"Hi," I replied, eyeing him skeptically. There was an air of familiarity with him that I couldn't place. Los Angeles sometimes felt like a huge version of a small town.

*Do I know him? Did he apply to work at Breakers?* I wondered, analyzing his face. His ominous, dark eyes, scruffy, dark hair, and orange tinted skin gave him a bit of a disheveled look, but he had a remarkable smile that set me at ease. *No, that can't be it.*

"I heard what she said to you. She was rude."

"Jokes on her. I love my fat ass," I replied, winking at him.

"I like you." His broad shoulders shook as he laughed to himself. "I'm Evan. Having a good time?" he asked casually, pushing the sleeve of his black dress shirt back up toward his elbow. His tattoos caught my eye.

I'd stayed to myself all night, nursing the same glass of champagne for almost an hour. Our phones and other electronic devices had to be left in the car. Most of the women I'd come in contact with were either nervously talking about nothing or meanly bashing the other women in the room. I didn't want to be a part of any of it so I sat at the bar alone. Evan was the first person to try to engage me in a real conversation. And for the first time all evening, I felt comfortable.

I backed up and leaned against the wall directly across from him. Tilting my head to the side, I smiled. "Zoe. And no, not at all."

His smile widened. "Why not?"

"This whole thing is crazy. I can't believe I'm here. I really think I'm having a quarter-life crisis because this just goes against everything I believe in."

He tucked his head down a bit and chuckled. "What do you mean?"

"Reality TV, dating shows, pitting women against each other to compete for a man, superficial conversations with even more superficial people. Everything that *The One* stands for is pretty much near the top of my bullshit list."

His teeth were straight and white, resulting in a captivating smile. It was almost buried in his unruly beard, but the moment I noticed it, I couldn't look anywhere else. He ran his hand down the side of his face. "So why are you here?"

"That's a good question." I smiled, not quite understanding why I was confiding in the stranger. "Quarter-life crisis strikes again I guess. This isn't me at all. I don't do things like this and I don't make rash decisions. I'm not at all a risk-taker. And I just made two huge life-altering decisions in a two-week time span. The first one, I won't get another opportunity to change it until later. But this, I could still stop this train wreck. I could just leave right now..." I shrugged.

"But here you are."

"Here I am."

We were both quiet for a second before he lifted his broad shoulders innocently. The sound of Koko's favorite musical group filtered down the hallway toward us.

"In the spirit of not being completely negative, the music isn't bad," I offered.

His smile grew. "You like the music?"

"Yeah, that's been the only thing getting me through this." I gestured to the party. "Well that and..."

I hesitated to tell a stranger that I was moved and compelled to meet Julian Winters because of his words. So I tried to change the subject. "My best friend loves Super Casanova. Have you heard of them? They're pretty good."

"I know what you're doing and you're not getting away with it that easily. The music and what? I won't judge. A couple of people in the kitchen were saying that the contestants get a thousand dollars for each round they complete or something like that. Everybody has to make a living somehow. No shame in that."

"It's not the money. It's..." My sentence trailed off and I looked at the ceiling before returning eye contact with him. "My best friend signed me up without my consent and then I told my parents that I was going to do the show. So I'm here so I won't be a liar."

"You get more and more interesting by the second, Zoe." His hands seemed to bury deeper into his pockets, elongating his torso as he stared at me intensely. "I think there's more to it though. You don't seem like the type of woman to do something that you don't want to do."

I smirked at his perceptiveness. "You don't seem like the type of man to beat around the bush."

He laughed. "Okay, you're right." He pushed his sleeves up on his elbows again. "You're not like anyone else I've met tonight."

"Well, I stand out for a number of reasons," I countered playfully, casting my gaze toward the group of women that could be seen mingling.

"That's the truth."

I turned my head in time to see Evan's eyes traveling up

my body.

*Okay, maybe I should head back.*

When our eyes met, I couldn't read his expression but I could feel his interest. A flush came over me.

*I should definitely head back.*

A waitress with a tray full of shrimp sauntered between us, giving him a long glance on her way from the kitchen to the party. I waited until she passed before telling him goodbye.

"Well," I started. "I—"

"So I'm not going to bother trying to ask you for your number since you're here for a chance to be with that music guy..." He paused as if waiting for me to dispute his claim.

I lifted my left eyebrow and waited for him to continue.

He smiled. "I figured. But I guess I just have one question. There's a room full of women, women like you, all here for him. What is it about this guy?"

"He intrigues me," I answered without hesitation. "Some of these women are already saying that they love him. They don't know him to love him." I shook my head. "That's what I hate about these shows. Just complete bullshit. But I am intrigued by Julian Winters. I know I didn't sign up for this, but after getting acquainted with his work, I had to try to meet him. Anyone who writes poetry for a living is someone I need to know."

"Poetry? I thought he was a musician. A songwriter or something."

"He is a poet," I argued. The dreaminess in my voice caught me off guard, but I pressed on. "He's talented at what he does and obviously, he's made a good living doing it. But he is a poet."

Evan didn't say anything immediately. He slipped his hands back into the pockets of his black pants. "So if I were a poet, would I have a shot?"

I didn't know why, but I liked him. Although I wasn't immediately attracted to him, there was something about his confidence, the way he spoke, and his smile.

I pushed away from the wall and flashed my teeth at him. "I thought you said you only had one question?"

"Yeah, but—"

A small group of women passed between us, interrupting his sentence. I didn't pay attention to the group until I heard the grating voice of one of the women I encountered in the bathroom—the blonde bitch in the pink dress.

"That's her," she uttered mockingly, right before opening the bathroom door. "Look at her. She definitely has a better shot with that dirty looking waiter than she does with Julian."

She disappeared into the bathroom so fast that I didn't even have a chance to respond.

A couple of the women with her snickered, one looked horrified and the shortest one looked like she had spaced out. But all of them followed her into the bathroom.

My eyes met Evan's and he looked genuinely surprised. "Dirty looking?"

With a shake of my head, I sighed. "And that's the perfect example of why this isn't my sort of thing."

"Dirty looking?" he repeated, looking down at himself. He lifted his hands away from his body.

I gave him a small smile. "Don't listen to her. You're not dirty looking. Your tan is just a little..." I lowered my voice and walked across the hallway. I rested my hand on his arm, right above his elbow. I was surprised by how muscular his arm felt under my light touch. "I don't think you rubbed in the self-tanner as well as possible, that's all. You're not dirty looking, though. She's a bitch. Don't listen to anything she says. You saw a woman who didn't fit in and engaged her in conversation to make her feel better about being here. You are a good person and any woman would be lucky to have a shot with you."

Oddly enough, his brilliant smile made my insides warm. I dropped my hand from his body.

"So does that mean I have a shot at you?" He asked teasingly.

I laughed, walking backward. "Are you a poet?"

"So you only date poets?"

"I'm here, aren't I?" I winked before spinning on my heel and striding back to the party.

My conversation with Evan was exactly what I needed to get my head back into the game. He was easy to talk to and he reminded me why I showed up to the event.

*Julian Winters.*

As much as I denied it to Koko, I was looking forward to meeting him. Initially, when I came to terms with the fact that I had agreed to do the show, I was interested in meeting him and getting on TV so my parents wouldn't be disappointed in me. But after doing my research, I was genuinely intrigued and wanted to know more about him, about his art, about his talent.

I spent time reading his lyrics and each one made me feel like I knew him a little better. Maybe he was making up all of the tales of everlasting love or soul-crushing heartbreak, but his ability to make me feel with each skillfully placed word did something to me. There weren't many personal details about him on the web. But I read a bunch of articles about his music and through his music, I felt like I knew more than any random article of facts could tell me. The lyrics felt like they were his truth and I hadn't been moved like that in a long time.

*Probably not since I got my book of Pablo Neruda poems from Grandma,* I considered as I walked around the perimeter of the party.

For thirty or forty minutes, I slowly made my way around the outskirts of the room. I overheard bits and pieces of conversation, never hearing anything that interested me enough to stop and engage. I sipped on a glass of champagne that was offered to me and observed my surroundings.

Looking at the women gathered, I couldn't tell what Julian's type might be. But there were a lot of blondes in the room.

"Hello!" A man in a tuxedo addressed us with a salute as he entered the open space from the hallway. He looked like a real-life Ken doll with his overly gelled blonde hair and his tanned skin.

"Hello," he repeated, his booming voice echoed from the wireless microphone he held in his hand. Cheers and excited squeals erupted throughout the room. I looked around in confusion.

*Who the hell is this?*

Everyone but me seemed to know who the man was. I clapped politely for a few seconds, before resting my forearm on the back of the leather smoking chair I was standing next to. As women around the room seemed thrilled, I was still waiting for him to appease my curiosity.

"For those of you who don't know, my name is Bryce Wilson. I am the host of The One," he introduced himself, sweeping his free hand out dramatically. He grinned as he took in the second round of applause.

"Thank you, thank you. Please, take a seat," he directed us.

A hush fell over the room and a few excited squeaks could be heard as everyone scrambled to an available chair. I slipped into the chair I was leaning against. Crossing my smooth legs, I finished the champagne remaining in my glass. Twisting the stem of the glass between my fingertips, I could feel my nerves starting to get the best of me.

*I'm going to tell my parents the whole truth as soon as possible, no matter what. This isn't like me. Running from the bar. Lying to my parents. Participating in this bull—*

"You are all here because we saw something special in you. On paper, you each held qualities that our eligible bachelor is looking for in a significant other. For those of you who are familiar with the show, you know that usually there are twenty-four women selected for interviews and then that number is slashed to twelve who appear on the actual show. This season we are doing it a little differently."

Gasps rang out even though Bryce hadn't specified what was different this time around. The tension in the room became thick as the reality of the situation settled in. Some of us were going home and some of us were staying.

*Here we go.*

"You may have noticed that there are fifty of you here. And you may be wondering how we are going to interview you all tonight since we've had this cocktail party for the last two hours." He paused and smiled.

But the pause was for a little too long. It was like the pauses they do on television when they are about to drop a bombshell.

*Wait a minute.*

I scanned the room until I located several black orbs around the room. There was one in each corner of the room and one in the center, attached to the chandelier. I froze.

*They are recording this. This is going on TV.* I sat up a little straighter and tried to act natural. I placed the empty champagne flute on the small table beside me. The uptick in my heart rate made me feel unnecessarily guilty. *Did they catch the conversation in the hallway with the waiter? They wouldn't have cameras on the way to the bathroom and the kitchen area. Would they?*

"You've actually been interviewed all night!" Bryce yelled, causing confusion to sweep through the room.

Everyone started talking at once. Well, almost everyone. I relaxed a bit in my chair and let out a short, dry laugh.

*They may have recorded us, but I wasn't subjected to any interviews. I didn't talk to anyone except for—*

My thoughts were cut short when three members of the wait staff came down the hallway and flanked either side of Bryce. I didn't realize I was holding my breath until it was confirmed that none of the three men who walked out happened to be the waiter I was talking to in the hallway.

"These men who have been interjecting themselves in your conversations and offering you more of those delicious finger sandwiches all night are not who you think they are. No, ladies. Let me introduce you to your interviewers. We have James, Omar, and Scott. Best friends of Julian Winters!"

I clapped along with the rest of the women. Each of them gave us a wave and I noticed how uniquely handsome they were.

"These men have been asking questions, getting first impressions, and looking for the best match for their best friend. They have helped whittle the list down from fifty to twelve," Bryce announced, allowing the tension to swell.

*Nothing sobers up a room full of women competing for the same man like telling them that they are being judged on their actions when they didn't know they were being judged.* I put my hand over my mouth as I laughed to myself again. *I know my antisocial ass is getting sent home.*

When I arrived at the beginning of the evening, I initially tried to make an attempt. But after the third superficial conversation, I couldn't take it anymore. I was pretty sure I came off as disinterested and stuck-up since I didn't interact with anyone.

*Well anyone besides—*

Evan walked out as if the universe wanted to finish my thought for me. A sense of uneasiness worked its way through my body as I tensed. I breathed a sigh of relief when he immediately took a right toward the bar.

Phew.

My eyes followed him as he tucked himself into a corner near the bar. I didn't know why the thought of Julian knowing my conversation with the waiter made me uneasy. Maybe it was the fact that the waiter was flirting and I may have been a little flirtatious back. Maybe it was the fact that my voice betrayed how Julian's lyrics made me feel. Maybe it was the fact that I was a little embarrassed that after all the shit I talked, I kind of wanted to be selected.

I looked at my empty glass. *I drank the kool-aid.*

"If we are getting rid of thirty-eight of you tonight to make sure the most compatible matches get through, we couldn't make that decision without additional help," Bryce began merrily, using his hands excessively.

I stopped listening to what he was saying and focused on how he was saying it.

He seemed rather excited about sending thirty-eight women home. Living locally, I gave up an afternoon and a little bit of my self-respect. Some of these women put in leave of absences to their jobs. Some of these women walked away from their family and friends for possibly two months. Some of these women gave up a lot for the chance to be with a man they don't know. I cast my eyes around the room and for the first time, I kind of felt for them.

*Putting your life on hold for the hope that this man that you don't know could be the one.* I shook my head. Even though

I couldn't do it, I understood the sentiment behind it. *The hope of love is such a powerful motivator.*

"...so without further ado, the following women will be asked to immediately move into the house for a chance to get to know Julian Winters. We believe that one of these twelve women will be... The One."

# Chapter 4

"That's perfect," Koko commented as she finished applying my makeup. "Open."

My eyes had to adjust to the brightly lit makeup trailer again. Between the overhead lighting and the vanity lights around the mirror, I had to blink several times to get everything into focus.

The room was brightly lit and colorful. The walls were a vibrant blue with the name Julia Jones scrawled in purple. From the high tech sound system to the chrome makeup table and storage drawers, the trailer was fully customized.

My eyes focused on my best friend. Her eyes were lined in charcoal with long lashes attached. Her jet black hair was dyed blue at the ends as an ode to her new boss. Her all black outfit with blue combat boots was cool and apparently comfortable since she'd been on her feet doing makeup for the last three hours.

Once she finished my lipstick, Koko made eye contact with me. Her grin stretched across her face as she took a step back and analyzed her work. Her happiness was so evident.

She worked her ass off and she made it. And working with the makeup guru herself was the coronation of her success.

*And I couldn't even keep my shit together long enough to take the bar.*

"This is big time," I whispered so Julia Jones wouldn't overhear me as she stood at the back of the trailer washing makeup brushes. "I'm so proud of you."

"Thank you! I love you, girl!"

"I love you too. You deserve this and so much more," I said as she spun me around in the chair to face the mirror. When I saw myself, my jaw dropped.

I didn't wear makeup often and when I did, it was heavy eye makeup and minimal everything else. Although I still looked like me, I looked like a photo-shopped version of myself.

"Wow. Koko...I look amazing!" I leaned forward. "What kind of voodoo magic is this? I went to church last Sunday so I don't need those problems," I joked, scooting to the edge of my seat.

Koko laughed and out of nowhere, Julia laughed too.

"This kid's laugh is amazing!" She commented lightheartedly before she called another contestant in for makeup.

"I know it's more makeup than you're used to and I know you're worried that you're going to get it everywhere. But I've set it with this sealing spray. JJ swears by it. And you're going to be on camera, with optic zoom, so you're welcome."

I stared at my face. My skin was smooth, almost creamy looking. My full lips were slathered in a matte red. My light brown eyes and natural long lashes were played up with black liner and smoky shadows. With my hair already done in an elegant up-do, I felt beautiful...and not regular, everyday beautiful, but TV beautiful.

"You like it?" She asked anxiously.

"Like it?" I looked at her in the mirror. "I love it! I feel like I look like I'm in high definition."

She squealed. "You will be!"

We hugged and after a wave goodbye to Julia, I hustled out of the trailer. I had already stopped in wardrobe and my dress was being steamed before being delivered to my room. I felt like I had more than an hour to burn so instead of going through the side entrance, I followed the cobblestone walkway and took in my surroundings.

*Holy shit.*

My stomach churned with nerves. It wasn't like the feeling I had the night before the bar. The nerves that caused me to wring my hands were because I was so hell bent on running from the bar and the future that I ran in the complete opposite direction. And I had no idea what to expect.

I wanted to meet Julian because there was something about his lyrics that connected with me. But was coming on the show the only chance I had to meet him? Maybe, maybe not. All I knew was that coming on the show was so completely unlike me.

*I'll do the song and dance they need me to do tonight and then I can quit the show. I just want to talk to him. I can leave at any time. I just need to spend a little time with him, talking to him.*

When Bryce Wilson called my name along with the names of eleven other women, I couldn't deny the sense of excitement I felt. My crush had become a real, tangible thing and the thought of meeting the mystery man to talk to him about his music and his poetry made me feel exhilarated.

As quickly as I hyped myself up about meeting Julian Winters, the enthusiasm came crashing back down. The high of being on the show to get to know the man who wrote

"Breathe You" shattered quickly when the realization hit that it wasn't a meeting or a date, but a competition.

We were all given the call time of ten o'clock Friday morning to report to the mansion, located in Calabasas, California, about thirty-five minutes away from Los Angeles. A limo was scheduled to pick us up from Sway Luxury Resort, the high end downtown hotel where all of the out of town women were staying. I took a taxi to the hotel and chose that moment to call my parents to tell them the truth.

Because of the three hour time difference, they weren't up yet. I thought about leaving a voicemail message apologizing and telling them everything, but instead I just apologized and promised to explain everything once I was able to use my phone again. Then, I tucked my phone away in a pouch that I dropped off to Koko's desk as soon as I arrived on the property.

The six bedroom, four and a half bathroom house was breathtaking. It had a fitness room, a study, a formal room, a deluxe kitchen, and a fully loaded bar located in the living room. There were other rooms, but the doors were closed and locked. There was a pool and a hot tub and another fully loaded bar on the back patio. A garden maze and fountain were situated on the far side of the property between the show mansion and the neighbor's property. It was incredible.

After spending the first two hours getting a tour, selecting a bedroom, and being told where and where not to go, we were shown how to attach our microphones and where the stationary cameras were located. We were told that before each Bracelet Ceremony we had to visit hair, makeup and wardrobe. We were also given the rules and regulations. It was information overload, but I was confident I'd figure it out. And then they pushed us into hair and makeup.

"Excuse me! You're in the way!" A man barked, shaking me

out of the recollection of the last twelve hours of my life.

I whipped around and then immediately jumped from the walkway into the perfectly manicured grass. Pushing an oversized cart with camera equipment and boom mics, he grumbled and groaned as he seemed to be pulled behind the cart as he traveled toward the outside entrance that led to the basement.

I looked around and the hustle and bustle of one hundred or so production people working together to create this fantasy was fascinating. Everything was staged. It was as fake as I always thought it was, but seeing the effort that went into it was mind blowing. From script writers to story producers, men and women worked together to create the reality that is then chopped and screwed in editing for millions of Americans sitting at home.

"Hey, you! Out of the grass! We just sprayed it!"

My eyebrows flew up. I held my hands up in surrender as I scurried back over to the walkway. "Sorry!"

Determined to get out of the way and to clear my mind, I took a nerve-settling walk to the far side of the property. By the time I reached the lush greens of the garden, I already felt better. The cool breeze felt good against my warm skin.

Entering the garden, I decided that instead of getting lost in the maze, I would take the more direct route to the fountain at the center. I needed to relax and calm myself. If I got lost in a maze and was late back to the house, that would've just caused more stress.

*I'm definitely going to need to get my makeup and my hair touched up,* I realized as I unzipped my light jacket and pulled my white t-shirt away from my body.

I stopped in mid-step as the shrubbery ended and opened up to a massive concrete fountain. Water spouted from the top and then cascaded over the ridges of each subsequent basin. Closing my eyes, I inhaled deeply and then exhaled the confusion I felt.

*What am I doing?*

"Hey, what are you doing here?"

The masculine voice caused my eyes to fly open and my heart to pound. My head was on a swivel as I looked in the direction of the sound.

"I was asking myself the same thing," I mumbled honestly as I craned my neck to see if I recognized the man in the alcove.

I blinked, unsure of what I was seeing. I took tentative steps toward him.

*Is that...is that Julian?*

Wearing a pair of navy blue jogging pants with the matching jacket, Julian Winters was sitting on a concrete bench in the little alcove. He had a pair of black and red headphones pushed off of his ears and resting around his neck. A notebook occupied the space beside him. He wore black aviator sunglasses that somehow softened his chiseled features. He looked more like a mix of the boy in the picture Koko and I saw online and the man we were showed a picture of that morning. With each step I took toward him, he became even better looking.

His skin was the color of a rich almond cream and contrasted nicely with his short, black hair. His nose was narrow and symmetrical, anchoring his features. He didn't have the five o'clock shadow covering his chiseled jawline that attracted me in the photos. But when his full lips parted into a smile, I decided that the beard would've only distracted me from the most attractive thing about him.

His smile grew with each step I took and that smile was everything. He was officially the most attractive man I'd ever seen in my life.

## The One

The nerves I felt about being on the show dissipated as soon as Julian and I were face to face. He had a calming demeanor and that effect wasn't lost on me. The knots of anxiety that made me second-guess my decision to be on the show unraveled in his presence. For some reason, seeing him alone, with his notebook made me feel like I was seeing the real Julian and not Julian Winters, the star. And that made my heart race.

He held out his arms in confusion. "Are you trying to escape?"

Taken aback by his question, I couldn't do anything but laugh. "Honestly, I needed to get away. It's crazy over there."

He let out a chuckle and the sound reeled me in. "Tell me about it. That's why I came out here to write."

Something stirred in me. His writing was the main thing that attracted me to him.

*Well, until seeing him in person,* I conceded, forcing myself to keep staring at my reflection in his glasses so I wouldn't check him out.

My attraction to him went from an emotional attraction that stemmed from his ability to make me feel every single word he wrote and rolled into a sexual attraction that stemmed from his ability to make that jogging suit look like that.

I couldn't see his eyes behind his sunglasses, but I could feel his gaze sweeping over my body. Heat rose from beneath the surface of my skin. I shifted my weight from one foot to the other as my body reacted without my consent. I cleared my throat, pointing to the notepad. "You write when you're stressed?"

He paused as if surprised by the question. He nodded, replying slowly, "I do."

I lifted my eyebrows. "You haven't gotten very far."

"You're right." He smirked, appearing to hold back a laugh.

"Do you mind helping me with something, Zoe?"

*HE KNOWS MY NAME!*

I grinned, just barely keeping the ridiculous giddiness that tickled my insides under wraps. "Of course," I replied as coolly as possible.

He gestured for me to come closer and then he patted the bench beside him.

I ran my hands down the side of my jeans before I sat next to him. We were close, but not touching.

He licked his lips and my eyes automatically zeroed in on them. They were full and undeniably kissable. Realizing I was staring, I jerked my eyes back to his. I was certain I'd been caught, but if I had, he didn't indicate that he'd seen me. Turning my head toward the fountain, I stared straight ahead.

*I need to calm down.*

"This garden is nice," I mentioned for no reason in particular.

"Great place to escape," he added.

Sneaking glances with my peripheral vision, I saw him reach up and pull his sunglasses off. He tucked the arm of them into the collar of his shirt. I put my hands on the cool concrete on either side of my knees and gripped the edge of the bench. Even the way he removed his glasses was sexy.

I swallowed hard, trying to get my brain to stop focusing on him. I had to coach myself up. *It's your turn to speak. Stop eyeing him and respond.*

"I'm surprised more people aren't here," I offered, keeping the conversation going. I was glad no one else was around, but surprised sounded a little less anti-social. It wasn't until after the words left my mouth that I realized that surprised didn't fit either.

"Surprised or relieved?"

My head swung his way and my jaw dropped. I let out a

short laugh. "Am I that transparent?"

When he turned his head and our eyes met for the first time, all the air along with all the amusement left my body. His eyes were grey, an intense shade that seemed to mimic the rolling shadows of overcast storm clouds. They were epically hypnotic. It was too much, but I couldn't get enough.

My heart thundered in my chest. Pressing my palm harder into the concrete, I felt nothing but the intensity of his gaze. The silence between us only made the tension thicker. His eyes pierced me as if he could see into my soul. The energy between us was undeniable.

He blinked several times before dropping his head to his notebook.

"I'm working on something and when I get stuck, I like to bounce ideas around." Julian picked up his pen and tapped it against the empty pad. "Would you mind giving me feedback?"

Fixating on the fountain, I watched the water dance. I ran my hands over my thighs, trying to shake the feeling of Julian looking into me like he had. "I can definitely do that."

"I want you to listen to this and tell me how it makes you feel."

I chanced it and looked over at him. He slipped his headphones from around his neck and stood. Throwing his long leg over the bench, he straddled it, facing me.

Instead of handing me the headphones, Julian flipped them upside down, letting the headband hang under my chin. His fingertips grazed my skin as he ensured the ear pads covered my ears. A shiver ran through me. His eyes searched my face and his hands lingered on the headphones for a second too long. As if snapping out of it, he sat back, giving me a thumbs-up after he hit play on his phone.

The music started and he turned it up gradually. I closed my eyes so I could focus on what I was hearing and not be distracted by anything. I first heard the agony of the strings and it was sexy. So sexy, in fact, that I felt my body reacting to the music. Violin strings strained against someone's needy bow while guitar strings were plucked at a painstakingly slow rate. The song built from there and then ended the same way it began.

I opened my eyes and found Julian studying me. I didn't take into consideration that even though I closed my eyes to block him out, he could still see me. I looked down as I slipped the headphones off and noticed that his paper was no longer blank. Unfortunately, since it was upside down, I couldn't make out the words.

"It's almost distracting how beautiful you are," Julian commented, flipping to a new page in his notepad and slipping his headphones around his neck. Not giving me a chance to reply, he continued. "What did you think of the music?"

My stomach was still quivering from his words. "It's sexy. There's no other way to describe it." Wound up with a mixture of excitement and sexual tension, I started gesturing with my hands for emphasis. "From the way the strings sound like they're crying out to the way the drum kept that steady, consistently pounding beat. It sounded like sex. It kept building and once it climaxed, it wound down like a heartbeat slowing."

Julian ran his hand over his head, ruffling his hair. "First of all, hearing you describe it is sexy as hell. I like that you're conducting the music as you talk about it." A light chuckle escaped his lips. "But that's perfect. That's exactly what I hoped you'd feel. I just didn't think you would be able to put it into words like that." There was a bit of awe in his voice that made me curious.

Playfully, I crossed my arms and narrowed my eyes at him. "Oh because I'm a contestant on *The One*, you didn't think I'd be able to string together a coherent sentence?"

"That's not it at all." Amusement still danced in his eyes.

I stood up and kicked my leg over the bench so that I was straddling it and we were facing each other. I folded my arms again and glared at him. I couldn't help the smile that tugged at my lips, but I did my best to look intimidating.

He reached out, pulling my elbow until he freed my arm. Taking my smaller hand between his larger ones, he said, "I don't think that just because you are incredibly sexy and devastatingly beautiful, you can't also be smart with a great personality."

"An amazing personality," I corrected, my heart in my throat.

"My mistake, an amazing personality," he laughed, conceding my point. "It wasn't that I didn't think you could string a sentence together. I just didn't expect you to be so spot on." He shook his head. "Everything I thought when I produced the song is what you said. You hope someone gets what it is you're saying, but you never expect it to be word for word what you were thinking. That's unreal."

I cocked my head to the side, gazing at him. "Great minds think alike."

The silence enveloped us comfortably and the moment felt nice, but intimate since we were facing each other. We seemed to realize that we were still holding hands at the same time and quickly untangled our fingers.

I fixed my hair.

He grabbed his notepad and pen.

Julian bit down on his bottom lip. "Thanks for taking a listen. I needed an unbiased opinion. I'm figuring out which music I'm going to use on my album and which music I'm going to sell."

I smiled. "I can imagine that being difficult. You work hard on a track and then you have to decide if you're going to sell your hard work and run the risk of them ruining it with a crappy song." I pursed my lips. "My opinion is that you keep it."

He smiled, placing his pen and notepad on the bench space behind him. "Thanks, that helps."

"I'm glad I could help. So what's typically the next step in your process?"

"Next, I write. After I have the music, I use that to inspire me."

An excited flutter ran through me. "Are you going to start writing right now?"

Silently, his eyes shifted from my face and swept over the landscape. After what felt like minutes, he reached behind him and grabbed the notepad. When he looked up, I thought I saw a flash of vulnerability in his eyes. He glanced down at the bound papers, opening to a page with writing on it.

*Was that too much? Too pushy? Too forward?*

Unsure of how to react to the look in his eyes, I backtracked. "I'm sorry if I came off...strong maybe. I was just really excited about your writing and your process. I know you're stressed which is why you're out here so I don't want to put more pressure on you. If you want to write, I can leave you to it."

He met my gaze and whatever I saw in his eyes earlier was gone. "No, it's cool. I like having you here." His smile was small, easy going. "It might help me through this block."

"Maybe you're just having writer's block because you're doing this show. The stress of it all could be blocking your creativity." I paused for a beat. "Maybe you should go to your happy place and relax. I can go and let you get back to—"

Before I could finish my sentence, he shook his head. "Right now, with you, is the only time I haven't felt stressed about all of this."

I tried not to smile too hard. "Well good. I'm glad," I replied almost shyly. "And I feel the same way."

"Good."

Glancing at his notebook, I gestured with my head. "So, what do you have so far?"

The corners of his lips crept up sexily. "I have the first verse and I just wrote down a couple of thoughts for the second while you were listening to the beat."

I rubbed my hands together and lifted my eyebrows. "Okay. Let's hear it."

Julian laughed, disconnecting the headphones and pressing play on his phone. The music started pulsating through the speaker and he closed his eyes and belted out.

The sound of his voice blew me away. It was layered, husky, and raw. The way the melody of his voice carried over the music and tied together in perfect harmony made my heart swell. But his words took my breath away.

When Julian laid out his desire for this woman, he toed the line between implicit and explicit, love and lust, want and need. His lyrics felt different than his other stuff, more specific and real. But nonetheless, his wordplay captivated me. By the time he finished the first verse, I had to check to make sure drool wasn't dripping from the corners of my mouth.

"I started this yesterday and I've been stuck here ever since," he pointed out after he concluded.

I exhaled shakily and found myself at a loss for words.

His eyebrows lifted as he waited for me to find my voice.

I swallowed hard. "That was incredible, Julian. I mean, I— wow."

His face lit up. "Thank you."

"No, I don't think you understand." I put my hands on his knees and leaned forward, bringing my face closer to his. I knew I sounded like a swoony fan, but his talent was so attractive. "That was incredible. You are incredible. Your talent, your words, your emotion...God, your emotion."

His eyes dipped to my lips and lingered. "Thank you."

I wanted to close the six or seven inch gap between us and kiss him. The urge was so overwhelming, I started to shake. But I remembered that I was one of twelve women trapped in a house to compete for his affection.

*Like Tate, he is weighing his options. I came here to get to know him, not to fall for him.*

Rocking back, I removed my hands from his knees and clasped them in front of me.

"So, um, what do you have written down to start the second verse?" I stared at his notepad, trying to cool down.

He didn't respond so I looked up. His smirk grew.

"What?" I poked him in the middle of his chest. "Will you sing a little bit of the end of the first verse and then go into the second for me? Maybe if I hear what you're working with I can help you figure something out," I requested.

He obliged, maintaining eye contact and something clicked.

He sang passionately while staring directly into my eyes. His voice carried the melody with such sincerity that I paid closer attention to his newfound lyrics.

"Stripped down, I see you
All of you
Down to your core.
And looking in your eyes
It's no surprise
I want you much more."

I smiled at him as he continued, the words seeming to flow out of him. I ignored the way my heart pounded in my chest. I ignored the way every inch of my body burned hot for the man who was exposing himself to me. There was something so vulnerable about how emotionally open and unguarded he was being. Once he finished and the music on his phone faded, he broke eye contact, jotting notes down in his notepad.

"That sounded amazing. The lyrics teetered between lust and love and the music is almost erotic. It was great. You didn't need any help at all," I gushed. "I'm sorry. I probably sound like an obsessed fan. I swear I didn't know who you were a couple of weeks ago."

"No. You don't sound obsessed." His eyes glowed as he put his hand over his heart. "And ouch."

I stifled my giggle. "I just meant that I've heard your songs, but I didn't know they were your songs. Your songs are everywhere. But what you just did, that was something different. And it was special because you were the one actually singing it. It sounded personal."

He stared at me, chest rising and falling steadily. "It sounds like you heard me."

"Maybe you just needed someone to listen to you."

"Maybe I just needed you to listen to me."

I was drawn to him. "Maybe."

As the quietness descended upon us, something was definitely brewing between us. It could've been the music or the lyrics or both, but it made it difficult for me to resist him.

*And it's probably for my own good if I didn't get too attached considering I'm on a dating show where he decides to date multiple women at once to weigh his options. Kind of like Tate wanted to do.*

Julian was the first to break the silence. "I don't know

55

where that came from. I had been stuck all day. That never happens to me."

"What inspired the song to begin with?"

He smirked as if he had a secret. "A conversation I had at a bar."

"Well it must have been a good conversation," I joked, ignoring the pit that sat low and heavy in my stomach.

*Great. More competition.*

He seemed to sense where my mind was going. "She helped me see what it was that I wanted and needed in a woman. It gave me perspective. And since I usually use my life as inspiration and I had this beat that I hadn't released yet, I thought why not?"

"That's something I was wondering about." I took the opportunity to change the subject. "Are all of your lyrics true to life? The song about 'Ass Everywhere' comes to mind." I wiggled my eyebrows suggestively.

Although the title was a little too on the nose for me, it was a surprisingly poetic look at living a life where women offered up their bodies first and their hearts second and their minds last.

He shook his head with amusement. "I've experienced some crazy shit, but depending on who I'm writing for or what I'm being asked to write about, I work with the artists to help tell their stories. 'Ass Everywhere' is true for DJ Ox. I hung out with him and from what I saw and what he told me, that's the life that he's living. The songs that I've written that are solely written by me, those are true to life. I leave a lot of me in all of my songs, but it takes the spin of whoever the artist is. When I write what I feel, real or imagined, I put myself in the situation. That's the only way it feels true." He let out a little laugh and turned his head toward the fountain. "I shouldn't be telling you all of this, any of this. I'd appreciate it if you'd please keep it to yourself."

"Hey," I uttered, reaching up and touching his face. I turned his head back toward me. "I would never tell anyone anything you told me."

He grabbed my hand from his cheek and kissed the inside of it. The electricity crackled between us. I let out an audible breath.

*Is this what swooning is?*

The kiss scorched the skin of my palm and coursed through my entire body. Butterflies started at the base of my stomach and fanned out.

"You are going to kill it on this show," I murmured, shaking my head and gently pulling my hand out of his grasp.

He smiled, but his eyebrows furrowed. "What do you mean?"

"You are going to own *The One*."

"Why do you say that? You have to give me a reason."

"I can give you five."

"By all means..." He lifted his upturned hands.

I lifted my pointer finger in the air. "First of all, look at you. You're sexy as hell and you're so comfortable with who you are as a person that you made me comfortable with you on sight. Second of all, you have a house full of women who don't know you and are already saying they love you. Third, you are sweet. That hand kiss is the stuff shows like *The One* are made of. That hand kiss is the stuff unrealistic expectations are made of. They're not going to be able to have another bachelor after you and you're going to completely fuck things up for every man in America. Fourth, your personality really is amazing. You're funny and intelligent with just the right bit of a sarcastic edge." I stood up, lifting my leg over the bench and backing away. "Everyone is going to love you. You are going to thrive on the show."

Julian rose to his feet and my head dipped back as I kept eye contact. He appeared to be six feet tall and hovered over my five foot seven inches.

"Well, if that's the case, why does it sound like you're telling me goodbye?"

His face conveyed a myriad of emotions—confusion being the one I picked up on first. I thought I saw flashes of disappointment, but I wasn't sure if that was wishful thinking or not.

I continued backing away from him, creating a safe distance between us. "I'm not telling you goodbye. I'm still a contestant so you'll see me in a couple of hours."

"You know what I mean." He stuffed his hands in his pockets. "Why are you abruptly walking away right now?"

Holding up all five fingers, I admitted the truth. "Fifth, there's something about you."

His eyes seemed to laser focus into me and my voice faltered as I continued.

"You're a poet and you truly have a gift. I could watch you work out song lyrics for hours. You have a way with words that completely sucks me in. And it would be too easy and too risky for me to go down that rabbit hole. So Julian Winters, I bid you adieu. It's been real."

Without giving him a chance to respond, I turned on my heel and jogged out of the fountain area and moved quickly through the garden. For a brief second, I was disappointed that he didn't run after me or at least call my name. But then I thought about the setup of *The One* and the premise behind it.

*Why would he chase after one woman he just met— regardless of how crazy the chemistry is between us—when he has eleven more women ready to throw themselves at him?*

As soon as the thought entered my head, I shook it off.

*I've been here for less than twelve hours and I'm already getting caught up in the bullshit. I don't need him to run after me. I chose to walk away. And I chose to walk away for a reason. A good reason.*

Sighing, I picked up the pace and moved toward the house. The faster I moved, the harder I breathed, and the hazier my mind became. My heart beat was out of control. Slowing down near the well-lit trailers, I peeked into the makeup trailer to see if Koko was still around. I needed a touch up and some best friend talk.

Fortunately, she was alone and cleaning up when I burst through the door.

Koko took one look at me and waved me into the trailer frantically. "Come here! Close the door!" She washed her hands and pointed to her makeup chair. "What the fuck happened to you?"

I plopped down in the chair and allowed her to dab my face with a moist toilette. My heart was still racing, but I wasn't out of breath. It was him. The way he looked at me. The way his fingers brushed against my skin.

I squeezed my eyes shut. "The worst possible thing that could happen on day one of this bullshit happened."

She gasped, covering her mouth with her hand. She lowered her voice. "You fucked him on camera?"

"No, worse. I fell for him off camera."

# Chapter 5

After telling Koko everything that happened, I followed the walkway back the way I came until it led me to the French double doors of the side entrance. I heard yelling before I even walked through the door. The noise was to my immediate right, in the sun room, so I peeked in. A producer seemed to be strategizing with two contestants. The contestant that was doing the yelling was Tori, the blonde bitch from the cocktail party the night before. Shaking my head, I rolled my eyes and continued moving through the house.

"Zoe!" Mya, my newly minted roommate, sighed with relief as she popped up from behind me. She lowered her voice. "Where have you been?"

I smiled at the brunette beauty. Mya sat beside me in the limo and while everyone else was talking incessantly, she didn't feel the need to talk. We silently observed everyone else and when someone said something ignorant, we looked at each other and smiled.

Our friendship and roommate status was born in that

moment.

"I'm just getting back from a walk and getting my makeup touched up," I replied on our way to the spiraling staircase. "But I went to wardrobe earlier and my dress should've been delivered by now."

"Well, I just left wardrobe and I got cursed out because I waited until the last minute. But I went when they called me! Aren't we supposed to be down in the living room at six? I still have an hour to get ready!"

I smiled, amused. "Yeah, exactly. I got yelled at when I stepped on the grass earlier. I think everyone is high strung because it's the first show." Once we got up the stairs and entered our bedroom, I continued. "This is supposed to be reality TV, but there isn't anything real about it. Everything is micromanaged. This producer keeps asking me if I have time to speak with her before the cocktail party tonight."

"Is it the one with the short haircut?" Mya asked, sitting in the middle of her bed.

"That's the one." I shook my head, kicking off my shoes and sitting on the edge of mine.

"She cornered me too, but I was heading to wardrobe so she said she would stop by our room before six."

I groaned, letting my head fall back. "I need a nap before I can deal with this bullshit."

"Unfortunately you don't have time for a nap, but hopefully once we get ready, it'll be too late for her to try to feed us lines."

"Is that what they're doing?"

"I think so. I saw Bailey reading a script. A script!"

We sat on our respective beds and talked about what we expected. When Mya said she heard one of the ladies in the house caught a glimpse of Julian, I remained silent. For some reason, it felt right to keep it a secret. I didn't want to share my time with him with anyone else in the house. So I nodded and smiled at what our housemate said Julian was wearing—she was wrong.

Where I held the anti-reality TV perspective, Mya was the hopeless romantic that thought reality TV dating shows were real. Although we had two polar opposite views, we somehow found ourselves meeting in a new point of view that teetered between appalled by how fake everything was and excited to spend time with Julian.

We'd just finished getting dressed when there was a knock on the door. Mya and I immediately looked over at each other blankly. It took the second series of knocks before she walked over and opened the door.

"Hi guys. I'm Jamie," the producer introduced herself as she eased into the room. "I just wanted to talk to you about tonight. How are you feeling? You're meeting Julian Winters!"

My stomach fluttered, but I didn't say anything. Mya yelped.

Jamie smiled, but it seemed forced. "From what I can tell, he's a great guy. I am assigned to you two and I just want to make sure you two make it to the finale. And the best way to do that is to have a game plan."

"Game plan for...?" I asked, cocking my head to the side.

"To win." The inflection in her voice made it clear that she thought the answer was obvious. Jamie looked back and forth between the two of us. "How are you two going to approach this?"

"I'm going to be myself," I answered before giving her a tight smile and walking back to the mirror.

My hair and makeup were utter perfection, but the dress was exquisite. The wardrobe department had chosen dresses specifically for each contestant based on a style profile that was in the application. Whatever Koko filled out for my style was enough for them to get the exact dress I would've picked for the night.

*I mean, it would be the dress I'd pick if I had thousands of dollars to spend on one dress.*

It was black and fitted, hugging my generous curves. It was floor-length with a thigh high split and the sweetheart neckline showed off my breasts without being over the top. I paired the chiffon number with my red pumps.

"So I want to talk to you both about tonight." She held up two small microphones that needed to be clipped to our dresses. "And I came to mic you up. Just a reminder, when the battery pack is green, it's live. When it's red, it's off. If it's blinking red that means we're trying to locate you. It takes a few minutes, but there's a sensor that gives us a general idea of your whereabouts."

Mya tossed her hair over her shoulder and held her hands out at her sides. "Where am I supposed to put it?"

Mya's white skin-tight dress had a high neckline, but was completely backless. While on me, the dress might've looked overly sexualized. On Mya and her smaller curves, the dress looked sexy, yet elegant.

"I will tuck it right on your shoulder. For the most part, your hair will cover it," Jamie answered, problem solving on the fly. She walked over to Mya and started putting the mic on her. "I also wanted to give you both a few tips. You may want to play up who you are."

She finished pinning the mic on Mya and moved across the room to me.

"What do you mean?" Mya asked, fixing her hair.

Avoiding eye contact with me, Jamie pinned the mic on the inside of my sweetheart neckline. I looked down and it was almost undetectable.

"Thank you," I murmured, still waiting for Jamie to answer Mya's question.

She took a few steps back and looked between us. "Well," she started slowly, almost nervously. "You two need to play up your personalities. All of the women have notes and tips that will help them stay in the game longer. But for you two, you need to...play up your personalities."

*Play up our personalities? She doesn't even know us to say... Wait... Is she saying what I think she's saying? No, she can't be. That's not even legal.*

I felt my eyebrows come together. "I feel like you're taking the long way around to the point you're really trying to make."

"Yeah," Mya agreed, putting her hands on her hips.

Jamie sighed, the fake smile that was plastered on her face fell. "Okay, fine. Mya, what are you? Mexican? I need you to play up the fiery Latina in you. And Zoe, you need to be the sassy black girl. You know..." She snapped her fingers in a Z-formation in the air.

I was in shock. I looked at Mya, whose mouth was agape and eyes were watering.

Everything in the room froze in time as Jamie's words echoed in my ears. My mind was spinning and then my shock gave way to anger.

"First of all, you will not try to force us into stereotypical roles. We are going to be who we are, period. So to say we need to 'play up our personalities' is bullshit code for us to perpetuate your small-minded idea of who we are. You don't know us to know if we're 'fiery' or 'sassy' so to assume that is problematic. Second of all, the Civil Rights Act of 1964 prohibits you from even coming to us with this. That case against that other reality show was dismissed only because it focused on casting decisions and how it affected the First Amendment. But the First Amendment does not protect overzealous producers actively violating our rights. Third, I'm a woman, not a girl. Don't make that mistake again. And fourth, fuck you."

Jamie shook her head. "I didn't mean to offend you guys. I just want to be honest with you. I've been working on reality dating shows for the last ten years and minorities don't last long on these things."

Mya spoke up. "Isn't that Julian's decision? He wouldn't have selected us to be on the show if we weren't viable options."

Jamie shook her head and tucked her short hair behind her ears. "Julian isn't the only one making the decisions. His decisions are taken into advisement when he fights for a girl to stay, but at the end of the day, this is a business. Robert Brady is the creator, writer, and executive producer. This is his business. And the only way to keep him happy is to keep the ratings up. And the only way to keep the ratings up is to give the people what they want." She shrugged. "And unfortunately, they want fiery and sassy from the two of you."

"I'm not doing it. And it would be in your best interests to not say shit to me for the rest of my time here," I replied dismissively.

"I'm not even fiery. I don't have a temper. I'm a librarian not some sexy temptress!" Mya turned away from us and headed to the mirror. She dabbed at her eyes. "It's almost six, we have to go downstairs."

Jamie backed away from us, stopping at the door with a sympathetic look. "Look, I didn't want to be the one to have this conversation with you guys. My girlfriend is African American and I know how this sounds. I understand why you'd be mad. But the only way to stay around long enough for Julian Winters to get to know you and fight for you to stay is to do what will keep the network happy from week to week. Think about it."

The door closed with a light click behind her.

Walking toward the door, I took a deep breath in order to calm myself down. "Are you okay?"

"No," Mya answered, her eyes were pink and watery from the tears she was holding back. "Because she's right."

"No, she's not."

"Yes, she is. Have you ever seen one of these shows? We're going to be the first ones to go. We're going to have to take drastic measures to get noticed!" Her weepy voice broke.

Thinking about Julian, I remembered how his eyes traveled up my body. I remembered how he spoke to me, sung to me, opened up to me.

"Don't listen to that bullshit, Mya. I'm not going to be anything, but myself. I would advise you to do the same. You're great. You have depth and you're beautiful. Don't doubt that."

"But this is Julian Winters!"

"And you're Mya..." *Crap! Last name is...? What is her last name!* "Santos?" I guessed, my voice elevating and my smile unsure.

I was ninety percent sure I was correct.

Mya's teary expression gave way to delight as she started to giggle. She lightly touched under her eyes before turning and walking toward me. "You forgot my last name."

"Well, in my defense, we met this morning."

"Oh God, why does it already feel like it's been at least two weeks since we arrived?"

I nodded, walking out the door. She was right. "This isn't normal."

# Chapter 6

The bright lights of the chandelier competed with the production lights. I tried not to be nervous, but I couldn't stop thinking about the fact that I was being filmed. More than that, I couldn't stop thinking about the fact that I was about to see Julian again in front of a camera.

*Focus,* I told myself, shifting my weight nervously. *I'm on camera.*

"Ladies, we're going to have you each enter from this door here," Bryce explained, gesturing toward the main entrance. "Julian will be stationed at the bottom of the staircase. You will enter, greet him and then move along to the back patio where there will be music, drinks, and a few things to nibble on. Once everyone has had a chance to meet and greet Julian, he will come out here and you will have your chance to make a connection. He will be getting rid of two of you tonight if he feels you are not...the one."

Bryce smiled toward a camera without actually looking at the camera until someone yelled, "Cut!"

"Okay, ladies, follow me," a petite woman with braids

called out. We fell into step behind her in the order we were placed in. She led us out the side door and down the cobblestone walkway. "Okay you're going to line up in order and the golf cart will take each of you one by one. Once you are in the cart, the camera and mics will pick up everything you say and do so just act natural. Good luck."

She signaled and the sound of a golf cart against the pavement could be heard. None of us said a word as the cart moved closer to pick up the first contestant.

*Bailey.*

Bailey was a pretty blonde from the Mid-West with an adorable accent. She was very sweet, but seemed to be easily influenced. In the few hours she had been in the house, she was bullied out of the room she wanted and talked into cooking lunch. After that incident, Mya and I told her that she could hang with us, but she wanted to be part of what she considered the 'in' crowd.

It was five minutes before the next cart came to pick up the next contestant. I was seventh in line and it felt like an eternity before the cart came to get me.

I climbed in and clasped my hands in my lap. My stomach twisted into knots the entire thirty second trip to the front of the house. The gentle bell that chimed on the cart seemed to be announcing my arrival as well as heightening my anxiety. My body was tense. I inhaled and exhaled deeply in hopes of calming myself down.

*I have nothing to be nervous about. I'm just going to gracefully jump out of this cart, strut into the house and meet Julian for the second time. Sure we have chemistry and he's incredibly good looking and he has this amazing way with words that really makes me want to throw my panties at him. But he's just a guy. A guy ready to meet twelve women. A guy that I've already met, talked to, and hung out with so I'm really making this a bigger deal than it is.*

I attempted to shake off the jitters that were completely unlike me and took another deep breath.

It didn't help.

I climbed out of the cart and saw a cameraman readjust his position and realized that the jitters weren't just because of Julian. It was because I was being filmed. Everything I did or said was being captured for posterity and for the entertainment of viewers everywhere. If Julian really was everything I imagined him to be, I would be sad to be sent home, but it wasn't like I was in love or anything. If I did something to embarrass myself or my family, that would haunt me for the rest of my life and ruin my career.

I took my time walking to the house, my focus on not tripping. I could handle the scarlet letter of H for hypocrite for appearing on a show that I trashed for years. But I couldn't handle being on the blooper reel of said show. I had to draw the line somewhere.

Pushing one of the double doors open, I caught of glimpse of him. I hesitated before I stepped in.

*Damn.*

Somehow, Julian Winters looked even better than he had earlier. Wearing a black tuxedo that had to be custom fit to his body, Julian's broad shoulders were on display. Seeing him from that distance, I could see he was easily six feet tall with an athlete's body. The man I saw in the garden was good looking, open, and vulnerable. The man standing in the in the foyer was absolutely breathtaking, confident, and in control.

He let out a low whistle. "Wow." The word was low enough that I didn't think he meant for me to hear it and loud enough to make my heart skip a beat.

I took a few tentative steps into the foyer, trying to get the drumming in my chest under control before speaking. We just looked at each other, wide-eyed, before either of us made an attempt at a greeting.

"Hi," we said at the same time in the same tone of voice before laughing.

Our laughter broke the spell and the nerves and anxiety went away instantly. Something about his laugh made me feel at ease, like we were back in the garden with no microphones, no cameras, and no group of eleven other women.

"I'm Zoe." I moved across the room and reached out to shake his hand.

If possible, his smile grew. "I'm Julian."

The moment our hands touched, something happened.

It would sound too cheesy to say that sparks flew, but I didn't know another way to describe it. Maybe it was Julian or maybe it was the scenario, but the knots in my belly turned into butterflies. And I couldn't see it for myself, but I felt like I was grinning foolishly up at him like a pre-teen staring up at her celebrity crush.

*Get a grip.*

I exhaled. "It's very nice to meet you, Julian."

*Oh my God, why is my voice so breathy? I sound like I'm trying to seduce him!*

"It's very nice to meet you as well, Zoe."

Whatever was crackling between us was distracting me and kept me from thinking straight. I felt myself becoming flushed so I pulled my hand from his grasp.

I pretended not to notice and not to be affected when I saw disappointment crease his features.

"I have something for you." He reached over to a table and picked up a white gold charm bracelet. He stepped closer to me, eliminating all pretense of personal space. With his free hand, he reached for my right arm and trailed his fingers from my elbow to my hand. Turning my palm upward, he ran his thumb over the inside of my wrist.

I shivered.

"Thank you for being here," he whispered, putting the charmless charm bracelet on me. Once it was clasped, his grey eyes found mine and I lost my train of thought.

Unable to tear my eyes from his, I swallowed hard. "Thank you for having me."

*It's not just me. He is having this moment with twelve other women tonight,* I reminded myself, controlling the wind under my sails.

With his hand still encircling my wrist, he applied a little pressure. "Tell me something you're passionate about."

"Poetry," I admitted almost breathlessly.

His eyebrows flew up. "Really?"

Finding my natural voice, I redirected. "Yes, really. Why does that surprise you?"

He gave me a playful look as if he was flashing back to earlier. "I'm not saying it surprises me. I'm just saying I'll have to test your poetry skills and knowledge later."

I grinned. "I'd like to see you try." He let out a short sexy laugh from deep in his chest so I continued. "And what about you? What are you passionate about?"

He smirked. "You're the first one to ask me that. I have to say my work. I'm very passionate about my work."

"I can tell. Reading the lyrics to the songs you've written, it shows."

"You read the lyrics?" Julian's eyes searched mine quizzically. His thumb stopped its gentle caress against the inside of my wrist.

*Did I not mention that earlier?*

"Well, yeah. I wanted to get to know who it was that I was going to be meeting. So I read your lyrics. And when I looked at the words, not listened to the songs, but looked at the words, it read like poetry to me."

There were so many things his eyes were telling me, but I was too overwhelmed by the darkening of them to understand a single one. He dropped his gaze and took my other hand into his. When he made eye contact again, I saw it and I understood it. "I appreciate you saying that, Zoe. It means a lot."

The sincerity in both his voice and his eyes made me smile. In a reality TV setting where everything was faked, that moment was real. He seemed genuinely caught off guard and appreciative of my compliment. I wanted to elaborate, but I could hear the bell of the golf cart as it made its way up the pavement.

"I know you have other women to meet so I'll leave you with something special that hopefully you'll remember me by." My smile widened as I began quoting my favorite Pablo Neruda poem.

I knew that most of the viewers at home would think it was sexually charged and aggressively flirtatious. But I hoped that Julian would get it, especially after the song he shared with me earlier in the day.

If he was the poet that I felt that he was, the poet that his music indicated him to be, he would appreciate more than just the sexual attraction and desire on the surface of the poem. Even if he'd never heard it before, I hoped he'd get the meaning behind it. Hopefully he'd see the poem represented a desire to know someone fully, a desire and a motivation to seek them out to know them fully. The poem was intense, but it was my favorite and if I was going to go home, I wanted it to be on my terms.

I didn't doubt my decision to quote the poem until I was finished and I couldn't read Julian's expression. His lips parted, but didn't say a word.

*Okay, that didn't go over as expected. But at least if I'm going to leave tonight, I'll leave looking flawless and quoting Pablo Neruda. It'll suck that I didn't get a chance to know him, but—*

His hands slipped up my arms slowly, unhurriedly, making goosebumps cover my skin and stopping all train of thought. Once reaching my elbows, he followed the same path back down before enveloping my hands with his. "Pablo Neruda," he stated softly.

My heart, definitely, and my entire body, possibly, trembled. I was so surprised that he knew the poem, I couldn't do anything but laugh.

He winked, joining in with my laughter. "Didn't think I'd know that, did you?"

"I have to say...that is impressive," I returned, backing away from him and letting my fingers slide from his grasp.

"We'll have to talk more poetry at the party."

"I look forward to it." I turned on my heel and strutted toward the back patio.

I put an extra sway in my hips and I could feel his eyes on my ass. I smiled even harder. The feeling of his eyes on me made my entire body tingle. I sighed happily.

*Yes.*

Once I got around the corner, the judgmental eyes of six women burned into me. With glasses of alcoholic beverages in their manicured clutches, they eyed me up and down. The feeling of their eyes on me made me cringe. I sighed irritably.

*No. Hell no.*

Instead of sitting with them, I made a beeline for the bar. Looking around, I noticed there was no camera in the little nook where the bar was hidden.

The old man behind the bar grinned. "What can I get for

you?"

I glanced down at his nametag and then back to his face. "Hi Bart! How are you? I'll take a glass of champagne please."

"I'm doing pretty good for an old man. How are you? Are you excited?"

I rested my elbows on the bar top and I smiled. "I'm doing well." I looked over my shoulder and saw the woman who had just walked in get the stink eye from the rest of the group. "I'm excited to get to know Julian. I'm not excited about the rest."

"Everyone always feels the same way. But when you're stuck in here with no phones, no televisions, and nothing to do, you make friends."

"Or enemies."

The old man laughed. "I suppose you're right." He handed me my drink and then gave me a sympathetic grin. "They need you in the filming areas so you can be recorded during the cocktail parties. You have to go back to the group."

"You mean I can't hang out with you until Julian is done?" My tone was playful.

"I'm afraid not. But I'll be here until the Bracelet Ceremony is over. Then drinks are a free-for-all." He shrugged.

"Thank you, Bart."

He gave me a wave and I headed back to the patio area. I stood on the outskirts of the area and the same woman talked without taking a break or allowing anyone to get a word in.

"...guess his type. I would assume he likes variety." A nameless brown-haired, blue-eyed woman spoke using her hands a lot. She seemed chatty.

*I will call her Chatty Cathy.*

"That's funny. I was almost positive you said that you didn't understand how they would let in those two because they are fat," Tori pointed out in a voice full of fake concern. "Or did I hear you wrong?"

Chatty Cathy gasped. "No! I mean, not like that." She looked at two other women whose names I didn't bother to remember and whose bodies didn't deserve to be ridiculed. "I didn't say you were fat. I said you were chubby. That's all." She glared at Tori. "Tori said you weren't going to be able to find clothes to fit in wardrobe and I said they have chubby sizes too. I didn't mean it like that." Her eyes watered and she put her hands to her cheeks. "They were all there! They heard me!"

Tori stood in her sequenced gown and her blonde hair stacked on top of her head as if she were royalty. She was a mean girl who was trying to pit people against each other. I would've assumed it was to get into their heads to ruin their conversations with Julian at the party. But since my run-in with her at the interview, I knew that she was just a stone cold bitch.

When Mya walked in, most of the women were too engaged in the argument to give her the death stare. Two still managed to do it though.

I shook my head and signaled for her to follow me to the canopy on the outskirts of the sitting area.

"Tough room," she muttered after she passed the rest of the women. I lifted my eyebrows and made a face.

We were only a few feet away, but it offered enough privacy that we could discuss things privately.

"Two things...where did you get that?" She pointed at my drink. "And what is this argument about?"

I pointed to the little nook on the other side of the patio. "Bar is over there. Bartender is Bart. He's sweet. And this fight is because Tori and some of the others were just being shitty to the two women who are by the fire pit now." I shook my head. "This is why I don't bother learning names."

"Exactly." She grinned. "Can I tell you about my meeting with Julian?"

"Of course," I answered genuinely meaning it at the time.

"So I walk in and he says 'hey beautiful' and I say 'hey yourself handsome' and then I give him a hug! His arms are...mmm, yummy! He lifted me up in the air a little."

I felt the pit growing in my stomach with each word. My mouth felt a little dry so I took a swig of my champagne.

She hugged herself with her arms. "Then he asked me what I was passionate about and I said working out was a passion of mine and he kind of checked me out and nodded like..." She gave me a smoldering look while checking me out and she nodded slowly. "Just like that! Almost like, yeah I can tell. And then he said he'd come find me inside." Her face beamed with happiness and hope.

My mouth was still dry and the pit in my stomach had turned into heavy knots rooting me to my seat.

It was weird hearing about Julian having a flirty exchange with Mya. But it was even weirder that I felt so weird about it.

*I met him four or five hours ago. He's not my man.*

I cleared my throat and smiled brightly. "That's good, Mya. Sounds like it went well!"

"Yes! Thank you. Let me grab my drink so I can hear about yours!" Mya's small frame spun around and darted to the other side of the patio.

*I'm not a jealous person,* I reminded myself. *Julian is going to flirt with other women. That's the premise of the show. It's way too early for me to feel any kind of way about it. He's a guy. He's just a regular guy. Just a regular guy who knows Pablo Neruda off of the top of his head.* I sighed. *This is insane.*

By the time Mya returned and I gave her a brief recap of

my exchange with Julian, leaving out the poetry part, Bryce and Julian stepped out onto the patio.

"Ladies," Bryce called out to us. We all gathered around as he continued. "Welcome to your first Bracelet Ceremony. You've all had a chance to meet Julian. Now you will begin what we call the Bracelet Ceremony Cocktail Party. You will mix and mingle with our bachelor and give him a chance to get to know you. At the end of the party, we will have the ceremony. You've each received a bracelet and each week, if Julian chooses you to stay in the competition, you will receive a charm. If you do not receive a charm at the end of the ceremony, you will need to say your goodbyes to not only one another, but also to Julian. On the up side, you are free to keep your bracelet!" He gave the camera a cheesy grin before casting his gaze over us. "This week, Julian has a First Impression charm which will be given to the person who made a great first impression." He turned to Julian. "Are you ready to find the one?"

"I'm as ready as I'll ever be," Julian answered, looking around, seemingly overwhelmed. He flashed a smile that was so mesmerizing that I almost didn't notice that it didn't reach his eyes. "Hold on."

Julian walked around where we were gathered, past the cameraman and camerawoman who were on opposite sides of our group, and beyond the pool to get to the gate. Not missing a beat, the camerawoman was only seconds behind him when she got through the gate.

Confused murmuring commenced while I silently stared at the gate.

*Is he getting cold feet? Is he quitting? Does he not feel like the one is in this room?*

After fifteen minutes, Julian returned through the gate with a bottle of water and a determined expression on his face. He ran his hand through his short, slicked back hair.

"I apologize about that. Where were we?"

Bryce repeated the last few sentences of what he had said and then asked Julian again if he was ready.

Julian nodded. "Absolutely. I'm ready to find the one and I believe she's in this room right now."

*Was it a coincidence that he looked right at me when he said it?* I looked around to see if anyone else noticed. *Okay cool...so it was just in my head. Got it.*

Bryce announced that he was leaving and he would be back for the Bracelet Ceremony. The moment he left the patio area, Tori positioned herself in front of Julian.

"I'm going to go ahead and steal you for a minute," she said, looping her arm around his and leading him out of the eyes and ears of the rest of us.

"Well, she didn't waste any time," someone remarked.

That comment opened the floodgates. Interestingly enough, the people who were hanging around Tori the most had the most to say as soon as she left the room.

"The claws are coming out so I need another drink." Mya mouthed. "You?"

I shook my head and pointed to our seats from earlier. She gave me a thumbs-up and then headed for the bar.

"Who does she think she is? I'm going to give them three minutes and then I'm going to go find them and interrupt. I need time with him, too," Chatty Cathy announced.

A pale, redhead with bright green eyes and an exotic brunette with plump lips egged her on even though those two were the main ones I saw with Tori.

*Maybe I should've gotten another drink,* I thought as I made my way to my seat.

"So what do you think of Julian?" A producer with a camerawoman in tow asked just as I sat down in the chair.

I was caught off guard and I froze. The camerawoman seemed to zoom in on my confusion.

"It's okay to talk directly into the camera. Throughout the show we like to do confessional interviews. They're just private moments with the contestants to get a sense of what they are feeling as things are going on."

"Oh, okay."

My mind instantly replayed the moment our eyes met for the first time and then when he recognized the poem. The corners of my lips turned up and as hard as I tried, I couldn't control my grin. My first impression of him wasn't the Tom Ford model that was standing in the foyer. My first impression wasn't the introspective man writing his way through his stress in the garden. My first impression of Julian was in print. So I went with that.

"My first impression of Julian is that he's deep. There's more to him than meets the eye. I'm looking forward to getting to know him."

"What do you think about the other girls?"

*Girls? These are grown ass women. Sure some of them are childish, but it's a little demeaning to refer to them as girls.*

"I don't."

"What do you mean?"

I smirked. "I don't think about the other women in the house."

The camerawoman laughed as Mya walked up. Shifting the camera's focus to Mya, she was asked the same question. "So what do you think of Julian?"

Mya's entire face lit up as she detailed her interaction with him during her meeting.

I watched her and the more she talked, the more uncomfortable I became. It dawned on me that the look on her face probably mirrored the look on my face as we talked about the same man.

*What am I doing?* I sighed, letting my head drop back. *What am I doing here?*

Forty minutes had passed and almost everyone had stolen a few minutes with Julian. Most of the women were interrupting other women in order to get their turn. I figured, once everyone had their turn, I'd take mine and I wouldn't have to worry about being interrupted.

On my way back from the bar, I stopped in my tracks when I noticed the last woman who went off with Julian talking to another woman. The drinks were flowing and only one person was sloppy drunk. I took a sip of my champagne and casually looked around the patio. Everyone had taken a turn.

*It's now or never.*

"Zoe."

The unexpected sound of Julian's voice sent a chill down my spine.

I turned around to face him. My smile matched his. "Julian."

He held out his hand. "Will you accompany me?"

"Of course." I intertwined my fingers with his and the tingling started in my fingers and traveled up my arm.

I allowed him to lead me to a private section of the property. The pathway was lined with flowering bushes and lights. With each step, the noise of the women chattering disappeared and it was just me and Julian.

*Well us and them.*

I put my glass to my lips and glanced at the cameraman, two producers, a production assistant and someone with a clipboard.

"Have you adjusted to all of this yet?" I asked, squeezing his hand as we slowed to a stop.

We sat down on a bench under a beautiful stone archway that was wrapped in ivy.

He laughed. "Not at all. I think it'll take some time to get used to it all."

"Are you enjoying yourself at least? Because that's what matters."

"I am." He looked down at our intertwined fingers before meeting my gaze again. "One of my favorite memories so far was when this beautiful woman walked up to me and recited a poem."

"Someone stole my move?" I gasped in mock surprise.

Julian chuckled. "Beautiful, sexy, smart, funny...you're the total package."

"I would agree with that." I grinned, finishing my glass of champagne and placing it on the ground. "And you're not so bad yourself."

"Not so bad?" He paused as if he was thinking about it and then he nodded. "I'll take it."

"So, what brings you on the show?"

"Well, I work a lot and when I do get some downtime, I want to spend it with someone special. I don't want to spend the time that I have searching bars, online, whatever or with someone who isn't right for me. So it just so happened that I had planned a month to write, no recording, no producing, just writing and this opportunity fell into my lap. Because the timing was so perfect, I felt like I had to give it a shot."

I nodded, soaking in the information. "When things line up like that, you have to take the shot."

"Zoe, I—"

"Cut!" One of the producers yelled as the cameraman swung the camera from his shoulder and started messing with it.

With a sharp intake of breath, I jumped. The flurry of activity took me by surprise. Julian rubbed his thumb across the side of my hand, calming me.

The producer put a walkie-talkie to her lips. "Are you getting this? Something is going on with Tim's camera. It just happened. Yeah. Okay. We'll be reset in five minutes. Tell someone in electrical to fix the damn camera in the damn archway. That's the whole reason we have this bullshit on the side of a house. Yeah. Well, we have everything about why he's here. Yeah. I know. Yeah..."

I turned my head back to Julian and found him still staring at me. My face instantly heated.

"We only have a few minutes where we aren't being recorded." His voice rushed and his hand covered his mic. "So let's do this for real. What would you say is the worst thing about being here?"

I crushed the small device between my palm and my chest, smothering the sound of my voice. "For the most part, it's one person in particular. Hands down. But in general, it's the people. It's like they see a camera and a handsome man and they lose their minds. What about you?"

"I'm sure I can guess who you're talking about." He smirked. "For me it's being contractually obligated to do what's in the best interest of the show." He looked over his shoulder at the crew members before leaning in a little closer. "I know this isn't your scene. All night, you've been off to the side observing. Earlier today, you went for a walk. So what made you decide to go through with this?"

"You're right. This isn't me. I think reality dating shows are complete bullshit." The words flew out of my mouth. "But when I started reading the lyrics to songs you've written, that's what did it for me. For some reason, I felt like I needed to be here. You are a poet. The things that you can do with words...intrigue me. That's why I'm here. Because I couldn't stop thinking about you. I kept wondering about who you were and what you were all about and what inspired you to write with that much emotion."

He let out a breath that seemed to sag his broad shoulders. "Wow, thank you for that." He squeezed my hand and leaned closer, giving me a boyish grin. "I can't even put into words how much that means to me, to hear you say that. Every song I've ever written started as a poem. I add the hook and chorus later. But for you to pick up on that." His eyes bore into mine, not just looking at me, but looking inside of me. "No one has ever picked up on that before."

My heart faltered. His words were dripping in sincerity and vulnerability. I had no idea the conversation was going to get so real, so fast. There was no pretense, no expectations, no hidden agendas. It felt like he'd let me in on a secret that he didn't know he wanted to tell.

I looked over my shoulder to see if they were still working on the camera. When our eyes met again, I felt something pang in my chest so I tried to lighten the moment. "Well, I love poetry. I guess I just have an eye for talent."

His deep chuckle from the barrel of his chest made me smile and broke the spell he was casting on me. He shook his head at me. "We don't have much time before we're back on camera. Where are you from?"

"Virginia. Chesterfield, Virginia. But I live here now. You?"

"Rockville, Maryland. But we moved here when I was twelve. When did you get here?"

"Seven years ago. If you didn't write, sing, and produce, what would you do?"

"I'd be a lawyer. What do you do for a living?"

"Bartender." I shook my head, slowing our hurried exchange of information. "Wait a minute, you want to be a lawyer?"

"I would if music didn't work out. I went through a long trial early in my career and I got really into it." I must have been making a face because he leaned back a little and asked, "You have something against lawyers?"

I stifled the giggle with my hand. "No, not at all. It's just that I'm about to be a lawyer!"

"No way! You're in law school now? While you're here?"

"No, I'm done with school. I just have to take the bar and then...I can practice law."

That sentence gave me hives two weeks ago. But for whatever reason, sitting with Julian, holding his hand, and talking to him about it didn't make me want to freak out.

"That's awesome, Zoe. Wow! You are...wow. When do you take the bar?"

"July. I could've taken it a couple of weeks ago, but..."

He searched my face, inching closer. "But what?"

"I choked," I admitted. "I completely choked. I was—"

"Camera is back. Check your feed!" The producer exclaimed loudly into the walkie-talkie, startling me again. She lowered her voice and turned her back to us to add, "They've been whispering while we've been down so replay your sound feed. Oh. Yeah. They're covering their mics."

Julian frowned playfully. "She knows we can hear her right?"

Ignoring us, the producer yelled, "Action!"

A mutually understood look passed between us as we uncovered our microphones.

"Tell me something weird about you," he asked, changing the subject.

There was a twinkle in his eye as if we shared something special that no one else knew and my smile widened. If I wasn't so impressed by how much we had in common, I would've swooned over the look he gave me.

"Hmmm...something weird. Well, I love the smell of rain."

"The smell of rain? I don't think this is going to work out," he deadpanned.

I threw my head back and laughed. "It's the smell of plant oils and soil mixing with the rain droplets. It just smells so fresh and new."

"Yeah, okay," he joked, causing another round of laughter to bubble up within my chest.

We were joking back and forth when the producer indicated that he needed to wrap it up.

"Well, Zoe. Despite the fact that I now find you incredibly weird, I have something for you anyway." Julian reached into his tuxedo pocket and pulled out a charm. "It's the First Impression charm and I want you to have this." He pulled out the white gold rose charm and held it in the palm of his hand. "Will you continue on this journey with me to find the one?"

"Absolutely." My voice managed to keep its cool, but I felt inexplicably giddy.

He had inched closer and although it was unnecessary, it was welcomed. His fingers brushed against my skin as he snapped the charm onto the bracelet. We were inches apart and my body was reacting to his, but I was keeping it under control. It wasn't until he looked up at me that my heart rate got the best of me.

Julian's eyes lingered on my lips. "I'm happy that you will still be here. I look forward to getting to know you better."

Maybe it was how talented and easy to talk to Julian was or the fact that he knew Pablo Neruda. Maybe it was the seclusion of being locked down at the mansion for the longest day of my life or the fact that the last two days had been consumed with the excitement of getting to meet him. Maybe it was the overtly romantic backdrop and the soft lighting that added to the ambiance or the fact that Julian was one of the most handsome men I'd ever seen in real life. Or maybe it was the fact that he hadn't stopped touching me since he asked me to come to the archway with him. I didn't know the reason, but when he leaned forward, the other women, the entire crew, the apprehension of being on *The One,* the camera, it all disappeared.

Our foreheads touched and his nose just barely grazed mine. His eyes were half-closed and darkened with desire.

"Can I be honest about how often I've thought about kissing you?" Julian breathed, his full lips mere centimeters from mine.

His champagne coated breath tickled my skin. His hands were warm and while one had remained intertwined with mine, the other traveled up my arm, over my shoulder to cradle my neck.

My eyes closed and I let out a shaky breath. I couldn't hear anything over the pounding in my chest. Everything I felt was vivid and intense. I couldn't pull away if I wanted to.

After what felt like a thirty second wait, I trembled at the first brush of his lips against mine. The kiss was slow, allowing us to relish in the feeling. He pulled back slightly, hovering just over my lips so that they were barely touching. My eyes opened to find his conveying the same confusion that was whipping through my brain.

*What the hell was that?*

Our tongues hadn't even touched, but my body was on fire, my heart was rattling in my chest, and butterflies had turned into bats in my belly. That was essentially a peck on the lips, yet it sparked something and resonated deep inside of me. I'd never experienced anything like that before and from the look in his eyes, he hadn't either.

He licked his lips and I knew he was about to kiss me again. I let my eyelids flutter closed.

"Excuse me?"

My eyes flew open and although Julian and I startled apart,

we never stopped holding hands. I jerked my head in the direction of the voice and Tori stood on the walkway with her hands on her hips.

Once she had our attention, she closed the three feet of distance between us and stood directly in front of the bench. Giving her attention to Julian, she said, "I'm here to steal you away for a minute since the Bracelet Ceremony will be starting soon."

"Oh, okay," Julian said agreeably. He turned to me and I could see the confusion mixed with disappointment creasing his features. He squeezed my hand. "Thank you for spending some time with me, Zoe."

I flashed him my best smile. "I enjoyed every second of it."

Our fingers unraveled slowly and his eyes lingered on me for a beat too long.

Tori must have noticed as well because she reached for his free hand and tugged it. "Ready?"

Letting me go, he stood and gave Tori a charming smile. She pushed her obviously fake breasts out and threw her hair over her shoulder. Julian bent his arm for her to hold onto as they walked toward the patio with the cameraman and others in tow. The reality of the situation set in.

*I am on a reality television dating show. Even if it feels real, it's not,* I reminded myself as my emotions knotted in my gut.

I stood, brushing the back of my dress off and squaring my shoulders. Acutely aware that while I didn't see the second cameraperson lurking, they were.

*I can't let myself get swept up in the moment again. I wanted to meet him and I did. I wanted to know more about his artistic process and the First Impression charm gave me a few more days to do that. And then I'm out. It's too easy to get caught up in my feelings in this environment.*

I leisurely followed the path back to the patio trying to

convince myself that I could still walk away from the show and Julian anytime I wanted.

# Chapter 7

The Sunday sunlight poured through the window, bathing the room in a Southern California glow. I stretched my arms and legs out under the thousand count sheets.

*Now these are sheets.*

Since the bullshit that took place at Friday night's Bracelet Ceremony, I spent all of Saturday in bed. It wasn't because I was avoiding confrontation. I was just tired so I slept.

We didn't have plans to see Julian on Saturday so besides to shower and eat, I didn't feel the need to hang out anywhere else besides my room. It wasn't as if I was interested in interacting with anyone else.

*I mean I expected things to get crazy, but after the first ceremony? That's unreal.*

On Friday night, once I returned to the patio and people caught sight of the charm on my bracelet, the whispers and cattiness directly aimed at me ramped up. I didn't enjoy it, but it didn't bother me either.

At the beginning of the Bracelet Ceremony, Bryce Wilson called me to the front and announced that I had gotten the

First Impression charm and the women clapped as if they were happy for me. It was the fakest thing I'd ever seen.

One by one, women were called to stand beside me, but the only one I was concerned about was Mya. She was called last, leaving two of Tori's minions with whom I never conversed with to be sent home.

After the ceremony, Julian left the mansion and all hell broke loose. Tori tried to bait me into an argument and when I didn't cave, she told everyone that Julian and I had kissed. If I thought the shade I was getting was bad when they saw the First Impression Charm, news of the kiss sent them over the edge. Because I didn't want to talk about it and said I was going to bed, opinions and insults were thrown at me as I ascended the stairs.

*Even Mya was a little distant with that news.*

I sighed and flipped over so that my back was to the window. I opened my eyes to see if it helped tone down the brightness in the room.

"What the hell?" I yelped, sitting up in bed.

Mya was sitting on the edge of her bed staring at me with bloodshot eyes.

My outburst caused her to jump. "You scared me! But I'm glad you're awake."

I groaned, falling back into the safe haven of the sheets. "I'm not awake. The bed is pretty much where I will spend most of my time so I think I should spend more time getting acquainted with it." Snuggling into the pillow, I found a comfortable spot and relaxed into the mattress. Tucking the sheet and comforter under my chin, I asked, "Why are your eyes red?"

"Are they still red?" She dropped her head and put the heel of her hand against her eye sockets.

"What's wrong, Mya?"

She sighed. "I almost went home last night."

"But you didn't."

"But I almost did. And I was thinking about what Jamie said and I..." Her sentence trailed off and she looked down at her hands. She started picking at her nails and then she peeked up at me. "What if I'm not enough?"

I pushed myself up so that I could face her and she could see that I was sincere. "Mya, you are enough. Period. And that has nothing to do with a man, a show, or anything else. You are enough."

"I've been divorced for three years now and the first time I'm really ready to put myself out there, I get chosen last." Her voice broke and she buried her face into her hands. "It sucks."

"From the little bit I know of you, you work six days a week in a library in a small town. You don't come into contact with many eligible bachelors because you don't go anywhere. Mya, you are beautiful and well read. You are kind and sweet. You don't hang out with bitches."

My last point received a snotty, crying laugh. She wiped her face and lifted her head up. "Thanks."

"You don't have to thank me for telling you the truth."

"I just really feel like Julian is the one and I don't know how to express it without coming off like an idiot. I really made a fool of myself on Friday. Maybe it was the drinks but..." She sighed. "How did you do it? How did you get him to be interested in you?"

It was an odd question to ask and an even odder question to answer since we were interested in the same man. I felt my stomach twist because prior to the beginning of the show, I sat across from Mya and I thought, 'if Julian is as good as I think he is and he doesn't pick me, I hope he has enough common sense to pick Mya.' Then I met him, spent time with him, held his hand, connected with him, and we shared the hottest PG kiss in the history of kisses. And everything changed.

I didn't know what to say. I wanted to reassure her, but I also didn't want to encourage her to pursue the man I was interested in.

*What kind of shit is this? Is this why they force us to share rooms? They want us to get close to each other and then endure this kind of torture?*

I pulled my shorts down so the people who were watching the video feed didn't get a free show and walked to Mya's bed. Sitting down, I put my arm around her shoulder and I told her the truth. "I was myself. I don't know how else to describe it. I was myself and he seemed to appreciate it. And that's what you deserve, Mya. You're great. You need to be yourself and have someone fall in love with the amazing woman that you are."

"But I want Julian to fall in love with the amazing woman I am."

I didn't know what to say because saying 'I don't' didn't seem appropriate.

Fortunately, the banging on the door saved me from having to respond at all.

Mya wiped her eyes and I stood, padding my way to the door. Stopping briefly at the mirror, I adjusted my tank top. I smoothed my coiled hair down as some of it had come from the ball on top of my head. I looked back at the bed and saw the scarf that must have slipped off during the night.

"You okay?" I mouthed to Mya.

Once she nodded, I pulled the door open and found a note taped to the door. Pulling it off, I opened it and read it aloud.

"There are two dates scheduled for today. One will be the group date and will take place during the day while the other will be a two-on-one date which will take place immediately afterward. Julian and Bryce will arrive at one o'clock in the afternoon. Dress in what you would wear on a first date."

The note seemed to perk Mya up. "It's a little after ten. Do you want to go downstairs to eat and then get ready?"

"I'm not really hungry. I was just going to grab a protein bar."

"Oh... Okay." Mya avoided eye contact and sat back down on the bed.

Something was up.

"Mya...? What's going on?"

Apparently while I was sleeping yesterday, Mya went downstairs and overheard Tori and a couple of other women talking about her.

"She said that my body was weirdly proportioned and that's why Julian wasn't into me. But the worst part was when she said, 'how does it feel to know that you're probably the one going home today?' And the three of them just laughed."

"They are trying to get in your head." I walked over and grabbed my toothbrush. "They wouldn't even have said anything to you if they didn't think you were competition. Let me brush my teeth and then I'll go down with you."

By the time we had gotten downstairs, no one was in the kitchen for breakfast except for a woman I'd never seen before.

"Good morning," Mya and I said to the woman sitting at the kitchen table staring out of the window.

"Good morning," she greeted us back, turning to give us a small smile. Her skin was a creamy, golden honey with a smattering of freckles across the bridge of her nose. Her hair was a reddish brown frizzy mass of curls. She looked familiar, but I didn't recognize her from the night before.

*But it's not as if I was making an effort with the other ten women.*

Deciding to give this new person a chance, I marched over to the woman and I stuck out my hand. "I'm Zoe."

"I know. You got the First Impression Charm," she replied, shaking my hand. "I'm Nicole."

Looking at her big brown doe-like eyes, it hit me.

*Ohhhhh...This is the woman Chatty Cathy and Tori called fat. Her hair was straight and she didn't have freckles on Friday. Did she?*

"I'm Mya. Your hair was different on Friday, right?"

She looked over at Mya who was making a bowl of cereal. "Hi, Mya. Yes, I straighten it every day." She looked down. "But I just haven't gotten around to it yet. After last night, I just didn't feel like doing much of anything, you know?"

"Tell me about it," Mya agreed, sitting down at the kitchen table with her. "Being chosen last on Friday which rolled into being bullied and dealing with Tori and her clique on Saturday made for a rough weekend. So I feel your pain."

"Everyone is going to see them call me fat. America is going to be watching and judging me. Even if they didn't immediately think I was fat, once it's out there, I'm going to be forever known as the fat one." Nicole put her hand on her belly. "I've lost sixty pounds in the last year. I work out every day. I eat healthy six days a week. I have a little extra body fat that I can't get rid of and I was okay with it. Until last night..."

"Listen," I interjected, hoping to break up their pity party. "Tori is a bitch. She is a mean, unhappy person who makes herself feel better by belittling others. She said some crap to you Friday and to Mya on Saturday. She called me fat when I first met her Thursday at the cocktail party interview." I shrugged. "Fuck her. Everybody is shaped differently and that's what makes us who we are. And you two do realize that you wouldn't be here if Julian didn't find you attractive, right? Her opinion does not matter. You're not here for her; you're here for him. She's clearly insecure about her own body which is why she keeps taking shots at body types that don't look like hers."

"Is that right?" Tori's grating voice screeched from behind me.

Mya and Nicole's eyes widened as they looked beyond me.

I didn't bother to turn around as I continued. "I don't know why, but women will attack other women's physical appearance before anything else. And unfortunately, we take that putdown the hardest. It's sad. If some insignificant person like Tori called you dumb and you know that you're not, you'd let that roll off of your back. But for some reason, you both know that you're beautiful, yet you allow this bitch to tell you otherwise."

"I'm right here," Tori snapped.

"See? Insignificant."

Mya and Nicole tried to suppress their stunned giggles, but failed.

I turned on my heel to find Tori, a cameraman, a boom mic operator, a producer and a few other crew members watching in amusement. Well, everyone but Tori was amused.

*I guess that's making it on TV.* I lifted my eyebrows at Tori. *Good.*

I picked up a bottle of water and a protein bar and walked out of the kitchen.

After a long hot shower and a super sneaky trip to the makeup trailer to tell Koko what happened, I was standing in front of the mirror analyzing my first date outfit.

The stretchy black skirt was fitted and highlighted the curve of my ass beautifully. My off-the-shoulder grey t-shirt had black watercolor splotches and added a casual vibe to the sexy skirt. I pinned my hair to the side, showing off my favorite pair of black diamond hoop earrings. Spinning in the mirror, I felt like my outfit was enough to standout without being over-the-top.

"You look hot," Mya commented as she entered the bedroom.

I looked over at her in a pair of skin tight jeans that sat low on her hips and a cropped white top that exposed her flat belly. "So do you!"

She picked up a soft pink blazer and slipped into her five inch pink pumps. "Thank you. I was worried it would be too much and then I saw Bailey and thought I was overdressed."

I laughed. "I think that's part of the whole process. If we are all told to wear something for a first date, they are probably looking at what we consider first date appropriate."

I slipped into my platform booties and we headed downstairs with the rest of the women and more crew members than I had seen at one time in the house.

At one o'clock on the dot, we heard Bryce and Julian walk in before we actually saw them. And even though I knew Bryce walked in, I wouldn't have been able to tell the police what he had on if he went missing.

Julian looked incredible in a tux. It was as if a tailor used Julian's body to design tuxedos for all mankind. But casual Julian in a pair of grey washed denim jeans and a black button-up that fit his body just right was hands-down my favorite. Julian Winters was a piece of art.

"Hi everyone!" Julian greeted us.

I was so busy devouring the visual image of him that I couldn't remember if I even opened my mouth to respond.

He looked around the room, giving us each eye contact. "I hope you are all ready for a fun group date! Anyone excited?" He waited for the cheers to die down before he continued.

"The party bus is outside so let's go."

Julian extended his arm, indicating he wanted us to go through the door before he did. One by one, we exited the room, each hugging him on the way out. I made a point to make my way over to him slowly so I could be last. It was my best chance to steal an extra second with him if I could. But Tori must have had the same idea as she hung back, too.

Wearing a dress so short, I was almost positive I was going to see her ass, Tori stood with her arms crossed and her eyes narrowed at me. Seeing how much I got under her skin, I smirked and moved toward Julian, allowing her to be last. At least that way, she could see for herself what type of chemistry we had.

When it was finally my turn, I forgot all about Tori when he wrapped his muscular arms around me. It was the first time we had embraced and I relished it. My face nuzzled his chest, breathing him in. I wasn't sure if it was his body wash or his cologne, but it was a manly scent that was powerful without being overwhelming.

"Hi," I murmured, looking up at him. "You smell really good."

Bending down so his lips were on the shell of my ear, he whispered, "And you look absolutely incredible."

His compliment tied my stomach in knots. His lips just barely touched the shell of my ear causing me to shiver. His breath tickled my skin giving me goosebumps. But when he picked his head up and looked at me, my knees felt weak.

He licked his lips and the urge to kiss him overwhelmed me. I swallowed hard.

And just as fast as the moment came, it went.

Julian pulled his arms from around me and rested his hands on my hips. As he held my gaze, he squeezed. I knew he was trying to tell me something, but I wasn't sure what.

Letting me go, he turned his attention to Tori. I started to walk off, but as I put on my oversized sunglasses, I glanced over my shoulder. Unintentionally, I froze when I saw Tori's body pressed up against Julian's like a second skin.

*Or a leech.*

I turned my head quickly, not wanting either of them to see me looking. As soon as I whipped my head around, a camera was in my face. It had probably been there the whole time, but I was so concerned with what Julian and Tori were doing, I didn't notice.

Comforted by the fact that my sunglasses masked my eyes, I rolled my shoulders back and allowed my lips to turn up into a smile. I walked out of the mansion without a second look.

*I cannot let these people keep catching me in my feelings.*

Due to my delayed time in the house, the seat beside Mya was taken. I found myself wedged beside Chatty Cathy with the last available seat on the other side of me. I sighed when Tori got in and slid her slim body right next to mine.

"Where do you think we're going?" Chatty Cathy asked aloud to no one in particular.

I tuned her out and stared directly at the back of the driver's head. I just focused on the shape of it and the apparent slickness of his baldness. I distracted myself from what she was saying, with whom I was sitting, what I was doing, where I was going and most importantly, what I was feeling.

I didn't want to be, but I was bothered. I was bothered by the fact that Julian was technically dating everybody. But it bothered me even more that Tori was still a contestant. I was bothered by the fact that I was being forced to compete for Julian's attention. But it bothered me even more that I couldn't walk away as easily as I thought. I was bothered by the fact that in two brief conversations, Julian had stirred up some feelings inside me. But it bothered me even more that

I couldn't seem to control those feelings around him.

The party bus slowed down in front of an old, rustic looking bar called Saul's Den. It wasn't like most of the swanky bars in L.A. It had character. The driver opened the door and we climbed out, surveying our surroundings.

Julian stood at the entrance, smiling proudly. "You've all had the pleasure of meeting my best friends. This bar was the place where we used to go when we turned eighteen. It was the place we celebrated each of our birthdays for about five years. I had my first drink here. At the age of twenty-one, of course."

The sparkle in his eye let me know that he probably was able to get drinks before he was legally allowed to drink. I smiled...and then I pursed my lips.

*He will not keep luring me back in with his awesomeness. I'm not getting drawn in by his coolness and his cute little smirks and his sparkling eyes and his gorgeous smile and his incredible body. He's over there smiling and reminiscing like the tease that he is. So no. Nope. I'm not letting him suck me in anymore. This is how people end up getting made to look foolish on these things. They get too caught up too fast.*

We followed him into the building and I took in the clean, but sparsely decorated bar. It was modern with flat screens all around, but the wooden décor had a rustic look that felt homey.

Julian gestured to five tables, each with two seats. Mya and I must have noticed the layout at the same time because we immediately looked at each other and then snaked our way around people to stand next to one another.

Julian grabbed a bucket off of the bar and held it out. "So you're going to pull one of the darts out of here and hold it up."

I pulled out red. Mya pulled out green. I knew immediately

that was a bad sign.

"Now," Julian said, returning the empty bucket to the bar. "Find the person who has the same color dart as you and select a table, but don't sit down. Line up here."

I was disappointed that I didn't have Mya as a partner, but I would've been straight up livid if I was stuck with Tori.

"Looks like we're partners," Bailey said, walking up behind me. Her thick blonde hair was pulled into a high ponytail and her floral print dress left little to the imagination.

I smiled and nodded.

We selected our table and I noticed that Mya was stuck with Tori. I gave her a sympathetic look.

Lining up shoulder to shoulder facing the DJ booth, Julian walked in front of us like a drill sergeant. I was at the end of the row and the closer he came to me, the harder it became to focus.

Julian stopped right beside me. "One of the main reasons my friends and I came here were the cheap drinks, but also because of this." He pointed to the DJ booth and a buzzer went off.

An older, jolly looking man with a ruddy complexion pumped his arms in the air as he stood from behind the booth. "Ladies, it's Trivia Time! You can call me DJ Saul and we are going to do some traditional pub style trivia and the winners get to go on a duo-date with Julian Winters."

I glanced at Julian who was looking at DJ Saul with amusement. His hand was covering his mouth, but his cheeks and his eyes gave away his smile.

DJ Saul hit the buzzer again. "And as an added bonus, if you win, I'll tell you what this superstar was like as a little scrawny ass twerp hanging around with his little scrawny ass friends."

I laughed loudly. And because I was the only one who

laughed period, all eyes were on me.

DJ Saul pointed at me. "She gets it. The rest of you need to loosen up. Now eyes up here and let's go over the rules!"

Still giggling, I shifted my gaze to Julian and noticed he was checking me out. My eyebrows lifted in surprise. From the corner of my eye, I watched him suck on his bottom lip as he took me in. With each second that ticked by, I felt the effects of having his undivided attention. Although I knew he was attracted to me from the moment we met, this was a more sexual look he was giving me. I didn't feel objectified by his lingering gaze. I felt wanted. I felt desired. I felt empowered by his attraction.

DJ Saul was still going over the rules, but when Julian's eyes made their way up my body and locked with mine, I couldn't hear anything but the sound of my heart beating. He knew I had caught him staring and he didn't try to hide the want in his eyes.

"Julian, you ready?" DJ Saul called out, snapping us both out of it.

Julian blinked rapidly as if he was clearing his head and smiled at the man. "Yes. If everyone is good on the rules, let's go!"

We headed back to our tables and were given paper and pencils. For an hour, DJ Saul asked us questions ranging from pop culture to politics. It was a good thing that Bailey and I were partnered together because where she excelled at pop culture and movies, I excelled at current events and music. Unfortunately, neither of us knew much about sports. But what I did notice was that Bailey was a lot smarter than she let on. Between rounds music was played and drinks were served. At the end of three rounds, we turned our papers in and waited for the points to be tallied.

"Okay, the winners of the duo-date..." DJ Saul said with the same conviction as Bryce Wilson. "Zoe and Bailey!"

Bailey clapped happily bouncing in her chair. Even I glanced down, distracted by her breasts' near escape from the low cut dress. I felt my eyebrows come together and I shook my head.

*If Koko was here, she'd understand the humor in this. Did no one else even see that?*

Shifting my gaze to Julian, I saw him give me an amused grin with his eyebrows almost to the middle of his forehead. With that look, I knew he had seen it too and that he also thought it was funny. Just when I thought I was alone, he found a way to make me feel like he got me. I couldn't help but beam with exhilaration.

Bryce appeared from seemingly nowhere and opened his arms wide. "Congratulations Zoe and Bailey! Julian will take it from here." He turned his attention to the other women. "Better luck next time ladies. Follow me. We are headed back to the house."

The sound of wooden chairs angrily scraping against the floor seemed to echo since DJ Saul stopped playing music.

Julian walked the other women to the door, hugging each of them before they left. Once the door closed behind Tori who made sure to give us a death glare as she hugged him, Julian flashed us a smile.

"Follow me please," he said as he held out his arms for us to take. With us attached to each arm, he led us to a back door I hadn't seen before. "After you."

I walked through the door first, followed by Bailey, followed by Julian, followed by the camera crew.

I gasped. Two seconds later, Bailey gasped.

Red rose petals littered the floor of the banquet room. White tablecloth covered tables lined the room against the wall and were covered in candles. One black tablecloth covered table was situated in the middle of the room with white candles and red roses gathered on the far side. The three chairs at the table were a reminder that this was not a solo date.

"This is beautiful," I gushed.

Julian put his hand on the small of my back and led me to the table. It wasn't until that moment that I realized that I was addicted to his touch. I looked over at him and noticed he had his hand on the small of Bailey's back too.

I sighed and kept my thoughts to myself.

Once we were seated, DJ Saul, who insisted we call him Saul, brought out an appetizer sampler for us to share.

"This smells amazing," Bailey remarked, reaching for the mozzarella sticks.

"Wait," Julian and I insisted at the same time.

The moment the word was out of our mouths, our head whipped toward one another.

I narrowed my eyes at him and pulled out my hand sanitizer. He laughed, leaning forward and grabbing the bottle that was strategically placed and hidden within the floral candle arrangement.

We burst out laughing again and the sense of ease and calm came over me immediately. It was something about Julian that I couldn't put my finger on, but he had a way about him that just made me feel comfortable.

As the laughter died down, I glanced over at Bailey whose face was red.

*Crap, I hope she doesn't think we're laughing at her.*

After squirting hand sanitizer into our hands and then his own, Julian smiled. "Okay, now let's dig in."

The cameraman circled around us and then situated himself right above the side of the table where the forth chair would've been. Eating on camera wasn't something I was looking forward to doing so I picked up my glass and sipped my water.

Julian looked at me and winked before turning his head in the other direction. "So, Bailey, where are you from?"

"I'm from Wisconsin," she answered awkwardly. "Where are you from? Oh, I mean, I know California, but I mean...where?"

I tuned them out while he spent time getting to know her. It was awkward feeling like the third wheel on someone else's date.

*On second thought, I will have a mozzarella stick.*

I didn't know if I was bored because their conversation was boring or if I was feeling a little left out, but I had resorted to reading and re-reading the menu until I knew for a fact that I was ordering the Cobb salad and that the secret ingredient in the marinara sauce was crushed red pepper flakes.

"So Zoe, what do you think of this bar?" Julian had turned his attention to me.

Putting the menu down in front of me, I clasped my hands on top of it. "This place is exactly the kind of place I would expect you to hang out. It's attractive and deceptively cool. It has more depth than anyone realizes. And it's comfortable."

Light flickered in his eyes as his smile grew with each of my descriptions. He nodded before he asked, "What do you mean comfortable? That could be a good thing or a bad thing."

"It's a good thing." I smiled back at him, leaning slightly in his direction. "You know those places you go where you can be yourself completely. Those are comfortable places. I feel like this is your comfortable place."

He licked his lips before bringing the glass of water to them. "What's your comfortable place?" His eyes added more weight behind the question than I think was intended.

*With you,* I replied in my head as a knee-jerk reaction to the hypnotic way he was looking at me.

He smirked as if he knew what I was thinking. His eyes were begging me to say it aloud, but I stuffed that thought into the deepest part of my psyche.

I broke our gaze which brought me back down to reality long enough for me to coach myself.

*Okay Zoe, reel that shit in. This is the third time, THIRD, you're having a conversation with this man. He is not your comfortable place. He is the place you return to because you had a good time before. This isn't your Café Nervosa, your Central Perk, your Cheers. This is the popular hangout that everyone wants to get into and you are just one of the many who are on a wait list.*

I blinked several times to break the spell before making eye contact again. "Home. My comfortable place is home."

"They say, 'home is where the heart is.'"

I shook my head in disbelief that he said that. My face grew hot. I didn't know how to respond so I just laughed. "Um, thank you for that," I replied, cocking my head to the side. "You are ridiculous."

The goofy smile on his face made me certain that I had the same goofy smile on mine. Seconds passed and we were just smiling at each other and it wasn't until Bailey cleared her throat that I realized how in our own world we were.

"Are you two sure you haven't met before the show?" Bailey asked with a laugh. Although her voice was playful, her upturned lips didn't reach her narrowed eyes.

I shook my head. "No, I've never met anyone like Julian Winters."

As soon as the words came out of my mouth, I realized what it sounded like. I opened my mouth to backtrack, but Julian's hand found my knee under the table. I sucked in a sharp breath in surprise.

Julian looked at me. "And I've never met anyone like Zoe Jordan."

Feeling a blush coming over my skin, I became acutely aware of how the exchange looked outside of our bubble. I widened my eyes indiscriminately and tilted my head fractionally.

Quickly, he turned away from me and smiled at Bailey. "And I've never met anyone like you, Bailey."

She grinned and then looked down. "I'm glad to be here. With everyone being so pretty and smart, it is hard feeling like I'm not standing out in the group, you know?"

"Hey, look at me," Julian said softly. "You stand out just fine. You are beautiful and obviously, you're smart. You two won the trivia date! So no matter what happens, your beauty and your intelligence remains the same."

Even though his words weren't directed at me, those words were so similar to something I would say that they wormed their way into my heart and I couldn't deny it anymore. I liked him.

Saul came by to take our late lunch orders. Squeezing my bare knee one last time, Julian let go of me and I missed the heat of his hand immediately.

The rest of the meal was uneventful. Julian seemed to be more cognizant of splitting his attention between the two of us. I learned a lot about him and even though I didn't share a lot of personal stuff, Bailey shared enough for the both of us.

At the end of the date, we said our goodbyes to Saul and climbed into the town car that was waiting for us. The sun was starting to set and it was truly a beautiful day. With the three of us situated with Julian in the middle, the ride back to the mansion was prolonged by an accident on the freeway. But that wasn't the most interesting part of the twenty minute trip.

Bailey, likely emboldened by the wine, took charge of the conversation with Julian. She talked, flirted, and giggled her way through the entire ride to the house and I didn't say a thing. To the cameraman who was sitting in the front seat and filming through the window, it may have looked as if I had given up or that Bailey was dominating the date at that moment.

Bailey was beautiful and with her hair up in that ponytail and her makeup done impeccably, she looked high fashion. Her outfit wasn't my style, but it showed off her biggest assets. Straight men tended to like to look at breasts so I could see her thought process in that wardrobe selection. And she seemed to be playing dumb for some reason, but as her trivia teammate, I saw through the act.

So, on the surface it may have appeared as though Bailey was gaining traction on me. But I saw the way Julian looked at me tonight and he didn't look at her like that. There was no spark between them and the fact that he discreetly held my hand while talking to her during the car ride let me know where his attention was truly focused.

At one point, I did wonder if he was holding her hand too. But when I saw him pick up a bottle of water and keep it in his hand for the remainder of the ride, I knew that he wasn't. So I closed my eyes and relished in the feeling of his hand sensually stroking mine. I rested my head against his shoulder and felt his body react. I squeezed his hand and smiled, letting the two of them enjoy their conversation about nothing.

*No seriously, they weren't talking about shit.*

# Chapter 8

"Zoe, we need you," a woman I hadn't seen before called out to me the moment Julian finished hugging me and Bailey goodbye.

Bailey raised her eyebrows and I shrugged.

She opened the door to the house and another crew member seemed to grab her for questioning as well.

"Do you feel like since you got the First Impression Charm and then the duo date, you are in a good place with Julian?" The producer asked as the cameraman got set.

*Hell yeah!*

"I feel as though things with Julian are solid," I answered, channeling my mother and giving nothing away.

"Are you worried about what the other women are saying about you in the house?"

*Hell no.*

I smiled politely. "Not in the slightest."

"You've been described as stuck-up, pretentious, and not at all Julian's type?"

*Seriously?* I looked at the seven or eight crew members and tilted my head slightly. *This is how it is huh?*

"Julian doesn't think that. And more importantly, I don't think that."

I could see the frustration in her face and body language since she wasn't getting the reaction she was hoping for and that made my smile widen.

She bristled. "Well, I was just asking because the ladies in the house were debating that. If you'd like, I can tell you which ones."

*What's funny is that that's probably the only honest thing she's said this whole time.*

I let out an amused sigh. "There's no need."

She looked at me blankly and tightened her thin lips.

I widened my eyes innocently. "Is there anything else? I'd really like to get inside."

"Cut," she said with an attitude.

Giving them a wave goodbye, I turned on my heel and stalked into the house. As soon as I walked in, I caught the tail end of Bailey's confessional interview.

"Well," she twirled the end of her ponytail with her fingers. "I don't know..."

I shook my head and kept going. I didn't understand what Bailey thought she was gaining from dumbing herself down, but that truly was none of my concern. I needed to focus on what I need and what I needed most was a break from the house. It had only been a weekend and I was already about to lose my mind.

"Oh look. It's not quite six o'clock yet and you're already back here," Tori called out as soon as I reached the steps. I looked over and she was walking out of the living room flanked by the redhead and a cameraman. "Aw. I guess things didn't go well tonight. See, Tiffany. I told you she wasn't any real competition."

I opened my mouth to respond, but I decided against it. Tori wanted a reaction out of me and I refused to give it to her. I glanced at the redhead, Tiffany, before shaking my head and jogging the rest of the way up the staircase.

*These people are going to drive me insane. I need some alone time.*

I was determined to lose the cameras and my microphone and go for a walk. The only two people who would actively try to find me would be Koko, who didn't work on Sundays, and Mya. And as much as I enjoyed Mya, I needed to get away from everything related to the show for a few minutes. I just needed to breathe.

When I entered the bedroom, I found Mya sleeping. The last few rays of the sun were trickling into the room so I moved quickly, but quietly, so to not wake her up. Creeping over to my side of the room, I opened the bottom drawer and pulled out a pair of black yoga pants, a white tank top with the words 'Work It' emblazoned on the front. Making as little noise as possible, I ducked into the huge walk-in closet—one of only two places in the bedrooms where cameras weren't stationed. Once I was dressed, I eased my way into the bathroom to wash my face, brush my teeth and to take the pins out of my hair. After fluffing my curls, I grabbed my jacket, re-attached my microphone and tiptoed out of the room.

No one was in the hall, but I knew the cameras were watching me so I played it cool. My adrenaline was pumping like I was doing a covert mission when all I truly wanted was to have a few minutes to myself—not on camera and not recording my every word. I heard music coming from the patio area and figured the women were outside enjoying themselves. I'd made it just past the kitchen when I was spotted.

"Zoe?" The Mid-West accent called from behind me.

My sneakers made a subtle squeak as I abruptly stopped in my tracks. Turning, my eyebrows flew up. With what appeared to be a silk robe in her hand, Bailey stood in the middle of the hallway wearing an itty-bitty bikini.

"You like?" Her smile stretched from ear to ear as she spun around in a circle.

Her nipples were covered by small triangles and the majority of her ass was hanging out. She was as naked as humanly possible while still being able to be shown on network television.

"What are you wearing?" I asked, almost in disbelief. The swimsuit didn't appear to be functional. "Can you even swim in that thing?"

"No, not at all!" She shook her head and made a face as she pulled on her colorful robe. "It's for Julian. It's for the cameras. It's also for my competition to start taking me seriously."

"If you want to be taken seriously, stop dumbing yourself down. You're clearly a smart woman."

She made a face and gestured to the sun room. I turned, continuing down the hall and entered the room. She was on my heels, closing the door behind her.

"Will you turn that off please?" Bailey pointed at my mic.

I turned it off and then looked at her in exasperation.

*What's with all the secrecy? Didn't we just spend all afternoon together?*

Crossing my arms, I glanced at my watch as if I wasn't contractually bound to the show and the mansion for the next three and a half weeks. I lifted my eyebrows in question. "What's going on?"

"You tell me. Do you know Julian?" Her tone was a little more curious than accusatory.

I cocked my head to the side. "For the second time, no."

"Don't worry. My producer said that this room doesn't have cameras because of something with the wiring. That's why they come in here to strategize sometimes."

"I'm not worried about the cameras. I'm wondering why you're asking this again. We told you at the bar that we didn't know each other."

"Well, there's something there. It's only been a couple of days and it was like you two had known each other for months. I felt like the third wheel on your date."

I uncrossed my arms and stuffed my hands in my jacket pockets. "I mean..." My sentence trailed off as I lifted my shoulders. "I don't know what you want me to say to that."

I didn't know what to say. Julian and I clicked. I couldn't and wouldn't apologize for the chemistry between us.

Bailey shook her head. "No, it's fine. Julian is sexy, rich and in the industry, but we don't have anything in common. And during the cocktail party, I tried to kiss him and he brushed me off."

I bit the inside of my lip to keep from smiling. Memories of his kiss and the way he touched me as we kissed made my insides warm.

"Why are you telling me this?" I asked.

"Because I'm here for me. I'm not here for Julian. And I think we can help each other. We can form an alliance."

"I'm not here to play games, Bailey."

"Who's playing games?" She pointed at the door. "No one else was at the duo date. No one else saw what I saw, Zoe. You two have something that seems genuine. But have you seen the show before? In a few days, everyone is going to be calling him their boyfriend. I will be flirting with him and playing the part, but trust me, I don't want him. I just need the camera time and a few more shots of me in this on camera will seal the deal."

"Why would you tell me all of this though? It makes no sense. You could've kept this to yourself and went about your business. I don't understand the motivation."

"In this alliance, you would just need to play your part. It'll succeed with just two, but three would be nice. Remember, three is not a crowd if everyone wins." She walked to the door swinging her ponytail behind her. With her hand on the doorknob, she turned, gesturing outside with her head. "Everyone else out there wants the man you want and a man is only as faithful as his options."

She smiled, untying her robe and letting it drape open. "I figured you would rather have the hot girl who is not trying to steal your man in the competition rather than the hot girls who are." She opened the door and peeked out. "Think about it."

With that, Bailey sauntered away. The sound of her ditzy giggle rang down the hall as she loudly claimed to be lost.

I had so many thoughts running through my mind at one time that I just stood in a stunned silence for a minute.

"Wow," I breathed.

It was too much for me to process and the information I had just learned wasn't computing.

*An alliance? What does that even look like? Why would I even need one? If Julian and I are meant to see where this thing goes, it'll be because that's what we choose, not because of an alliance.*

Exiting the room, I didn't see any production staff or camera crew members anywhere around so I slipped out of the side door. Moving stealthily and staying close to the house, I eased my way around until I got to the side where the darkened hair, makeup and wardrobe trailers were parked. With my eyes trained on the garden maze, I slipped undetected behind the overgrown rose bushes.

Floodlights and decorative lamps lined the garden. It was early evening so the blue sky glowed with touches of orange. It was almost dark enough for the lights to come on, but not quite. I slowed down as I followed the path and right as I entered the maze, I heard a click and a buzz.

Startled, I paused, questioning my decision to leave my mace hidden in my luggage. Once I realized it was the solar night lights gearing up, I let out a relieved sigh and continued through the blankets of greenery. Every few feet another section of flowers would be on display. It was quiet and I was alone with my thoughts.

*No cameras. No microphones. No petty bitches. No random ass alliance talk. No—*

"Ah!" I hoarsely screamed as I turned the corner and came face to face with Julian.

He startled, yanking his headphones off of his head. "You scared the shit out of me!" He started laughing. "I thought I was out here alone."

My hand covered my chest and I felt my heart racing. "I think I'm having a heart attack," I huffed as I tried to catch my breath.

He laughed harder as he reached out for me. I swatted his hands away with my one free hand. I tried to glare at him, but my amusement kept pulling my lips upward. My heart rate started coming down, but when our eyes locked, it sped back up again.

"Why did you scream like that?" He put his fist to his mouth in an attempt to stop, but his shaking shoulders and inability to speak gave way to more laughter.

"Stop it," I demanded through clenched teeth before I started laughing too. "Shh! We have to be quiet!"

Five minutes later, we'd pulled ourselves together. I wiped

the tears from my eyes and placed my hand on the tightness of my belly. It felt like I had done a thousand crunches.

"So how did you manage to get out here without a camera crew following you?" Julian asked, looking around us. "You are out here alone, right?"

"Yeah, I had to sneak out." I pulled my jacket open, flashing the battery back for the microphone. "I turned my mic off and everything. I just needed to get away."

He was quiet as if he were contemplating something. Reaching out his hand, he took mine. "Well then, let me take you away."

I fell into step with him as we headed in the direction he was coming from. We made small talk about everything from favorite movies to passport stamps. The conversation was so good and so funny that I didn't realize how long we had been walking until I peeked over the hedges toward the house. It looked like it was on the other side of a football field.

"You don't watch much TV?" He asked after I told him I hadn't seen *The One* or any of the other shows he asked me about.

"I used to. Studying for the bar was a full time job. And then working at the bar was my part time job. When I had free time, I wanted to do something different. But when I did watch TV, I watched shows from the nineties that I used to watch with my mom. *Frasier, Martin, Friends.*"

"Okay, Martin and Frasier I watched reruns of those. Pretty funny."

"Pretty funny?!" I exclaimed, throwing my free hand in the air. "Try hilarious."

He squeezed my hand, looking down at me. "I think you're hilarious."

"I think you're a flirt," I returned with a soft smile. I continued to take in my surroundings. "Were you headed to the house earlier?"

"No, not at all. I was heading to the fountain." He let out a deep breath that kind of sounded like a laugh. "I'm not going by the house unless I have to."

"What's wrong? Overwhelmed with beautiful women throwing themselves at you?" I bumped my shoulder into him playfully.

"The whole thing is a bit more than I bargained for," he admitted, shaking his head. "It was my own fault though. I probably should've watched a few early episodes before signing up."

He tugged on my hand and we cut through two tall walls of shrubbery that was off of the maze path. Even though the lights only barely made it through the greenery, Julian moved seamlessly through the darkness.

"Wait, you were giving me grief and you've never seen the show before either?" I asked, moving closer to him as the path became narrower.

He slowed to a stop. "Get behind me."

I suppressed the urge to scream as I did as he commanded. Clutching at his t-shirt and burying my face in his back, I waited for him to tell me what was going on.

*It's a spider. I know it's a spider. We are walking through this glorified lair and—oh my God, there are probably spiders in my hair!*

"What are you mumbling back there?" Julian asked in amusement. He reached back and grabbed my hands, wrapping them around his waist.

I didn't know what to do so I didn't move at all. But each time he breathed, I could feel his firm abs contracting and constricting. Each time I breathed, I couldn't smell anything but the soft scent of his masculine body wash. Having my breasts crushed against his back and my head cradled

116

between his broad shoulders, I was having trouble not melting into him, let alone answering his question.

The squeaking noise of a gate being opened jostled my brain enough to kick start it back into gear. "Where are we?"

"Check this out." He walked through the gate and after I made it through, he locked it.

My eyes widened as I looked at the large house several yards in front of us. "Is this where you're staying?"

"Yeah. But I spend most of my time over here." Instead of walking toward the house, he grabbed my hand and pulled me toward a huge glass gazebo. As we got closer, I noticed the brown leather furniture and the cream and brown stone flooring.

"This is incredible." I marveled at the glass and mahogany structure. It was even more stunning than the house, which was also beautiful. But the gazebo was a piece of art.

He opened the door for me to enter. "Welcome. Have a seat. Make yourself at home."

The lights were low, giving the place a romantic glow. It was bright enough to see the rich luster of everything, but it was dim enough to really appreciate the tiniest bit of light in the horizon.

"This is beautiful. Seriously." I spun around in a circle, taking in everything.

"Not as beautiful as you."

"Are you flirting with me?" I asked once my eyes landed back on him.

He moved toward me. "Every chance I get."

I put my hand on my chest and fell to the couch as gracefully as possible. "Okay fine, it happened. You have officially made me swoon."

He laughed, but I was completely serious. It wasn't just what he said. It was how he said it and how he looked while he said it. He had a way with words that touched me in my heart and soul.

*And also in a few other places that have needed to be tended to for far too long.*

Needing to get ahold of myself, I changed the subject. Pointing at a picture of an older couple in frame, I asked, "Are these your parents?"

Julian sat down with half of a cushion separating us. "Yeah, that's them." He smiled with pride. "Mom and Dad are also known as Susan and Brian."

I studied the picture. "Where did your dark features come from? They look like they both have blonde hair and really fair skin?" I wondered curiously. Only the tips of their hair were showing because of the hats they wore. But even still, Julian didn't resemble them at all.

"My biological father is Puerto Rican. My mom had a one-night-stand with him a week before she met my dad. She was pregnant, but she didn't know it. As soon as she found out, she told Dad everything. He married her and said I was going to be his son in every way that mattered. Signed the birth certificate as soon as I was born." He smiled at the memory. "So that's why I don't look like him, but that pale man, with the grey hair that he still calls dirty blonde, is my dad."

I put my hand to my chest and let out sigh. "I love that so much. Real love stories. Complicated love stories. Those are the stories that have so much depth. It's easy to love someone when it's easy. It's real when you love someone when it's hard. Tell me more about them. Where was this picture taken?"

He told me about Susan and Brian, two teachers who spent their summers finding adventures to get into. The picture he had on the table was taken in December when they celebrated Christmas in Aspen. As he told me stories about them, I learned more about him. Hearing how his parents loved each other, how much he respected their love for each other, and how much he wanted to end up in a relationship like theirs, made me believe that Julian was relationship material.

*Maybe he isn't in this to date around. Although, when you are dating several women at the same time, you are still dating around.*

"Your parents seem awesome."

"Thanks, they really are. Now, tell me about yours."

I launched into my origin story and concluded with the fact that my parents have the kind of love that I want to find one day. And although the conversation was good, the topic of love shifted the air in the room.

With our heads back on the couch, we were able to look through the glass ceiling and see the stars beginning to shine.

"It is so beautiful in here. Is this where you come to write?"

He smiled and nodded. "It's easy to get inspired in here."

"I'm sure. I didn't realize that they had you staying right next to us. I guess it makes sense for you to be close by though."

"Yeah, I have to be on set early so being next door made it easy. They want me to go over treatments before episodes. Can you believe that?"

I scoffed. "I never thought that anything about reality TV was real, but I didn't know it was staged to the point of scripts and treatments and all that craziness." I shook my head. "I don't know what I got into."

"Me either. I should have watched the show." He smirked. "Lesson learned."

"So you've never seen the show before either?"

"I only saw the final episode of last season. It was two-hours of my life that I couldn't get back, but I wanted to understand what it was that I was being offered. And before I actually signed on, I heard the couple got engaged so I knew there was a method to the madness."

"Is that what your end game is? Getting engaged?" As soon as the words passed my lips, I heard them.

When his eyebrows flew up, I froze.

*Oh shit, oh shit, oh shit. That definitely sounds like I'm planning our wedding or something. Ugh! I sound like the women in the house proclaiming to love him after a weekend!*

Sitting up straight, I started gesturing with my hands. "No no no no no! I'm sorry, that came out completely wrong." I shook my head profusely for added emphasis. "I just wanted to know what you want out of this experience, not if you're ready to get engaged. That sounded...That came out all wrong."

"So basically, you're asking me if I plan to propose to you?" Julian deadpanned, his eyebrows furrowing in mock confusion.

I squeezed my eyes shut and pursed my lips. "You just took a slightly awkward question and made it into an abomination so thank you for that."

We laughed for a few moments and I collapsed back against the couch. Silence surrounded us briefly.

"I don't have an end game," he answered, his voice low. "I took this opportunity to meet someone that I can be myself around and know they are here for me and not the money. To meet someone who can look at my life's work, the thing I'm most passionate about, and see me in it. Someone who already has their life together and having me would be a bonus and not an opportunity. Dating in L.A. is hard enough without all the extra pressures of being in the industry. I can't tell you how many dates I've been on where she will casually mention that she's always wanted to be a singer."

I put my hand on his shoulder. "So is this not a good time to play you my demo?"

Julian's expression was a mix of shock and horror before he lurched toward me, grabbing and tickling me.

I laughed, squirming across the couch until somehow I ended up in his lap. Sliding back, I dropped to the leather cushion yet my legs still remained draped over his thighs. He rested his arms across them and placed one hand on the outside of my thigh and the other on the outside of my calf.

"Let that be a lesson to you," he warned, a mischievous glint in his eyes.

I started to reach up and touch his hair, but decided against it.

*If I touch his hair, I'm going to pull his face toward me. If I kiss him, I'll end up taking off his clothes. If I take off his clothes, we're fucking. It's a slippery slope so I should probably keep my hands to myself.*

Instead, I covered his hand with mine and caressed his skin. "I hear what you're saying though. It sounds like you've had some pretty bad dates and I think it's really cool of you to try something new. And you know more about the women in the house than you would someone you'd meet at a bar or in the club." With an impish smile, I admitted, "I must confess that I questioned the seriousness of someone who would come on a show to find love. But that was before I read your work and then met you."

"I get that, but I'm serious about this process. I'm looking for something special. You can hook up with anybody. But you can't settle down with just anybody."

"So when was the last time you hooked up with anybody?" I asked, watching him to see if he'd panic because of my question.

Without hesitation, he answered, "It's been awhile. Early November. It was with an ex that I have no interest in rekindling anything with, but I have needs and she was in town."

"I get that." I waited for him to ask me when the last time I had sex was but he didn't. So I asked a follow-up question. "How did things end with your ex?"

He laughed. "She is a great person, easy to work with but we weren't compatible. We were together because we were both trying to make it in the industry at the same time. But when it came down to it, when I was getting dragged through the mud over that copyright infringement suit, she bailed. And when I won and started making a name for myself and my checks got a little bigger, she wanted to reconcile." He shook his head. "It was my first lesson on loyalty and four years later, I'm ready to actually find someone."

I searched his face. There was no bitterness, no anger. My heart faltered. "Sometimes you have to go through something like that to really understand what it is that you want."

He was quiet for a beat and then smirked. "It's funny...when my manager brought *The One* opportunity to me, I was a little skeptical of what kind of women came on shows like this." He squeezed my thigh. "Yet here we are."

My stomach fluttered. "Here we are."

Julian ran his hand from my calf to my ankle and then back to my calf. Heat radiated from his hand through my yoga pants and up to the apex of my thighs. "I want to know more about you, Zoe Jordan."

I licked my lips and his eyes dipped momentarily causing me to squirm in my seat.

"What do you want to know?" My voice was softer than I expected.

# The One

"When was your last relationship?"

"It ended almost three years ago."

He stared at me, into me. "Do you feel like talking about it?"

I slipped my fingers through his and tilted my head to the side. "Tate and I dated for about four years. We talked about getting married. He purchased a ring with the intention of proposing sometime during graduation weekend. He was going out of town for the NFL Draft, so he had scheduled all of his exams early. He wasn't going to be back until graduation weekend. Oh, I forgot to mention, he was the star running back on our football team and even though he wasn't invited to go to the televised Draft ceremony, he thought it would be cool to all be in the city and do all of the Draft Day events. There were four of them that went and they were all expected to be drafted but in the late rounds. And fortunately for them, they were all drafted. They came back and were rock stars on campus. We were supposed to meet at a party and I just knew that he was going to propose. But when I got there, he broke up with me. He said that since he's a professional football player, he didn't want to tie himself down. He said that it wasn't fair to commit to one woman when he was going to be moving to New York and it made more sense for him to keep his options open."

"Well damn." Julian looked like he was at a loss for words. "Just like that?"

I lifted my shoulders. "Just like that."

"He did you a favor. Any man who would drop you at the first taste of success isn't the kind of man who deserves a woman like you. You're beautiful, funny, smart, educated, kind and sexy as hell. I've only known you for a weekend and I can't stop thinking about you. But good riddance. He's an opportunist and he will always be chasing the high of being with you."

"Thank you." I grinned, putting my palms on my flaming cheeks. "I smile so much when I'm around you. You have a way with words that just..." My sentence trailed off as I struggled to put it into words. "I like it. I like being with you."

He removed his hands from my legs and scooped me up in his arms, shifting me into his lap.

I gasped at the quick movement. "What are you doing?" I exhaled the question so softly that I didn't know if he heard.

Our faces were inches apart and as I sat atop him, I realized that somehow during the shift in position, I ended up with my arm around his neck. The electricity between us crackled and I wanted to simultaneously back away and be sucked in closer.

*It really wouldn't take much to twist my fingers in his hair and kiss him silly. I shouldn't do it, but it really wouldn't take much for me to—*

He licked his full lips. I watched his tongue linger at the corner of his mouth for a second before disappearing again. I was mesmerized by that action and how badly I wanted to kiss him. A wave of heat coursed through my body. I forced myself to raise my eyes to his and my heart stammered.

"What are you doing?" I breathed, even though the answer didn't matter. I decided instantly that being wrapped in his arms didn't require a reason. The real question should've been 'why didn't you do this sooner?'

"I have to tell you something." He lifted his hand and tugged at a lock of hair that had curled its way onto my cheek. "And I wanted to hold you close, just in case what I tell you changes how you feel about me."

*What is he about to say?*

"I'm not going to lie. That warning makes me nervous." Although my tone was joking, I was serious. I paused, trying to read his expression and realized he was serious. He was

124

more serious than I'd ever seen him.

I put my hand to his chest, feeling the rise and fall of his quick breaths. "But in the short time that I've known you, you've always made me feel so comfortable. So I hope that you are comfortable enough to tell me anything."

"I am. No one knows what I'm about to tell you except for my boys and Bryce. And none of them even know the whole story."

Nerves caused every worst case scenario to filter through my brain. "Just tell me. I won't tell anyone if that's what you're worried about. I just want to know."

*He's married. Or he has kids that he doesn't take care of. Or he's a serial killer who only kills bad guys. Or—*

"I was at the cocktail party interview last week and I wasn't supposed to be there."

I let out a sigh of relief that bordered on a giggle. "Okay? You had me worried. Why would that change how I feel about you?"

"I only got Bryce to agree for me to be there if I didn't talk to anyone. I was supposed to observe and then leave. But on my way out, I saw another pretty face that I hadn't seen earlier in the night while I was discreetly making my rounds. I knew I wasn't going to be able to get to everyone and I was okay with that. But when I saw her, there was something different about her."

My stomach knotted.

"Her style was different. The way she carried herself was different. She was different. But what really stuck out to me was that she was genuine. And in that environment, when you see someone do something nice for the sake of being nice and not because she's on camera or any of the studio heads were around."

My instincts were to climb out of his lap. As hard as I

resisted his charms, I let him get under my skin and it felt like he was telling me that he had already met someone.

I took a deep breath and unraveled my hands from around his neck, feebly attempting to remove myself from his locked arms.

I cursed silently as I felt stinging behind my eyes. It was way too soon for me to be invested anyway. *This is what I get.*

I nodded, avoiding eye contact. "I understand."

"I don't know what's going on in that head of yours, but I don't think you do." His head moved to try to catch my eye. "Look at me."

Swallowing hard, I met his gaze and blinked rapidly. Being that close, that intimate with him threatened to push the tears over the edge. And then the fact that I was about to cry was about to make me cry.

I didn't understand why I was having such an emotional reaction. Whenever I'd see previews of these types of shows where women are crying over a man they knew for seventeen minutes, I would roll my eyes in disgust.

*And then here I am doing the exact same thing.*

I liked him, but I wasn't in love with him. I knew him, but at the same time, just barely. But I felt connected to him in a very real way. And I allowed myself to get excited, I allowed myself to get caught up in the flood of emotions he brought out of me. I let myself want it a little more than I even realized.

"Look at me. Please," he begged, gripping my hips tightly before holding me in place. When his hands moved, I felt him interlock his fingers and rest them at the top of my ass. "I didn't want anyone to know who I was so I couldn't get the makeup team to disguise me. So I bought a wig, a beard, brown contacts and some dark self-tanner."

The worried look in his eyes perpetuated the fear I felt within me and it took a few minutes for what he said to resonate.

My heart rattled in my chest. "You were Evan?"

He nodded. "Evan is my middle name."

My forehead tightened as I felt my eyebrows furrow in confusion. "So you already knew who I was?"

"No. Not that night. I didn't really know who anyone was. I was actually leaving when I ran into you in the hallway so it was purely coincidental. I told them I would be in and out. I picked a bunch of women based off of their packets, but I wanted to make sure the best possible matches were in the house. So I was just there observing to see who I got a vibe from. And the only person I felt anything for was you. The only person I feel anything for is you."

It was as if his entire purpose in life was to steal my breath away.

"Julian," I breathed softly, overwhelmed with the rollercoaster of emotions I was experiencing.

I was at a loss for words. It made no sense that we would have the connection that we had because we'd known each other for essentially five minutes. But it was there. And it was real.

"You don't have to say anything. I've been thinking about this since the moment we met so I just wanted to let you know before all of the stuff we have to do tomorrow."

I searched his face, fingers caressing his neck. "I don't understand why you would think any of that would change how I feel about you."

"Because you mentioned that the worst part of being here is one person in particular. I assumed you meant Tori."

My left side of my lip quirked up. *I love that he just gets me.*

He continued, "Yeah, I thought so. I didn't want you to think that I saw and heard the way Tori spoke to and about you at that cocktail party and still wanted her to be here. There are some things I can't really speak about because of the contracts that I signed, but know that she's here because I was outvoted."

His eyes burned into me and my gut told me that there was more that he wanted to say. He ran his hands through my hair and then twisted his fingers in the back of the thick mass. Guiding my head forward, he stopped when our noses brushed up against each other.

His breath tickled my skin and his touch set it on fire. Our closeness weakened me as I felt my body's desire to give in to my many, many wants when it came to Julian Winters.

"Julian," I murmured, in a needy voice that I didn't recognize.

*Kiss me dammit!*

"Promise me that no matter what, you won't forget that at the end of this, when it's all said and done, you're who I'm taking home," he uttered so softly that my entire body reacted.

"What's going on, Julian?"

He let his lips brush against mine briefly. I let out a little whimper when I realized I couldn't lean in for the kiss. His firm grip in my hair kept me hovering just above his lips as he delayed kissing me.

"Tell me you understand. Promise me, Zoe."

Staring into the greys of his eyes, there were so many emotions flashing through them. I felt so conflicted. On one hand, what he wanted me to promise him felt like something that someone would say before they do something that completely contradicts that. But on the other hand, when I thought about the way his arms gripped me protectively, his eyes drank me in appreciatively, and his voice held the promise he was looking for from me, I didn't believe he would ruin whatever was just starting to develop between us.

I didn't know what else to do so I nodded.

Finally, his lips crashed into mine and I moaned my approval into his mouth. Our tongues moved together in an effort to try to see who wanted who more. As the kiss deepened, I felt a vibration ricochet throughout my entire body.

"Did you sneak your cell phone into the house?" Julian asked between kisses.

I shook my head and continued giving and receiving the best kisses of my life.

And then realization struck.

My heart hammered in my chest as we pulled apart. I opened my jacket and saw the blinking red light of the microphone. "Oh shit! They are trying to track me."

Scrambling to our feet, we ran out of the gazebo and made a beeline for the gate. He opened it for me, and after letting me walk through first, he grabbed my hand and we sprinted. Once we made it back to the discreet opening that led to the maze, we peeked out. I saw a few people with flashlights in the distance heading toward the garden. We ducked back into the hidden pathway.

"Okay, I'm going to make a run for it," I informed him, pulling my hair back into a low ponytail.

"I can walk you back to the house."

I shook my head. "And that would just start stuff and after Tori told everyone she saw us kiss, I'm sure that would just make things worse in the house."

"Tori." Julian scoffed, a grimace on his handsome face. "As soon as I'm able to, she's gone."

*As soon as he's able to?*

I looked down at the buzzing battery pack. "Crap! I have to go." I launched myself at him, wrapping my arms around him tightly. "Until tomorrow."

He tilted my chin upward and kissed me with enough passion to get me through the night. "Until tomorrow," he whispered between kisses.

With one last fleeting glance, I took off running toward the house. Staying on the outermost edges of the maze, I followed the well-lit garden path at full speed. Once I was far enough away from Julian that it didn't look suspicious, I decelerated to a brisk walk and turned my microphone back on. The green light lit up quickly.

Less than three minutes had passed when Jamie the producer appeared on the other end of the straightaway. She gave me a wave. "We've been looking for you," she called out to me, her voice echoing. "Where have you been?"

I didn't respond until we were in closer proximity.

"I went for a run."

"Oh!" Jamie's surprise bordered on judgmental as her eyes surveyed my soft, curvy body.

"Okay Jamie, you can dial back the shock on your face."

She laughed, lifting up her hands. "I'm not shocked that you went for a run, I'm shocked that you went for a run this late."

# Chapter 9

Monday morning, we sat in the living room wearing jeans and matching white t-shirts waiting for someone to fix the chandelier. The broken bulb was bothering the creator of the show so production stopped while the team in charge of the set took care of it. The house had been operating with a few screws loose since I made my way back from Julian's gazebo the night before.

At some point while I was out, all of the women converged at the pool and drank a lot. New friendships were forged, two huge arguments broke out, chairs were thrown into the pool, and someone's blonde hair extensions ended up in the garbage disposal. By the time I'd arrived, crew members were swarming the house, getting it pretty for filming. Someone must have missed the broken bulb during clean up.

Sitting on the loveseat next to Mya, I nudged her with my elbow. "Is everything okay?"

She gave me a small smile. "I guess I'm just nervous."

I reached out and patted her knee. "It's going to be fine."

Someone yelled "Action!" before I could say anymore.

Bryce and Julian walked into the room and we all cheered their arrival. Julian was wearing jeans and the same white shirt with the same black heart in the middle. His sunglasses were hanging from his collar and his hands were lodged in his pockets. He just looked effortlessly cool.

"Hello ladies!" Bryce exclaimed, unusually animated. "So I'm sure you're all wondering why you're all dressed the same. Well we are about to tell you. But first, I want you to pick a partner."

The sound of women calling each other's names engulfed the room. Mya and I just looked at each other and linked arms.

Feeling the eyes of someone on me, I glanced up to find Robert Brady staring at me just off camera. We held eye contact for a few seconds before Bryce pulled my attention away.

"Now that you have your partners, I'm going to let Julian deliver the good news." Bryce clapped Julian on the back with a huge smile on his face.

"We are going to Black Heart Studios today. We're making music!"

My eyebrows flew up and Mya and I danced in our seats excitedly. A couple of ladies squealed. Some jumped up. Tori went over to Julian and gave him a big hug to which he reciprocated with a huge smile.

The energy in the room changed at that point.

He looked around the room, giving us each eye contact. "Are you all as excited about this as I am? I hope you are all ready for a good time!" He waited for the cheers to die down before he continued. "The party bus is outside so let's go."

Julian didn't stand around waiting to give us individual hugs as he did at the beginning of our last group date.

Instead, he led the charge outside. Once standing in front of the house, we noticed there were two town cars right behind the party bus. We were lined up like we were told to do before filming began and a camerawoman stood on one side of us, while another stood near Julian.

I looked around suspiciously. *Something is about to happen.*

Julian slipped on his sunglasses and flashed a smile. "As you can see, most of you will be traveling on the bus. But I'd like to invite Emma to ride with me in the town car."

My stomach twisted. I sucked in a sharp breath, but recovered by politely clapping and smiling as Chatty Cathy, real name Emma apparently, made her way over to Julian. Even though I knew that he couldn't necessarily pick me for every one-on-one, private moment, it still bothered me to not get picked.

I tried to be discreet as I watched Julian place his hand at the small of Emma's back as he escorted her to the car. He opened the back door for her to enter and she thanked him by running her hand down his chest. She must have said something funny as he laughed before closing the door behind her. He walked around the back of the car and climbed in on the other side without a second glance at the group.

Unfamiliar feelings whipped up inside of me as I struggled to hold on to the smile that was keeping my shit together. The two camera crews were panning over the group, waiting for us to say or do something. Who Julian picked to spend his time with was who he picked to spend his time with, but how we reacted to his decision, that would be the thing that followed us around for the rest of our lives. With a deep breath, I pushed everything I was feeling down.

*Don't give them what they want. Let the drama queens do*

*their thing and—*

"I can't believe he picked her," Tori complained into the camera. "I really can't. But I guess that's part of why I love him. He is always so generous to the needy."

I rolled my eyes.

"Was that eye roll because you agree with Tori, Zoe?" The producer standing beside the camera man asked.

"No, not at all. That eye roll was because of Tori. Who's that mean and petty for no reason?" I shrugged.

"What about you, Mya?"

"Emma seems nice, but she isn't me. I'm not worried," Mya said, winking at the camera crew.

*Go Mya!*

I stifled a surprised giggle. I wasn't sure what had gotten into her, but I liked it.

"Okay everyone else, over here," Bryce shouted, standing at the party bus, ready to usher us in.

The nine of us climbed into the bus followed by a camerawoman and producer. Bryce gave us a few made-for-TV assurances before he exited the bus and got into the town car directly behind the car with Julian and Emma.

Just thinking about the two of them in a car together with the windows pretty much blacked out bothered me all over again. Pushing my sunglasses onto my face, I closed my eyes and tried to focus on something other than Julian. But without my phone, entertainment or music, all I'd been able to think about for the last four days was Julian.

*This is how it happens. This is how reality TV ends up making a fool out of every single woman on these shows. It cranks up people's emotions by creating the illusion of a relationship, ensuring the man that we're in a relationship with is effectively dating several other women at the same time, pitting the women in question against each other for attention and affection, and isolating them from the real world.*

As I listened to Tori detail her trip to Cabo San Lucas, I'd never thought I'd actually miss the news. I turned to Mya and frowned.

She frowned back.

We talked quietly about life back home, but every ten minutes Tori would get extremely loud, causing us to not even be able to hear each other. An hour into the trip and I couldn't take it anymore.

"Tori—"

"We're here!" Ana announced, her face practically pressed to the window. "I've always wanted to record my music! I wish I would've thought to bring my business cards."

I looked around the bus and it seemed as though I was the only person who heard it or took concern with it. Even the producer, who was busy talking to the cameraman, seemed to not catch that bit of information. I knew I was sensitive to Ana's comment because Julian just told me that his fear was meeting someone like that. But I had to tread lightly because telling anyone what Ana said had the potential to be misconstrued as me being jealous or trying to throw her under the bus.

*Even though I'm just trying to look out for Julian.*

The bus slowed to a stop and we filed out of it quietly. The red brick building looked like a converted warehouse. It had no windows, only a steel door complete with a big black heart on it. We were waiting and in position when the town car pulled up. Cameras focused on us and our reactions while a separate camera trailed Julian and Emma as they strolled up. His arm was draped around her shoulders with the kind of ease that is typically reserved for someone special.

*Someone like me.*

I couldn't deny the pang of jealousy that ate at my twisted gut. I was trying not to feed it. But as Julian and Emma walked by me, I felt invisible. So I endeavored to keep my distance from Julian during the date.

*If I'm going to end up without the guy, I for damn sure am not going to end up without my self-respect.*

Julian jogged up the five steps leading to the entrance and opened the door for us. As we entered the building, I noticed Julian patting everyone on the back. When it was my turn, I expected a signal, a whispered message, or any kind of acknowledgment of what we shared the night before. Instead, he patted me on the back like everyone else.

The pit in my stomach grew and my heart sank. I couldn't even pretend disappointment wasn't wreaking havoc on my insides. It wasn't so much that he spent the last hour with Emma. It was the fact that after spending that time with me last night, he acted as if I was invisible to him today.

*A mere sixteen hours ago, he wanted me to promise him that I knew that he wanted to ride off into the sunset with me. Yesterday, I was his one and only choice. Today, I'm one of many choices.*

My feelings were hurt, but I knew from experience that I was going to be okay. I closed my eyes and inhaled deeply and then I let it out slowly.

*Feeling better already,* I told myself until I heard the timber of his voice when he started to speak.

"I am in my element. This place is one of my happy places," Julian stated, glancing at me before training those gorgeous grey eyes on each of us. "When I was a kid, I dreamed of becoming a singer. Well, honestly, I dreamed of becoming a rapper, but that wasn't in my wheelhouse."

I snickered along with everyone else.

"I've always known that I would do something with music. I wasn't sure what or how it would manifest, but I knew I would do something. And I want you to get to know me better so one of the things we are going to do is put you in my shoes."

He paced before us causing the cameraman to adjust his placement. Someone in the camera crew signaled for Julian to stand next to the wall which had the black heart spray painted on it...which I was also leaning against.

Julian continued speaking as he walked toward the wall, his back to the camera. He looked at each of us, but when his eyes landed on me, he stumbled over his words.

I raised my eyebrows. *Interesting.*

A few feet away from me, Julian turned to face the camera, standing directly under the heart. "I know this may take some of you out of your comfort zone, but you and your partner are going to write and record a song here at the infamous Black Heart Studios!"

The sound of ten excited shrieks seemed to be magnified in the open reception area. The large space had a modern design with several seating areas and what looked to be soundproof glass walls as none of the people in their offices reacted to the noise.

"Oh wow!" I looked at Mya who was clutching my arm with her little hands and jumping up and down.

"Oh my God! Oh my God!" She kept repeating the phrase as she dug her surprisingly sharp nails into my arm.

"Ouch," I exclaimed with a laugh, swatting her away.

"Ladies, ladies!" Julian rubbed his hands together. His face was the epitome of happiness as he tried to get our attention. "You'll have an hour to write a verse each and then we'll get each pair of you into one of the studios to record. You will all be using the same track and the team with the best song will accompany me to a listening party tonight."

Another round of squeals and clapping followed.

He smiled and nodded then he calmed everyone's excitement down. "So if you look around the lobby, you'll find paper and pens at each of the tables and a couple on those couches near that fish tank. When I say go, your one hour begins." He paused for so long that I was convinced he was toying with us. Then he shouted, "Go!'

Fortunately, as soon as I was given my t-shirt and instructed to put on jeans, I decided to wear sneakers. A lot of the women wore heels so it didn't take much for me to spring into action to race to the couch in the corner. It was tucked away and seemed to offer the most privacy.

I plopped down on it as Tori, in five inch heels, slid to a stop in front of me. Her face was red with anger and exertion. "Move! I was headed here first!"

"Well I got here first, so I don't know what to tell you except better luck next time." I shrugged and then flashed a smile to Mya who took her time since only one of us needed to claim the seat.

"Excuse me," Mya said to Tori. "I just need to get by you so I can sit with my partner on our couch."

Tori let out a noise that was part growl and part scream as Mya eased by her in dramatic fashion.

The camera was in our faces in no time and somehow Julian managed to pop up discreetly behind the camera crew. He winked at me as soon as I noticed him.

I was statue-still, unable to move. I didn't know what to do or how to react to that. He had ignored me the entire day and then he winked at me as if everything was okay.

Julian cleared his throat and then flashed his sexiest smile. "Tori, the clock has started ticking and I think your partner is over on the other side of the room. You should head over there and get started."

Tori's tone and demeanor changed when the cameras arrived, but when she saw Julian, she transformed into a whole other person. "Julian, you're right. Will you walk me over there please?"

"Of course." He looked at us with amusement in his eyes. "I'm coming back to check on you two in a few minutes."

"Thanks, Julian!" Mya's chipper reply was the only response needed. "I'm looking—we're looking forward to it! So thanks for...thanks!"

Julian smiled sweetly at Mya's awkwardness. "You're welcome. I'm looking forward to it as well." His eyes shifted to me and held my gaze for longer than what was socially acceptable: "Zoe."

I cocked my head to the side. "Julian," I returned, inexplicably poised despite the butterflies that danced inside of me.

He chuckled as he took Tori's arm and escorted her across the room, the camera crew following closely.

"We have to win that date! We have to! Please tell me you can sing. Please!" Mya was a ball of energy. "I don't know why I keep making a fool of myself, but I do. And I can't sing and if I lose this date opportunity, it's over for me. I'm going to get sent home tonight if I don't win."

I looked at my insecure friend who had no idea how awesome she was and I smiled. "Mya, you're not getting sent home tonight—"

"Because you can sing," she interrupted with an abundance of hope.

"No, I can't sing at all. Like at all. But you're not getting sent home because you're going to stop thinking of Julian Winters as Julian Winters and start thinking of him as Julian."

"Look at him. Seriously." Mya pushed my arm until I looked

at Julian.

He was standing at the table of Tori and The Redhead, or as her name turned out to be, Tiffany. While Tiffany sat at the table, Tori remained clutched to Julian's side with her hand on his bicep.

Even though his arms did look good in that t-shirt, it was his smile that resonated with me. It wasn't just the perfect teeth or the softest, sweetest lips I'd ever tasted. It was that his smile seemed to radiate an innate goodness within him that I wanted to be a part of.

Mya sighed dreamily. "He's so hot and rich and could have any woman he wanted. He was probably the captain of the basketball team and the most popular guy in school. I was the librarian's assistant and president of the chess club. He's out of my league in so many ways, but I know that if he got a chance to know me, we'd make each other happy. Just reading his info without knowing who he was or how attractive he was, I fell in love with him. I haven't even liked a man since my ex-husband and I fell in love with the bio of 'Eligible Bachelor J.' Out of all the women who applied, there are only ten of us here. So maybe the producer was right. Maybe I have to do what I have to do to stay in the competition for as long as it takes for him to realize that I'm the one."

My feelings were conflicted and I didn't know what to say to her. Although I liked Mya and wanted to reassure her and keep her from selling out, my own feelings for Julian made it difficult for me to comfort her in the way that she probably wanted. I wasn't able to tell her that I hoped she ended up with Julian, but I was able to tell her a hard truth that she needed to hear.

With a deep breath, I ripped my eyes off of Julian who seemed to be entertained by Tori and Tiffany. Turning toward

Mya, I put my hand on her shoulder. "You have to get out of your own head. I don't know if it's the divorce or because we are in this weird competitive atmosphere, but Mya, you are worthy of real connection. And you won't have that with anyone if you aren't being completely yourself."

She kept her eyes on Julian for a moment longer before nodding. "Okay, let's write this song." She made a face. "Have you ever written a song before?"

"Today will be the first day. But I love poetry so maybe that will translate into a decent song."

"Okay good. But if we both can't sing, how are we going to pull that off."

"Let's get the song written and then figure the rest out later."

For the next thirty-five minutes, we each wrote a verse and then we settled on the phrase "I'm the one for you and you know that it's true" for the chorus. Julian checked on us at one point, but we shied away from showing him any of it because it was about him.

"Time's up!" Bryce Wilson called out. "Now, there are five groups and five available studios. You have one hour to record your songs. Once you're done, you will come back out here to meet the judges. They will listen and vote for the best song."

"Wait, so Julian isn't judging?" I asked Mya even though I knew she didn't know any more than I did.

She shrugged her shoulders and widened her eyes. "I don't know, but I'm even more nervous now. I thought he was the only one who was going to hear it."

"Well, him and the millions of people who watch this crap."

"Cut!" Someone yelled from the corner of the room and the two cameramen sat their equipment down. Lighting and camera crewmembers charged the boxed lunch table.

Black Heart Studios didn't allow filming equipment into the

studio area because of the clients that they had recording at the time. So for one full hour, the crew had some down time and we were able to embarrass ourselves without the extra pressure of it being televised.

We were all instructed on which studio we would report to and we excitedly went through the ominous black door.

"Knock knock," Mya said as she pushed open our private studio.

"Come on in." A woman with bright blue eyes, curly blonde hair and two arms covered in tattoos said as she rose from her seat. "I'm Jo, the engineer for today."

*Rock on,* I thought, greeting her with a firm handshake.

In my last semester of law school there was a case with a female sound engineer sued a label for sexism and I found out that ninety-five percent of sound engineers were male. So to see Jo as our engineer was a treat.

We immediately jumped into the conversation, explaining what we envisioned for the song as she played us the track.

"We were thinking something that kind of masks our voices and makes us sound better," Mya explained.

"Like auto-tune?" Jo questioned.

I leaned forward. "More like other people singing."

Jo laughed and tapped her finger against the huge sound board. "I think I have something. Which one of you wants to go first?"

Mya looked at me and pointed. "I need to shake the nerves out. You go!" She yelped and covered her face. "I don't think I can deal with the two of you looking at me through the glass."

I shook my head and sighed. "I'll go."

"I can hit this button and you won't see anything in here," Jo offered as I went in.

I looked at Mya's animated face and stifled a laugh. "Yes, please hit the button. I can't look at her and struggle to sing what I wrote."

Once I was in the booth, I put on the headphones and sat down on the stool. Flattening the paper on the music stand in front of me, I got comfortable in my seat. Squaring my shoulders, I adjusted the microphone and then I gave them an anxious smile and a thumbs-up.

The glass frosted and within seconds I couldn't see them anymore. Over the intercom, I heard Jo's voice.

"Let me know when you're ready."

I looked at the paper in front of me and my heart ached as I reviewed the lyrics. It was one part love letter and one part letting go hidden under a lot of metaphors that on the surface sounded like an angst-ridden stroll through the garden.

I took a deep soothing breath and then I shook my arms at my sides. "I'm ready."

The music started and I sang as if my life depended on it. Although I was able to carry a tune, it just didn't sound good when I did it. But after only four takes, I was done with my part and she played it back. Once I gave the thumbs-up on what was playing around the studio, I was instructed to exit the booth.

"You did great!" Mya exclaimed as soon as I walked through the door.

"Thanks. I was nervous once I got in the booth, but when I couldn't see anything anymore, I felt good. I know I wasn't in there sounding like Jill Scott or Adele or anything but when Jo worked her magic, I didn't sound like food going down the garbage disposal. So I'd say that's a win."

Mya laughed as she entered the booth. "You're so silly!"

She got settled in the booth and the moment the glass frosted over, there was a knock on the door.

Jo had on headphones, cueing up the music. I didn't know what protocol was, but I walked toward the door to open it. I was just about to reach out for the handle when it creeped open. When I saw who it was, I froze.

Being about a foot away from Julian overloaded my system with emotions and my stomach trembled. The seconds ticked by and each breath I took was hitching as I stared into his eyes.

"Zoe..." He whispered my name in a way that woke up every single cell in my body.

"Julian. I need to talk to you about—"

He looked over my head and then wrapped his hand around the back of my neck causing the words to stop on the tip of my tongue abruptly.

"Go to the room with the green door in two minutes. Make sure you're not followed." His voice was so soft and so fast that I was too focused on understanding him to notice that his face was coming closer.

He brushed his lips against mine and I could taste the sweetness of whatever he was drinking. The kiss was brief, too brief, but long enough to feel him breathe himself into me. He looked over my head, ensuring our moment was still just ours, and as suddenly as he appeared, he was gone.

I turned around and Jo was messing with the levels on the board and bobbing her head to the music. Scanning the room, I found a pen and I wrote a quick note on a fresh sheet of paper.

*Running to the restroom. Be back soon.*

After leaving it on the table, I slipped out of the room undetected. If they didn't know what time I left the room, they wouldn't be able to determine exactly how long I was gone.

Walking quickly down the hall, I kept looking over my shoulder to make sure no one saw me. When I got to the end of the hall, I could go left or right. Left had the restrooms and a few other doors, none of which were green. So I sprinted in the other direction, landing on the ball of my feet so my shoes didn't make any noise. When I saw the green door, I looked over my shoulder and then dashed inside.

The room was dark with a green light glowing softly from inside of the booth. I leaned against the closed door and waited for my eyes to adjust. When they did, I saw Julian's profile. He was standing in the center of the room and I couldn't see what he was doing, but I could tell he was concentrating. I saw the outline of his muscular body as he clicked a remote toward the booth. The light in the booth transitioned from one low green light to several. The extra illumination warmed the entire studio, but still kept it dim. The change made it so that I could actually make out Julian's facial expressions.

I wanted to ask him about him ignoring me. I wanted to ask him why he chose to take Emma's Chatty Cathy ass on the private ride. I wanted to ask him if he thought about me all night like I thought about him. I wanted to ask him a lot of things. And I planned to ask him every single one of those questions. But when he tossed the remote onto the green leather ottoman and then looked at me, I lost my train of thought. For a brief second, while my heart hammered in my chest, the connection between my brain and my ability to speak was rendered useless.

"You needed to talk to me about something?" He strode across the room to me, a smile playing at the corners of his mouth.

I tilted my head to the side. "Yeah...about how you've been ignoring me."

He smirked, shaking his head. "I haven't been able to ignore you since the moment I met you. What is this about?"

"It's about you ignoring me."

It was more complicated than that, but how was I

supposed to explain that I was a little jealous of him dating other women when we met on the set of a reality television show.

"When did I ignore you?" He closed the gap between us so that we were only inches apart.

I stared up at him. Even in the dim room, the way he looked at me rivaled any man I'd ever been with. I sighed, feeling myself being won over with just a look.

"Well you didn't ignore me," I backtracked. "But we had this amazing night together and then you come to the house today and you treat me like everybody else."

"You're not like everybody else. But when the cameras are rolling, I have to act like this is an actual competition. Even though I've already got my prize."

I paused, narrowing my eyes at him. I shook my head. "They wrote that in a script, didn't they?"

He tried to stifle his chuckle. He managed to do a pretty good job not making a lot of noise, but his shoulders shook uncontrollably. "They wanted me to say that during the live finale when I give the final charm. I told them no. I wasn't going to get through that line without laughing."

"Well don't use lame, discarded lines on me. Especially when last night you said one thing and then today—"

His face was serious as he interrupted me. "I meant everything I said last night. But as a soon-to-be lawyer, you know that I have to fulfill this contract. And I have to date around since this contract is for a dating show. That doesn't change how I feel about you though."

His eyes burned into mine and I knew he wanted to know if it changed anything with me, but he didn't ask.

*Does it change anything for me?* I asked myself, getting lost in his eyes.

"You're going to have to back up a few feet so I can actually think. And what kind of body wash or cologne do you use? Why do you smell so good all of the time?"

He laughed, backing up. He was about six feet away. "Is this enough space?"

"It is." I inhaled deeply and exhaled loudly. My body slacked against the door as I looked at him. "As I mentioned the other day, I'm not a risk taker. But at the same time, we have this connection that just...it doesn't make any sense. I've never met someone and knew instantly that I wanted to date them. I'm not saying we're getting married or anything, but I know I want to date you and I don't want to share you. There's just so much here, you know?"

He nodded in agreement and as I avoided eye contact, my truth just rolled out of my mouth.

"But you're also going to be dating other women, kissing other women, being affectionate with other women. And I have to compete against other women so I can try to win dates with you. And then to add insult to injury, I know firsthand that some of these women are complete..." I took a deep breath, pausing to refrain from saying anything I would regret. "If you're interested in me, there's no way in hell you're also interested in some of these women. You just can't be. And to top it off, I listen to women analyze and overanalyze your every look and touch and word and it gets in my head a little. If I'm hearing how you almost kissed someone, it makes me feel like...ugh!"

I let my head fall back against the door. "This show is bullshit and the only thing real about it is us. But we haven't been able to be us or be real with each other on camera because it's day four, date two and there are a whole lot of women left that you have to date. Which is fine, I guess, in theory. But it's hard because you're dating multiple women and at the end of the day, I'm just dating you. And I'm either supposed to be cool with that or leave. And...and then in the house, I'm supposed to either fight with the other women or act like we're friends and that it's not awkward that we all are into the same man. Those are the options and the producers are just looking for the best story. They don't give a damn about anybody's feelings. And I don't know about anyone else, but I have thought about you nonstop. But we don't get to date normally and get to know each other. If I don't win a date, I'm stuck in the house wondering if whoever you're out with is trying to give you a hand job in the back of the town car!" I threw my hands up in the air, meeting his gaze for the first time since I started my monologue. "I like you, okay? I like you a lot."

Silence filled the room, sucking out every other word except for the admission of my feelings. I felt him soaking it in. With each quiet moment, I felt my adrenaline from my vent session draining from me, but my heart still raced because of him. The intensity of his gaze pinned me to the door as I just stared at him wide-eyed, not knowing what else to say.

"I don't want to touch anyone else or kiss anyone else. Do you want me to tell you how much I like you again? Because I will." He licked his lips. "Because I do."

"Julian," I whispered, trying to break the hold he had on me so I could focus.

I watched his gaze travel down the length of my body. The air instantly became thick and I could feel how badly he wanted me. My body responded instantly. Although he couldn't see how wet he made me, my hardening nipples against my thin cotton t-shirt probably gave me away.

He stalked across the room and grabbed my face, crashing his lips against mine. With his hands around the back of my neck and his thumbs caressing the spot behind my ears, he kissed me hard and with enough passion to take my breath away.

Wrapping my arms around him, I moaned into his mouth. My body responded to his, curving toward him, into him. He pulled away briefly, resting his forehead against mine. Although we weren't kissing anymore, our bodies were still completely connected, moving in waves against each other. I could feel how hard he was and it took everything in me to not snake my hand down his torso just to see if he was as long and thick as he felt. My head was spinning and my eyes fluttered open.

"You can't do that." His breathing was ragged. "You can't moan like that again, Zoe. It makes me want to do things to you that I'm not going to be able to do in this studio."

*Oh yes please.*

Before I had a chance to respond, his mouth covered mine. His right hand left my neck and traveled down my shoulder. Once his fingertips hit the bare skin of my arm, fire burned through my entire body.

Impulsively, we moaned together, loudly, when our tongues touched. Shivers traveled up and down my spine. I found myself clutching his t-shirt in an effort to help me climb him. I wanted to keep our bodies connected and feeling him hardening beneath his jeans only intensified my urges. My heart thudded in my chest and because we were so close, I could feel his doing the same.

A deep growl from the base of his throat soaked my already wet panties.

He was rock hard and although he pulled out of the kiss and only our foreheads touched, I could still feel the heat of his hardness against my belly.

"We should stop," he said. His hands were running up and down my arms and his eyes were shut tightly.

I moved my hands from his back to his front, grasping his

t-shirt and feeling his hard abdomen. Resisting the urge to go south, I moved my hands north toward his well-defined chest until they were around his neck.

"We really should," I replied, gripping his short hair and pulling his lips to mine. My heart was drumming in my chest and something deep in my gut tightened.

His sweet lips moved against mine sensually, allowing me to relish in the taste of him. I nipped and sucked at his bottom lip causing him to relocate his hands from their grip on my hips toward the back pockets of my jeans.

Using the door as leverage, he lifted me by the bottom of my ass and never broke our kiss. I wrapped my legs around his waist and kissed him harder, deeper. I wanted him. I wanted him so badly that I didn't even think about the fact that we were in the midst of filming a show. It wasn't until I felt a vibration under my left thigh that I was even brought back to reality.

We separated our lips slowly, still in a daze. I untangled my body from his and he set me on the ground gently. His face was flushed, his lips were slightly bruised and his hair was a mess. It was the sexiest I'd ever seen him.

*I can only imagine what I look like right now.*

I started straightening my clothes and my hair as he pulled his phone out of his pocket.

"Shit," he cursed as soon as he saw the text message. He texted back and then put the phone in his pocket. "They need me back out there. The hour for the session will be up soon."

Panic set in. "Shit! How long have we been gone?"

"No more than fifteen minutes." He stared at me, reaching out and lightly touching my face with his fingertips. "You're beautiful. I mean, you're beautiful with the makeup and everything done for the cocktail parties, too. But right now, no makeup, wild hair, and your lips..." His eyes zoomed in on my mouth. His thumb ran across my bottom lip. "Your lips swollen from kissing me."

My heart skipped a beat. "Thank you." I put my hand over his and puckered my lips, kissing his thumb. "There aren't enough opportunities for moments like this."

"I know, I know. I will do whatever I can do to figure out how to make more time for us. I want to make you comfortable. I didn't really think about it like that, but you're right. I will be going on dates with other women and stuff, but think of it like I'm an actor, acting. So this is work."

*Work, my ass. Actors aren't getting real hand jobs unless they are in porn. He should probably amend his statement to specify that he meant television actor.*

I must have made an unintentional face because he planted another kiss on my lips. "I can't say anything more than this," he started, a brush of hesitancy on his face. "During my treatment meeting, I was told I was spending more time looking, talking and flirting with you than anyone else. So between the cocktail party and the bar date, they can see something between us so they'll be more mindful of it. I've been told I need to spread the love and that it's a show so I have to put on a show." He searched my face. "Are you going to be okay with that?"

*Probably not.*

His phone vibrated again. He checked it and he started moving and speaking quickly. "They're sending someone to come and get me so I'm going to leave out first. You leave a couple of minutes after me." He kissed me earnestly, urgently, and then dashed out of the room, leaving me winded.

I waited for two minutes and then flew out of the room like a bat out of hell.

Entering the studio, Mya was just coming out of the booth. "Hey! You missed it didn't you?" She went to sit on the couch and saw the note right after the words left her mouth. "Oh you went to the bathroom. Well, Jo is tweaking something and then be prepared to have your mind blown."

Jo finished ten minutes later and played the song titled "I'm The One For You." Had I not been in the booth, I would've assumed Jo contacted a couple of famous friends to help make the song better. Even though we didn't sound like Whitney Houston, we didn't sound bad. Mya and I were damn near unrecognizable on the track. Five minutes after our second listen, one of the crew members came by to pick up our love song. We had barely shut the door when Bryce Wilson knocked telling us they were ready.

A producer put microphones back on us before we left the studio area. When we entered the lobby we were in before, it had been transformed.

# Chapter 10

Three tables with Black Heart Studios tablecloths were arranged along the wall with the big black heart logo spray painted on it. Four people sat behind the tables. One was Julian, smiling at each of us as we walked through the door. The other three looked familiar, but I couldn't place their faces immediately. It wasn't until we were seated in the back, facing the judges, that I realized I'd seen them before.

"Is that the group Super Casanova?" I asked Mya.

"It could be. I'm not sure. I don't really listen to them. Is that the group with the guy with the high-top fade?"

"You know what? I don't know." I stared at the group members hard and the only man in the group didn't have that hairstyle. "It's my best friend's favorite group and we went to a show last summer. They're pretty good. I'm almost positive that's them."

"I'm not a fan of that type of music. I'm more into classic rock," Emma aka Chatty Cathy interjected from the other side of Mya.

I looked at her blankly. *I wasn't talking to you lady!*

Giving her a strained smile, I sat back in my chair. Production seemed to be having a meeting in between where the camera facing the judges was set up and where the camera facing us was set up. Lights were being adjusted and the squeak of music being cued up rang in the air.

"Action!" Someone yelled from behind the camera positioned near the judges.

Julian stood. "After all of that hard work, writing and recording, I hope you all have a better understanding of what it is that I do for a living. The woman I'm looking for doesn't have to be a great singer or songwriter. I'm just looking for someone who can appreciate the time and energy it takes because my job is my life. And I need to know that I have someone who gets it." He spread his arms out, gesturing to the people sitting with him. "So without further ado, let me introduce you to a few friends of mine. I've worked with you for...what is it, Londyn? The last six years? Seven years?"

The woman closest to him, presumably Londyn, laughed. "God, Julian, you make us sound old." She looked at the other two who had joined in with the laughter before looking out at us and the camera. "But yes, seven long years with this man as our go-to writing partner and friend."

Julian smiled and nodded. "So ladies, let me introduce you to my friends, Londyn, Marshall, and Hayden. Better known as Super Casanova!"

"I thought so!" I exclaimed to myself. The other ladies clapped and called out cheers, but when the producer in the back corner started waving her arms in the air, we increased our volume.

*I bet that's whose album listening party they are going to tonight.*

I tried to look beyond the camera as it swept over us, but it was hard to ignore. There were times when the camera was further away that it was a little easier to forget that I was being filmed. That was not one of those times as the cameraman was standing so close to us that it was hard to even get a great view of the judge's table. Fortunately where I sat, I could see Julian perfectly.

Still standing, Julian rubbed his hands together. "Okay, are you ready?"

We cheered.

"I said, are you ready?"

We screamed.

"Okay good! That's more like it," he laughed. "I'm actually not voting, but I am taking notes and listening carefully. Super Casanova will be voting on which song and lyrics are the best and they will choose the winners. And those winners will be accompanying me to the listening party of the surprise new album by Super Casanova!"

Again, we applauded. The producers in the corner threw their hands up, jumping up and down to encourage us to get louder. We did as we were instructed and as I was certain that it would appear as though we were all Super Casanova fans.

The first song started and because we all had the same beat, I sat in anxious apprehension until the first note of the song was sung. Looking at Mya, I was relieved it wasn't ours. But I soon realized that though the lyrics simple, the singing was amazing.

Although I knew my singing abilities were limited and that America would be hearing my garbled vocals over an intercom, that wasn't what made me a little anxious. My vocals, even if they weren't chopped and screwed into something tolerable, didn't expose me or make me vulnerable. The lyrics to my verse did.

For the start of the next three songs, Mya and I clutched

hands and tightened our faces. Once we heard the first word, we overdramatically breathed a sigh of relief each time it wasn't our song. On the fifth go-around, we did our same routine, but when we heard my voice, we squeezed each other's hands.

The words weaved languidly around planting the seeds of love and being scared of the conditions not being right for the flower to grow. I even managed to squeeze in a fertilizer line to shout out the show. It rhymed. It sounded good as a poem at least. But if Julian was only able to pull out a line or two, he would know it was me expressing how I feel about him.

*And that the show is bullshit.*

I swept my eyes around and saw the red head and Ana make confused faces at one another.

*Not surprised.*

As soon as my part was over, I looked up at Julian and he was looking directly at me.

My skin heated at the attention and I licked my lips.

He bit his bottom lip before shifting his gaze to other women and giving them his gorgeous smile.

As soon as Julian relinquished his visual hold on me, I could clearly hear and understand Mya's part. I knew her lyrics were very literal. She didn't claim to pick up on my metaphor; however, she started her lyrics out with her picking the flowers out of the garden and bringing them to him.

*So maybe she did know.*

Once the final song was played, the judges took fifteen minutes to deliberate and the contestants were given the ability to go on a bathroom break. I didn't have to go so I stayed back with a few other women and just took in my surroundings.

*This is a really cool experience,* I thought to myself as the hustle and bustle of a recording studio surrounded me.

# The One

I tried not to stare at Julian, but it was hard since he was right in front of me. I watched the production crew set up shots and then I glanced at Julian. I watched the cameraman and a producer interview Super Casanova and then I glanced at Julian. I watched Nicole do a confessional interview and then I glanced at Julian.

But that time, I caught him watching me. We smiled at each other and I bathed in the way he looked at me. We were in the middle of a flirtatious staring contest when Tori's shrill scream echoed through the building.

Julian wasn't just a talented, intelligent poet with a handsome face and sexy body to match. He was also an Olympic athlete.

Tori's scream lasted for about ten seconds and somehow, Julian made it from the judge's table to the bathroom on the opposite side of the room in that amount of time. He was already at the bathroom while I was still shaking off the scare that the scream gave me.

"What's wrong?" Julian shouted, grabbing her shoulders and giving her a quick once over. "Are you okay?"

She started crying and pointed to the bathroom. Julian, suddenly flanked by two body guards, two producers and a camerawoman, knocked on the bathroom door and then announced that he was going to come in.

I craned my neck to see around the people clamoring over to see what was going on.

Tiffany opened the bathroom door. "No one else is in here, come in. Ana's in the big stall. I think she's having a panic attack."

"Get the medic!" The female producer called out as she entered the bathroom after Julian and one of the bodyguards.

The camerawoman hesitated and the male producer, still

outside of the bathroom, said something I couldn't hear. The camerawoman made a horrified face and shook her head. He whispered something again. That time, she only deliberated for a minute before she entered the bathroom to film the medical emergency.

*Poor Ana. Can't even have a breakdown in peace.*

I didn't care for Ana, but I hoped she was okay.

"She's probably faking it," Emma noted, folding her arms across her chest. She tossed her chestnut brown hair over her shoulder with a whip of her neck. "All three of them are liars. Ana, Tiffany and especially Tori..."

Chatty Cathy was at it again as she started gesturing wildly with her hands and talking a mile a minute. The medic rushed into the building and just as he was about to enter the bathroom, Julian, carrying Ana, exited the bathroom. The camerawoman came out next; camera focused on Ana's reddened face. The body guard and producer followed.

"Are you kidding me?" Emma exclaimed, snatching my attention away momentarily. "Are you seeing this?"

Trying to figure out who she was speaking to, I looked between Samantha, Emma's side kick who was standing next to her, and the woman sitting beside Samantha. I didn't remember her name, but I remembered that it started with the letter L.

*Lacey? Lily?*

"Leah, stand up and look at this bullshit! Julian is carrying Ana like the fucking baby she is. And then..."

*Leah! That's it. Trying to keep these names straight is work!*

I don't know why Emma was so riled up and angry but it made me laugh. I turned away from them so I could watch the action.

Mya and Nicole were the only contestants not in the room when everything went down because they opted to use the restroom that the "mean girls" weren't in.

"What's going on?" Mya asked me as soon as she was close enough for me to hear her. "What happened?"

"Tiffany said Ana had a panic attack," I answered, gesturing with my head to the scene playing out in the back.

Ana was sitting on one of the couches with the medic taking her blood pressure. Julian sat beside her, holding her hand. Tori positioned herself beside Julian while Tiffany sat beside Ana.

"Hmmm," Nicole breathed, she looked perplexed by the situation, but didn't say anything.

"I just don't understand why we are wasting time with this. We all know she's faking it, right? Can we just agree that those whores are lying to get attention? She's just trying to get attention. Her song was shit and she's trying to get attention," Emma continued, still rattling on to anyone who was paying attention to her. "Samantha, you agree with me right?"

Samantha tucked her short black hair behind her ears and looked at Emma. "Yes."

The shy woman with the diminutive frame and porcelain doll features seemed to only talk to Emma. I didn't know if she was just introverted or if she just didn't feel comfortable around anyone but Emma. Samantha always sat attentively for Emma's rants. Outside of that, Samantha just faded into the background.

*Then again, she's always with Chatty Cathy so she might not have had the opportunity to speak.*

After twenty minutes of waiting for the hoopla surrounding Tori's gang, we had all sat down and were over it. Tori and Tiffany gave blow by blow accounts of what happened in the bathroom on camera, while Ana ate up being doted on while she told her survivor's story. Although no one except for

Emma said anything, I felt the tide turning from concern to annoyance. The tide had definitely turned for me.

*Mainly because we couldn't leave.*

Hearing Ana laugh jarred me out of my thoughts and an unintentional eye roll slipped out.

"I told you guys that bitch was lying. Look at her. If that panic attack was so tragic, why is she practically in Julian's lap?" Emma angrily muttered.

"Exactly." Samantha's response was very typical of her.

I whipped my head around to see what she meant. Ana definitely had her leg draped over Julian's leg. I pursed my lips and then turned back around. I didn't want to see anymore.

"What happened between you and Ana?" Leah asked cunningly as the second cameraman approached.

Hearing Leah initiate any kind of conversation always put me on high alert and I looked over at her. She was staring into her makeup compact and fixing her wavy, light brown with blonde highlighted hair. Even though Leah was unusually vain and a complete snob, she was beautiful and smart. And it was the beautiful and smart that put me on high alert with her because she had everyone fooled.

If the house was divided into sections, Section A included me, Mya and Nicole. I didn't know what happened while I was with Julian in the gazebo, but Mya and Nicole had become extremely close. After spending all morning in our room, I decided that Nicole was okay with me. Section B was Tori and her regular gang—Ana and Tiffany. Section C was Emma and Samantha who were apparently frenemies with Tori and her gang. Then there was Section D, the floaters and schemers, which included Leah and Bailey.

I knew Bailey's motives. Bailey wanted to be a star. She had a plan. She knew definitively that she didn't want Julian.

# The One

As we exchanged words at the coffeemaker that morning, I didn't want to admit that knowing that Bailey didn't want Julian made me like her that much more.

But Leah was a different story. Leah floated between Tori's gang of two and Emma's flunky of one. She made comments and talked shit about women in the house in such a calculated way that it seemed like an art form. Leah seemed to be in the middle of a lot of the arguments and fights in the house without actually being the person arguing and fighting. She reminded me of Tori, but more lethal.

On the outside, she appeared to be an angel. But on the inside, she was clearly an evil genius. She was sweet as she could be in front of Julian. But in the house, when she's relaxed and liquored up, she talked of Julian as if he was an accessory. She complained that most men didn't meet her standards, but that Julian was good enough for her. I was too distracted by Tori's overtly bitchy ways that I let a few days go by before I noticed Leah's covertly bitchy ways. She was clearly someone who that couldn't be trusted.

*I have to watch my back around her.*

"Did you not hear what she said about me last night?" Emma fumed. "She said—"

"Okay, everyone! I apologize for the delay, but Ana is okay," a location director announced, shutting Emma's rant down before it could get started. "Please return to your places." She paused for a minute while everyone else hustled to their designated places. We will return to filming in five, four, three, two, one. Action!"

Bryce and Julian sat at the end of the table while the camera filmed Super Casanova deliberating over who they were going to choose, making it super suspenseful even though they had already selected the winner prior to Tori's scream.

"Well first, we want to say that you all did a great job!" Marshall enthused, clapping his hands together. "You had two hours to pull off something that usually takes us at least a day or two. So give yourselves a hand!"

"Who do you think it's going to be?" Mya mouthed to me.

"I hope us, but number one was really good," I mouthed back.

She nodded back sadly.

Hayden jumped in after the applause. "The singers who sang this song will be escorted by our friend Julian Winters to our album listening party." She pointed to whoever had the music cued up and said, "Hit it!"

Super Casanova started dancing to the beat and when the vocal stylings of song number one burst through the speakers, Emma and Samantha jumped up and screeched.

Bryce Wilson laughed. "Well, then it seems we know who the singers are for song number one. Emma and Samantha, you two will be joining Julian tonight for the listening party. You will leave after the Bracelet Ceremony. So everyone, say your goodbyes to Julian and thank Super Casanova for being here with us today." He looked at us, but more likely the camera, and concluded, "I'll see you all tonight at the Bracelet Ceremony."

"Cut!"

The cameraman that was focused on the judges table stopped filming and started packing his stuff.

After a brief conversation with Julian, Super Casanova waved and we clapped as they departed. Julian was supposed to leave at the same time to do press for the show; however, he told the producers he was going to give us a proper goodbye first.

I smiled to myself hearing him say that because a proper goodbye would include his lips pressed against me.

"Did you hear how he told them he wasn't leaving without saying goodbye?" Nicole chirped to Mya.

"That's so sexy!" Mya replied giddily.

The air I was floating on depleted slightly. As much as I wanted to run over to him and kiss him, touch him, hold him, I couldn't. Not only could I not do that, there were other women who were probably thinking the same thing that I was thinking. I felt my smile faltering.

Julian was walking over to us and scanning the group with a smile. When his eyes landed on me, he held my gaze. I felt him questioning if I was okay. He scanned the group and then came back to me, his eyebrows moving upward slightly. It looked like he was coming straight toward me, but Tori ran over and pounced on him.

Since he was looking at me, he seemed surprised by her body colliding with his. Tori's heels made her almost his height and when she ran into him, she kissed him.

I froze. It wasn't jealousy that rippled through me; it was the familiar pain of disappointment.

And while I recognized that he didn't do anything, I couldn't help the way that I felt. I couldn't help the sting of seeing the man that I wanted being embraced by another woman. I couldn't help but feel like things were going too fast.

While others mumbled and griped about Tori's forwardness as they continued toward them, I was watching Julian. He placed his hands on her waist and shifted out of the kiss, hugging her instead.

Over her shoulder his eyes found mine and I looked away, swallowing hard. Until I could get myself together, I knew I didn't need to make eye contact with him.

Each woman made a point to hug him a little longer than the one before her. I hung back until I was the last one.

I closed my eyes for a second before looking up at him. He

wasted no time wrapping his arms around my waist and pulling me into him. Feeling him so close, smelling the scent of him, I allowed myself to melt into his body. I shut my eyes again and squeezed them tightly, holding in any sadness that wanted to slip out.

His mouth found the shell of my ear as he said softly, "I'm sorry. That won't happen again. I'll make sure of it."

I remained quiet, trying to decide what it was that I wanted to do next. *I could wait and let it play out like he said, going through the motions and then him choosing me. Or I could walk away now while I still can.*

I didn't know what was worse: the fact that I felt like there was a chance that I would wait it out for him and he wouldn't choose me or the fact that I still thought I could walk away.

I didn't say anything. I just held him. Anything I wanted to say, I wouldn't have been able to say anyway because we were both wearing microphones. My head was on his chest and I could feel his heart racing and I sighed.

*Maybe this is just as difficult for him as it is for me.*

I felt the absence of one of his hands on my back and then it relocated on my ass before sliding back up.

"Zoe?"

"You have to do what you have to do," I murmured, my heavy heart thudding against my chest. "Um, this is...I mean, it...makes good, um..." I cleared my throat to get my stammering under control. "Do what you have to do. Romance shows need romance. I think you need to really embrace it."

He pulled out of the hug to look at my face. He examined me carefully before realizing that some of the production crew had stopped packing up so they could watch us. I waited for him to drop his hands from me, but he didn't, he looked back down into my eyes.

I read his lips as he mouthed, "Are you okay with this?"

I shook my head.

He blinked, appearing to be stunned, confused, and maybe even a little hurt. His silence hurt me to my core.

I could see in his eyes that he was asking me if I was going to leave. I knew my emotions were getting the best of me and I didn't want to make a rash decision or say something I'd regret so I took a deep breath.

He moved his hand to my mic battery box and turned it off. He put his lips against my ear. "Meet me in the maze tonight. Midnight. We can talk there."

Not waiting for me to respond, he squeezed my hip as he turned my mic back on.

"Of course, I'll get you an autograph from Super Casanova tonight. Thank you for letting me know how much your best friend loves them," he said loudly with a wink. He turned and walked away as my laugh trailed behind him.

Crew members who were loitering around us, grumbled in disappointment as they also walked away. I knew he had said that to throw them off of what our conversation could've possibly been about, but the unexpectedness of it made me laugh.

*And how did he know that Koko loved Super Casanova?* I wondered, scurrying out the door to the party bus. It wasn't until I took that first step onto the bus that I realized when I had told him and my heart flipped.

*Ohhhhhh!* The memory of Super Casanova playing at the cocktail party interview while I was talking to Evan, who I didn't know was Julian at the time, popped into my mind and I stopped in my tracks. *I can't believe he remembered such an insignificant blip in the conversation.*

My heart flipped again. I was in my own thoughts, in my own world, as I sat down in the last remaining seat, next to

Bailey, in the middle of the bus.

It wasn't until I noticed people were looking at me that I realized anything was going on.

"Are you going to act like you didn't hear me?" Tori's grating voice erupted from the backseat. "I said, 'how were my sloppy seconds?'"

I turned around slowly.

*Who the fuck does she think she's talking to?*

I knew better than to engage with her. Despite everything, I knew how Julian looked at me. I knew how Julian looked at me when he was Evan. I knew that Julian wasn't looking at any other woman in the house the way he looked at me. I was able to see that, recognize that, but I responded anyway.

"You tell me." I shrugged. "The way he brushed you and that kiss off was sloppy and you definitely didn't kiss him first."

Mya, Nicole and Bailey laughed out loud while the others made noises, hyping up the situation. Tori looked stunned that I had actually said something to her. She was so flustered that she kept stammering on about how I didn't kiss him and that he wouldn't keep me around long enough for the home visit.

I turned back around and ignored Tori for the rest of the trip. I was disappointed that I wasn't able to keep my snarky comment to myself, but it felt good to shut her up. She had been a pain in my ass since day one and I was ready for her to go home. My only concern would be how my reaction would be edited and how it would reflect on my future career and on my parents.

# Chapter 11

When we were close to the house, one of the producers pulled out his phone and announced that the caterer had set up in the kitchen and that we had an hour to eat.

"After you finish eating, please report to hair, makeup or wardrobe, depending on the card that's on your bed. Cycle through all three and then be on the patio by six o'clock. The Bracelet Ceremony will only last an hour tonight because Julian, Emma and Samantha have plans and will be picked up at eight o'clock."

Emma and Samantha squealed with delight.

Apparently, Samantha didn't talk much so she could save her voice to sing. It was her voice that carried that song and that blew everyone away.

*I guess Samantha's not fading into the background anymore.*

We got off of the bus and stormed the kitchen. A caterer had set up various taco and fajita bars. After only having fruit for breakfast and then being gone longer than anticipated, every single one of us sat down and stuffed our faces. For at least the first ten minutes, no one even talked. We just ate. Once we were satisfied, production took the food out to the trailers so that they could eat as well.

"I'm so disappointed to not be going on this date," Mya complained as we climbed the stairs. "I think I'm going to start packing now."

I shook my head. "Don't put that negative energy in the air. If you pack your clothes, you're pretty much accepting defeat."

"You're right. Instead of accepting defeat, I have to do something else." Mya punched her right fist into the center of her left hand. "I'm not going home tonight."

"That's the spirit!" I cheered her on as we entered our bedroom.

I grabbed the yellow card from the center of my bed. "Wardrobe. Hair. Makeup."

I didn't know if Koko was purposely putting me on her schedule last, but it worked out so well. I loved knowing that I would be able to debrief with my best friend in a couple of hours.

Mya held up hers. "Makeup. Wardrobe. Hair."

I nodded.

Nicole knocked on the door and compared yellow cards with us. Mya and Nicole were excited to learn that they had the same shifts so they plopped down on Mya's bed and started talking excitedly.

I grabbed a pair of yoga pants and a plain white t-shirt and took it into my closet with me. Closing the door behind me, I stripped out of my clothes and pulled on the more comfortable attire. I stooped down to pick up my jeans by one of the legs and a folded piece of paper fell out of the back pocket. After stuffing my jeans and t-shirt into my laundry bag, I reached down and picked up the paper.

# The One

*I didn't put anything in my pockets today.*

Flipping it over, I didn't see anything on the outside to alert me to what could be on the inside. Opening it up, I immediately noticed that it wasn't my handwriting.

*To The One in the garden:*
*I feel you.*
*Intimately*
*In too deeply*
*Intrusively*
*In you I see me.*
*I feel you.*
*Infiltrate*
*Penetrate*
*Worth the wait*
*Years I would wait*
*I feel you.*

I read the words scrawled on the yellow notebook paper three times with my heart in my throat each time. I read the poem the first time too fast, not sure what it was in my pocket. As I read each word, something deep within me woke up, but I couldn't stop myself from rushing through it. The second and third time, I read it slowly. I let each word wallow in my heart and then imprint on my soul.

The steady beat of my heart sounded like a drum. I couldn't hear anything else, but his words on repeat to the cadence of my heartbeats. My chest rose and fell as I took it all in.

The poem was sexual, emotional, and spiritual. In two short stanzas, he summed up the intensity of our connection. It wasn't just sexual attraction driving whatever it was between us. It didn't matter that it had been four days since we'd met. I'd never felt stronger feelings toward another man.

I read the poem again.

Clutching the paper to my chest, my eyes stung with tears. I was overwhelmed.

The delicate knock against the closet door forced me to get myself together. "Everything okay in there?" Mya's voice sounded concerned.

"Yeah." I had to force myself to sound normal. "Just getting laundry together," I replied, folding the letter quickly. I stashed it in my cross body bag and then slung it over my head.

I walked out of the closet to see Mya and Nicole looking at me suspiciously.

"I'm probably going to do laundry tomorrow since there's nothing planned." I sat on my bed, facing them.

"On days we don't have dates, I feel like I'm going to die of boredom. I wish we had a TV or something," Nicole complained.

Mya responded but I didn't hear her. My mind had circled back to Julian Winters, who was looking more and more like the man of my dreams.

"Earth to Zoe," Mya said, in a sing-song tone.

I didn't realize I'd been staring at my hands in my lap. I snapped out of it, looking up quickly. "I'm sorry. I have a lot on my mind. What did you say?"

They giggled. "We're going to head to the makeup trailer. Do you want to walk out with us?" Nicole offered.

"Yeah, let me get my shoes on."

I put on my sneakers and then we left the house. We split up on the sidewalk and I made my way to wardrobe. I knew I wasn't going to the listening party with Julian, but I wanted him to be thinking of me the entire time he was with Emma and Samantha.

Over the next sixty minutes, I finished my wardrobe and hair styling for the night. I selected a form fitting, dark blue dress with accents of pink and mulberry patterned throughout. The light pink pumps and matching light pink accessories pulled the look together. I felt beautiful in the outfit because the material and color were flattering against my skin and the cut of the dress was sexy. For my hair, it was styled in a bun on the top of my head. The pink pearl hair accessories were utilized to hold my thick hair in place and also to bring the look together.

When I arrived at the makeup trailer, Koko was alone. Her mentor had just finished someone's makeup and was taking a break. That was the second best news I'd heard all day.

"You look great!" Koko exclaimed, eyeing me.

"Thanks. You too!" I replied, noticing how pulled together she looked in her blue jersey knit dress and black tights. "Are you fucking with someone on set?"

Koko threw her head back and laughed. "Because I have on this dress? Come on!"

I sat down in her chair and narrowed my eyes at her. I pursed my lips, questioning her with my silence.

"Come on, give me some credit. I would never!" She pointed to my microphone that was dangling from my shirt and shook her head.

"Oh, no." I gestured to my microphone. "I turned this off earlier in wardrobe. Who is it?"

"Oh, well if that's the case. Bryce Wilson."

"What?" My jaw dropped.

She started prepping my face as she began, "JJ introduced us during my first interview so we've known each other for a couple of months. We've been friendly and because we've attended some of the same meetings and the show started, we've been seeing each other a little more frequently. Some of us all got together the other night after the meeting. Bryce was there and we got drinks and then we got flirty. I teased him because on camera he's so proper and off camera he is a surfer or something. He says 'dude' all the time. Way too much. But it's so cute and funny. He said he liked me teasing him and I told him that wasn't the first time I'd heard that. Nothing happened that night. But then yesterday, he came in here to get his makeup done and JJ had to leave to meet with a vendor. So he and I started talking and then I started doing his makeup and then...one thing led to another."

I had to grab her wrist so I could open my eyes again since she was doing my eye makeup. I moved my head away from her brush. "Wait...wait wait wait. In here?"

She grinned. "In the bathroom and then in his trailer." She lowered her voice. "And then again in his SUV."

I wiggled my eyebrows. "Nice! I mean, yeah, it's reckless because this job is huge for you. But that's hot and sexy."

"Yes it was." She started working on my eyes again. "He was good, better than I thought he would be. But just hearing people walking around outside and the threat of almost getting caught was..." She sighed. "Remember that time you fucked your study partner in the Breakers bathroom?"

I laughed because it caught me off guard. "Yes—"

"Hey! I'm trying to do your lipstick, hold still."

"Then don't ask me questions!"

As she was finishing my makeup, she filled me in on everything she had going on.

"All done!" Koko announced, spinning me in the chair with a flourish.

I opened my eyes and smiled. "You are excellent at your job, my friend."

"Thanks. Now spill. I'm done with making your lips even more kissable for your man."

She was joking around, but her saying that made me grin.

"You have that lovesick look in your eyes already. Tell me everything!"

I told her everything. From the gazebo date to the poem, I filled her in. It took twenty minutes, leaving her almost no time for us to really get into it.

Koko's eyebrows were in the middle of her forehead for the entire breakdown. "Wow," she said for the eleventh time. "He obviously loves you, but what's blowing my mind is that you love him, too."

Although my heart rate increased, I rolled my eyes. "Don't be ridiculous! We just met four days ago. But if I'm honest, I know it's completely unlike me, I do like him...a lot. More than I should." I shook my head. "It's crazy and I don't know what to do about it. It's risky, you know?"

"Well, love is risky business in general. And yes, you avoid risks at all costs, but I don't think you should avoid this. After everything you've told me, it's clear to me that you two are into each other, 'love-at-first-sight' into each other. You're going to be here for the entire three and a half weeks and you two are probably going to get paid a million dollars to do one of those *The One: Wedding* specials."

I laughed despite myself. "You are ridiculous. Seriously, Koko. I'm trying to tell you something serious and you're making jokes."

"I'm serious, too! You should see your face right now. You have it bad."

I looked at myself in the mirror and she was right. My eyes were wide and sparkling. My smile was goofy, yet radiant. My face was flushed, despite the high-definition makeup that was smoothed over my skin.

*I do have it bad,* I realized, examining myself in the mirror. *And this lipstick color is now on my must-have list.*

"What's the name of this lipstick?" I asked.

She pursed her lips. "Denial."

I laughed again. "I miss you. It's so hard living in the house." I pouted. "We've been roommates for seven years. I think they should allow you to stay with me. I have separation anxiety."

"Even if Julian was my type, which he's not, they wouldn't let me in. They already have an African American woman and a Mexican American woman. A Japanese American woman would make three minorities and that's just too much diversity for one show," Koko joked, rolling her eyes. "And after what Jamie said to you, I can only imagine what she would say to me."

"Right? I'm still pissed about that." I looked at the time. "I have to go." I stood up and hugged her. "I wish I could come over here and chat more without it looking suspicious."

"Me too! But we're going to have to figure something out tomorrow because you need to tell me everything that happens at midnight."

"I know! I'll definitely find a reason to come back. Tomorrow is the first day they air the show right?"

"Well they've only had the *Before The One* Special air on Sunday and that showed the interviews."

I made a face. "How was it?"

"Well, you weren't on it much. It was—"

The knock on the door interrupted her words as Koko and I turned to see who was coming in.

I felt the corners of my lips turning upward. "Hi Bryce!" I greeted him as he walked in. "I was just leaving." I turned to my best friend and winked. "Thank you again. See you later!"

I ran out of the trailer and back to the house in no time. When I burst into the room, Mya was dressed in a sexy teal dress and primping in the mirror.

"Zoe! You only have fifteen minutes."

"I know, I know." I rushed over to the dry cleaner bag

hanging on the wall. "Makeup ran long. That dress is sexy, by the way."

I grabbed the dress and I ran into the closet to change. Emerging a few minutes later, Mya proceeded to whistle.

"Oh, I love that color on you. You look really good!"

There was a knock on the door and a deep voice called out. "Five minutes to six, ladies!"

"You ready?" Mya asked, making her way to the door.

I gave myself one last look in the mirror and nodded.

*Ready as I'll ever be.*

I didn't know why I was so nervous. It was as if the poem had completely thrown me off. As production rattled off information, I clutched my glass of champagne. Letting the liquid settle the twisting in my belly, I breathed through the overwhelming mixture of feelings. Even when Bryce arrived on set looking happy and refreshed, I could only manage a smirk. When we were told to mingle and that Julian would arrive any minute, I got a refill.

"You're quiet tonight. Everything okay?" Mya asked as I finished my second glass of champagne.

"Yeah, of course. How are you?"

"I'm ready!"

"Good!"

Mya, Nicole and I stood on the sidelines, watching an argument brewing between Tori and Emma based on something Leah said. The fight was heating up and the camera was catching every moment of it. Although I couldn't hear them, I saw some of the crew excitedly looking on and celebrating what they saw as a must-see TV ratings boost. When I watched the way they talked to each other based on Leah's insinuation that one of them said the other didn't have chemistry with Julian, I saw the demise of female unity and empowerment.

I looked at the fight and imagined impressionable young girls watching these shows and feeling as though female friendship took a backseat to finding a man. I looked at Bailey and imagined girls believing that being pretty was more important than being smart and interesting. I looked at Leah and imagined girls thinking that being strong meant being manipulative.

*And then there's us.* I looked at Mya and Nicole as they giddily told a story. *Impressionable girls will look at them and think that they are in love with someone they've never taken the time to get to know. Or they will look at me and see a hypocrite and think that falling in love after a few days is possible.*

I groaned and considered getting a third glass of champagne.

Even though I wasn't facing the door leading to the patio, I knew the moment Julian was near. The air shifted in the room and my eyes focused on the entrance. Ten seconds later, Julian walked in wearing dark denim jeans and a white button-up shirt.

*Damn, he looks good.*

After greeting us and talking to us as a group for a few minutes, Tori grabbed him and led him away. Each woman alternated between interrupting someone else's time and snatching him as soon as he returned from his time with another woman. I hung back, wanting to go last again, hoping to not be interrupted.

"Zoe, can I steal you away?" Julian asked as the rest of the women looked on. It was the first time he had chosen someone to go off with. There were still two women besides me who hadn't gone yet and I was hoping to be last. But what was I going to say? No?

"Yes, of course," I enthused, allowing him to help me off of the couch.

As soon as my hand was in his, the nerves, the knots in my stomach, and the anxiety melted away. I saw Mya staring at me and although I didn't think she would be thrilled, she looked flat out irritated.

Julian led me into the house. We walked into the kitchen where two cups of hot cocoa that a producer just poured were sitting at the kitchen table. I saw the reflection of the producer running away in the window. I looked over at Julian, curious as to if he had planned it, and he just smiled. When we got to the table, he pulled the chair out for me and I sat down.

"Thank you," I said, feeling overwhelmed by my feelings for the man who had just sat down across from me. But with his smile and my hand comfortably still tucked in his, I was able to simultaneously wallow in my feelings without feeling stressed or anxious about it.

"Of course."

We sat on the same side of the table and the camera crew was on the other side. I had so many things I wanted to say, but was unable to with an audience.

"Name three things that we appear to have in common," I asked, unable to ask if he truly thought he could see a future with us.

Turning his body slightly, he unraveled our hands and put his arm around me, resting it on the back of my chair. His fingers danced up and down the curve of my shoulder. Our faces were floating around that danger zone where intimacy is intensified through either the telling of secrets or the sharing of kisses.

"We seem to have the same sense of humor. There have been times over the last few days when something will happen and we will be the only ones laughing about it. We're both hard working and dedicated to our work." He took a sip of his hot cocoa and then licked the foam away before looking at me again. "And poetry."

The storminess of his eyes left me utterly speechless for ten seconds. I swallowed hard.

"What three things would you say?" He asked, holding me captive with his gaze.

My voice shook slightly. "Our love of music and movement. I notice when music is playing how you move because I find myself doing the same thing all of the time. The importance of family. We both love our families and believe in family and love and..." Just saying the word 'love' to him made it hard for me to breathe. I cleared my throat. "We both communicate very well...which is probably why we have this shared love of poetry."

"I'd agree with that," he said slowly, staring right through me. "Because poems are the ultimate expression of how someone feels so that does go hand in hand."

I nodded, adding softly, "Poems are driven by emotions and passion."

"And truth."

I had butterflies in my stomach, in my chest, and everywhere else. My entire body felt like it was going to take flight.

He licked his lips and my eyes zoned in before shutting. I didn't remember who leaned forward to initiate the kiss, but when our lips met, I felt lightheaded.

The kiss was tender, more like a brushing of our lips than a passionate declaration of desire. It grew into something more worshipful with each passing moment. His hand that rested on my shoulder tightened its grip while his other hand cradled my head. While one of my hands was trapped between us, my other hand clung to his shirt.

The sound of a chair screeching across the floor burst our bubble, snapping us out of our moment. Our bodies tensed at the realization that we had an audience. We pulled out of the kiss, but he rested his forehead against mine.

"If we were in the real world, what would a perfect date look like to you?" He asked, his cocoa breath danced across my face causing me to smile.

"If it's someone I've been dating, candlelight dinner at home with—"

"Julian?" Mya's voice interrupted, causing us to break apart. "I need you."

Julian turned his head, giving her a smile that didn't reach his eyes. "Hi, Mya. Yeah, sure." He looked at me. "Thank you for spending some time with me, Zoe." Intensifying his gaze, he continued, "And I meant to tell you that midnight blue is your color."

My stomach flipped as I heard his emphasis on the word midnight. Solidifying our plans to meet, I nodded as I said, "Thank you."

He turned around and offered his arm to Mya. "How are you? You look beautiful."

"Thank you. I wanted to see if you had time for something a little more...sexy," she flirted, tossing her hair over her shoulder.

They left out of the kitchen, followed by the camera crew. I sat at the table in shock. Mya was generally quiet and reserved, but she came on to Julian like some sort of sex kitten. But as quickly as the shock of Mya's personality shift wore off, thoughts of meeting Julian at midnight and really talking infiltrated my brain and shook me up.

I remained in the kitchen until the Bracelet Ceremony. We were gathered and arranged in two rows. There was an issue with the way Leah's dress looked in the front row so she was switched around with Bailey. Once we were staged correctly, Bryce and Julian entered the patio area.

"Hello ladies! Welcome to the Bracelet Ceremony," Bryce announced, clapping his hands together. "Emma and Samantha, you won the contest today so you automatically get to hold on for another week in hopes of becoming 'The One.' Once you get your charms, please go straight upstairs and change into your outfit for the listening party." He turned to Julian. "Now, Julian...the floor is yours."

"You all look beautiful tonight," Julian began. "I wish I would've had more time to spend with each of you, but we have a tight schedule." He took a deep breath. "So I guess we will begin."

A sense of calm came over me. Because I was meeting Julian at midnight, I didn't need to worry about him getting rid of me. His reassurance over hot cocoa was enough for me to feel secure that I didn't have anything to worry about.

Julian reached over and picked up a musical note charm. "Zoe."

I knew I wasn't going home, but I didn't expect him to pick me first. He smiled at me and I saw nothing but adoration in his eyes.

Before I was able to take a step, someone yelled, "Cut!"

The set exploded in murmurings as Robert Brady marched onto the patio.

"What's the creator doing out here?" Mya turned and hissed at me from her perch on the front row.

"I have no idea," I replied even though a part of me did.

My stomach sank as I thought about how I saw Robert Brady staring at me earlier in the day. Whatever he was discussing with Julian in hushed tones wasn't going over well with Julian. His jaw was locked as if his teeth were clenched and his arms crossed his broad chest defensively. The heated discussion came to an end with Robert walking off seemingly satisfied and Bryce patting Julian on the back.

"Okay let's get set," the same voice called out. "In five, four, three, two, one. Action!"

Taking a deep breath, Julian reached over and picked up a musical note charm. His demeanor, his facial expression, and his body language had changed. He still smiled, but his smile didn't reach his eyes.

"This first charm goes to..." He looked at me and I could see in his eyes that something was wrong. "Samantha." He shifted his gaze to Samantha who was on the second row with me. She made her way between Bailey and Tiffany and walked gracefully up to Julian. "Will you continue on this journey with me to find 'The One'?"

"Yes," she squealed, allowing him to clasp the charm onto her bracelet. They hugged and then she went inside to get ready for their date.

Julian called Emma next, followed by me.

When I moved toward him, I felt Julian's energy. I stood before him and when he looked me in my eyes, I saw the anger or frustration or whatever was clouding his features before giving way to peace. "Zoe, will you continue on this journey with me to find 'The One'?"

Staring up into his eyes, I answered without hesitation. "Yes."

He clasped the charm on my bracelet, letting his fingers linger on my skin longer than necessary. We exchanged smiles and then I took my place on the other side of Bryce.

As he cycled through the rest of the women, I watched the production crew as they milled around. Some seemed to be working, but others looked on with clipboard or tablets taking notes. It felt as though some were staring at me, but with the group being so close together, I couldn't really tell.

"This is it," Bryce interjected, bringing me back to the actual ceremony. "One of you is not the one."

I looked and saw Leah and Nicole on the chopping block.

"Leah," Julian called out.

Leah moved forward and they had their moment, but my eyes were glued to Nicole as she broke down crying. I didn't know why that made me sad, but it did.

Once the ceremony was over, Julian left with Emma and Samantha. The rest of us were left to our own devices.

I went into the kitchen to get a bottle of water and when I turned around Leah was standing behind me. Because I was lost in my own thoughts, when I saw her I jumped.

"Leah, shit, you scared me," I informed her.

"Oh, sorry," she said in a way that let me know that she was not at all sorry. "So, you and Julian, huh?"

I didn't respond because I didn't know what she was trying to say. So I stared at her with a quirked eyebrow. "What are you asking?"

"So it's clear you've made quite the impression on Julian. Everyone is talking about it. Even Mya, which surprised me."

*Oh, okay, I see. She's trying to make drama happen between us. She must have just acknowledged me as a threat. Got it.*

I nodded, walking away. "Cool."

When I was almost out of the kitchen, she added, "Do you think that it's crazy that Ana has a sixteen month old baby at home and she's out here looking for love? Shouldn't she be home taking care of her child?"

"Have a goodnight, Leah." I didn't bother to turn around. I headed straight to my room.

I grabbed my headphones and iPod and proceeded to take a long hot bubble bath. Listening to songs didn't do anything to stop my mind from drifting to Julian. I didn't know how long I ended up being in the bath, but when I got out, my fingers were pruned.

Mya wasn't back from wherever she was hiding and although I knew she probably took Nicole's leaving hard, I wanted to spend some time with my own thoughts before she came back. After putting on leggings and a sexy bra and panties set, just in case, I climbed into bed and let my body get sucked into the depth of the mattress. I pulled the sheets up and the time seemed to creep by slowly because I was anxiously awaiting midnight. As soon as I felt sleep coming, Mya burst through the door. Flipping on the light and making a lot of noise, she stopped as soon as she saw me peering at her.

"Sorry! I didn't know you were sleeping so soon." Her words were slurred.

"No worries," I said, sitting up in bed, rubbing my eyes. "Are you okay?"

She stumbled to her bed and then collapsed. "I'd be better if Julian was here," she giggled. "He's so hot!"

My eyebrows furrowed. "Mya, how much did you have to drink?"

"Enough!" She groaned. "I think they have an open bar every day for a reason. No snack food, but drinks for days!" She did a little dance. "Do you know what's crazy?"

"What's crazy?"

"How it is obvious to everyone that Julian is really into you."

I didn't know what to say to that so I just looked at her.

She started laughing. "Don't be shocked. It's a good thing. And honestly, it's not a surprise that Julian Winters has a thing for you. You're great and you have your shit together and you don't have all this baggage."

"Mya, are you sure you're okay?" I got out of the bed in my black leggings and soft pink t-shirt. "Do you feel sick?"

"No, I didn't have that much to drink. I'm good. Just drunk, but not drunk drunk."

"Do you want help getting out of your dress?"

"Yes please!" She sat up and threw her hands in the air like a child.

I unzipped her dress and she held it up so it didn't fall, exposing herself to the camera. I helped her slip on an oversized t-shirt. She climbed into the bed and I tucked her in. "Are you good?"

"I'm good, I'm good. Are you good?" She reached up and grabbed my hand. "I heard what happened."

"I'm good. I don't know what you're talking about though," I answered slowly, looking at her skeptically. "Are you sure you're okay?"

Mya gave me a look of pity as her eyes fluttered closed. "It really is a good thing that he likes you. I mean that so much." Her lip started quivering as her eyes seemed to shut for good. Her voice became lighter with each word. "But I hate that the only thing that gives the rest of us hope for a relationship with Julian is that the show isn't going to let you win."

"Wait, what?"

No response.

I stood there looking at my roommate sleeping peacefully wondering if I heard what I thought I just heard.

"Mya?"

Light snoring.

# Chapter 12

I was glad that I put on a jacket as the breeze was a little chilly. I stuffed my hands in my pockets as I quietly followed Julian to the gazebo. I spent most of the walk in my head, trying to figure out how to approach him about what Mya said. I wasn't trying to throw her under the bus and I wasn't trying to start anything, but if it was true and someone with knowledge of the show told her that, I wanted to know.

Once we walked through the narrow walkway to the fence, Julian reached for my hand.

Intertwining our fingers, I felt that familiar pull to him, that immediate connection to him. I sighed.

*As soon as we get inside, I'll talk to him about it,* I assured myself.

"The closer we get, the quieter you get. Are you having doubts about sneaking out of the house?" His playfulness pulled a smile out of me.

I looked up at his handsome face and my stomach flipped. "When we get inside, can we talk?"

He looked at me, clearly unnerved by those three little

words. "Is everything okay?"

He opened the door and gestured for me to walk through the door. I had only taken two steps before stopping in my tracks.

My eyes swept over the dimly lit room. Moonlight poured into the room, cascading light through the glass windows. Rose petals surrounded a small table that was placed in the middle of the gazebo. Three big white candles sat on the table, fire flickering at the wicks. Slow R&B music played lightly through speakers hidden in the walls. The smell of chocolate wafted through the air.

I spun around just as Julian closed the door behind us. Even with the beautiful layout before me, he was the reason my heart skipped a beat. In a pair of sweat pants and a tight t-shirt that showcased his muscles and the half-sleeve of tattoos on his arm, he was gorgeous. And knowing that the gorgeous, amazing man before me might have put together the most romantic layout for me was almost enough to make me cry.

"What's this?" My voice was so light that it lost itself in the music.

"This," he said, stepping forward. He cupped my face. "This is the date you deserve."

He planted a sweet, lingering kiss against my lips. When he pulled away, he gazed down at me. My heart thumped between the kiss and the way he looked at me.

I wrapped my arms around him. "You are an incredible man."

"And you are an incredible woman." He pecked my lips and then spun me around. Wrapping his arms around me from behind, he kissed my neck as he guided us to the table. He pulled out my chair for me and I sat.

The expensive looking bottle of wine he poured from was

beautiful, but I'd never heard of the brand before. He filled our glasses and upon tasting it, I knew it was the most delicious thing I'd ever tried.

I looked around in awe. Taking another sip, I gushed, "This is so thoughtful, Julian. Really. Thank you."

He walked to the small refrigerator and pulled out a huge slice of cake. "Do you like chocolate drizzle on your cake?"

"That sounds good." I unzipped my jacket and pulled it off as he brought the cake and chocolate to the table. "Julian, this is amazing. When did you have time to do this?"

"I made a few calls and then once I had everything I needed, I put it together when I got back from the listening party."

I had a visual of Emma and Samantha on his arm. "How was that?" I tried to make my voice sound natural and unbothered.

"It would've been better if I would've been there with the woman I wanted to be there with." He picked up a fork and cut a piece of cake. Offering it to me with a slight movement, he fed me the decadent desert. "I was there, but I wasn't there. I smiled for the cameras. I did what I needed to do. But this was the date I was looking forward to."

I swallowed and smiled. "You always know the right words to say, don't you?"

He took a bite of cake and nodded. "I just speak the truth."

"This cake is the truth," I returned, picking up the other fork and spearing another piece for myself.

We finished off the cake as we talked about our life prior to the show and the things we wanted to do after the show.

"What kind of law did you specialize in?" Julian asked.

"I specialized in Corporate Law, like my mom."

He nodded, studying me. "What kind of law do you want to practice? Or do you even want to practice?"

I let out a breath and even though I didn't know how to verbalize the feeling his question gave me, I wanted to try to answer it.

"I do want to practice. I joke that it was a quarter-life crisis, but seriously, I think it is." I put my hand over my mouth and let out a little laugh. "I think I opted out of the bar because it felt like too much pressure. I was either going to pass it or fail it. I was either going to start a career or spend six months drowning in my parents' disappointment. And then I've been flirting with the idea of Entertainment Law and... I just got in my own head. I'm not a risk taker at all so spending my whole life wanting to do Corporate Law and then feeling like I want to change to Entertainment a couple months before the bar...it was a lot. It's still a lot. And I still ended up doing something rash by not taking it at all. I don't know..."

*I'm rambling.*

I bit my lip. Placing my fork down on the empty plate, I kept my eyes trained across the small table at him. I smiled, shaking my head. It was crazy to me that I felt so at peace in the moment, yet two weeks prior, that line of questioning had me throwing a bag together and fleeing to Virginia.

A smile played a Julian's lips. "What?"

"People usually automatically assume that my mom's path is my path, too. I like that you didn't and that you cared enough to ask."

*I like that you see me.*

"I like that you open up to me." His eyes diverted from mine and he chewed his bottom lip. "You, uh, you wanted to...talk to me about something?"

A series of heart palpitations kept me silent for a moment. "It's not important," I answered, rashly deciding against bringing up what Mya said at that moment.

I rationalized my decision by reminding myself that I just

wanted to enjoy my time with Julian since it was so limited.

*I'll probably be over here for a few hours so I can work it into the conversation later.*

He didn't look like he entirely believed me, but he didn't push. His eyes gave him away though. There was a certain vulnerability in the way he looked. Finally, he nodded.

Picking up a remote control to turn up the music, Julian stood. Stretching out his hand toward me, he implored, "Will you dance with me?"

I smiled, placing my hand in his.

He pulled me up quickly, causing me to collide into his chest. I giggled until he wrapped his arms around me. At that point, my body melted into him. With my ear to his chest, I closed my eyes and listened to his heart. His hands ran through my hair and then moved down my back as we moved to the music.

"I love your hair down."

"Mmmm. Thank you," I murmured into him. I inhaled his scent and then sighed.

He chuckled to himself. "What are you doing?" He asked, kissing the top of my head.

*Not being creepy, I promise!*

"Just enjoying this. This is nice. This is..."

*Perfect.* My eyes flew open as soon as the word entered my mind.

"This is what?" He asked softly, his hands running up and down my back.

"This is...the sweetest thing anyone has ever done for me." I looked up at him. "Thank you."

"You don't have to keep thanking me." He kissed me before pulling away. "I have something else for you."

As he went over to the shelf, I refilled our wine glasses and walked them two steps over to the couch. Placing the glasses on the end table, I smiled as he walked over to me with a gift box the size of his hand.

My jaw dropped. "You did not get me a gift."

He smirked. "I did."

"I can't accept it." I stood up and gestured around to the table and the petals. "I told you six hours ago that my ideal date night was a candlelit dinner with rose petals and you executed it. That is gift enough."

He took a step closer to me and grabbed my hand. "You being here, spending time with me is my gift from you so please accept it." Turning my hand palm up, he placed the gift in my hand.

I tried to contain my smile, but I couldn't. I clutched the box to my chest with one hand and I grabbed the collar of his shirt with the other. Pulling his face closer to mine, I pushed my lips up to meet his. I moved my mouth over his in appreciation, in adoration and in absolute lust.

"You're going to have to stop kissing me like that," Julian groaned lightheartedly as I pulled away.

I giggled and started opening the gift.

"This is for you to write down all of the poetry inside of you," he whispered, fingers toying with my curls.

Seeing the small, brown leather notebook, I glanced up at him and let the flood of emotions wash over me. I flipped through the blank cream pages. "It's beautiful." I choked the words out while hugging my gift. I let out an overwhelmed breath. "That's really sweet."

I put the notebook on the end table beside the wine glasses and then reached up to wrap my arms around his neck, hugging him tight. Standing on the tips of my toes, I rested my cheek against his chest. He pulled me so that I was flush against his body. As he moved his hands over my back, somehow his fingers wound up underneath my t-shirt, stroking my bare skin. His movements were purposely slow. His fingertips brushed the waistband of my leggings, causing goosebumps to explode over my skin. I was instantly wet from his light touch.

My entire body was on fire from his fingers stroking my skin. It made me think how hot he would get me if he stroked me elsewhere. That thought alone flipped a switch inside of me as I slipped my fingers into his short hair, tugging his head back slightly.

The way his grey eyes flashed and bore into mine, it was as if he could see the sexual nature of my thoughts. I took one shaky breath after another as I tried to slow the flood of emotions I felt. I slid my hands down his chest and wrapped my arms around his waist to see if I could get him closer. While I went down, he went up, running his hands up the side of my body until his hands were around my neck. The sexual tension only intensified.

*I didn't come here for this,* I thought, feeling him hardening against me. *But God, I want it.*

"Zoe, we should stop before things go too far too fast," he breathed, staring at my lips.

I licked my lips slowly. "You're right."

If anything, our grip on each other tightened.

My heart felt like it was going to beat out of my chest. Our faces were just inches apart, but I knew if we kissed in that moment, it wouldn't just be kissing. It would've evolved into something else entirely. We teetered in that space, incrementally closing in on one another and then retreating. That tortuous back and forth sent shivers down my spine.

"We should stop." He swallowed hard and I watched his Adam's apple move. He dropped his forehead to mine, making it harder for me to breathe. "But I've never wanted anything as badly as I want you."

"Julian," I moaned breathily, my voice barely above a whisper.

He groaned in response.

The desire in the deep guttural noise rendered me speechless. The knowledge that he wanted me as badly as I wanted him and the feeling of his hands around my neck was a heady combination.

"And I want all of you, Zoe. I want your mind. I want your soul. I want your body. God, I want your body." His eyes closed as his thumbs caressed my jawline. Our noses brushed together when he opened his eyes again. "But I will wait for it. If you give me your mind and your soul, I'll wait for the rest. I—"

My mouth crashed into his, interrupting his sentence. All of the pent up sexual tension between us exploded. We kissed each other hungrily, urgently. His tongue played with mine in a way that made me long to feel it all over my body. That thought alone gave me chills.

As the kiss intensified, we pulled each other closer, moved against each other harder. It took everything out of me to pull away from his lips just long enough to pull his shirt over his head.

As soon as the cotton barrier was gone, I allowed myself a mere thirty seconds to take in his shirtless state. Taut muscles in his chest and abs, broad shoulders and well developed biceps were on display. I drank him in and briefly glanced at the half sleeve of tattoos on his arm.

*Damn. And I thought he looked good with clothes on.*

It was apparent that Julian thought I was taking too long to return to our kiss as he tilted my head so our mouths could find each other again. I let my hands play over his muscles, feeling the ridges of his chest and the definition in his arms.

My rational mind shut off and my carnal needs took over

as my hands dropped lower and lower down his sculpted abs. Untying the cord keeping his sweatpants in place, I let the material slack on his hips before I ran my hand over the length of his hardness. I only opened my eyes when he broke the kiss to let his head fall back. The low groan that erupted from him when my fingers wrapped around his sizeable girth and squeezed caused my entire lower body clench deliciously.

I let go of him to remove my own t-shirt. As soon as the shirt was over my head, Julian's mouth was on me. He parted my full lips with his tongue and kissed me hard and deep. I wrapped my arms around him and returned his kiss with just as much power.

Grabbing me by my round ass, Julian picked me up, sliding me up his body. The placement forced his cock to lodge itself right at the apex of my thighs. I could feel how hard he was and I knew he could feel how hot I was. That only turned me on more.

Placing my feet back on the ground, he trailed kisses from my lips across my cheek and to my ear.

"I let you have the shirt," he grunted, gripping my hair, tugging on my tight coils, exposing my neck. "But you're going to let me take every other piece of clothing off of you."

I squeezed my legs together in want as I let out a mewling noise, nodding my approval.

Twisting me around, he nibbled on my collarbone as he used one hand to unhook my black lace bra. Slipping his fingers underneath the straps of my bra, the light material easily slipped down my arms and to the ground. He ran his hands down my arms as he trailed kisses down my spine.

Light feathery kisses sparked instant goosebumps in their wake as he reached my leggings. Hooking his fingers into the waistband, I felt his breath tickle my skin as he took his time stripping the material down over my ass. He stripped my G string down slowly.

"Fuck..." His low growl gave me chills as he uncovered me completely.

The feelings of the damp lace material peeling away from my skin caused another round of chills.

"Lift," he demanded, helping me out of the rest of my clothing. "Lift."

Running his hands up my smooth legs, Julian massaged my thighs and hips. When he was fully standing, he pulled my ass into him and I instantly rotated my hips, grinding on his dick. He sucked in a sharp breath and flexed his fingers into my full hips. He dug in, holding on tight as I continued to move against him. The feel of his dick strained against the cotton material, spearing my ass, was too much for me to resist.

Turning around, I watched as his eyes devoured my naked body. I took distinct pleasure in the worshipful way he salivated over seeing me completely bare for the first time. When his eyes traveled back up and locked with mine, I reached out and pushed his sweatpants and boxer briefs down to the wooden floorboards. He stepped out of his clothing and his grey eyes darkened sexily.

Unable to resist, my eyes traveled from his handsome face to his hard cock that bounced solidly as he closed the gap between us. My lips parted as it seemed as though he was throbbing right before my eyes.

*Good God,* I thought as I reached out to touch him. He was hot, heavy and throbbing against my palm. I was impressed and completely mesmerized by him.

"It's not too late to slow this down." Julian's pained whisper called to something deep inside of me.

"Yes, it is."

## The One

Before the words had a chance to settle between us, Julian kissed me roughly. The passion that emanated from the kiss set me ablaze. I wrapped my arms around his neck and stood on my tip toes in an attempt to get his cock to rub the exact spot. His hardness speared me just below my belly button and I had to physically restrain myself from dropping to my knees and sucking him off.

With my eyes closed, it allowed me to just feel what he was doing and anticipate what he would do next. Julian grabbed a fistful of my hair and tugged my head back. With my neck exposed, he trailed feathery kisses from my nape to the sensitive spot behind my ear. When he got to my earlobe, he nibbled and sucked gently. It was so sexy, but the throbbing between my thighs competed for attention against the sensuality of his actions.

Drunk off of desire, I opened my eyes woozily as I felt him press his forehead against mine. He backed me up until the back of my legs brushed against the leather couch. Then he kissed me again, harder, deeper.

When he pulled away, he stared into my eyes and my breathing faltered. His fingers found my nipples and he gently pulled and twisted them before allowing the wet heat of his mouth to suck each one. I moaned loudly as his mouth alternately covered each nipple and flicked them with his tongue.

When I felt like I would scream from being teased, he kissed down my belly, dropping to his knees. He nuzzled his nose against my skin and inhaled deeply.

"I've been fantasizing about the way you taste since I met you."

Before his sentence was complete, his fingers had already found the most sensitive part of my body. He slowly stroked me. He looked up at me, watching my face as he moved over my wetness. I moaned, letting my head fall back.

"Sit down," he demanded softly.

My body was under his control and I was splayed on the couch before I knew it. His finger had found its way back against my clit, before dipping inside of me, causing me to rotate my hips against his movements. His actions would've definitely put me over the edge, but he slowed down, keeping my orgasm just out of reach.

"You like that?" he whispered as his mouth joined his finger.

I purred as he added another digit, hooking upward into my g-spot. With his tongue alternating between flicking and sucking my clit, I felt myself tipping over the edge. My stomach quivered and my thighs started shaking. I came. I came hard. I came loud. Pleasure radiated from my clit and shot through my entire body as he continued to pump his fingers, extending the ride.

When my body finally trembled for the last time, I tried to gather my thoughts, but all I could hear was my heart racing.

"Wow..." I breathed as I continued to be frozen in the contorted position on the edge of the couch.

For a second, my eyes wouldn't open all of the way. Peeking through my lashes, I moaned in satisfaction. I heard Julian's sexy chuckle as he kissed up my belly, between my breasts and up my neck. When his lips finally returned to mine, we both moaned hungrily as I could taste myself on his lips. My arms wrapped around him as we shared sloppy, passionate kisses.

His kisses were the energy boost I needed as I sat up, never separating our lips. I pulled out of the kiss, letting my lips hover over his as I gazed at him.

"Sit on the couch," I murmured, sucking on his bottom lip.

After a minute of feverish kisses, he rose to his feet. Unable to help myself, I kissed and sucked the head of his dick. He growled so loudly, I startled. Pulling off of him, I licked my lips and waited for him to sit down. He just stood before me, stunned. I wrapped my hand around his shaft and pumped two times, sucking him into my mouth again.

"Sit down," I repeated sexily as I climbed to my feet.

He sat down and I maneuvered myself in front of him, he eyed me hungrily. Reaching up, he ran his hands down my chest, over my breasts. He stopped momentarily, pulling at my aching nipples. I bent at the waist to allow him to put one in his mouth.

"Mmmm," I sighed as he massaged my heavy breasts.

His hands continued down my body until they rested on my hips. He gripped them firmly before moving to my ass. He squeezed each cheek before massaging his way up and down the back of my legs. Palming the back of my thighs, he pulled me closer to him, kissing the length of my pelvis, from hip bone to hip bone.

"Julian…" I moaned, aching for him.

"I love to hear you say my name like that. Say it again," he demanded roughly, biting at my rounded hips.

"Julian…" I repeated softly, sexily. His reaction fueled my desire.

Groaning, he removed one of his hands from the back of my thighs and stroked himself. I watched his hand move up and down his shaft. I watched his thumb swipe across his saliva soaked head.

My breathing became increasingly labored as the seconds ticked by. Feeling empowered by my effect on him, I pushed Julian's shoulders and he allowed himself to be rocked back.

Looking down at him, I ran my hands over my body, watching him watching me. The way his eyes, hands, and mouth worshipped me over the course of the night turned mc on to the point that my wetness was starting to coat my thighs. I spread my legs and played with myself as he watched.

His grey eyes glinted with unbridled lust as he said, "I want to be inside of you. I want to stretch you out and make you mine. I want you so bad it hurts."

Climbing onto the couch, I placed each leg on either side of his thighs. His hands went from my breasts to my hips and held on tightly. I waited until I felt him so overcome with want for me that he was slowly trying to thrust upward. When I couldn't take it anymore, I let myself go.

I sank down onto his swollen cock. With each inch, he filled me, stretching me, connecting with me. The sheer pleasure that erupted from my core weakened me as I came instantly. I grunted and struggled to keep my eyes open as I squeezed him deep inside of me.

Julian grunted a string of expletives, but I only barely heard what he said due to the fact that my heart was pounding and I was crying out.

"Fuck, Zoe. I almost came." His breath was coming out in harsh gusts. He held me in position, not allowing me to move. "You are so fucking tight."

Gently, I lifted myself up and down in his lap.

He grunted from deep inside his chest. "Fuck...and wet."

I was still tender from my unexpected orgasm so I had no problem moving slowly. Raising myself up unhurriedly allowed me to feel every vein and ridge. I felt like I was experiencing every single inch of him inside of every inch of me. My heart skipped several beats and my stomach fluttered from more than the burning desire between us. It was more than that. And I knew it the moment our eyes met.

With one hand on my hip and the other palming my breast, he guided my movements. He held my gaze as I rode him.

The tenderness gave way and everywhere our bodies were connected, I was on fire. Allowing the rhythm to build, he watched me grind down on him. I felt sexy and wanted which made me ride him harder as I moaned his name repeatedly.

I bounced on him, making my ass clap against his thighs. He grabbed my hips tightly and started thrusting upward. His breathing was ragged as he continuously hit a spot so deep inside of me, I felt my third orgasm coming on.

After a minute, Julian rolled us over, keeping himself inside me. With one of my legs over his shoulder and the other around his waist, he repositioned himself over me. He continued thrusting, but this time in long, hard strokes. In the new position, I was submissive. Allowing him to control the tempo and not knowing what was going to happen next turned my nipples into stiff peaks.

He leaned down and suctioned his warm, wet mouth on them, intensifying every feeling he was giving me.

"Julian," I whimpered, feeling the third orgasm build.

"Fuck, that's sexy," he grunted before increasing his speed. "Say it again."

When our lips found each other again, we moaned in unison. Hitting that new spot deep inside of me, I clenched tighter, causing him to groan loudly.

"I feel it, baby...I feel you," he grunted against my mouth, as he drove himself into me harder with each stroke. "You want to get off again...and I want to get you off again." He sucked in a sharp breath. "Let me know when you want me to pull out."

My mouth fell open and my toes curled. Hearing his words, his knowledge of my body, and his desire was accelerating my impending orgasm.

Without warning, Julian got rough, ramming into me hard. I could hear my wetness each time he slammed into me, triggering a new wave of pleasure inside of me. I barely heard him murmuring about how good I felt when he reached between us and used his thumb to stroke my clit. That pushed me over the edge.

My head tilted back in ecstasy as pleasure took over and I had no control. My pulsating body arched violently. Crying out, I tightened and convulsed around him. His muscles, slick with sweat, flexed in response. My orgasm spread throughout my body as I writhed beneath him.

"Oh God," I panted through sloppy kisses. My body was still shaking.

"Tell me when," he grunted into my mouth as he kissed me with wild, reckless abandon. "Fuck, I...can't hold it."

I was so turned on by him, by my body's reaction to him, and by the depth of my feelings, I murmured back to him. "Don't pull out."

His strokes and his breathing were erratic and I wasn't sure if he heard me or if he wanted clarification. His kisses were a mixture of unrestrained hunger for me and for the release he'd been chasing. "Where...do you...want it?" He moaned as I felt his solid balls connect with my skin with each, deep thrust.

"Inside me," I answered honestly.

Deep guttural groans ricocheted around the room as Julian increased his speed seeming to hear what I said that time around. The new pace caused an aftershock of sorts as I started to spasm, extending the mind blowing pleasure that pulsed through me. Seconds later, Julian exploded inside of me and my trembling body went limp.

Overwhelmed, emotionally exhausted, and thoroughly fucked, I blacked out.

I eased out of my unconscious state, the sound of violins swirling around in my head. My body felt warm and my muscles were tight. I heard the steady thump of a heartbeat and I knew I was on Julian's chest. Inhaling, I smelled a sweet and salty mixture in the air.

*Chocolate and sex.*

Opening my eyes slowly, I saw the candles flickering and the rose petals. Beyond that, I saw the dusky sky full of stars. I felt like I was dreaming.

Julian had his arm around me, writing awkwardly. I lifted my head an inch off of his chest and his focus shifted from his notebook to me immediately.

"Good morning sleepyhead," Julian greeted me with a smirk.

My head snapped up. "Wait, what? It's morning. I've been sleeping all night? What time is it?"

Julian's chuckle was deep and sexy.

I tried pushing myself up, but my body felt like a wet noodle. He was able to keep me restrained with just his relaxed arm resting on me. And he was laughing too hard to answer my questions.

"Julian," I whined with the knowledge that I didn't think I could walk and rolling off of the couch in order to get up might have been my only option.

I looked at him, one hand over his eyes and his body quaking underneath mine. His amusement struck a chord in me and I started laughing along with him.

Five minutes later, we were smiling goofily at one another.

"What was so funny?" I asked, smiling up at him. I poked his chest playfully. "I think I passed out."

"You did, but only for a few minutes. I twisted us around and had just gotten you settled onto my chest when you woke up."

"So it's been what? Five minutes?"

He chuckled again, nodding. "We actually spent more time

laughing than you were actually out of it."

Shaking my head, I groaned. "I could've sworn it was hours. I've never had that happen before. I've never experienced anything like that. That was...wow."

Picking my hand up from his chest, Julian brought it to his lips. "I feel the exact same way."

Butterflies fluttered in my belly as I lay naked on top of Julian Winters after what was absolutely the best sexual experience of my life.

*This is the kind of sex that will ruin me for other men.*

From the beginning to the end, I'd never been so fully and totally satisfied and well-fucked in my life.

"Um, it's a little late for this, but I don't have any STDs and I'm on birth control."

He smiled, kissing the inside of my palm. "I also don't have any STDs, but I'm sure they put that in the packet of information."

I nodded and we both cracked up. I rested my head back on his chest.

"This is the craziest thing I've ever done," I admitted, amusement tinging my words.

He was quiet for a moment as he stroked my hair. "The show or me."

"Honestly, both. I've never had unprotected sex with anyone except for the ex I told you about. And that was after year three started. Not after day three. And then being on this show, being with you, it just..." My voice trailed off.

I felt a change in his breathing. He turned so that I slipped to the back of the couch, sandwiched between his body and the cushions behind me. His arm cradled my neck while the other one adjusted our newly intertwined legs. With one hand trapped between us, my free hand rested on the side of his naked body. His free hand lightly grazed the skin of my arm.

# The One

I watched his face as his eyes followed his hand en route to my shoulder. I could tell he was thinking.

His voice was lower, huskier. "It just what?"

Angling myself so that my lips touched his ear, I admitted softly, "It scares me."

He turned his head, pressing his forehead against mine. Our noses touched and as we stared into each other's eyes, I felt as though I was breathing in his essence. It was intoxicating being that intimate with him. He moved fractionally so that his mouth was up against mine. "You scare me."

I kissed him tenderly before asking, "Why?"

"Because I knew it was a long shot for you to be here and stay here. You said up front that this wasn't your scene. I believe you said something about competing for me." He kissed me again for a longer period of time, causing my body to respond. "But let me tell you, there's no competition, Zoe. There's just you. There's only you."

I knew what he meant. I knew what he was saying to me. And in his arms, I believed him wholeheartedly. But a house full of women and a stack of reality television paperwork said otherwise. And as hard as I tried to get it out of my head, I heard Mya's drunken voice tell me that the creator wasn't going to let me win.

*So where does that leave me?*

I didn't know what to say so I recited *Drunk as Drunk* by Pablo Neruda and then I kissed him. I put everything I felt, all of my emotions, into that kiss. In return, he kissed me in a way that caused a rattling in my chest.

After cleaning ourselves up, I pulled on my t-shirt and he pulled on his boxer briefs. For the next two hours, we talked about our pasts and our futures. We talked about places we wanted to go, trips we wanted to take, and things we wanted to do together. We spent more time talking than we did kissing, but we spent a significant time kissing.

I'd never been with anyone who made me feel beautiful from just a touch, just a look, just a kiss. At one point, he pulled me into his lap and held me, kissing me softly, stroking my hair, and I felt safe. I'd never felt as safe as I did in Julian's arms.

"I love it out here. I can see why this is where you spend most of your time," I murmured against his neck with a sigh. "But I should go."

He held me tighter. "Or...or...you should stay. We should go in the house. We should climb in the bed."

I giggled sleepily. "I wish. I have to get back in the house before they notice I'm missing."

"Had I expected things to go down like this, I would've set this up in the house anyway."

I lifted my head and put my hands on his face. "Tonight was magical." I paused. "And I don't say stuff like magical."

He chuckled in a tired baritone before kissing me.

Julian insisted on walking me back through the garden so we strolled, hand-in-hand, with the stars shining over us. At the edge of the garden, I argued with him because he wanted to walk me all the way to the house and I thought it was too risky. Our goodbye was long and drawn out since we weren't going to be able to see each other. He had to do press from the show and would be gone until Wednesday night. He promised to come to the house when he got back since the next group date wouldn't be until Thursday and he couldn't go that long without seeing me. I jogged back to *The One* headquarters on cloud nine.

I snuck into the mansion a little before five o'clock in the morning. Fortunately, I was able to get inside the house without being detected. Although it was really late...or really early, I heard voices somewhere within the house.

I froze.

*Who the hell is up right now?*

I tried to focus my breathing and slow my heart rate as I stood in the darkened hallway. I'd come too far to get caught. Taking measured steps, I moved down the hall toward the staircase. With my back against the wall, I knew that the foyer was the trickiest part of my escape and return because most rooms and hallways on the first floor seemed to converge at that point. As I prepared to make my move, crying caught my attention.

"Is that really what people are saying about me? Just based off of the interviews?" It sounded like Ana's Romanian accented voice.

"Yes," a masculine voice replied. "And we won't know how it shakes out until this week gets going. It could go either way."

"This is humiliating! I hate losing." She whined. "I don't understand. Leah talks the most shit when the cameras aren't around. She's the real mean girl. I don't get it. How is she the frontrunner? I'm prettier than her!"

"You are. But when you have ten sexy women in the same place, you have to find other ways to stand out."

"That's what you told me on Friday so I've been doing what you said. You told me to stick with Tori because the mean girls always make good TV and get more screen time, so that's what I did. Why do I have the lowest approval rating?"

"You don't have the lowest approval rating." He sounded exasperated.

"I wanted to tell Julian about my—"

"No," he said, cutting her off mid-sentence. "Not right now. If you do, people will judge you and because you're not ranking as high as I would've hoped, that's not going to help."

Ana sighed, "I feel like I'm lying or I'm ashamed and I'm not either. I just wanted to wait until we at least had a few more conversations before I dropped it on him. He may not be ready for it."

"You wanted me to help you win and that's what I'm trying to do. I'm holding up my end of the bargain. I know you're worried. But know that I'm as invested in you winning as you are so I've been pouring over the feedback to predict how this week will go."

Ana giggled a little. "Well you do seem more motivated over the last few days." I heard a smacking noise and I couldn't quite figure out where it was coming. "How do you think this week will go?"

I'd heard enough. They seemed to be entrenched in conversation so I thought making my move would be in my best interests. I stretched my legs, taking long steps, to reach the staircase as quickly and as quietly as possible.

"Well, I'm not sure. On Thursday, the episode will air where you talked shit about Bailey and Zoe while they were out," the man explained, causing me to freeze at the bottom of the steps at the mention of my name. "...and then when they got back, you played drinking games with Bailey. You're going to look fake."

"I like Bailey. And I don't have an issue with Zoe. Tori does, not me! I was drunk and I said that stuff because someone asked me what I thought of them winning the date. And earlier, you told me to answer like I was Tori," Ana whined.

I carefully creeped up the first couple of steps and then paused.

"I know. I didn't realize Jamie was still going to be doing one-on-ones or I would've found you so we could've powwowed. But even then, I didn't expect Bailey and Zoe to poll so high. But you have the chance to turn this around, Ana.

That's why I'm meeting with you in the middle of the night...so we can fix this."

"Yeah, is that the reason why?" Ana's voice got lighter.

I heard a smacking sound again. *Wait, was that what I think it was?*

"You said you'd fix this." Her voice bordered on baby talk. "Please. I'll do anything."

The man seemed to turn into a political strategist in two point five seconds. "Well, the top three women in the house who are polling the best have one thing in common. They kept to themselves at the cocktail party interview. They come off as nice in their own ways and people like nice... at first. But nice is boring. You seemed to rub people the wrong way initially. Your first impression isn't as strong, but you will grow on them."

"What can I do?"

"Your panic attack stunt helped—that'll buy you sympathy. Now you have to ramp it up a bit. You need to set yourself apart from Tori. You can't afford to be in her shadow with your numbers so close."

"What do you mean?"

"You're going to have to make her your bitch."

I took the steps slowly, trying to balance my weight on the balls of my feet. I continued that method, only stopping once more when an interesting bit of information was revealed.

"Tori?" Ana hissed. "If Leah is winning the popularity contest, and Bailey and Zoe are second and third, why would I worry about Tori if she's in the middle with me?"

"Leah is so far ahead, based on the numbers, that Robert Brady is already declaring that she will be who Julian ends up with. He's already working up storylines that will push the two of them together. I am trying to help you turn the tide so that you—

I didn't linger around to hear the rest. I had made it to the top of the staircase and I was exhausted. I glanced at Mya who was snoring drunkenly on my way to the closet. My mind revisited what I'd learned as I changed my clothes. Climbing into bed, I let what Mya said earlier and what Ana's producer had just told her enter my thoughts.

*Julian and Leah?*

I pushed the thought out of my head as I felt my body drifting off to sleep before my mind. With my eyes closed, I pushed out Leah and the other women, the show, the fear, the doubt, the negativity.

*I will not focus on anything, but what I feel. Everything else is just noise. The creator wanting to push Julian and Leah together will not overshadow Julian telling me he wants me.*

I replayed my time with Julian from beginning to end. I felt warm all over just thinking about it. The five hour stretch that I spent with Julian was the best I'd ever had and it wasn't just the fact that he put together a candlelit dinner. It wasn't just the fact that he communicated with me and compelled me to share myself with him. It wasn't just the fact that we could laugh and play together. It wasn't just the fact that his dick was exquisite and our bodies worked well together. Although those were all great things, it was the best night of my life because Julian Winters made me feel something I'd never felt before.

The sound of my heart started lulling me to sleep and I didn't have the strength or energy to push out the thoughts that creeped in.

*You're falling for him.*

Even if I wouldn't verbalize it, even if I had the willpower to deny it in the morning, that night, somewhere between midnight and five o'clock in the morning, Julian Winters made me fall for him.

# Chapter 13

Tuesday, I slept in. Mya wasn't feeling well so we both spent most of the day in bed. She slept while I alternated between daydreaming about Julian and reading my Pablo Neruda book of poetry. Even when we left the bedroom to eat, we didn't really run into anyone. To us, it was an uneventful, boring day.

Wednesday, Mya and I decided to venture out. We'd learned that we were dead wrong about Tuesday being uneventful and boring. Because apparently, on Tuesday while we slept, shit went down.

Eating burgers and fries for lunch, Mya and I sat at the kitchen table discussing politics when a camera crew strolled in.

"Ladies, would you mind talking about something a little more...interesting?" A producer asked as soon as they heard our topic of choice.

"And what would be more interesting?" I returned, my eyebrow quirked in annoyance.

"Boys?" Mya remarked sarcastically.

I laughed before popping a fry into my mouth.

In an effort to dumb us down as a collective whole, they made a habit of telling us to converse about Julian or the other women in the house. We were urged to not talk about substantial things because it was deemed boring. And although they didn't blatantly encourage us to drink, we were offered drinks with every meal. And with nothing else to do in the house and an endless supply of self-serve alcohol, a lot of the women drank heavily. I suspected the endless supply of alcohol was to make us more emotional, more volatile, and less prone to an intelligent conversation.

*Which is why I stuck with bottled water most of the time.*

As Mya and I ignored the cameras and continued our conversation, Leah strolled into the room. She didn't speak and neither did we. The producer's smile widened as he signaled to the younger guy with a clipboard. The camera swung around and focused on Leah.

My mind instantly went back to the conversation Ana was having when I snuck in. The early feedback rooted for Leah. I wasn't the jealous type. I could admit that she was gorgeous—her hair was thick and wavy, her skin was blemish free, and although her sense of style was a bit boring and traditional, she knew how to work her assets.

Wearing short shorts that showed off her long, toned legs, Leah smiled at the camera and gushed about Julian.

*I wonder if whoever her handler is told her she was the front runner.*

"What are your thoughts about what happened with Tori and Ana yesterday?" The producer questioned Leah.

"I thought it was sad that two people who had become such good friends had a big blow up like that. Ana instigated it, but Tori took it too far. I just don't see Julian wanting to be with the type of women who would be so trashy."

I looked at Mya and she appeared just as stunned as I felt.

The camera crew followed Leah and her short shorts out of the kitchen and into another room. Once the coast was clear, Mya speculated about what could've happened. My gut told me that it had something to do with the conversation I overheard. But if I shared that information, I would've had to explain why I was lurking in the shadows at five o'clock in the morning. So I remained quiet.

The Ana versus Tori debacle was the only thing anyone talked about on Wednesday until we were all prepped and told that Julian was stopping by for an hour. We were given an hour to get ready and told to look very casual as if we were lounging around.

*Clearly that means leggings.*

After dressing and preparing for his visit, we were pushed into the living room and forced to answer questions as a group.

"What do you think Julian is looking for in a woman?"

"What do you think you have in common with Julian?"

"Would you move to California to be with Julian?"

"If you had to choose someone, outside of yourself, to be with Julian, who would you choose?"

"Can you see yourself falling in love with Julian?"

The questions mixed with the alcohol and as the questions progressed, the answers became more emotional. With each refreshed glass, the women became more talkative and more open. I drank my bottled water and remained quiet. As long as they were getting the content they needed from other contestants, they didn't notice that I wasn't participating.

"I have a surprise for you," Bryce Wilson addressed us, rounding a corner into the living room, catching everyone by surprise. Robert Brady also entered the set, but he remained off camera. "Julian is going to be here a little later. But since you're all gathered here now, I'd like you to meet someone who can maybe give you some insight into Julian Winters."

We all exchanged looks, but waited with expectation for more information. Bryce flashed a smile to the camera and waited a moment, presumably they'd edit in a commercial break.

Clapping his hands together, Bryce cast his gaze over us. "I'd like to introduce you to Lillian Pierce, Julian's ex-girlfriend."

The mood in the room shifted abruptly. I'd never heard a silence so loud. My body tensed.

"Hello everyone!" Lillian greeted us as she strolled into the room. "I'm Lillian! As Julian's only real relationship, I'd be happy to give you any insight I can."

I blinked blankly, unable to join in with the chorus of unsettled hellos. Her looks gave me pause.

With the face of a model, Lillian Pierce was stunning. She had a warm honey skin tone that had a radiant glow. Her bright blue eyes sparkled. She had lustrous dark blonde hair that cascaded down her back in soft waves. Her one-piece romper was trendy, but sophisticated.

"She looks just like Leah," Mya hissed under her breath. "Leah 2.0."

My stomach twisted violently as I nodded as discreetly as possible. I was thinking the same thing.

"Lillian will be having one-on-one time with each of you before heading back to Black Heart Studios: Nashville. So, let's get started! Ana, you're up first."

Ana smirked cunningly as she rose from the loveseat and followed Lillian out of the room.

As soon as they left the room, everyone seemed to start speaking at once. The cameras panned over us and the crew members seemed giddy. They knew getting us together as a group to wait for Julian would be awkward. They knew cracking open bottles of wine and encouraging us to answer questions about Julian would be tense. But throwing in Lillian, who looked like the show's frontrunner, was stirring the pot.

*And they are getting exactly what they want.*

Samantha started crying, spiraling into a weepy insecure mess as Emma comforted her.

Tori and Tiffany picked apart Lillian's overall appearance in unnecessarily catty remarks.

Leah seemed uncomfortable, staring into a compact mirror and primping herself.

Bailey and Mya speculated what we would learn from Lillian.

And I couldn't stop thinking about the concerted effort the show was planning to take to push Julian and Leah together.

*Even if America didn't love her, she is clearly Julian's type.*

The amount of alcohol consumed in that hour was ridiculous. It didn't take long for me to realize that they were calling women to chat with Lillian alphabetically.

"Last, but not least, Zoe," Lillian beckoned with a faint smile.

I followed her to the frequently unused study. Two mahogany leather wing-backed chairs were angled toward one another. We each took a seat.

"Zoe...how are you?" Lillian started, crossing her legs.

I smiled. "I'm well. How are you?"

"Tired!" She giggled, tossing her hair over her shoulder. "We don't have much time so shall we get to it? Tell me what it is you like about Julian?"

"He's the second best man I've ever met. And it's a close second so that's really saying something."

She seemed amused. "Who's the first?"

"My father."

"So, no daddy issues. That's good, very promising."

I thought that was an odd response, but I smiled politely.

Lillian clasped her hands in front of her. "So tell me more about what you like about Julian."

"I like that he's so together and focused. He knows what he wants. He's a go-getter. And we have a lot in common."

It was quiet as she looked at me, compelling me to explain myself, my feelings. "Go on," she encouraged gently.

"I don't know what else you want me to say." I paused before adding, "He's intelligent, annoyingly so at times. He's funny." My body warmed and my lips turned upward. "But not just funny, he's witty and he has incredible timing. He's sweet and affectionate. He's poetic. He has this way with words that just speaks to me. He..."

I blinked through the haze and my stomach flipped. I'd realized I was rambling on camera in front of his ex-girlfriend like a lovesick crazy person. Shifting in my seat, I pulled myself together.

"He's a great man and I've been enjoying getting to know him," I concluded.

Lillian's facial expression was unreadable. "Well, is there anything you'd like to know about Julian?"

I thought about it and the barrage of questions immediately popped into my head. *You wanted to reconcile at one time, do you still? Did the sex in November rekindle some feelings for you? Does he have a type? Are you his type? Why did you break up with him? Do you regret it? Why are you here?*

"No, thank you." I gave her a kind smile. "Anything I learn about Julian, I want it to be from Julian. I appreciate you taking the time to speak with me though."

Lillian looked at me long and hard. Her lips slowly turned upward as the seconds ticked by. "Well, well, well. This is a first."

I didn't know what to say to that so I didn't say a word.

Lillian's smile evaporated. "You're serious?"

I nodded. "Yes. I'm good. If I have questions about anything, I like to go to the source."

She leaned forward and lowered her voice. "You have a chance to hear about him from the perspective of his only ex, the only person to be in an actual relationship with him. What's a better source than that?"

"He is. He's a better source."

She nodded slowly. "Do you love him?"

*Ummmmmmmmmm...*

"After six days? That's a little fast don't you think?"

Lillian giggled to herself before looking at the producers. "I think we're done here. I have to get going."

We got up to leave, allowing the camera crew to rush out before us. The group of four bolted from the study in the direction of the living room where the rest of the contestants were located.

Lillian lightly touched my elbow before we made it down the hallway. "Zoe, you never answered my question."

My heart rate accelerated as I turned to face her. "What do you mean?"

*I knew exactly what she meant.*

She glanced behind me. "Listen," she started, her eyes darkened. "A couple of these girls are clearly here for the money or the exposure. Some seem to genuinely like him and even claim to love him. But let's be honest, they don't even know him." She paused, folding her arms over her relatively small chest. "But you, you speak about him in a way that I recognize. Because it's how I speak about him."

"Okay...?" I crossed my arms over my chest and tilted my head to the side.

She took a step toward me and lowered her voice. "I've known Julian for a long time and in the four years since we've broken up, do you know how many times he's been in a relationship? Been in love? I'll tell you. None. I'm his first love, his only love."

"If that's the case, why is he here? And why are you telling me?"

Tossing her hair back, Lillian scoffed. "I'm trying to help you out, kid. I saw it in your eyes when you talked about him. You're in love with him. And I get it. He has that effect. But I'm trying to save you from heart break. None of the other ones seemed to even know him, but you do. And if you're this invested now, how hard do you think it'll be when the show's over, the romance is gone, and he resumes his life with me?"

I shook my head, letting out a humorless laugh. "Do you hear yourself? I'm not discrediting what you two had. Had. Past tense. But if he wanted to be with you, do you think he would've gone through all of this to be on *The One*?"

"Oh Zoe..." Her voice dripped with condescension. "You're obviously beautiful and well-educated, but you're not being very bright right now. So let me break it down to you. Julian took this opportunity because he is making the leap from producer to musician. Every single episode is not only a promotional opportunity for him as a man, but also for him as an artist." She paused, smirking. "He's going to choose that poor man's version of me, Lena, Leah, whatever." She rolled her eyes. "And then once this show is over, we will be together again."

My blood was boiling, but I kept my cool. "I'm not going to continue to have this conversation with you. Julian knows what he wants."

Lillian took a step back. "Yes he does. Me. And in November, when he was recording in my studio, he pretty much told me so." She winked. "Don't say I didn't warn you." She turned on her heel and walked off.

I didn't give her the satisfaction of reacting. I headed toward the living room and once I heard the front door slam, I closed my eyes and let my head drop back.

*That condescending bitch!*

I told myself that I only had to wait twenty-four hours for the next Bracelet Ceremony and my opportunity to discuss with Koko what happened.

I sat on the edge of the couch and the excitement swirling around the living room earlier in the night was diminished by Lillian's visit.

"Hello! Anyone home?" Julian's deep voice rumbled through the hallway, cutting over the feminine voices speaking.

My heart jumped at the sound of his voice and my emotions swirled inside of me uncontrollably. I sucked in a deep breath.

In jeans and a t-shirt, he strolled into the living room evoking my body's immediate response. His eyes landed on me instantly. The irritation of my interaction with his ex-girlfriend still didn't quell how I felt about him.

"Everything okay?" He asked after everyone greeted him. He looked around as if he could see it on our faces.

All of us looked at each other before Emma spoke up. "We had a visitor before you arrived."

Julian looked confused, his eyebrows furrowed. "Who?"

"Lillian," Ana spat.

His jaw clenched. "What?" He turned toward where a group of producers were standing behind the camera. "What?" He growled.

"Cut!"

Julian stormed over to the patio area where Bryce was

standing in deep conversation with Robert Brady. We were left in a stunned silence as we craned our necks to see if we could see what was happening. When all three men started walking back from the patio less than ten minutes later, we scrambled to get back in our seats.

Julian looked pissed, but he smiled anyway. "I'm going to spend some time with you one-on-one for a bit. I'm going to start with..." He glared in the direction of Robert and Bryce before he turned his stormy grey eyes onto me. "Zoe."

I stood, grabbing on to the hand that he extended to me. He didn't say a word as he stalked out of the living room, me in tow.

The camera crew followed us as he led us to the study.

"Julian," I started as soon as we were in the room. I tugged his hand, compelling him to look at me. "Hey, Julian, look at me."

He turned around and I saw the anger and frustration embedded in his features.

I put my hands on the sides of his face, staring into his eyes.

It only took a few seconds for his face to change completely. His face relaxed, rage and aggravation evaporated. The tension in his body gave way and he exhaled roughly.

"Hi," I whispered, putting my arms around his neck.

"Hi." He smirked, pulling me into him. "Thank you."

"For...?"

"For being you."

I gazed up at him adoringly, biting down on my lip to keep from smiling so hard. "You are a sweet talker."

He put his lips to my ear. "I missed you. I thought about you the entire time I was gone."

The fluttering in my chest cavity made it hard to suck in air.

He spoke so softly that the production crew waved their arms frantically to get our attention. The words 'we can't hear you' were written on a piece of paper clipped to a clipboard.

I cleared my throat and gestured with my head to the sign.

He sighed. "You want to have a seat?"

I grinned, moving my body against his as discreetly as possible. "Not really."

He laughed. His hands ran up and down my back and then rested at the curve of my ass.

Standing on my tiptoes, I planted a quick peck on his lips. "Now, what was that whole thing about with Lillian?"

He clenched his teeth and closed his eyes for a few seconds. I patiently waited for him to answer.

"There's no reason for her to be involved with this so she shouldn't have come. But more than that, the show shouldn't have contacted her without my permission." He shook his head. "She can be intense. Did all of you have to meet with her?"

I nodded. "And she was a delight," I answered sarcastically.

He grimaced. "I can only imagine. Did she say anything out of line? Scratch that. What did she say that was out of line?"

"Oh, you know. A little of this, a little of that." Subtly, I tilted my head toward the camera. "She did ask if I wanted any dirt on you. I declined."

"What dirt would she have? This is crazy. We broke up when we were twenty-four. We've run into each other a handful of times over the last four years and only one time did we have a real conversation." He gave me a look. "And that was in November."

Her words irritated my soul. I lightly cleared my throat. "Yeah, she mentioned November."

He closed his eyes and his jaw tightened. When he looked at me again, I saw nothing but sincerity and genuine affection. "I apologize. When we hung out in November, the meeting served its purpose. If I would've thought that meeting would've led to her popping up here on The One, I wouldn't have had that meeting with her. And I don't want my ex negatively impacting anything with my future."

My heart stopped.

*Did he just call me his future?*

I felt giddy. "Julian..." I dragged his name out dreamily. "I appreciate you saying that. But how I feel about you is pretty solid. And considering you're dating me and eight other women, I can handle the ramblings of your obsessive ex."

He looked into my eyes for a long time. "I'm sorry. I really am." He hesitated before he mouthed, "For all of it."

"You can make it up to me," I flirted, temporarily forgetting the camera because I was caught up in his eyes. "I can think of some ways."

"Zoe Jordan, you have no idea," he growled, slapping me on my ass.

"Julian Winters, I think I do."

We both laughed.

Grabbing my face, Julian moved his mouth over mine sweetly. I felt myself smiling against his lips.

"What are you smiling about?" His hands crept a little further down on my ass and he dropped his forehead to mine.

"You make me smile. Just being with you makes me smile."

There was a short knock on the door before Tori walked in. Although our foreheads separated, we were slower to remove our arms from around each other.

Julian sighed in disappointment faintly. "Hi, Tori."

"Hello...do you have a few minutes?" She asked sweetly.

"Of course. Just give me a minute to say goodbye to Zoe, please," he replied before looking down at me. "Our time is up, but it was a pleasure as always."

"Indeed it was," I returned, wanting to kiss him but knowing I couldn't. The door slammed shut and I looked over to see that Tori finally left the room. Meeting his gaze again, I held him tighter. "I'm looking forward to tomorrow's date."

"As am I. Any extra time I get to spend with you is nice. I wish we had more time tonight." He gave me a look.

*Is he telling me to meet him tonight?*

"Me too." My response was a little unsure.

We walked hand-in-hand to the door and he gave me a chaste kiss that left me wanting more when we parted ways. Tori walked in immediately after I took one step over the threshold and I happened to look back in enough time to see Julian give her a big hug.

My stomach turned.

All of us had to remain in the living room until everyone had their few minutes with Julian. Once he had spent his time with each of us individually, he sat in the living room with us, drinking and talking as a group.

Seeing him interact with the other women offered both reassurance that he didn't look at anyone in the house the way he looked at me and a reminder that he could. Bailey's voice rang in my head watching him with Leah tucked under his arm, Ana clutching his other hand, and Mya sitting on his lap.

*A man is only as faithful as his options.* I rolled my shoulders back and tried to clear my mind.

I tolerated the vapid conversations and the flirty commentary that whirled around me. Sexual innuendos were being tossed his way and with his quick wit, he would reply accordingly. But watching him being affectionate made my stomach turn and at that point, I switched from water to wine.

At the time that Julian was supposed to leave, Leah volunteered to walk him out. I grumbled obscenities internally. A few other women grumbled audibly. But Robert Brady smiled like a Cheshire cat from the patio.

One of the camera crews followed the two of them and we were free to leave the area. I wanted to head straight to my room, but I was intercepted by a producer.

"Zoe, will you follow me for a minute. I want to show you something."

I looked at Mya and shrugged.

When she started to follow me, the producer said, "No, just Zoe this time."

Mya and I looked at each other suspiciously before looking at the producer. "I'll wait for you right here," she told me.

"What's this about?" I questioned as I followed the familiar looking man through the foyer.

"Think of me as your best friend," he answered. "You and Julian have a lot of chemistry."

I didn't know if it was a question or not, so I hesitated before replying, "We do."

"It really jumps off of the screen. But in person, sometimes it's like you two are the only people in the room."

I smiled despite myself. "That's a good thing."

"Definitely," he nodded, stopping at the big, picturesque window. "He only has that with one other woman."

*If he does, I don't see it.*

"Oh really?"

He moved the satiny curtain fabric to the side, but left the sheer panel in place so it took me a second to see what he was showing me. I gasped.

Julian had his arms around Leah and she was gazing up at him. I moved the sheer panel to be sure. The camera crew had their backs to the window so it was unlikely that Julian or Leah would look my way. I'd hoped that I wasn't seeing what I thought I was seeing, but there it was right in front of me. I'd never seen him embrace any of the other women the way he embraced me. I'd never seen him look at another woman the way he looked at me.

*God, this must be what the other women feel like when they are around us.*

My heart broke as he laughed. He ran his hands over her back as he hugged her tightly. She lifted her head from his chest, but kept her arms firmly in place. Julian looked down at her and then over her head. I tried to follow his line of vision, but the corner of the house was blocking my view. He looked down at her face again and hesitated.

*Don't do it. Don't do it. Don't do it.*

He pressed his lips to hers and a piece of me broke. A little small piece of me chipped off and died. I didn't even know I had reacted outwardly until the producer put his hand on my shoulder.

"Are you okay?"

"I'm fine," I lied shakily. In truth, I was heartbroken. I dropped the curtain back into place and started to walk away. "Thanks for the heads up."

I went upstairs and it wasn't until Mya came in thirty minutes later that I realized that she was waiting for me.

"Where did you disappear to?" She asked with her hands on her hips. "What did Leah's handler want?"

I peered at her from under my comforter. "Wait, what? That was Leah's producer?"

She nodded.

*That's why he wanted to show me that! That makes so much more sense now.*

"He wanted to intimidate me."

"What?" Mya's eyes widened and her mouth fell open.

"He just wanted me to know that Leah is the frontrunner."

"Well it makes sense that Julian is into her." Mya sat on the edge of her bed looking a little dejected. "She looks exactly like his ex. If nothing else, we know that Julian is attracted to her."

"Yep."

"But what gets me is that she has a bad attitude. She's rude and condescending and snobby." She let out a frustrated laugh even though her eyes were watering. "But Lillian was the same way so maybe she's perfect for him. I don't even know why I bother at this point. I should just give up and go home."

I didn't have it in me to be encouraging since I was stuck in my own feelings. So I kept it simple and said, "I feel where you're coming from. If you want to stay, you should stay."

"That's easy for you to say," she snapped.

I closed my eyes and let out a loud sigh. *I am not in the mood to have this conversation.*

"It's not easy for me to say, but I'm telling you that I understand where you're coming from and that you have to make the best decision for you." My tone was even, even though it felt like she was baiting me.

Mya's frustration seemed to mix with a bit of jealousy as she unleashed on me. "You have no idea what it's like. Julian validates you. He makes sure you know you're important. He goes out of his way to seek you out. He is always looking at you. He is always finding reasons to touch you. So, excuse me if I don't want to hear 'I understand' from you!"

I sat up in bed, irritated. "Listen Mya, I understand that you're upset, but right now is not the time. I'm really trying not to say anything I'm going to regret so I need you to take that bullshit somewhere else."

Mya stood up. "Gladly!"

She stormed out of the room, slamming the door behind her.

*My only friend in the house has just lost her damn mind.*

*Koko won't be back until tomorrow and I'll have to wait all damn day for a legit reason to go to makeup and see her.*

*And Julian...fucking Julian.*

I tried to push thoughts of him out of my head, but I couldn't stop seeing him with Leah, holding her, kissing her. I squeezed my eyes shut and still, that's all I could see. I tried to will myself to sleep, but Lillian's words floated through my head, giving sound to the disturbing visual images.

*He's going to choose that poor man's version of me, Lena, Leah, whatever. And then once this show is over, we will be together again.*

It was a long night.

# Chapter 14

I held my champagne glass to my lips and let the cold bubbly cool my warm insides. Sitting on the bench under the romantic stone archway, I looked at the ivy twisted around the structure. It looked real, but I knew it wasn't.

*Like this show.*

I shook off the negative thoughts that had plagued me for twenty-four hours. It affected my sleep pattern which prompted me to question if I wanted to stay in the competition. It affected my relationship with Mya which was how I was able to pack my bags without her knowing, just in case. It even affected my performance on the group date earlier in the day.

It was a cool date. We took a guided tour through the abandoned zoo at Griffith Park. Julian seamlessly weaved among us. With my sunglasses on, I paid close attention to how he interacted with everyone else. The hand on the lower back, the arm slung over the shoulders, and the smile. His smile was my kryptonite and that alone pissed me off even more.

# The One

When we were together, we held hands and discussed the stops on the tour. Julian told me that he could see it in my eyes that something was wrong. I told him I'd tell him at the cocktail party because I didn't want to ruin the vibe of the date. I could tell that my answer bothered him, but he didn't press it. He still made his rounds, always coming back to me and holding my hand. By the fourth time, we didn't talk at all. We held hands and he stared into my eyes until they watered with the hurt I felt.

Needless to say, when the tour guide selected the winner for the one-on-one dinner date, it wasn't me. I wasn't surprised at all. I was surprised; however, that he selected Leah. She didn't do anything to warrant the win, but I suspected the creator of the show had something to do with it.

So even if I wasn't already in my head about Julian and Leah, after we returned from the date, I spent the rest of the day in the house listening to the other women complain about Leah getting the first one-on-one date and what that meant. It was hard to listen to, but when I retreated to my room, it was all I could think about.

When I talked to Koko during my makeup session, I told her everything and her advice was to somehow get away from the cameras and turn off the microphones and really talk. I didn't know if that was going to be possible, but we both agreed that I couldn't say everything I needed to say on camera or with a live mic.

As I sat alone on the stone bench under the romantic archway, I looked absolutely fabulous in a backless emerald green gown. My hair was pinned up in an elaborate way that elongated my neck and highlighted the sexiest part of the dress. I felt beautiful on the outside and like a hollow mess on the inside. I felt the emotional breakdown starting to happen and I refused to look like Samantha, who had been crying off and on since Lillian's arrival the day before.

I waited until Samantha started crying and Tori and Emma got into an argument over something Leah said and I turned off my microphone and slipped away unnoticed.

*What do I really have to cry about? I did this to myself. I was just supposed to come here and meet him. I was just supposed to come here and pick his brain about his work. I was just supposed to be on one show so that I wouldn't be a liar. I wasn't supposed to develop feelings for him. I wasn't supposed to...*

Instead of finishing my thought, I finished my third glass of champagne. Sitting the empty glass on the ground beside me, I took a deep breath. It was the first time all day a camera wasn't hovering around me. I felt like I was able to be emotionally free like I needed to be without someone watching me, judging me, speculating, or assuming. What I shared with Julian was deep. To think that I was wading in the deep end on my own wrecked me. To have it wreck me on national television would be far too humiliating for me.

I put my hand in the pocket of my gown and felt for the letter I'd written. I breathed a sigh of relief that it was there. The thought of it ending up in the wrong hands made my skin crawl.

*No one could begin to understand. I didn't understand.*

It was just seven days ago that we met, but Julian and I instantly had this rare bond that fast-tracked our intimacy. We just clicked and it was like we'd known each other our entire lives. We didn't have to be anyone or anything other than who we were as our unguarded selves. I'd never experienced that before.

What I was feeling made no sense due to the time period we'd known each other. But I was also aware that everything was heightened by the lack of connectivity with the outside world. *The One* created a scenario that deliberately forced the acceleration of feelings or presumed feelings.

Everything I did in the house for the last seven days straight was focused on him. The other contestants and I were given nothing to do but drink, talk and think about a man twenty-four hours a day for days on end. The goal was always focused on getting us to generate feelings for him. And I knew that coming in. I knew that and I was determined to avoid the slippery slope that led to embarrassing breakdowns and everything that made for must-see TV. But for a second, after the most mind-blowing series of orgasms I'd ever experienced and a look that stole my heart, I let myself hope.

*I always knew this was a possibility,* I told myself, closing my eyes. *At the end of the day, there are a lot of us and one of him. He has a choice where our only choice is to stay or leave.*

Unfamiliar emotions swirled within me and I felt my eyes filling with tears. I inhaled deeply. The sound of women laughing and talking was faint and far away. With no distractions, no witnesses, no cameras, no clues, I was able to breathe. I was able to let out how I felt as the first of hundreds of backed up tears I refused to shed trickled down my cheek.

*This is too much. I have to leave.*

"Zoe, Zoe, Zoe."

The deep sound of Julian's voice woke up all of my senses. His presence pulled something out of me that I couldn't explain. Wiping the tear away as quickly as possible, I looked up at him, just high enough to avoid making eye contact.

*God, he's beautiful.*

The things that man could do with a tux were unbelievable.

His body was made for clothes...and for nakedness.

*His body is incredible. And he's incredible. And—nope. Focus. Just breathe.*

"Hey," I said, forcing myself to sound as normal as possible.

He was on me before I knew it. Pulling me up from the bench, I was wrapped in his arms before I had time to process. I inhaled his scent and my eyes fluttered closed briefly.

Putting his forehead to mine, he searched my eyes and I had to look away. "Zoe, what's wrong? Please talk to me."

I stared at his mic, tapping it.

"I turned it off when I saw you sitting over here."

I took a shaky breath and gripped his biceps. I was overwhelmed and off-balance. "Can we sit down please?"

He ran his hands down my bare back and I shivered. "Yes, of course."

Holding my hand, he waited until I was seated before straddling the bench, facing me. I stared straight ahead and I felt his eyes on me. My body heated under his gaze and I let my eyes close, relishing in it. I didn't know how much longer it was going to last.

Julian spoke first, still running his fingertips up and down my spine. "Is this about Lillian? Because she's—"

"It's not about Lillian. Well, not completely," I interrupted, still staring at the ivy. I let my head fall back as I blinked back tears. "How's the album coming along?"

"The album? I'm sure we don't have much time alone. Do you really want to know about the album?" I heard the anxiety in his voice. The hand that rubbed my back dropped off of me and I felt the loss immediately. But the hand that held mine squeezed tighter. I still didn't respond so he sighed. "The album is almost done. I have a couple of songs that I need to record so I can add them."

"Did you come on the show to find love or to promote your album?"

Out of the corner of my eye, I saw him gaping at me. I knew I was good at burying the lead, but it seemed like he was more taken aback by the fact that I had to ask the question as opposed to the actual question.

"I knew Lillian had something to do with this," he muttered under his breath, scooting closer to me. "I don't know what Lillian said to you, but my manager told me about *The One* gig while I was in Nashville recording. My manager asked me if I wanted to do it and I flat-out said no. She was around when he told me it would be good for my career. I said I'd consider it based on the audience numbers and potential for branding, marketing, and product placement. When I initially considered it, yes, it was a business opportunity. But I didn't sign the contract until after I did research and read about how some of these guys actually found something real. I watched an episode and I agreed to do it. I thought if I didn't meet anyone, at least it would be good promo for my album. But I'm here for the right reasons. Especially after meeting you."

I believed him. Without even looking at him, I felt his sincerity through the way he spoke and the way he gripped my hand.

I nodded. "I believe you."

"Why would you let an ex that I barely speak to put doubt in your head about me?"

"It's not like that, not exactly. She just kept talking shit before she left and then I saw the way some other things played out and..." I shook my head as my voice broke off.

A silent sob threatened to ripple through my body, but I swallowed it back down. I knew Julian felt it roll through me by the way his hand protectively rubbed my back and shoulders as I shook. I closed my eyes tightly to keep the tears at bay.

Exhaling, I pushed forward. "I have feelings for you. Real feelings. And I can't explain it and I don't understand it, but I have them."

"You know I feel the same way." He let go of my hand and reached out and gently turned my head his way. "Like I told you the other day, whatever this is between us, I feel it and I've felt it since I pretended to be a cater waiter. There's something real here."

Having him say those words to me, while looking in my eyes, pushed me over the edge. My bottom lip quivered and I bit it to stop. My eyes burned with unshed tears and I tried to turn my head away from him before any fell, but he held me in place.

"Don't hide from me, Zoe," Julian uttered in a painfully soft voice, causing my breath to hitch.

A tear fell, slipping down my cheek. The look on his face when he saw it broke my heart. The confusion, the fear, the frustration and the hurt that I felt played out over his handsome features. Using his thumb, he wiped the tear from my cheek.

"Zoe..." My name on his lips sounded like a plea. I heard him, but his voice was competing with the sound of my heart beating like a drum.

I broke and a shuddering intake of breath forced at least two more tears to fall before I managed to pull myself together to continue. "This situation is too much for me. You've made me vulnerable. And you can't be vulnerable in a situation like this. It's too risky."

His finger stroked the curve of my cheek. "I'm in this with you."

"Are you?" I questioned so softly I thought he didn't hear me at first.

## The One

When I felt his body stiffen, I knew not only had he heard me, I'd hurt him. And hurting him was the last thing I wanted to do. He didn't answer for a second, chewing on his bottom lip.

"Don't do that. Don't question how I feel about you." He let go of my face and ran both of his hands through his hair. "I'm in...I'm in this, Zoe."

I ran my fingertip under both of my eyes to ensure that my eyeliner didn't run even though I knew they only used long lasting, water resistant makeup specifically for dramatic cries and emotional breakdowns.

My face trembled as I stared into the greys of his eyes. I gestured between the two of us. "No, I'm in this. For you and only you."

He grabbed my face, bringing it an inch or two away from his. "Are you listening to me? I'm sitting here telling you that I want you and only you. I..." He gaped at me in disbelief and let his sentence trail off.

His frustration with me and the situation was apparent.

"You want me and only me?"

His eyes squinted slightly and his eyebrows furrowed. He let my face go, returning his hand to my lower back. "Yes. That's what I've been saying. You say this isn't about Lillian, so what is this about?"

"It's about you and Leah."

"There is no me and Leah. She won the date. That's it."

"So, did you kiss her?"

He hesitated and my heart stopped. "I don't have feelings for Leah."

I swallowed around the lump in my throat. "Julian."

Resignation on his face, Julian shook his head. His jaw tightened. "How did you find out?"

"Does it matter?"

His eyes were closed as he nodded, fuming. The tension in his body was coming off of him in waves. "It does. It matters a lot. I was supposed to have more time to explain before you found out about it."

When his dark lashes flapped open, the pain in his eyes drew me in and punched me in the gut. "It didn't mean anything," he stated firmly.

My heart throbbed painfully. I put my hand to his face and he leaned into my touch.

"It didn't mean anything," he faintly repeated as his features slowly relaxed. "Robert and some producers told me in the treatment meeting that I needed to kiss her. Well, they said that I needed to show more affection to other women in the house. So, I said I'd do it. It wasn't until later that they said it needed to be her. Others could come later. But that night, it needed to be Leah. Something about the numbers and ratings and I don't know. So later, I..."

His sentence trailed off. He put his hand over mine as it rested against his cheek. He turned his head to kiss the inside of my palm, giving me butterflies. Pulling my hand from his face, he intertwined our fingers.

"You kissed her outside when she walked you out."

He nodded. "I told them if I did it, it would have to be kept under wraps for a couple of days. They gave me their word. They had Leah sign something. They said that for twenty-four hours, it would be kept between the four of us. That's why it pisses me off that someone leaked it. I was always going to tell you. I hope you know that I would never keep something like that from you. I was hoping you'd either win the one-on-one or you'd meet me tonight, but I was always going to tell you. I want to build something with you, Zoe, so I wouldn't keep anything from you. I wouldn't lie to you or betray your trust."

Seconds passed and we just stared at one another. His words penetrated my heart and dug into my soul. He said everything I didn't even know I wanted him to say. He had me. I had so many emotions churning inside of me that it was stifling. I couldn't breathe.

Without warning, I moved forward and pressed my lips against his. It was an impulsive, involuntarily reflex to his words. He responded instantly, wasting no time deepening the kiss and letting his mouth move over mine seductively. My arms circled around his neck, pulling him closer. His hands traveled on separate missions with similar results.

One hand roamed over my back from my shoulders to my lower back pulling me closer to him and igniting my bare skin with his touch. His other hand stroked my cheek and worked his way down my neck. My nipples hardened thinking he was on his way to stimulate them. But he rested his hand over my heart and kissed me with so much passion that I moaned.

Pulling out of the kiss, my chest heaved as I stared at him. He rested his forehead against mine and we sucked in air, trying to catch our breath. His hand was still over my heart so while I played with his hair with one hand, I put my other hand over his heart. His breathing matched mine. My heartbeat matched his. And in his eyes, I saw the way he looked at me and I recognized it as the look my dad gives my mom.

Something passed between us and it made me tremble with a nervous energy I'd never experienced before. My stomach flipped and flipped on a continuous loop. My heart stopped and started erratically. My skin was enflamed. I'd never felt anything so intense and it scared me. I tried to shake it off, but I couldn't quite stop the fluttering that traveled from my belly to my chest cavity. Feeling overwhelmed, I tried to break away or at the very least, avert my gaze. But I was powerless to do either. I was powerless to the feelings. I was powerless to that moment. I was powerless.

"What the fuck is going on?" Bryce Wilson hissed angrily, shattering our moment and scaring the shit out of us.

We didn't have time to respond as he continued, "They have a fucking search party looking for you, Julian. They thought you were pissed about what they asked you to do..." He glanced at me in the least discreet way possible. "They thought you went home so Robert and his assistants are on their way to find you. They didn't tell any of the women you were missing. They just said that you pushed the Bracelet Ceremony back an hour so the crew is on break, too. You better be glad that I'm the one that found you." He shook his head.

As much as I wanted to interrupt his scolding to point out the hypocrisy of his own inappropriate work relationship, I knew it wasn't going to help. If anything, it might've jeopardized Koko's job and I wouldn't ever do that.

Julian looked unbothered by either the search party or getting caught sneaking around with me. "I needed to talk to Zoe. I'll be at the front door in a few minutes."

Bryce's eyebrows flew up. His Ken-doll features looked exasperated. "I like you, dude. I do. So I'm going to be straight with you right now. Zoe is a beautiful woman—smart, funny. I read the bio and she's top notch so I'm not saying you're not making the best choice for you."

"I'm right here," I muttered in annoyance.

"...What I'm saying is that your contract is for you to date multiple women and choose one at the end. People don't tune in after you make your decision which is why the show ends with a live finale in which you choose. I told you on the first date you needed to chill out, but it's getting bad now. People are noticing. This happened one other time and ratings dipped. Robert sued the fuck out of that dude. Dude literally had nothing left to give when Robert got through with him. Robert's not a bad dude, but he doesn't play with his money. And ratings equal money, so be careful."

"I hear you." Julian stood and the two men gave each other the handshake-hug combo that men often did. "Thanks for looking out. I'll be up front in a minute."

Bryce looked at him as if he'd lost his mind. "See you soon, Julian." The emphasis on the word soon wasn't lost on me. He was telling him to hurry his ass up. "Bye, Zoe."

With his head on a swivel, Bryce left us alone and headed toward the house.

Extending his hand out, I allowed him to pull me to my feet. He pulled me flush against his body and I rested my head in the crook of his neck. He held me, resting his head against mine. "I'm sorry," he whispered. "I wish I would've had a chance to tell you and you didn't have to hear it from someone else. I should've known that that was why you were pulling away from me. But I don't want Leah. I don't want anyone, but you. You know that right?"

I nodded. Opening my mouth to say what I had started to say before we were interrupted, I choked. I exhaled instead. The words on the tip of my tongue wouldn't drop. So I swallowed them instead and settled for squeezing my arms around his middle tighter.

His chest expanded as he squeezed me with the same amount of force.

"We should get back out there," he pointed out, kissing my forehead.

Again, I nodded, nuzzling him at the same time.

He pulled out of the hug and put his hands around my neck, cradling the back of my head. Resting his forehead against mine, I saw that look in his eyes again and I knew.

My eyes watered instantly.

*I've always wanted someone to look at me like this.*

He searched my face and his lips parted. I didn't know if I wanted to hear what he was going to say. I didn't know if it was going to make things harder or easier. I had already put myself in the precarious position that I was in. So instead of waiting for him to speak, I placed a kiss against his soft lips.

My intention was to give him a peck since we had to split up and head to the house. But somehow, my mouth opened slightly, inviting him in. Once the invitation was there, I wanted nothing more than to taste him. He tilted his head and lightly sucked on my top lip before tentatively exploring my mouth. When our tongues touched, I gave in to everything I felt for him. The desire, the emotions, and the sorrow all culminated into that kiss.

I brushed my hands over his well-defined chest, his perfectly sculpted abs and finally over the hardening bulge in the front of his pants. I just grazed him before getting the letter out of my pocket. He maneuvered his tongue in such a way that almost made me drop the letter, but I was able to keep it together long enough to slip it in his pocket. Returning my hand to his bulge, I applied more pressure to the touch. He moaned into my mouth and his fingers flexed against my scalp. Spurred on by his reaction, I stroked him through his pants. With a sexy growl that started deep in his throat, he tore his lips away from mine and backed up.

His eyes flashed with unbridled lust and that look alone soaked my panties.

"We can't do this now," he rasped, letting his gaze drop to my lips. He adjusted himself. "As bad as I want you, I can't go to the production trailer with my dick hard."

The mental image of that was hilarious. I laughed and within seconds he joined me.

He ran his finger down the side of my face. "Once I check

in with them, I'll let you know if they plan on being here late. If they are working with the usual overnight crew, I want you to meet me at midnight. I want to show you my house. I want to make sure you know how I feel about you."

I stared into his grey eyes, my heart swelling with each of his words. I believed him. I believed every word he said. But that didn't make it any easier for me to be in the position that I was in.

"If you don't walk away now, I'm not going to be able to let you go," I whispered.

He chuckled to himself before dropping a kiss against my lips. "The feeling is mutual."

I stood under the romantic stone archway with ivy twisting up and around it and I watched him move further and further away from me. I looked toward the sky and tried to breathe through the feelings to make sure I was making the best decision for me.

By the time the first couple of women came out of the house, I was already sitting off on the far side of the patio, in my go-to nook.

A camera crew followed Ana and Tiffany as they had a conversation about Tori being a bully. They pretended to debate if they were going to tell Julian. Based on their conversation while I was trying to make a snack earlier in the day, they had already made their decision. When Tori came out, they changed the subject abruptly.

I rolled my eyes.

Samantha and Emma came out of the house and Samantha was actually smiling. When I'd left, she was sobbing so that was a positive. With Tori and her minions busy making derogatory comments about everyone and Emma and Samantha consumed with their conversation, the five of them didn't notice me at all.

*Which works out well because they won't know how long I've been gone or when I came back.*

Bailey strolled out onto the patio and she spotted me immediately. She didn't call attention to me as she went to get herself a drink. With her glass of wine filled to the brim, she made her way to me and sat down.

After a long gulp, she smiled at me. "Where have you been hiding?"

"I've been outside the whole time. That's a big glass."

"I bet." She winked and turned off her microphone. She pointed to mine and I nodded, indicating that it was off. "To put up with these bitches, I need it."

I couldn't do anything but laugh.

"Well during your hiatus, while you were 'outside,' you missed a lot." She could only use her one free hand to do an air quote. "Everyone turned on Leah because she was bragging about kissing Julian so Tori and her henchmen joined forces with Emma and Samantha and it was the most hilarious thing I'd ever seen. Leah is a bitch, but she's smart and Tiffany kept using words she clearly didn't know the definition of so it was really funny." She shook her head as she took another sip. "But when Mya got involved, my jaw dropped."

"What? Why did Mya get involved?"

"Probably because you weren't there to stop her from meeting with her handler."

I closed my eyes. "Oh God, what happened?"

"She let Leah bait her into an argument with Samantha. Of all people, Samantha!"

I laughed, nursing the champagne. I thought I wanted to be alone, but Bailey's story was helping calm my nerves.

"Anyway, your roomie goes off and gets in Samantha and Emma's faces. I mean she was playing the hot-headed fiery

Latina like a professional. I've taken acting classes so it didn't take me anytime to slip into the sexy, dumb blonde role. But she was in character, to the max."

"I wonder why she is acting like that."

Bailey pursed her lips. "The same reason I'm doing the dumb blonde routine." There was amusement in her blue eyes. "I respect that you didn't cave and you're still getting the guy. Being a stereotype is exhausting. Part of me wants to yell I graduated from an Ivy League School when some of the crew talk to me like I'm an idiot. But my producer told me that if I want to stay around, this is what I have to do. I imagine Mya was told something similar."

"Yeah, Jamie told us to play the part. We both said no."

"Well no worked for you. As confident as Ana and Leah both have been over the last couple of days, I think they know you are their main competition. Are you ready to admit there's something between you and our boyfriend yet or are we still keeping that a secret?"

I blinked innocently. "What kind of wine is that?"

Bailey laughed loudly. "Okay, okay. Well, just so you don't get blindsided by the news, Leah's kiss story sounded fake. She stuttered and fumbled her way through how he kissed her to the point that I don't think anyone was even listening to her story anymore. She said they made out for twenty minutes. But she was outside with him for ten." Bailey rolled her eyes. "Bitches."

Being reminded of that bit of information, no matter how fabricated, tore me up inside. The visual of Julian laughing with Leah, holding her in his arms, and kissing her was too much for me. The anger of a woman kissing my man mixed with the out of control feeling of not being able to do anything about it. And just to make me feel that much more out of my element, little fragments of jealousy shrapnel wedged into my spirit deeply. It was in that moment that I started to really freak out.

*The only thing I know for sure is how I feel about Julian and that this whole thing is killing me. So maybe it is time for me to go. Maybe this whole thing was to take me out of my comfort zone so I can get my shit together. Maybe I was so scared that I wouldn't pass the bar, I threw myself into the complete opposite direction so now I need to focus. Maybe—*

"...Earth to Zoe," Bailey sang, waving her hand in my face.

I blinked, I could feel the panic on my face.

She gave me a look. "No cocktail party. The Bracelet Ceremony is about to start."

I looked over and all of the women were gathering in the center of the patio.

"Turn your mic back on," I whispered as we made our way to the center of the patio. I hit my button as discreetly as possible.

Bailey hit hers, winked, and then seamlessly slipped back into her dumb blonde routine. "This wine was so good. It tasted like grapes!" She announced loudly, holding up her empty glass.

I rolled my eyes and couldn't help but smile at her.

"Hello ladies! Welcome to the Bracelet Ceremony," Bryce announced, smiling brightly. "Leah, you won the contest today so you automatically get to hold on for another week in hopes of becoming the one. Julian gave her the charm on their one-on-one today. So Leah, you can come on up." Once Leah stood on the other side of Bryce, he turned to Julian. "Now, Julian...the floor is yours."

"Again, it must be said, you all look especially beautiful tonight," Julian began. "You each bring something special to our interactions and I just want to acknowledge that." He took a deep breath as he picked up an elephant charm. "First up...

Zoe."

My heart pounded against my chest and I thought it might explode. With each step I took toward him, I felt my grip on my emotions slipping faster than my grip on reality.

"Zoe—"

"Can we talk for a minute?" I interrupted as quietly as possible even though the microphone still caught every word. I just didn't want the other women to hear me.

Julian's face froze and I could see him tense up. "Of course."

Even if the women didn't hear me, they knew something was up because they started murmuring.

With his hand on my lower back, Julian guided me into the mansion, through the foyer, and to the study.

"Can we have a second?" Julian barked as a camera crew member bumped into him as he tried to open the door for me.

They didn't say anything, but they allowed us to go into the room alone.

Julian slammed the door behind him and the force didn't allow the door to catch so it remained cracked. I was going to say something, but when I looked at Julian, the look on his face silenced me.

*I guess whatever happened when he went to the production trailer did not go well.*

"Dammit! We just need a fucking minute!" He unbuttoned his jacket and ran both hands through his hair. He looked at me, really looked at me, and I saw the moment that he knew something was wrong. His face transformed from irritation with the camera crew to confusion about why I needed to talk.

"You're shaking," he pointed out, rushing to me.

Putting his hands around my neck, he put his forehead

against mine and we just held each other's gaze. The electricity between us was palpable and I felt myself succumbing to my feelings. I knew what I had to do, but having him so close made it hard. Inhaling his scent, feeling his touch, and staring into his eyes, I was left powerless to my emotions. In general, I knew I had to be firm and do what was in my best interests. In actuality, I knew I would do just about anything Julian asked me to do.

*Which is part of the problem.*

I took a deep breath and channeled my mother. The words ended up tumbling out of my mouth. "I need to leave the competition tonight."

Although his hands still held my face steady, he moved his head back. "The competition? You need to leave the competition?" He spat the word competition out as if it tasted bad.

"Yes. And the way you say it is the way I feel about being a part of it. So I need to leave."

He chewed on his bottom lip as he stared at me. His eyes were filled with anger and hurt. "Are you serious?"

"Yes."

His jaw tightened and he brought his face within inches of mine. "Because of a kiss? Because I kissed someone else, you want to leave?"

It was more than that, but the less I had to admit on air, the better. "Yes."

"You know..." He glanced down at my microphone and then closed his eyes. He released his grasp on me and walked toward the book case letting out a deep roar. The silence that followed scared me more than his outburst.

It sounded as if the entire house stopped breathing.

"Julian."

He sighed and turned around. Lacing his fingers, he rested

his hands on the top of his head. His face was flushed, his jaw was set in a hard line and his eyes were reduced to slits. "I'm sorry I yelled," he uttered hoarsely. "I'm just so frustrated because I can't talk to you the way I want to talk to you." He scrubbed his face with his hands and then exhaled.

I closed the six foot gap between us. Running my hand down his jacket lapels, I peeked at him through my lashes. "Listen to what I'm saying. I can't stay because this situation is too much for me. It has nothing to do with you or how I feel about you. It's just too much for me."

"Okay," he said slowly. He refused to look me in the eyes as he continued. "I've said everything that I could to you. I've laid it out as much as I possibly can. And you still want to walk."

Pain lanced through my entire body because he was hurt and he still didn't understand. But of course, he didn't. Having the microphone on and having to be mindful of everything I was saying, made it difficult to express my feelings without making a fool of myself. "It's not that I want to leave. It's—"

"I get it. You don't have to explain."

I swallowed hard. "No, but I want to explain. It's just hard putting myself out there like that."

"I don't want to have this conversation anymore. You've made up your mind to leave; I can't do anything about it." His tone had no inflection and he still wouldn't look at me as he spoke.

I wrapped my arms around him, hugging him. I leaned back to make him look at me, but he wouldn't. "Julian, please."

"What do you want me to say, Zoe?" His jaw clenched. "I kissed Leah and apparently I'll be kissing other people over the next few days, weeks even, and you don't want to put yourself at risk of...I don't even know anymore." His chest rose and fell rapidly.

My eyes watered. I knew if he would just look at me, he would get what I was trying to say. It hurt me to see that I hurt him. I turned off my mic and then hit the power button on his battery pack when he muttered, "I should probably get back to the women who actually want to be here."

It felt like a slap in the face and I recoiled away from him. "What?" I couldn't breathe.

Finally, he looked at me. Grabbing me and pulling me back into him, I saw the hurt in his eyes and I was pretty sure he could see the hurt in mine. Against his chest, I could feel his heart racing.

"I shouldn't have said that. But I'm not going to beg you to stay, Zoe. If you don't see—"

"Stop," I murmured, shaking my head. "I just...it isn't...I..." I stammered my way through the beginning part of three different sentences before my eyes started to sting with tears. I quickly blinked them away.

Maintaining eye contact with him, I lost the ability to speak. Without the fear of the mic, I thought it would be easier, but it wasn't. My mouth opened and closed twice without a word escaping. We just stood there, breathing each other in. He searched my face and I searched his.

*I just need to say it. Firm and to the point.*

I placed my fingertips against his cheek. The contrast between his smooth skin and the prickliness of his stubble stimulated my nerve endings. I let the ends of my finger skate along his jawline and stop at his chin. My lips parted as I allowed my finger to move up and skim the curve of his mouth.

*I'm going to miss the things he would say...and do with this mouth.*

My heart fluttered, but I pushed past the nerves. "I'm

leaving because I can't handle watching you with other women. This thing between us is real. And I tried to deny how deeply I'm in this because it's only been a week. But the truth is, my feelings have gotten to the point where I can't just sit around and watch the man that...I can't be here, even if you're pretending with them. I..." Feelings I was trying to keep buried attempted to bubble up to the surface. I closed my eyes. It was hard for me to say because it was hard for me to believe. My voice broke. "I'm falling in love with you so I can't do this show anymore."

His eyebrows flew up in apparent surprise.

"Julian!" Robert Brady stormed into the room with a flurry of people and camera equipment with him.

Julian's eyes jerked from me to the door. His hands fell away from my body and moved toward Robert, trying to meet him before the crew could get settled. "We just need a few more minutes. Please."

"I have a show to do and you disappearing for an hour and now spending twenty minutes in the middle of my Bracelet Ceremony to focus on one woman. Did it make for a shocking moment when Zoe didn't accept the charm? Yes. But then you disappear for almost thirty minutes. So I'm paying the salary of over a hundred people, but it's possibly worth it because I'm getting good video and sound on this end, right? Wrong! It would be good TV if your microphones were on. But since you've turned them off, you are not only in breach of your contract, you're wasting my money and my time!"

Julian's eyes flashed angrily and I'd only seen that look on his face once—when he was blindsided by Lillian's visit. "Robert, now is not the time. I've taken your shit because this is your show and I'm doing the best I can. But I'm tired of you trying to hold that over my head. The contract is to do the show. I didn't guarantee anything beyond that."

"Your contract guarantees you do a dating show, not a relationship show. You date multiple women, not one," the series creator sneered, throwing his hands in the air. "Do you want another high profile lawsuit?"

Robert's snub was clearly directed at me and I felt awful. There were about twenty production crew members gathered in the study and the silence that followed was deafening.

*I don't just need to leave the show for me. Clearly, I need to leave the show for Julian too. I don't want to be the cause of anything bad happening to him. I don't want to hurt him. And I don't want to get hurt. I bared my soul to him and... Was he about to freak out when I told him I was falling in love with him? Oh my God...This whole thing is a mess.*

I backed away, my hand on the center of my belly as it twisted violently. Adrenaline was pumping through my veins and as I watched what was happening before me, I knew it was in the best interest of both of us for me to leave. I let my adrenaline push me in the direction of the door.

"You don't want to spend money on that, do you? Because I have enough money to keep you tied up in court for years." Robert's chest was puffed out and he was obviously trying to get in Julian's head. The room was silent for a second before he deflated. "We still have three more weeks of shooting and we can get along just fine. But don't waste my time or my money. Stick to the script."

Julian was a few inches taller than Robert and way more muscular so I could see why he wasn't intimidated by the smaller man. His eyes were trained on Robert and his voice was almost menacingly low as he warned, "We know what this is really about and I'm not going to tell you again. Your script is a suggestion. You're not going to make my decisions for me."

I'd heard enough. With the no one paying any attention to me, I snuck out of the room, out of the mansion, and out of the competition.

I quit.

# Chapter 15

I was dropped off at Sway Luxury Resort Hotel where I was expected to be holed up until *The One* finished airing. When I rushed out of the mansion hours before, I thought I was going to jump in the limo and be taken home.

Unfortunately, the limo driver called someone in production and they picked me up in a golf cart and whisked me down the long driveway. Twenty minutes later, a camera crew arrived on a cart.

Jamie hopped off of the back and brushed her short hair back into place. "Hi Zoe. We have to do one for the road." She turned and pointed to her lighting guy who flipped a switch and flooded me with artificial light. "That was quite the interruption back there. Why did you decide to break things off with Julian?"

"It wasn't like that," I answered honestly, looking around for my ride. "It's complicated."

"You and Julian seemed to get along really well so it was quite a shock when everyone learned that you were leaving."

"It's complicated."

"A lot of people are saying that Leah is the one to beat. What do you have to say to that?"

"No comment."

"If you had to pick someone for Julian, who would it be?"

I stared at Jamie for a long time, sadness coming over me quickly. *Me,* I thought, my heart sinking.

"I don't want to answer any more questions," I whispered, looking away from them. I took a couple of steps into the road.

"That's enough. We got what we need," Jamie ordered, walking over to me.

The cameraman put his camera down and loaded it back into the case.

"Zoe," Jamie put her hand on my elbow and I turned to her. "I know we got off to a rough start, but I'm glad you didn't take my advice. I was rooting for you."

My lips turned upward into a smile. "Thank you."

She stepped closer and lowered her voice. "Just between me and you, you had this in the bag. The reason Robert Brady is so pissed off is because everyone can see that Julian Winters is crazy about you."

After Jamie and the crew got up the driveway, a town car packed with my bags picked me up. An executive producer rode in the car with me and explained that for the next three weeks, I would be restricted to one floor of the hotel. The rooms were set up in a way to promote ultimate privacy to 'grieve the loss of the relationship.' But the common areas were open if we needed to talk to one another.

Although I had access to a television, no internet or phones were available to me. There was a community room with a full kitchen and fully stocked pantry, a small gym, laundry drop off, and a request bin for anything else. She explained that I had to attend the obligatory reunion special that aired the day after the live finale and that would be the next time I would get fresh air. Everything else she rattled off was exactly the same as the living conditions in the mansion.

I was shuffled into a private elevator and walked out into a well decorated hallway. The rooms were spaced out and allowed for a lot of privacy. I could hear a pin drop so I assumed I was alone. I made my way to my room, pulling my suitcases behind me.

After unpacking and taking a long, hot shower, I dropped into the king-sized bed as the adrenaline started to drain out of my system.

*It was fight or flight.*

When I was in the town car, I knew for sure my decision was fight. I was fighting for me and what I needed and I was fighting for things to be easier for Julian. But as I stretched across the bed, I worried my actions were more in line with flight than fight. I worried that I'd made the biggest mistake by walking away from Julian before we could finish our conversation. I justified leaving abruptly because he was going to be sued if I stayed around. But a small part of me felt like I left abruptly because I was scared of what his response to what I said would be.

*If he said he was falling in love with me, I wouldn't have left. I would've stayed and died a little each time I saw him with another woman. If he said he wasn't falling in love with me, I would've died...of embarrassment, mortification, and a broken heart. There's no win for me.*

Seeing that it was approaching ten o'clock, despite my better judgment, I got out of the bed and wandered into the living room. I flipped on the TV and with the remote in my hand I had a decision to make.

*Do I want to torture myself?*

I sighed, knowing the answer before I even asked the

question. Finding the channel that aired *The One,* I went into the small kitchenette area and grabbed a bottle of water and a bag of popcorn.

I made myself comfortable, but as soon as the theme music for *The One* started, I fidgeted. Everything about the situation was uncomfortable.

"How do people even watch this crap?" I muttered to myself as I moved around, unable to find a cozy spot on the couch.

When I heard the words 'last time on *The One*,' my stomach quivered. I watched with rapt attention as the highlights from Tuesday's episode flashed across the screen followed by a direct roll into a shot of all of us after the first Bracelet Ceremony. After I went upstairs, Tori and her cronies sat downstairs and talked shit about me.

"Oh, you bitches," I whispered.

I wasn't surprised because they had started prior to me leaving to go to my room. But I was surprised that Mya stood there and said nothing. The first ten minutes of the episode seemed pretty consistent with what happened. I was pleased with the way I looked on TV. I looked good, I handled myself well, and I didn't do anything to embarrass myself or my family.

Two weeks ago, that would've been enough. That was all I was expecting to get out of it. But I was ten minutes into the episode and I couldn't turn it off. I was mainly intrigued by the one-on-one conversations, especially with Julian, and situations that I only heard about after the fact, like the big blow up that happened on Saturday while I stayed in bed.

I cringed as I watched Tori, Ana, and Tiffany rip into Mya as Leah watched with a sinister smile. I laughed as I watched Bailey strut into the room, taking the heat off of Mya so she could escape upstairs. I stopped breathing for a second whcn Julian first came on the screen and then my heart went wild.

*Dammit.*

As the Sunday Trivia Date at Saul's Den replayed on the screen, I realized it was edited. Although it still caught Julian checking me out, it didn't show the frequency of our flirtation. But most notably, there was a moment in which Bailey's entire breast almost fell out and Julian and I looked at each other at the same time. It was doctored to look like he was staring at Leah and having a moment with her.

*How do they get off stealing my moment with Julian and giving it to Leah because she couldn't generate her own?*

My anger faded away as they captured the two-on-one date. The editing department did a good job of making it seem as though Julian split his attention between Bailey and I equally. Remembering the moment, I pulled my knees up to my chest and gazed at the TV like a lovesick puppy.

*I miss him.*

The after the date interview with Bailey was hilarious. The after the date interview with me caught me by surprise. I thought I was playing it cool when I answered the question about the connection between me and Julian. My voice was steady, but I might as well have had hearts in my eyes and a damn 'I love Julian' t-shirt on my body.

I dropped my head into my hands as I groaned. My head snapped up quickly when I heard Julian's voice.

"I had a really good time tonight. Bailey is pretty, sweet, and fun to be around. Zoe is..."

He smiled into the camera and he appeared to get lost in his thoughts.

*"Zoe is special. She's beautiful, intelligent, funny, and deep. I love the way she thinks. She's..."*

He nodded, biting his bottom lip.

*"She's a good one. She's a keeper."*

He stammered as he corrected himself, widening his eyes.

*"They—they are keepers. Both of them."*

The rest of the episode encompassed a fight I didn't know about between Tori and Emma, a montage of Bailey dancing in her bikini, and the group date at the recording studio. Although I had no doubt that the rest of America was rolling their eyes with me as the screen showed Ana's panic attack. She was gasping for air and the moment Julian picked her up to carry her out of the bathroom, she was breathing just fine.

During the playing of our songs, the camera caught Julian and I staring at one another. But when he winked at me, they zoomed in on a smiling Bailey. I noticed a lot of the moments Julian shared with me from across the room were edited to appear as though he was looking at other women.

The show only spent five minutes on the awkwardly hilarious two-on-one date with Samantha and Emma. It was funny because it just showed time lapsing as Emma talked. It kept cutting to Julian and Samantha who were just sitting there looking bored not saying a word.

Even though the two-on-one date happened after the Bracelet Ceremony, the date was shown first. The two-hour episode ended with the Bracelet Ceremony and I watched Julian's face. Maybe I was biased, but I didn't think he looked at anyone the way he looked at me.

As the ending credits rolled and outtake clips played, I saw me and Julian at the kitchen table staring at one another. My heart clenched and even when they moved on to other clips, I was still thinking about Julian. Not that I'd ever really stopped, but seeing his face made me wish I was able to redo the last six hours.

I didn't know what I would do differently, but I knew the heartache that had started to set in was threatening to make me cry. I shouldn't have watched, but I couldn't help myself. When it said tune in on Tuesday for the next episode of *The One*, I knew I would.

I turned off the television and then dragged myself to bed. I was ready to feel the hurt and disappointment that I felt after Tate. But it didn't come. Instead, I felt hollow and completely empty. Tate wanted to be free so he could date around with new women that success brought him. Julian wanted to be with me but he was obligated to date around with new women due to his contract. I didn't expect Tate to do what he did and even though I did expect Julian to date around, I didn't expect to catch feelings for him. With Tate I felt hurt and disappointment and after it was over, I didn't miss him. With Julian I felt loss and emptiness and a complete denial that it was over.

*This is for the best. At the end of the day, this is for the best.*

I had to remind myself that it was for the best when I woke up the very next morning, but without any remnants of adrenaline in my system, it was harder to believe. I hardly left the bedroom for the next two days. Friday and Saturday were a blur of waking up, wallowing in my feelings, showering, continued wallowing in bed, and then restless sleep. I read and reread Julian's poem while alternating between crying and resisting the urge to cry. I didn't leave my suite at all. On Sunday, I at least sat in the living room. I tried reading my book of Pablo Neruda poetry, but when I got to the poem, *Absence*, I broke down and cried. I was emotional partly because of the beauty of the poem, but mostly because that poem was what was written on the note I snuck into Julian's pocket.

*Is it normal or healthy to miss someone this much after such a short period of time? Is it normal to fall in love with someone in such a short period of time? The One is not normal. I don't know what this show did to me, but this is not normal.*

On Monday, I had the energy to venture out of my suite. Not that I had the ability to go far being restricted to one floor, but it was a change of pace. I went to restock my kitchenette with some goodies and I ran into Nicole in the lounge area. She told me that Samantha had been sent home the night I left and that someone else had moved into the suites on Saturday night, but she didn't know who.

I asked about the first two women and she said that only top ten went to the suites.

We talked for a while and we figured out that the layout of the place and the privacy of the rooms were probably set up to give everyone time to grieve the breakup. I told her I was still wanting alone time, but we made plans to watch the next episode of *The One* together in the lounge.

When Tuesday morning came, I couldn't think about anything else except watching the show. Based on where Thursday's episode ended, I knew the upcoming episode was the one where I left. Just thinking about it made me want to reconsider watching it with someone else. I knew I was going to get emotional.

Tuesday late afternoon, I decided that watching it with someone else was going to force me to keep it together and really watch the episode.

Tuesday, with seven minutes left until nine o'clock, I paced back and forth in my living room in just my leggings and a t-shirt. I shook my arms at my sides.

"Okay, I can do this. I can do this," I mumbled under my breath as I opened the door and headed to the lounge.

"Hey!" Nicole chirped, waving me over to the couch. She looked comfortable in a pair of pajamas. "I thought you had changed your mind."

"Hi." I gave her a tight smile. "I'm here."

I grabbed a bottle of water and sat on the other end of the couch.

"I didn't want to say anything, but I'm dying to know...how are you here?"

"It was for the best." I took a sip of water before changing the subject. "And I like your hair."

Although I wanted to shift the focus away from me, I really did like her hair. Nicole's curly, reddish brown hair was braided and it looked cute on her.

"Thank you," she replied. She looked like she wanted to say more, but the theme music for *The One* started. "It's starting!"

When I heard the words 'last time on *The One*,' I sucked in a deep breath. We watched with rapt attention as the highlights from Thursday's episode flashed across the screen followed by an argument.

"Tori really is a bitch," Nicole stated from the other end of the couch.

Without looking over at her, I nodded. "She really is."

Tori was onscreen talking to the cameraman about how

hard it was to be in the house with a target on her back because everyone was jealous of her.

"Is she serious?" Nicole commented with a sarcastic tone.

I couldn't do anything but shake my head.

The next scene was an argument brewing between Tori and Ana while they were by the pool. Tori had said something that the camera didn't catch and instead of laughing like she ordinarily would do, Ana got mad. Ana called Tori a bitch and Tori called Ana a string of derogatory words that the network bleeped out. Tiffany stood between them looking shocked. Emma and Samantha walked out to see what was happening, followed by Leah and Bailey.

"Where were you?" Nicole asked.

"I was upstairs reading," I answered, the light flutter of butterflies tickled my belly as I thought about how I was actually upstairs in bed reliving the best night of my life.

After the commercial break, all of the contestants were sitting in the living room talking. My eyes always found my image whenever I was on screen. It amused me that it was so clear that I was not having a good time unless Julian was around.

"Oh my God!" Nicole screeched as soon as Lillian appeared on screen. "I would die!"

Watching Lillian with each of the women was interesting because the edited version of Lillian was coming off as sweet. She was saying all of the right things to pretend to be supportive of Julian being in a relationship with someone who wasn't her. I was beginning to think that they were going to skip her sit down with me to protect her image when my face flashed on the screen.

Lillian asked me if I loved Julian and the camera zoomed in on me and I finally saw what Lillian saw. My heart pounded in my chest. I didn't know how to feel about my truth being exposed on national television. Even as I turned the question back around on her, it was so clear that I was in love.

It went to commercial break soon after and I felt Nicole staring at me.

"Wow."

I didn't even want to address her 'wow' so I didn't respond, hoping she would move on. But she didn't. I just continued to feel her eyes boring into the side of my head. After an entire commercial ended, I sighed and turned toward her.

"Wow! I mean, it's crazy, but I love it. It makes so much sense," she squealed, putting her hands to her chest. "I didn't even think that happened in real life!"

"You didn't think what happened?"

"Love at first sight!"

"Come on, now." I rolled my eyes. "Stop."

She started to say something, but the commercial break ended. "This isn't over," she giggled.

The conversations with Julian were cut short, but the one with Julian and Leah was the most riveting.

"So I met your ex-girlfriend. She's a peach," Leah joked as she crossed and uncrossed her legs in short shorts.

*"I heard,"* Julian replied dryly.

*"You were clearly not pleased that she was here."*

*"Clearly."*

*"Well I just want you to know that I'm here for you if you want to talk about it. I'm a great listener."*

Julian smiled. *"Thanks. But I don't want to talk about her.*

*How are you?"*

*"I'm doing quite well actually. Thank you for asking. I've been trying to stay out of the fray."*

*Julian let out a sexy little laugh. "The fray? I don't think I've heard someone your age say 'the fray' before."*

*Leah giggled. "Well, maybe you should hang around me a little more and I'll expand your language."*

*"Oh my language needs to be expanded? By you?"*

*Leah shrugged. "You'd be surprised by what I could teach you." She gasped, covering her face. "I just heard how that sounded!"*

*He smirked. "You knew how that sounded when you said it."*

*"I'll never tell."*

The flirty banter bothered me, causing a pit in my stomach. But when Leah asked Julian if she could walk him out, my skin started to crawl because I knew what was coming. I wanted to leave. I wanted to head back into my room. But I knew I would obsess about it even more if I didn't see it.

Julian and Leah hugged. I knew the kiss was coming because he brushed the hair off of her shoulders while she held on to him. I tried to control my breathing so I wouldn't react. But when the camera zoomed in on his lips brushing against hers, a sound escaped my mouth.

"Are you okay?" Nicole asked.

I nodded, my eyes glued to the TV.

As they said their goodbyes, I watched Julian's eyes to see

if he looked at her the same way he looked at me. But with my eyes beginning to water, I couldn't really tell.

The episode moved along as I remembered it. Nicole gasped and made comments, but I couldn't stop thinking about the kiss. Much like I was unable to stop thinking about the kiss while on that abandoned zoo group date. A close up of my face on screen made me realize that it was highly likely that I had the same expression on my face as I watched it.

During the one-on-one with Leah, Julian was his charming self. There was an ease and comfortability between Julian and Leah and it bothered me. I didn't feel like he looked at her the way he looked at me, but there was definitely something there. It rolled to a commercial break and I regretted not watching the show alone in my room.

Nicole turned her entire body to face me. "Okay so...that took a turn I didn't see coming."

"That's reality TV for you."

The awkward silence filled the room and even though *The One* was torturing me, I was grateful when it came back on. Until I saw images of the cocktail party and the announcement that Julian had pushed it back. While the camera caught snippets of women speculating what was going on, I zoned out, remembering our conversation under the stone archway wrapped in ivy. And my heart rate increased.

Everything slowed down when the Bracelet Ceremony began. I watched the surprise and the hurt play out in Julian's face. I watched the giggles and laughter of a few of the women behind me. But what really blew my mind was that part of the conversation we had in the study was captured.

"Was the camera outside of the room or something?" Nicole asked as we watched the scene play out through a crack in the door.

I nodded, my eyes watering. "Yeah," I whispered.

Although the camera only caught me as I walked across the room to Julian, the audio prior to me turning our microphones off was clear.

"You didn't want to be in the competition anymore because you love him."

I didn't answer, but I closed my eyes and let my head fall back. The scene ended with Julian saying, "You've made up your mind to leave; I can't do anything about it" and was immediately followed up with the conversation with me at the end of the driveway.

*So all of that other stuff with Robert Brady was cut out?*

I ran my hand down my face a couple of times and sighed. Part of one episode and watching *The One* was already stressing me out.

The Bracelet Ceremony began and although Julian smiled, his eyes looked sad. He seemed hurt and that hurt me.

After Samantha was sent home, the ending credits rolled and I felt like I'd been through the ringer.

"So...are you okay?"

I stood up. "I think I'm going to head to bed."

Nicole stared at me in disbelief.

Lifting my eyebrows, I gave her a tight smile. "Okay, have a goodnight."

She let her head drop back in irritation before she jumped up. "Wait, please! I've been here for a week without anyone to talk to. We can't talk to anyone outside of each other. We are trapped on this floor for another few weeks. Can we please talk for a while? I need adult interaction right now. And I understand if you don't want to tell me everything because it's just a friendship of convenience, but dammit Zoe, can you please just talk to me? I'm going out of my mind."

Although I knew I wasn't going to confide my entire life story to Nicole, I liked her and she had a really good point. I couldn't imagine how I would've felt if I was here and didn't see or talk to anyone for days on end.

I gave her a small smile. "You're right. But tonight was a lot to take in. Do you mind if we talk for a few minutes and then we can talk for longer tomorrow?"

"That's fine. I'll take anything I can get," Nicole conceded, sitting back down on the couch.

I sighed. "I know you want to ask so let's get it out of the way."

"You're in love with Julian?"

*Well damn... She just jumped right to it, didn't she?*

I pursed my lips. "Next question."

Nicole laughed. "Did you leave because of Leah?"

I sighed, choosing my words carefully. "It wasn't necessarily because of Leah. It was because of how I was feeling."

"Do you regret it?"

I swallowed hard. "Sometimes."

She reached over and squeezed my hand. "For what it's worth, the way you two looked at each other, no one else stood a chance."

I smiled. I hated to admit it, but after seeing whatever was happening between Leah and Julian, hearing that made me a little better.

"I liked Julian." Nicole smiled sweetly. "I didn't get a chance to really know him or anything, but I liked what I knew about him. But the night I left, I wasn't really sad about it. I get a thousand dollars, a month long vacation from life, and I met some cool people. I wouldn't want to be in a relationship with someone who clearly loves someone else."

"Me either."

"Whoever he ends up with at the end will always be competing with you."

"You're pretty good at this pep talk thing."

"I just don't want you to lock yourself in your room for another four days and then I won't have anyone to talk to anymore!"

# Chapter 16

I had been in the suites for over a week and as I looked around the marble and white community room, I smirked to myself.

*Two weeks ago, in the mansion, this would've never happened.*

"Please pass the pepperoni, Zoe," Tiffany asked, reaching her hand out as I passed the pizza box to her.

Sitting at the enormous conference room table, I looked around at the other women eating pizza. Nicole, Samantha, and Tiffany, who was the mystery contestant that came in on Saturday night, were sitting at the table with me, eating pizza and playing cards until *The One* came on. Maybe it was the cabin fever, but away from Tori, Tiffany was actually tolerable. I wasn't going to exchange phone numbers with her, but I also didn't feel the urge to punch her in the face.

*So that's a win.*

After Nicole and I watched *The One* together on Tuesday, we decided to make a thing of it. Samantha was over her "breakup" by Thursday's episode and Tiffany heard the three of us when she went to get ice so she joined in.

"It's about to come on! The brownies are ready. Are you coming?" Emma called out from the kitchen area. She had arrived on Wednesday night, completely unbothered by her "breakup."

The five of us, all wearing pajamas, spread out over the lounge area with a glass of wine as we watched Thursday night's episode of *The One.*

It had been a week of me being off of the show and I couldn't stop thinking about Julian. It seemed to get worse with each day. I read his poem daily. I used the notebook he gave me to write poems, thoughts and quotes that made me think of him. The recurrent theme that seemed to work its way into every thought was that maybe walking away only pushed him into Leah's arms.

The first moment I saw Julian's face my heart skipped a beat. He had an interview with the camera man and he said all of the right things about the women of the house, but I still saw a hint of sadness in his eyes. My heart yearned for him.

He was looking absolutely incredible as he took the women on the murder mystery date. The group date seemed a little more intimate with only six women left in the competition. They were dressed formally, sitting around a table for seven. Conversations ensued among all of them, but Leah was sitting next to Julian. I couldn't help but notice the amount of time they spent talking.

Tiffany started laughing and as soon as it cut to a commercial break. "The murder mystery was about a woman possibly killing her secret boyfriend and when she was accused of killing him, she said something about how she loved him in secret. Julian started talking about some poem and no one knew what he was talking about. Leah pretended she did and he asked her more about it and she had to admit that she was confused."

We all laughed, but on the inside I died a little.

*Sonnet XVII by Pablo Neruda. Julian is speaking directly to my heart right now.*

I didn't talk much during the episode. Tiffany and Emma spoke the most and Nicole and Samantha were hanging on to their every word. Every commercial break, I just stared at the TV with my heart throbbing. I wanted more Julian.

We watched as the women got into an argument while Julian was on the dance floor with Mya. Seeing Mya as the over-the-top flirty, sex kitten was odd, but fascinating. She was all over Julian, but from his expression, he was not interested in her. I wanted to avert my eyes when they kissed for the first time, but I couldn't. He was sweet and flirtatious, both before and after they kissed. But there was no spark between them.

*Or is that just wishful thinking on my part?*

It was odd watching an episode I wasn't part of because I didn't know the backstory. Everything that Nicole, Samantha and I weren't privy to, Tiffany and Emma were able to elaborate on. There were questions that I wanted to ask but didn't because as friendly as we had all been that day, I didn't have any desire to confide in them.

"Okay, so this is when I thought I really had a shot," Tiffany pointed out when the image of Julian asking her to dance flashed on the screen.

"I never thought I had a shot. That's why I wasn't upset about it," Emma added with a shrug. "Honestly, I didn't want him. It wouldn't have worked out."

"What?" Nicole, Tiffany, and I reacted at the same time.

"Well," Emma started, scooting to the edge of her seat. "I want—"

"Wait, guys, look! This is my kiss," Tiffany interrupted. "Watch how it goes from romantic to awkward in no time!"

The idea of watching Julian kiss yet another woman rubbed me the wrong way; however, seeing as though Tiffany was sitting in the same room as I was, I knew it didn't mean anything.

Julian asked Tiffany to take a walk with him while the judges were deciding which table most accurately solved the murder mystery. On screen, Tiffany wore a red dress that hadn't been really showcased until she and Julian were walking to the balcony. It was fire engine red and fit her body like a glove. Her red hair was piled on top of her head and she truly looked the best I'd ever seen her.

"I loved that dress," Tiffany noted, gazing at the television.

Julian and Tiffany conversed while they were standing on a balcony overlooking the ocean. A light wind seemed to whip at their clothing and Julian put his arms around her to keep her warm. She stared at him, dreamily. After a brief exchange that I couldn't really hear because I was focused on Julian's profile, they kissed.

The kiss looked soft and sweet. Julian pulled away and Tiffany moved in for the kill. She lunged at his mouth with hers and kissed him hard. He returned the kiss briefly, before gently pushing her away. The next scene cut to the women at the table. They were discussing how bad Tiffany's breath was after eating the garlic knots.

Tiffany dropped her head into her hands. "And no one told me until later that night."

"Not even your best friend Tori?" Emma's voice was dripping in sarcasm.

Tiffany snorted. "Not even my best friend Tori." She looked over at us. "One-on-one, Tori really is a sweet person. I don't know what it is about groups that make her turn into a bit of a bitch, but she was so different when it was just the two of us."

The five of us watched as Julian and Tiffany made it back to the table. Tiffany was glowing as her smile grew twice as wide. Julian went straight for his beverage and gulped it down.

"Oh they didn't even show when he kissed me!" Emma complained when the screen filled with images of them leaving as a group. As the commercial break started, she added, "The kiss was nice."

"Finish telling us why you didn't want Julian, who is arguably the sexiest man alive, to pick you?" Samantha asked. She tucked her hair behind her ear and stared at Emma as if she had two heads.

"No, it's not that I wouldn't have wanted Julian to pick me. Did you see his ass? Of course I would've liked him to pick me. But he had already picked who he wanted. I want a man who looks at me like I'm his world. I don't just want someone who tells me I'm special. I want someone who looks at me like I'm special. He didn't look at me like that." Emma pulled her legs up onto the loveseat she was sitting on. "I'll be thirty at the end of next month and I know what I want. So, I'm not saying that Julian and I couldn't have grown into loving one another. But when you see the guy you're dating look at someone else in that special way, you already know who he wants. It's just a matter of accepting it."

Samantha stuck out her tongue at me. "I saw him look at Zoe like that too and I still told myself I had a chance." She smiled. "But you're absolutely right, Emma."

"Thank God someone brought it up!" Tiffany flipped around from her chair closest to the TV, her red hair flying around her shoulders. "I didn't know what the deal was here and we were all getting along so I didn't want to rock the boat."

Everyone was staring at me. I looked around the room uncomfortably. "I don't know what to tell you."

"Tell us what happened between you and Julian," Emma insisted. "I know it had to be something big because you left the show. The producer I worked with told me that Julian got into a big fight for Zoe, but then he said he'd already said too much and wouldn't tell me anything else."

"Holy crap! A fight?" Samantha squeaked, putting her hands to her cheeks. "Did you know this?"

"Please spill," Nicole begged, her hands clasped together in front of her. "You did not say anything about a fight!"

I rubbed my eyes and groaned. "I don't know what to say. I really don't. It's hard to explain even if I wanted to."

"Just tell me this... did you two know each other before the show?"

"No!" I shook my head profusely. "Someone else asked me that, too. We just really clicked when we met each other. We had a really good series of conversation and then..." My sentence trailed off and I shrugged. I felt my lips curling up on the ends and even though I tried to stop it, talking about Julian never failed to make me either extremely happy or extremely sad. "I will say that whatever it was between us felt real to me."

"Real like you like him a lot or real like you love him?" Tiffany inquired, eyebrows sitting in the middle of her forehead.

I glanced at Nicole to see if she had anything to do with the line of questioning. She hadn't said anything about me loving Julian after I avoided her question on Tuesday. She frowned, discreetly shaking her head.

My heart hammered in my chest at the idea of saying how I felt out loud to people who weren't Koko. I didn't owe them an explanation so I wasn't required to tell them anything. But the fact that they saw what I saw only strengthened my resolve that what Julian and I had was real.

*But that's the thing, my heart and my mind are in a constant battle. In my heart, from the depths of it, I know how I feel. I know how I felt with Julian. And even if the words weren't enough, I know how he looked at me. But at the same time, as the practical, law-minded, daughter of Elise Jordan, I don't believe in fairytales or love at first sight...or taking risks where the odds aren't in my favor. Even if a little part of me thought that the house, the environment, the competition, exasperated my feelings, the fact that they hadn't gone away should tell me something. Although, technically, I am still in the same boat as I was in the mansion, where I am trapped in living quarters with women who dated the man I have feelings for.*

"...on the spot! Just tell us why you left," Emma offered.

I missed the entire beginning of her question.

*You know what? Fuck it. I'll just tell the truth. What will it hurt? Who will know? They can't talk to anyone just like I can't talk to anyone.*

"It was real. I felt it. He felt it," I answered, looking at the television as Julian's face flooded the screen as *The One* came back on.

"So why did you leave?" Samantha asked. "He was so hurt. I mean really upset."

"Samantha!" Emma cut her off sharply. She turned her face toward me. "It was—"

"No, finish," I interjected, looking between the two of them.

They were both silent so Tiffany jumped in. "Fine, I'll say it. Julian was pissed. He apparently didn't know you left for good until they started taking your luggage out. And then he went off. The Bracelet Ceremony started at..." she looked at Emma and then Samantha hoping they'd fill in. They didn't so she continued, "I don't know how late it got started, but it was late. He looked hurt. I mean, I didn't see him cry, but there were whispers that there were tears involved. I'm not really into men that cry, but I'd make an exception for those grey eyes."

"I love a sensitive man!" Nicole spoke up.

"See, what I loved about his reaction was that Julian wasn't just upset for no reason. He was upset because the one got away. The one. That's what I'm looking for. Someone who fights for me and cries for me," Emma sighed, giving me a swoony smile. "I don't know why you left Zoe, but I hope it was a damn good reason."

I stared at the TV, rooted to my seat.

*I fell in love with him. That's the beginning and the end of it. I left because I fell in love with him. I left because the idea of seeing him with other women was too much for me. I left because if he wants me like he says he does, we will be together. He said that at the end of this, I am who he will be taking home. So in a couple weeks, he'll pick Bailey and then no one will get hurt and she will get her shot at fame when they "breakup" and we will be together. That's what he said he wants to happen. Well that's what he said before I left abruptly without a real goodbye.*

"I know he didn't want me to leave the show." My voice came out in a hushed tone. Someone turned down the TV volume to hear me better. "But if I had to witness him kiss or touch or flirt or talk to any of you first-hand, a piece of my heart would break each time. And he was contractually obligated to date each of us so it was bound to happen."

I didn't mention the way Robert Brady pretty much forbade Julian from being with me.

"Do you think—crap! Next commercial break we are all over this," Emma exclaimed as she lifted the remote higher and turned the volume back up.

We watched as Julian and Leah sat down on the bench under the archway wrapped in ivy. They talked about places they'd traveled. As they discussed what they loved about different cities and Julian talked about his time in Italy, Leah leaned forward and kissed him. At first, Julian looked taken aback, but then his body relaxed. I swallowed hard. The kiss was different than the kisses he'd shared with other contestants. The other kisses seemed like work, seemed like he was doing what he had to do. That kiss with Leah seemed like pleasure.

My heart plummeted and my stomach twisted into knots. It felt like my insides had attempted to escape my body. The knife I felt wasn't necessarily in my back, but more so straight through the chest.

*I need to stop watching this show.*

"The music is making this seem way more romantic than it is," Nicole pointed out, obviously trying to lessen the blow.

No one else said anything as we watched Julian and Leah share a long kiss. When they pulled apart, the camera focused on their mouths only. She smiled and he smiled back. Although it didn't show their eyes, I figured they were staring romantically at one another.

*Probably the same way he would stare at me when we'd kiss.*

I tried not to freak out. Every curse word that tried to bubble from my mouth, I swallowed back down. As the toilet paper commercial's dancing puppy appeared, I felt vulnerable and exposed. But mostly, I was embarrassed. If I would've waited until the end of the show to respond to their questions, I wouldn't have felt so humiliated by Julian's betrayal. I would've felt devastated internally. But I wouldn't have felt so much like a stereotype externally.

*This is why I don't want to keep talking about Julian with them. The environment made me feel like what we had was special, but I've been gone a week and he's already moved on. And actually, this wasn't even taped tonight, so he must have moved on a few days ago!*

As the final moments of the show featured Tiffany's exit, everyone started turning toward me.

"I'm going to head to bed," I announced, untucking my legs from under me and attempting to get off of the comfortable couch.

"Hey, wait," Nicole said, reaching out for me. "Are you okay?"

I nodded, avoiding eye contact with everyone. "Yeah."

Nicole rose to her feet, looking at me. "Leah is sneaky and manipulative."

"Exactly, Julian isn't going to fall for her or her bullshit," Tiffany chimed in, kicking her feet in the air. "Do you know what Julian said to me before I got into the limo? After the conversation that they just showed, he asked the cameras to go away and he turned off our mics and told me that if I wanted my ex-boyfriend back, I should fight for him."

"What?" Samantha asked dreamily, her eyebrows pulling together curiously. "I love stuff like this! Start at the beginning."

Tiffany glanced at Samantha, putting her pointer finger up. "One second." She looked back at me. "The morning I left, Tori, Ana, and I were drinking and having a conversation that Leah walked in on. We had been talking about a lot of personal stuff since the cameras weren't around. When Julian said the thing about my ex, I asked him where he got that from. He said from Leah. So, FYI, Leah may have been gossiping to Julian about all of you bitches."

"Julian is not going to fall for a girl who gossips and is so obviously only interested in herself," Nicole joined in. "He's not."

"She looks just like his ex," Samantha said. "If he still wanted to be with his ex, he would be with his ex. He wouldn't be with that carbon copy." She looked around at us. "Right?"

"Right!" Nicole stared at me. "Don't worry about that kiss. You and Julian kissed on the first night and it was way hotter than that."

"It's fine. I'm fine," I lied, my voice cracking as I said it. I flashed them all a smile. "I'm just going to head to bed. It's late. I'll see you all in the morning. Goodnight!"

Nicole clearly didn't believe me, but she smiled anyway. "Goodnight, Zoe. I'm around if you need me."

When she said that, it made my eyes sting. I knew I needed to leave immediately.

"Goodnight!" Everyone called out happily as I waved heading out of the common area.

*Julian and Leah?*

My heart was racing. It hurt. It hurt so bad that I wanted to cry. The only thing that was keeping me from crying was the fact that I hadn't made it to my room yet. I knew they were trying to make me feel better, but I saw the way Julian relaxed into that kiss. It was almost as if he gave in to her while simultaneously giving up on us.

I'd gotten all the way down to my room when I remembered that I needed to grab a few more bottles of water. Turning around, I made my way back toward the common area when I heard Emma's voice.

"Something changed with Julian after Zoe left. It was like he had checked out. The way he looked at her, he didn't look at Leah like that. But—"

I stopped in my tracks. *Does she know something?*

"I know! It was irritating while we were on the show because I felt like I wasn't getting my fair shot. But no longer being in that environment, I think it's really sweet," Samantha interjected thoughtfully.

"But I think Zoe broke him or something and maybe Leah wore him down. It wasn't like it was with Zoe, but there was something happening between Julian and Leah. I think he might be gravitating toward her because of Zoe leaving. I don't think he likes Leah like that or anything, but I think he's trying to deal with the whole being dumped on TV thing," Emma continued.

"Do you think the thing between them is love or lust?" Tiffany asked, her voice full of wonder. She sounded legitimately curious. "I've never known anyone to fall in love at first sight."

"Love, definitely," Nicole answered quickly. "But more than that, I don't think it's any of our business to speculate what it is. Whatever it was, she is still clearly affected by it and from what you say, so is he. And we all saw what it was like when they were together. You can't deny that."

"That's true."

"I know the difference between love and lust," I said, walking into the kitchen area. I grabbed a couple of bottles of water while they sat in stunned silence. When I turned to walk out, I looked at them. "It's not lust."

I walked out, temporarily satiated by shutting that conversation they were having behind my back down. But with each step to my suite, I kept thinking about what Emma said.

*I broke him and drove him to Leah.*

I'd unlocked my door and was about to walk in my room when the elevator dinged. Curiosity got the best of me as I held on to the door handle waiting to see who was getting off of the elevator.

*Please be Leah. Please be Leah. Please be Leah.*

I lct out the breath I didn't know I was holding as I looked at the blonde woman dragging two huge suitcases. Dropping them with a bang, she flashed her bright blue eyes my way and smirked.

"Oh, look, it's the bitch who ruined Julian Winters," Tori sneered.

"And he still didn't want you so what does that tell you?" I returned, my lip curling in disgust.

I walked into my room, slamming the door behind me. I made a beeline for my suitcase. Opening the front flap, I pulled out the Manilla envelope with my contract for *The One* inside.

*I need to get out of here.*

# Chapter 17

"I am going crazy," Mya complained. "How did you guys manage to do this twice a week? I barely made it through Tuesday's episode. Tonight, I'm going to be thinking, well next week is me."

"Stop complaining! You got sent home after an all-expenses paid trip to Hawaii. I got sent home after dive bar trivia," Nicole scoffed, rolling her eyes.

As soon as Mya and I crossed paths, she ran up to me and threw her arms around me. We apologized to each other and it was like it never even happened. She admitted that she was a little envious of the connection that I had with Julian. I admitted that I didn't have the authority to dictate how she acted. She apologized for hoping I'd go home and verbalizing that on camera. I apologized for insinuating that she was a sellout for following Jamie's advice with no regard to the stereotype it would convey. From that moment on, when I felt like company, Nicole, Mya and I were inseparable.

*Not that it was difficult to be inseparable on one floor of the hotel, but it's the sentiment that counts.*

I stood in the kitchen eating a yogurt, listening to Nicole drill Mya for information about her last few days in Maui.

*If Tuesday's episode was when Emma was sent home, tonight's episode has to be when Tori is being let go.*

A smile played on my lips.

Tori had been a pain in everyone's ass since the moment she arrived at Sway's Luxury Resort Hotel.

*It has been the longest seven day stretch of my life...and I'd been in hotel captivity for two weeks!*

Unlike in the house, there was no big dramatic arguments or falling outs. Most of the women didn't like Tori so Tori stayed to herself in her room. Even when she would come out, she didn't stay long. Tiffany would split her time, but mostly, she would hang out with Tori.

Although Tori wasn't as argumentative as she was in the house, she was still a bitch. Nicole and I acted as if she didn't exist and countered her bitchiness with sarcasm and sass. Emma and Samantha steered clear of her altogether. And when Mya was cut on Monday in Hawaii, right before the home visit, she also acted as if Tori didn't exist. But since we all were forced into this odd bonding experience, we all, to a certain extent, had become family.

*We're just really, really estranged from one of the members of the family.*

"Why are you eating yogurt when I put cookies in the oven?" Tiffany said as she came into the common space.

I finished licking the spoon. "Because I wanted yogurt. And I'll probably have a cookie, too."

"Stress eating is not going to solve your problems," Tori replied strolling into the kitchen with her workout gear on. "It may even add unnecessary weight to that already rotund ass of yours."

"If it becomes a problem, I'll just get the number for your plastic surgeon," I replied gesturing to her surgically enhanced breasts as I threw away my empty cup of yogurt.

"But good use of your vocabulary words, Tori," Mya chimed in, winking at me.

Those were the first words that Mya spoke to Tori since she'd arrived and everyone in the kitchen snickered.

Tori rolled her eyes. "Whatever. Are we going to watch *The One* tonight or not?"

Mya lifted her cup to me and I lifted my bottle of water back at her.

Nicole, Mya, Tiffany, Tori, Emma, Samantha, and I sat down in front of the TV and watched as Tori began the episode being the biggest bitch that ever lived. She wasn't aware of it at the time, but the scene kept flipping back and forth between Julian watching her try to work with other people and cursing them out. It was probably funny to a large part of the audience to see Tori being outrageous, but I kept looking from the TV to Tori's face and even she cringed.

Tori gave us insight on different things throughout the episode and it was interesting. She explained how her producer told her that everyone had a role to play and to think about all of the true female stars of reality TV. She started listing the most well-known stars from shows that feature wives of the housewife variety and other dysfunctional relationship shows and she was right, they were all known for being the biggest bitch of the cast. She told us that she'd always had a reputation for being a bitch, but watching the scenes of her yelling at people on the salsa date was hard.

"I'm a bitch, but not, like, a mega-bitch," she explained, almost apologetically.

"Wait, was that an apology for the things you said at Salsa House? Because that shit wasn't right," Mya spoke up.

"What did she say?" Nicole asked, looking between the two of them.

"I was telling Leah and Bailey about my abuela and I told them this joke in Spanish that she loves to tell. And Tori started mocking my accent," Mya answered, quirking her eyebrow.

My eyes widened. "You talked shit about her grandmother?"

"I'm sorry about that. I really am," Tori apologized to Mya. She actually looked sincere as she glanced around the room. "I said I was sorry that night, too."

"Yeah, after the cameras were gone," Mya snapped.

The scene they were discussing played out on the screen and we were all riveted. What neither of them seemed to know was that Julian was in the next room talking to the manager and he heard the whole thing.

"Oh. My. God." Tori sat straight up and her jaw looked like it was unhinged. "He heard that!"

By the Bracelet Ceremony, Julian didn't need the cocktail hour to determine that Tori had to go.

"I can't believe he heard that. He probably thinks I'm horrible!"

No one denied it.

As the promo for Tuesday's episode teased about a vacation for the top four women, it flashed the faces of Mya, Bailey, Ana, and Leah.

Seeing Leah's face reminded me of last Tuesday's episode and how she was all over Julian.

*And he wasn't resisting her charms, either.*

I'd cried after watching that episode...just like I'd cried after watching Thursday's episode. The only reason I even agreed to watch Tori's episode in the common area was because I'd run out of tears.

## The One

Seeing Julian kiss Mya on their one-on-one was weird and difficult. I looked just above the TV so that I didn't have to actually see it, but I'd know when it was over.

*And no one would know that it was hard for me to see.*

He'd kissed the rest of the contestants with a little peck, which didn't rub me the right way, but it didn't make me emotional. There was one moment between him and Leah that hurt my heart, but it was foolish of me to think he would never hold another woman's hand.

Blinking rapidly, I shook off my feelings and tried to focus on the conversations around me.

"Well clearly, you know who didn't make it to the home visits," Mya joked, an inkling of disappointment coated her joke.

"Yeah, well you made it further than any of us, so that's a win!" Samantha cheered.

Emma was oddly quiet the entire episode. I looked over at her and she looked lost in her own thoughts.

"Are you okay over there, Emma?" I asked, leaning up to see her face.

"Yeah, I'm just thinking," Emma pondered. "This episode was all about Julian and Mya. Mya got the charm first. Mya won the salsa dance challenge. Mya was attacked by the big bad bitch." She pointed at Tori. "But Mya gets sent home the next episode. Do you think they are trying to throw us off track with who he's picking?"

"Yes," everyone replied in unison.

"That's the whole point," Tiffany clarified. "If you don't know who's going home or who Julian wants to be with, you're more likely to tune in week after week."

"It boils down to numbers," I added.

"Doesn't it always?" Nicole quipped.

We all dispersed soon thereafter, but Tori asked Mya to

stay back. I waited until Mya nodded that she was okay before heading to bed.

As I climbed between the sheets, I grabbed my notebook. I flipped through the entries. Page after page of poetry and thoughts on love and life filled the gift that Julian gave me. Every single entry was about Julian. Even the ones that were hypothetically about what I want in a man were about Julian. The ones about loss and heartache were about Julian. Picking up my pen, like every other night, I wrote the things I wouldn't say to anyone else. I wrote the thoughts I'd never admit to anyone. I wrote the words that my heart told me to write because in that small leather bound notebook, I was free.

I read the sentence I wrote repeatedly and when I closed my eyes, I continued to repeat the words from memory. From some hidden compartment I didn't even know existed, a fresh wave of tears burst from underneath my eyelids. When I finally fell asleep that night, my pillow was soaking wet.

The next day, my pillow was as dry as my eyes. My journal was closed and hidden between two books on my nightstand. My heart was tattered and hurt, but hidden in my chest so no one would see it.

Days in the hotel were even more restrictive and boring than in the house because we couldn't go outside. It was almost as if we had been taken hostage. So when something out of the ordinary would happen, we pounced on it. Unfortunately, most of the time, nothing out of the ordinary happened. But on Tuesday right after dinner, but before *The One* aired, we were drinking wine and watching a comedy when we heard the elevator ding. We'd discussed how it was weird that no one had arrived since Mya showed up a week prior. We figured that due to the home visits, maybe it was just taking a few extra days, but the suspense was killing us.

"Everyone cross your fingers that it's Leah," Nicole muttered under her breath as we all gathered down the hallway.

Everyone laughed.

But discreetly, I crossed my fingers.

"Hello ladies," Robert Brady called out as he strolled down the hallway as if he were in a hurry. "How's everyone doing today?"

We all exchanged pleasantries and then he rubbed his hands together.

"I'm here because one of the contestants, I won't tell you who, is coming to the hotel later tonight. She was sent home on Saturday, but we gave her some time to spend with her family before having her fly back here to pack up her belongings."

"Who is it?" Emma questioned, hands on her slim hips. "Come on, tell us. Who are we going to tell? We don't have phones or computers!"

Flashing a large smile, Robert ignored her request. "This week is your last week here."

We all cheered and clapped, causing him to laugh.

"Okay, okay, I get it." He held his hands up. "But this final week is important. There are two more episodes that air—tonight's episode and Thursday's. Then, next Tuesday, all eight of you will be picked up by a limo and taken to Lot A over at Dramatization Studios where we'll film the watch party reunion in front of a live studio audience." He rubbed his hands together.

"Wait, watch party reunion? I thought the contract stated that we just needed to be at the reunion?" I asked, forcing my voice to sound as normal as possible.

Robert looked at me and I couldn't tell if it was sympathy or annoyance in his eyes which just made me angrier. "The reunion is a combination of a live showing of the finale and a question and answer session with the audience." He paused. "It's the same as all the other seasons."

*How would I know that?!?! I don't watch shit like this! I* grumbled silently.

I bit my lip to keep from exploding.

*Now I'm going to have to watch Julian in a super cheesy romantic episode looking in someone's eyes and telling her that she's the one in front of a live studio audience. This is bullshit.*

Robert said a few more things that I couldn't focus on and then he left. Refilling our glasses, conversation ensued about who was likely showing up. I couldn't participate in the conversation because I was still reeling from the thought of having to be back on camera and watching Julian declare his love for some other woman.

"We have five minutes!" Mya announced, corralling us into the living room.

I sipped my wine, but I needed something stronger. Unfortunately, when the cameras were present, they stocked the bar with all the vodkas, whiskies, and rums anyone could ever want for, but in the hotel, without the cameras, we only had red or white wine.

*Just great.*

I plopped down on the couch and Mya and Nicole sat down on either side of me.

"Are you okay?" Mya inquired.

Putting the glass to my lips, I nodded slowly.

"You don't have to talk about it right now, but between now and Tuesday, get it all out so that we can go to the reunion and I don't have to worry about you," Nicole suggested.

With my eyes trained on the TV, I nodded again.

"It's on!" Mya yelled since Tiffany was taking the cookies

out of the oven. Looking around the room, she continued. "After the high of Thursday's episode, let's watch my fall from grace."

After a conversation with the remaining women in the house, Julian wanted to see what it would be like to go on vacation with each of them. When they were told to pack everything because they were going to Hawaii, they screamed. He explained to them that once they arrived in Hawaii, they wouldn't be going back to the house. From Hawaii, the final three would go home so Julian can meet their families. Then the final two would go to his home to meet his parents and he'd select the one.

Hearing him explain the process made my heart heavy.

*As of right this second, there are two women left because Mya is sitting right here and any minute now, someone else is coming in. So over the course of this week, Julian and the two finalists will be coming back into town to meet his parents and then he will choose who he wants to be with. And I have to sit and watch in front of the audience who will be in the studio and the millions who will be watching at home. I'm fucking screwed.*

The screen displayed picturesque aerial shots of Maui. The land, the water, and the people were incorporated to show the natural beauty. All four women joined Julian on a morning hike and when he left them, they seemed to get along a lot better without Tori around. But they were also much more emotional, crying about the attention he was giving the other women, complaining to him about feeling led on. Julian's frustration and indecision played out in his conversations with the camera.

He planned special one-on-one dates with each of them. I was able to tolerate the dates with Bailey, Mya, and Ana. But when Julian picked Leah up for their date, I excused myself and went to my room. I couldn't bring myself to watch it with other people.

Flipping on the TV, I sat on the couch in my darkened suite and watched as Julian gave Leah a lei made up of her favorite colors as they reached the beach.

*Don't let it be a romantic candlelit dinner for two on the beach.*

When I saw the table with the starched white tablecloth and pink candles to match her lei, my eyes filled with tears. A trio consisting of a guitar player, ukulele player and a singer started playing as soon as they approached the table. Julian reached out for her hand and asked her to dance.

My heart thumped against my chest as I remembered our night together. I closed my eyes briefly as I remembered the way Julian pulled me into his arms and whispered in my ear. I remembered the way Julian looked at me, telling me how he felt about me with his eyes. I remembered the way his lips found mine, softly at first and then rough with desire. A tear slipped from beneath my closed lids.

Opening my eyes, I caught Leah and Julian kissing and it felt like I'd been shot. I felt gutted.

Julian escorted her to the table and pulled her chair out for her. He sat down across from her. They looked comfortable together as they made small talk. When the chef brought out food, they ate in what appeared to be comfortable silence.

I sighed. The most fulfilled I'd ever been was in the silent moments between Julian and I. Being able to hear how much he cared about me or desired me was amazing, but being able to feel it in the silence around us when it was just the two of us was indescribable.

He took her back to his suite for coffee and conversation; however, unlike with the other dates, I wasn't sure if he'd slept with her. The other dates concluded and showed the women leaving. With Leah's date, it just showed them kissing on the couch and then an outside shot of Julian's suite. His muscular shadow stood in the balcony window for a second before he turned the lights out. After the commercial break, it was a Bracelet Ceremony on the beach.

I wanted to go out into the living room and ask Mya if she knew if Julian and Leah slept together. But I couldn't move myself off of the couch. I felt numb. I didn't know that I could possibly be in shock until I felt the tears dripping onto my chest as tears rolled down my face and dropped from my chin.

I was hurting. It was different than before. Before it was a more speculative pain whereas what I was subjected to at that point was definitive.

*Julian and Leah...are together.*

# Chapter 18

"He's a lying sack of shit," Ana wailed as she stomped through the kitchen holding two bottles of wine. She sat them down on the table.

Mya, Nicole, Samantha, Tiffany, Emma, Tori, and I sat at the conference room table with the paninis Nicole made sitting untouched on our plates as we stared at the Romanian beauty.

Ana arrived in the suites with a chip on her shoulder seven days ago and dramatically announced that she'd been robbed and that she wasn't going to talk about it. She didn't seem sad as much as she was angry. Every time we'd eat dinner together, she would let us know different things, little by little, and when we watched the episode in which she was sent home on Thursday, she was annoyed with that, too. She narrated the episode so passionately and so thoroughly that someone just muted the TV so she'd stop yelling. She kept almost telling us something and then ending the sentence with a squawking noise and punching the arm of the chair she was in. She was so over the top, yet had so much extra information that we didn't realize that we actually missed most of that episode because she was so distracting.

*It worked out for me because I didn't want to see Julian and Leah together.*

After a string of bad days, I'd promised Mya and Nicole I'd come out of hiding. Once I did, I was just as caught up with Ana's story as everyone else was. The only thing I was able to piece together from her scattered information was that she had gotten some bad advice. She said that a couple of times and then wouldn't elaborate. She would let us know a little bit of what happened each day and truly, I thought she just liked the attention. We had grown tired of daytime television and of being trapped so having a live-in soap opera was riveting.

It took her a whole week to admit what she had been alluding to, but with our determination to clean out their wine rack on our final day, she dropped a late lunch bombshell.

"I fucked him," Ana admitted.

My mouth hung open, even though I wasn't one hundred percent surprised. Everyone else gasped, shrieked and freaked out.

"How did you get away with it without anyone knowing?" Emma jumped up, hands in her hair. "There were cameras everywhere!"

"The cameras weren't in the sun room and on nights that Julian had to do promo stuff, the overnight shift was lax. Mainly just the editing guys."

Tori leaned back in the chair, a smirk on her face. "So in order to get to the final three to be with Julian Winters, you fucked your producer? Isn't that a little...slutty?"

"Hey!" Tiffany reprimanded, wagging a finger at Tori. "No slut-shaming. It was two consenting adults doing what they wanted to do."

"Yeah...besides, you've done a lot more for a lot less, Tori!" Ana gave her a look. "But just to be clear, that asshole said that he could guarantee me top two! Julian is going to pick either Leah or Bailey...the way things were looking before I left, it'll be Leah. So Leah gets Julian and Bailey gets her own show! That should either be my man or my show!" She took a gulp of the red wine.

*Ahhhhh...I thought so!*

I couldn't say anything out loud or then I would have to explain where I was coming from at that hour. But when I heard the way he was talking to Ana, something felt off. And I thought I heard loud kissing noises.

Questions, comments and concerns swirled the room between bites of our sandwiches and swigs of wine. It wasn't until we got an alert saying that the limo bus was coming to get us that we were distracted long enough to go get ready. Hair, makeup and wardrobe were going to be at the studio so besides shower, we didn't really need anything.

Even though I was probably dreading going to the reunion the most, I was packed and ready to go and was the first one on the party bus. Everyone else followed in quick succession.

Putting my headphones in, I tried to zone out while listening to a mix between Tupac and Maroon 5. I needed the sharp transition between artists to mimic the jarring emotions inside of me.

*I just have to hold it together for the rest of the day today and then I'll be home and I can put all of this behind me. I got over Tate just fine and moved on with my life. I can get over Julian,* I told myself as we pulled up to a gate.

Tori and Samantha had their faces pressed against the window in awe of being on a studio lot. Mya and Nicole never stopped their conversation with Emma and Tiffany. And Ana looked distressed. She stared out of the window, chewing one of her fingernails and bouncing her left leg up and down.

None of us were drunk, but none of us would've been under the legal limit to drive. The tipsiness levels varied and while it made most of the women talkative and ready to have a good time, it seemed to make Ana sad. But she may have started drinking before we got together for our late lunch.

*She did spend the entire week ready to burst,* I thought, giving her another once over. *Maybe we shouldn't have drunk so much.*

I moved seats and sat beside her. She looked at me and gave me a small smile.

"I was just about to ask you if you were okay," Ana said softly.

"Me? I was coming over here because you looked sad," I replied, my voice matching hers.

"You look like you're about to cry," she pointed out.

*Shit.* I ran my fingers under my eyes and then smiled.

"No, I don't," I argued, bumping her with my shoulder. "Are you really okay? Do you feel like he took advantage of you?"

She rolled her glassy eyes. "No, I seduced him. He told me he could get fired and he had a girlfriend...he said he didn't want to risk it. But I knew he'd never been with anyone as hot as me so I just kept coming on to him, hoping he'd break. And once he did, that's when I told him I wanted to make it to the final two. I told him that as long as I kept moving to the next round, we could keep playing. He said he could definitely get me into the final two. But it didn't happen." She shook her head. "Now I feel like I made an ass of myself on TV. I left my kids at home with my parents. I left my job. I left everything. And for what? I go home empty-handed."

I put my arm around her slight shoulders. "You can always be yourself on today's show. It's live so they can't do too much to edit it or anything. You can save your image tonight."

"Thanks." She gave me a bleak smile. "What about you? How are you going to handle things?"

"What do you mean?"

"You know exactly what I mean. I heard you couldn't even handle watching the date with Julian and Leah in Hawaii. How are you going to keep it together on live TV?"

*Does anyone know how to keep their mouths shut?* I grumbled in my head, looking around at the rest of the ladies on the bus.

I didn't have an answer. I didn't know what to say because I really didn't know how I was going to handle it. I didn't know how I was going to keep it together.

"Hey ladies!" Bryce Wilson welcomed us as he climbed onto the bus. "This is the finale! Are you ready?"

We followed him off of the bus and into the nondescript grey warehouse looking building.

"Right this way," Bryce directed, leading us through a few doors before we entered the right hallway. "Here's makeup, hair and wardrobe." He gestured to three different doors as he walked. "Here is the green room where you will hang out until you are called on stage. There's food and drinks in there already. You will probably get called two at a time to get pampered. But first, let me show you the soundstage."

We entered a smaller sized soundstage than what I was expecting. The live studio audience surrounded the mainstage on three sides. On the fourth side there was a huge projection screen.

"Look at this, dude. There is seating for about one hundred audience members. The finale episode will be projected on this screen for us all to watch together."

He pointed to two large black couches. "You will be seated here. Someone will bring us the seating order later." He pointed to the winged back chair that sat in the center with a

TV monitor right beside it. "This is my seat. We will watch the show right here if it's too difficult to turn your whole body around to see the projection screen."

He showed us a few more things before we were led back to the green room. We had only been in there for fifteen minutes when there was a sharp knock on the door. My stomach rolled from nerves as I knew it was the beginning of the end.

Koko stuck her head in the doorway. "Hi ladies! Zoe, I need to see you, please."

I rose to my feet and walked as normally as possible. Once I was out of the green room, Koko and I hugged so tightly I thought I was going to crush the smaller woman's bones.

"Do you know how much shit I have to tell you?" Koko hissed.

"You?! I've been freaking the fuck out because I have so much stuff to say and no phone to call you."

Koko all but pushed me into the makeup room. "At least when I went to Kyoto to visit my grandma for a month, I was able to use the phone to call you. This shit right here has led me to make some questionable decisions. You know you're my voice of reason!" She looked around and didn't see anyone. "Okay, JJ went on location to do their makeup early, but I think she should be on her way back soon. Let's say we have fifteen minutes so tell me everything. You fucking left? What the fuck? Dude, I had to find out from Bryce."

"Yeah, I know. I don't know. It made sense and then it didn't and then it did again. But I was falling for him, Koko. Hard. And I just couldn't take it anymore. Seeing him being affectionate with other women..." I shook my head. "I know that was part of what I signed up for but I couldn't take it. It was too hard." My voice broke.

"I'm sorry." Koko wrapped her arms around me, hugging

me and stroking my hair. "You really love him, don't you? I mean, I knew you loved him, but...you're crying. You don't cry. You're like the Elise Jordan of not crying."

I let out a teary laugh. "I've missed you."

"I've missed you too." She let me go and looked at me. "And just so you know, he has been miserable without you."

A tear rolled down my cheek that I swiped away quickly. "It looks like he's bounced back nicely."

I gave her a quick update of what had been going on and how the time at the suites had been. I told her how miserable I'd been and how I thought getting out of the show environment would make my feelings go away, but they didn't. I told her how all of us would watch the episodes together and the most recently kicked off contestant would tell the rest of the group the real scoop behind the episode.

"Was it weird? Essentially, everyone is just discussing how they ended up getting dumped by the same dude."

I smiled. "It was weird. Almost as weird as you saying 'dude.'" I poked her in her side. "So I take that to mean that things are still hot and heavy with you know who."

"I have to tell you all about that, but the short answer is yes. But more importantly, I need to tell you about Julian. Now listen, I've been watching the show, too and..."

"Koko, guess—oh!" Julia Jones burst into the room. Both of them stopping abruptly, Koko stopped talking at the sight of Julia and Julia stopped walking at the sight of me. "Zoe! Oh Zoe... how are you?"

I heard the sympathy in her voice and it made my skin crawl.

"Hi Julia," I replied, avoiding eye contact with her. I prayed I didn't look like I'd been crying.

"Hi JJ!" Koko greeted her boss with natural enthusiasm. "How are you?"

"I'm great. Really great. Fantastic actually! And I just got the news that this season has had the most viewers ever and we've been enlisted to do another season!"

"What? That's great! I know I heard that the um...one episode was a game changer for the ratings."

Something made me uncomfortable by the way Koko looked at me.

"Yes it was." Julia glanced at me. "Social media was all abuzz about it and it caught the attention of Marisa Brown. We've been tapped to do a major motion picture next month!"

"What?" Koko screamed, jumping up and down. "Wait, we? You mean we? As in you and me?"

"That's huge! Congratulations!" I celebrated with them. For the moment that I danced around the room with them, I forgot everything else having to do with the show.

The sharp knock on the door brought me back to reality though.

"I was told that you might have been in here," Jamie informed me as she stuck her head in the door. "You are needed in wardrobe."

I gave out congratulatory hugs before I followed Jamie out of the room. With each step, my stomach became more upset as the knots tightened.

Before I walked in the door, I looked at Jamie. "JJ had mentioned something about this season being the biggest to date."

Jamie instantly looked away. "Yeah, it has been a great season."

"What episode were they talking about being the game changing episode?"

Jamie looked at me. "Yours. When you walked away. It was all anyone could talk about online for a week. We had to re-air it on Saturday and from that point on, ratings have been through the roof. There are articles about..." She trailed off and then looked away.

*So one of the hardest things I had to do in my life has been reduced to online fodder.*

My throat was constricting and my mouth was dry. "Articles about what?"

"It doesn't matter."

"It does to me."

She sighed, looking around. "Just about how something must have happened off screen that people didn't see because you and Julian were really into each other and then you left out of nowhere. Then there was a long weekend stint that revolved around the idea of you must have had a boyfriend and you were doing it for the money."

*Oh my God, my parents are probably flipping out.*

"Can I call my parents? Please. If this has been going on all month, I need to tell them I'm okay."

She didn't say anything for what seemed like forever and then she whispered, "Follow me."

I followed her into a stairwell and she pulled her phone out of her pocket.

"You have to make it quick."

"Thank you so much." I hugged her because I was so grateful. "Thank you."

I dialed the home number for my parents and no one was home. I tried my mom's cellphone next.

"Elise Jordan speaking." My mother's clipped, professional tone sounded like music to my ears.

"Mom, it's me."

"Zoe, how are you?" Her voice shifted to warm and sweet in a matter of seconds. "I've missed you."

"I've missed you and Dad, too. I don't have much time, but I wanted to know if you've been hearing stuff about me." I looked at Jamie who was watching me carefully. "About me doing this for money or—"

"That's crap! Anyone with half a brain can tell by the way you look at the boy and the way he looks at you, that you weren't faking your feelings. When you're done with the show, we can go over the articles and file injunctions on the stories and sue them for defamation of character."

I laughed, wiping my eyes before the tears that formed had a chance to fall. "You always know what to say." I took a breath. "Thanks, Mom."

"Zoe, I have a meeting that I rescheduled so your father and I can watch this live finale together so I only have a few more minutes. Did something happen to you? Did someone do something to you? Is that why you left the show?"

"No, not at all! It's complicated. It just got to be too much for me. But no one did anything to me."

"Are you sure?"

"I'm positive. I swear."

She let out a sigh of relief. "Okay because I watched the episode three times trying to see if I saw anything different. I was going to have the firm on it if I felt anything was amiss."

I let out a short giggle. "Wow, you watched it three times and rescheduled a meeting to watch the finale. You and dad are those kinds of people now."

"As long as our daughter is one of those kinds of people who would be on the show, we sure are," she returned playfully. After a brief pause, she continued. "But I have to tell you something. I saw your face when you left the show. I don't know how this thing works, but if Julian is on the show tonight or if he calls in or anything happens where you can get in touch with him, you need to tell him how you feel."

"I did," I whispered softly. I looked down, praying Jamie couldn't hear my mother's side of the conversation.

"Do you love him?"

My heart clenched. "Yes."

"Then tell him how you feel."

"On national television? In front of everyone?" I wondered, fear paralyzing me. "What if it doesn't...go the way that I want?"

"What if it does?" She countered. "And yes, scream it from the rooftops on national television in front of everyone."

"I don't know."

"Do you have his number or another way to touch bases with him?"

"No."

"Then you need to seize the opportunities as they present themselves. So if you have to do it tonight, you have to do it tonight."

Jamie touched her watch frantically, giving me a 'wrap it up' signal.

"I'll think about it, Mom. But I have to go. I'm not supposed to be using the phone, but I really needed to talk to you. I just wanted to make sure you and Dad weren't disappointed in me."

"To be honest, we are a little disappointed..."

My heart started crumbling as the words hit me hard. I felt like I'd been kicked in my chest. Before I had a chance to respond, my mom explained her statement.

"We are disappointed because you gave up. I don't know what these kinds of shows are all about, but the chemistry between you and Julian couldn't be manufactured in the editing room. Even your dad admitted that the way you and Tate looked at each other was nothing like the way you and Julian looked at each other. And there's no bigger Tate supporter than your dad."

We both laughed.

"We are disappointed that you might miss out on something good because you got scared. We taught you to never give up. Not in life and not in matters of the heart. Giving up is the first step toward failure," she concluded, using her favorite motivational line.

"You're right. I love you, Mom."

"I love you, too, Zoe."

"Tell Dad I love him and I will call back once I get phone access again."

We said our goodbyes and I wiped my eyes. "Thank you, Jamie. I needed that."

"You're welcome." She rubbed my back before opening the stairwell door. "Do you feel better?"

"Much."

"Good. Now you are going to have to bust your ass to get ready in time. Can you do it?"

"I can do it."

My stomach was still in knots, but I believed the words that I said.

*I can do this. Right? Yes, I can do this. I can do this.*

# Chapter 19

"Stand right here," Jamie directed me. "Once Bryce says come on out, you will just walk up the stairwell and take the seat nearest him."

I nodded that I understood even though I was on the brink of a panic attack.

"How are you?"

"I'm okay. Better than I thought I'd be."

*Because technically pre-panic attack is better than full on panic attack.*

Jamie's mouth turned up into a smile even though her eyes were worried. "Well, you look great."

I smiled, appreciatively. "Thank you."

My makeup was natural, even though Koko still used the high definition foundation and my hair was loose and wild, the way I preferred it. I looked like myself. Even if I didn't feel like myself, I looked like me.

*The tense version of me.*

Nervously, I stood backstage teetering in black spiked

heels with silver studs all over them. The shoes made my legs look long and graceful, like a dancer, and also badass like a rock star. In a black and white checkered backless dress, I felt more like myself than I did in the gowns. The dress was sexy without pushing too many boundaries and flirty without being too over the top. It showed off my curves, but wouldn't be unbecoming of the future partner of L.A.'s top law firm. The only thing I was nervous about was the bodice inspired sweetheart neckline that only lightly covered me. My heavy breasts were held up by half of a package of double sided tape and the grace of God.

"Our first contestant needs no introduction. She is, after all, the woman who brought us the most powerful scene of this season. Maybe the most powerful scene in *The One* history," Bryce introduced. "Let's roll the clip."

The crowd exploded with excitement, cheering and clapping so I couldn't hear what footage was rolling at first. When the cheers died down, I could hear my own voice. I closed my eyes and visualized the scene as I listened to the audio.

"I need to leave the competition tonight," I said, my voiced sounded broken.

With anger and hurt in his voice, he asked, "Are you serious?"

"Yes." I sounded unsure.

"Because of a kiss? Because I kissed someone else, you want to leave?"

"Yes." I lied. It was more than that and the break in my voice gave me away.

"You know..." He let out a wail that sounded more painful than angry upon hearing it for the second time.

"Julian."

"I'm sorry I yelled," he uttered hoarsely. "I'm just so frustrated because I can't talk to you the way I want to talk to you." He sighed again and I heard the defeat in his voice.

"Listen to what I'm saying. I can't stay because this situation is too much for me. It has nothing to do with you or how I feel about you. It's just too much for me." My voice cracked with each word.

"Okay." Julian's tone was cold, flat, and almost despondent. "I've said everything that I could to you. I've laid it out as much as I possibly can. And you still want to walk."

"It's not that I want to leave. It's—"

"I get it. You don't have to explain."

"No, but I want to explain. It's just hard putting myself out there like that."

"I don't want to have this conversation anymore. You've made up your mind to leave; I can't do anything about it."

My tattered heart thundered in my chest as I relived the moment that haunted me for weeks. In the edited replaying of the scene, I heard things I hadn't heard before which dredged up feelings that I tried to force down for the duration of the live show. I sucked in a deep breath and held it for a second, hoping it would calm me down. But when Bryce called my name, I rolled my shoulders back and strolled out to the sound of applause.

After a quick kiss on the cheek from Bryce, I took my seat closest to Bryce and crossed my legs. "Hello!" I greeted him and everyone in the audience, flashing a huge smile.

Bryce ran his hand down the black tuxedo he wore to ensure it was still in pristine condition and settled in his chair. "You look beautiful. Thank you for being here."

"You look very nice as well. Thank you for having me."

*Not that I really had a choice.*

Bryce looked at the audience. "Next we have the woman who almost went the distance. She took our eligible bachelor home to meet her parents where we all discovered a bombshell. She is a mother! Roll the clip!"

As the clip played, I thought about how difficult it would be for me to leave my child or job for a period of time on just the hope that things work out with some guy I hadn't met yet. The clip was one of the many chunks of the episode we missed because Ana was telling us about a lot of other things that went down behind the scenes. In the scene being projected on the screen, Ana introduced her children to a surprised Julian. Although he looked completely surprised, he was also very good with those kids. Ana looked worn out before he did.

When Ana was called to come out, she sauntered out looking great. She gave me a wink when she got onto the stage. She was placed on the other couch, closest to Bryce.

Bryce went on to introduce the eight other women, playing a brief clip of their most notable moment on *The One* before each of them came out and took a seat. From the way the seating was organized, I was fortunate enough to be next to Mya.

Once everyone was on stage, there was twenty minutes before the video footage from Leah and Bailey's first meeting with Julian's family that took place over the last week would be showcased.

"Hello and welcome to *The One: Live Finale.* Before we show you part one of the finale, we are opening the floor to have your questions answered. Our live studio audience members have submitted their most pressing question and the creators and producers have chosen a few for the ladies to answer. Are you ready?"

The crowd cheered and stomped and yelled excitedly.

"Are you ready ladies?"

We smiled and laughed uneasily.

"Good!" He chuckled. "Let's do this!"

He opened up a sealed envelope and pulled out a handful of questions. "Oh! This is a good one. Question is for Ana... you seemed more angry than sad when you were sent home after the home visit. Do you think that's fair since you didn't tell Julian about your children?"

Ana eyed me for a second before turning on the charm. "I was advised by someone on the production crew to keep my children out of it, both for their protection and for Julian to get to know me, the woman and not me the mom." She positioned her body to the audience. "I'm sure many of the single mothers out there can agree that being a single mother is a rewarding, but all consuming job. When I meet a man, I want a man to make me feel like a woman. I've wanted to be honest with Julian this entire time, but I was told that Julian wouldn't be able to see me for who I am if I told him. I'd forever be seen in his eyes as 'the mom' and for the first time since my ex passed away suddenly, I wanted to be seen as Ana. I wanted to be seen as me."

The crowd's thunderous applause was the redemption that Ana clearly needed as her entire face lit up.

"It wasn't that I was mad at Julian and not sad about losing him. I was especially sad after seeing what a good father he would be. But I understood where he was coming from. He felt blindsided. And after thinking about it, I don't know why I listened to the crew members. But I did and I was mad at myself."

After the applause and Ana dabbing her eye with a tissue, Bryce asked the next question. "This is for Tori and Mya... Ladies, have you two squashed the beef between you after Abuela-gate?" Bryce chuckled under his breath. "Abuela-gate," he repeated to himself, clearly amused.

Tori and Mya, who were sitting directly across from one another, looked at each other before Tori gestured to Mya. "I've apologized to Mya both publically and privately. And I apologize to anyone who was offended by my actions. I'm a lot of things—bitch being one of them. But I am not prejudiced. So from the bottom of my heart, I'm sorry to everyone I offended with my recklessness. Also, I wanted to now take this take and apologize to Mya's abuela." She looked at Mya who gave her a smile and a nod. "Lo siento. Su hermosa abuela, lo siento mucho."

The crowd applauded.

"Last question before we tune in to see how the home visits went with Leah and Bailey. Zoe, this is for you. Oh..." Bryce looked at me, clearly uncomfortable by what was written.

My heart rate picked up. *What could be written on the page that has thrown him off so much?*

"Um...this question is..." He cleared his throat. "Zoe...do you love Julian Winters? Because it seemed like it. If so, how after so little time together?"

It was as if everything shut down and powered off. All I could hear was my staggered breathing and erratic heart beats. Everyone's eyes were on me and I didn't know how much time had passed between when the question was asked and when I started to have an out of body experience.

*Tell him how you feel.*

I heard my mom's voice in my head, urging me, rooting for me. I could see Mom and Dad on the couch watching this moment. I could almost feel my parents' disappointment in me if I gave up, if I walked away.

I took a breath and I answered. "Time won't permit the long form answer," I started, gathering courage along the way. "But long story short, yes. I love Julian Winters. The how isn't as important as the why. But to answer the question... You can't quantify your feelings in time. You don't have to know someone for a long time to feel and connect with their heart. Now would I marry someone I've known for a week? No. Absolutely not. But are my feelings real? Yes. Absolutely."

Mya grabbed my hand and squeezed it. Bryce gave me his Ken doll smile. And the overall crowd response was positive, but it was definitely a mixed positive reaction. While some cheered loudly, others said 'awww' as the reality of the situation settled in.

*I'm sitting on the couch because I'm not in the top two. I'm not one of the women Julian will pick.*

"Wow, very powerful words, Zoe. I wish we had time for one more question so this segue wouldn't be awkward." He paused and then looked at the camera. "But um...Thursday and Friday, Bailey spent time with Julian and his family. Saturday and Sunday, Leah spent time with them. On Monday, Julian had lunch with the ladies and then they were sent to two different locations to wait to see if Julian arrives today to tell them that they are the one. So without further ado, here are the home visits."

The studio darkened. The episode started with a sign that said 'Welcome to Palo Alto.' Once Bailey appeared on the screen, walking down the street, the live studio audience cheered happily. Her thick blonde hair bounced behind her as she moved. She had on jeans, knee-high, black boots, and a tight purple, blue and black sweater. The colors brought out her blue eyes and she truly looked gorgeous.

Bailey arrived at a bar and when she walked in, the camera panned over to Julian. He stood up and greeted her, kissing her lightly. He introduced her to his friends and when he went to the bar, his best friends, James, Omar, and Scott, each took turns asking her questions.

Bailey had dialed back the dumb blonde routine significantly, only using it in a flirtatious way. She held her own in conversations with his friends and when Julian returned, he seemed pleased with what he saw.

Leaving the friends, Julian and Bailey headed to a restaurant where a jazz band was playing. The music sounded familiar.

*That was one of the songs that played that night we spent together,* I realized, taking a deep breath.

After a romantic night at the jazz venue, Julian and Bailey headed into her room at the Palo Alto Bed and Breakfast. In the room, she stripped out of her sweater. In just a shelf bra that, admittedly, made her natural breasts look awesome, Bailey said something flirty and went into the bathroom to change. She came back out in a small red bikini and her thick hair piled on top of her head. Julian went into the bathroom and changed into swim trunks. His muscular body was on display and I saw a flicker of interest in Bailey's eyes.

I felt a nagging in my gut.

*Bailey wants to be a celebrity, not be with a celebrity. Or at least, not Julian Winters. That's what she said. That's what she assured me.* I swallowed hard as it showed Julian and Bailey in the hot tub.

Although the camera only alluded to things getting hot and heavy, I chose to believe that didn't happen.

The next scene showed Julian taking Bailey to meet his parents. The adorable couple in the photo in the gazebo came to life on the screen.

Brian and Susan Winters were great as a couple. They were really sweet and engaging with one another. They were also very warm and welcoming to Bailey. As much as Julian tried to do for them and serve them, his parents would not allow him to clean a dish or pick up a plate. Each parent took a turn talking to Bailey and at the end of the visit, they hugged her and told Julian they liked her.

The lights in the studio came back on and the crowd started with the 'oohs' and 'ahhs.'

I could feel the cameras and the eyes in the room boring into me. My skin crawled.

"Well, that was Bailey's home visit and it seemed like it went well. How do you think it went...Zoe?"

*Shit! Why me?*

I gave him a small smile. "I think it went well. Julian's parents, who are lovely, seemed to like her which is understandable because Bailey really is easy to like."

*I hope my voice doesn't sound as sad as I feel.*

Bryce proceeded down the couch asking the same question to Mya, then Emma and lastly Tiffany. He then pulled four more questions out of the envelope to ask and be answered.

"Wow, that was wow, Emma," Bryce overreacted, raising his eyebrows in shock as Emma finished oversharing in the fourth and final question.

*We're going to have to stop Emma from drinking anymore.*

Bryce calmed everyone down from the raucous laughter that Emma's story caused. "Now, we are ready to take a look at Leah's home visit with Julian in Palo Alto. Let's watch!"

Leah came onto the screen and the crowd cheered gleefully. She wore a turquoise dress with a black and grey polka dotted sweater. Her shoes also had black and grey polka dots. Her wavy hair was flowing in the wind as she made her way to a different bar.

The bar was casual so when Leah walked in, she stood out like a sore thumb. Her face as she scanned the dive bar was priceless. With her nose crinkled and her lips curled, Leah looked truly disgusted when two bar patrons exited the building and got close to her.

The camera panned to Julian and when he saw her, he rose to his feet. With her face lighting up, she pushed her way to him and jumped into his arms. Julian laughed and spun her around.

After introducing his best friends to Leah, she sat down and talked with them. The questions were rather tame and she answered each one flawlessly as if she had rehearsed. Julian stepped away in order for the real questioning to begin and when Scott mentioned something about Lillian, Leah's sweet mask slipped and she made a catty remark.

Omar smiled. "You think Lillian is a bitch?"

"Oh, I'm sorry!" Leah put her hands to her cheeks. "I don't know how that slipped out. It's just that she rubbed me the wrong way when we met. She was kind of brutal to me."

"So you think her sweet act is a routine?" James followed up.

"Certainly. I think she's phony because of the way she handled herself with me and the rest of the girls in the house. She was smiling in our faces, but in her eyes, she was looking down at us. Do you know what I mean?" She batted her eyelashes and smiled at the men.

"Looking down at you like the way you looked when you walked into this bar?"

Leah's face froze. "What?"

"We caught the way you looked when you walked in here." He paused. "You remind us a lot of Lillian. A lot," Omar explained. "You sure as hell look like her. We just wanted to spend some time with you to make sure your personalities weren't alike."

"She wasn't good for our boy." James leaned forward and looked at her hard. "And we don't want to see him end up in another situation like that."

Leah looked indignant. "I don't think Julian would have moved me along this far if he didn't feel the spark between us. We've built something special. I don't think he would have even selected me if he thought I reminded him of the bad portions of Lillian."

The men nodded.

"I agree with that," Omar stated with a laugh. He lifted his beer bottle to her. "We just wanted to make sure you passed the test. Cheers!"

Leah, Scott, and James all lifted their drinks and clinked them together. "Cheers!"

Julian returned and invited Leah to go with him to a restaurant. She took his hand and waved goodbye to his friends. As they walked through the door, the camera returned to Julian's best friends.

Omar made a face. "Hell no. If I don't know anything else, I know for damn sure that Leah's not the one."

# The One

Everyone in the studio cracked up laughing. I had been holding my breath since the moment Julian wrapped her in his arms and spun her around. The laughter was a good reprieve. I was feeling heavy hearted and anxious up until that point.

*I'm so glad someone finally called Leah out on her bullshit. I wish he would've done it when Julian was there, but my hope is that he will talk some sense into his best friend.* I exhaled. *Omar will receive an anonymous thank you card once this is all over.*

Julian and Leah entered into the same restaurant with the jazz band playing. When she complained that the music was too loud, Julian said 'okay,' but I saw the annoyance in his eyes. Instead of where he had planned a nice dinner, Julian took Leah up the block to a swanky French bistro. They ordered wine and through conversation, I saw the slow spark between the two of them as they talked about the commonalities in their lifestyles.

The spark wasn't as nonexistent as the one between him and Bailey and it wasn't as intense as the one between him and I. But there was a spark as they talked about places they've been and their experiences there. As this date was featured more prominently than other dates, I did notice that it seemed as though they were swapping stories as opposed to getting to know one another by unpacking those stories.

"Have you been to Paris?" Leah asked, looking around the bistro.

"Yeah. Every time I've gone, it's been nice. But I'm always so busy when I go. I'm making time to do something for me. There's this one thing I've always wanted to do, but there's never time to squeeze it in." Julian replied.

"Oh good! I love that you're so cultured. I'm tired of meeting men who don't have stamps in their passports. Paris Fashion Week was electrifying. We'll have to go together sometime."

Julian smiled, but on the one hundred foot screen, his smile didn't reach his eyes. "What year did you go to Fashion Week there?"

"Last year." Leah took a sip of wine. "Were you there?"

Julian's eyes lit up with amusement. "I was, actually!"

"Did you see when—"

"—the model fell and pushed everyone down with her?"

"Yes!"

They laughed together.

The knife twisted in my back so deeply that I sat up straighter to alleviate the pain. But things only got worse from there.

I watched as Julian fed Leah a bite of his chocolate éclair and then when Leah did the same with her strawberry one, she dripped a bit of sauce on the side of his mouth. Instead of getting it with a napkin, she used her mouth.

I wanted to vomit.

After dinner, Julian escorted Leah to the Palo Alto Bed and Breakfast. I was glad she didn't strip and take him to the hot tub, but she did 'slip into something more comfortable' and asked if he wanted to relax. He accepted and I was sure my eyes started to bleed.

I couldn't show any emotions or even close my eyes because I was positive a camera was pointed directly at me. So I was forced to watch Julian and Leah kiss and I felt like I was dying a slow death. I kept hoping it would cut back to Omar, but it didn't. It just showed Julian and Leah kissing and Leah closing the bedroom door with her foot.

I couldn't take anymore and I turned away.

The music changed and when I looked up, Julian and Leah were walking up to his parents' house. It seemed as though Leah rubbed his parents the wrong way immediately when she made a comment about their home being impressive seeing as how they were just teachers. Julian's mother, who was so sweet and doting with Bailey, glared at Leah as she repeated the word 'just.' Leah backtracked as best she could, but the damage was done.

Leah was good at bullshitting so it wasn't long before she had won Julian's dad over. She was still working on his mom when it was time to go. Stiff hugs were given all around and a pleasant goodbye followed. Brian Winters told the camera that he liked Leah. His wife stood beside him and smiled sweetly. When pushed, for thoughts on Leah, Susan Winters simply said, "Bless her heart."

Because I knew Susan was originally from the South, I snickered at the Southern insult.

The lights came back on and the crowd clapped excitedly.

Bryce turned toward the other couch. "What did you think about the home visit, Ana?"

"I think Leah is an underhanded bitch and I was pleased that both his friends and his family were able to see through her B.S.," Ana snapped, rolling her eyes.

"Wow!" Bryce kept his face as straight as he could, but his lips turned up as if he were holding in a laugh.

Half of the audience clapped and cheered. The other half let out shocked laughter.

Bryce moved on and asked Tori, Samantha and Nicole the same question. They answered with nicer versions of the same thing Ana said.

"I'm getting the feeling that those of you who actually spent time with her in the house, don't really care for her." Bryce stroked his chin as if he were really pondering the statement. "Audience, do you wonder why the comments for Leah seem so much harsher than the comments for Bailey in their pursuit for Julian's heart?"

The crowd cheered.

"Let's see who Julian has to choose from. Roll the tape!"

A video montage of Leah lurking around the house collecting information and reporting back to whoever was being talked about played and a few audience members gasped. The next series of clips were Bailey being extremely likeable and hot in her never-ending supply of bikinis, but saying the most ridiculously dumb things.

The segment was entitled Classy Bitch versus Bikini Ditz.

"I'm not okay with that," I spoke up, unable to stomach the title. I looked around. "Can someone remove that graphic? How did that even pass inspection?"

"What do you mean?" Bryce asked. "I thought you of all people would like how they poked fun at Julian's top two."

My heart hurt with the idea of Julian picking Leah, but more than that, my entire existence hurt knowing that I was a part of a show that referred to two grown women as a 'classy bitch' and a 'bikini ditz.'

"It's disrespectful. And as a series that thrives off of the participation of women." I gestured to all of us. "And off of the viewership of women." I gestured to all of the women in the ninety-eight percent female audience. "I would like to think *The One* would have a little more respect than that."

Even though Leah was a conniving bitch who lied and backstabbed her way to the top, a show that has profited off her devious ways shouldn't get away with disrespecting her. And Bailey was smart and beautiful and clearly a talented actress. She didn't deserve to be cemented as a 'bikini ditz.' She wore bikinis, but the cameras didn't have to follow her around as soon as she slipped into one. She purposely dumbed herself down because she was told that she would get more air time and that the audience loved a 'dumb blonde.' Neither of them deserved that.

The audience clapped with force until the graphic came down.

"I agree with you," Bryce stated, smiling when people started clapping for him as well.

After quieting everything down, Bryce asked us several more questions that ranged from what did we do all day to who did we think we would still be friends with in a year. I was still riding the high of standing up for what I believed in, I almost forgot what was coming next.

"On Monday," Bryce started. "Julian met with both women for brunch. Let's check in to see how that went."

The lights dimmed and the image that flashed across the screen was sexy. Julian was driving a black and chrome car that looked so expensive that I didn't know what make and model it could possibly be. He hopped out of his car to the delight of the valet parking attendant and entered the eatery in Downtown L.A.

Leah and Bailey were already there and they both jumped up when they saw him. Julian embraced both of them, kissing them on the cheek and he sat down. They made small talk for a while during brunch. When brunch was coming to an end, Julian told them that they would return to the mansion and on Tuesday they would both get dressed and wait for him at two separate locations.

"Do you know already who you're going to pick?" Leah looked nervous as she asked. I couldn't tell if she legitimately had feelings for him, but I knew that she felt like he was 'good enough' for her. She looked at him like she liked him.

Julian looked between Leah and Bailey. "If I did, would you want to know?"

Bailey looked happy, smiling. "I want you to take the next twenty-four hours and think about who you want to be with before making a decision. It's not proposing marriage, but it's serious."

Leah's mouth tightened. "Yeah, I would want you to wait and think about it. What you want, who you choose, is your decision. But I want you to know that I love you."

I couldn't read Julian's expression. "I care about both of you and I will see you very soon."

*Please pick Bailey. Please pick Bailey,* I prayed and silently begged.

If he picked Bailey, at the very least, I knew we'd have a chance. If he picked Leah, that would mean he was interested in seeing where that spark went.

# Chapter 20

"Are you ready to hear what our bachelor has to say?" Bryce Wilson yelled, getting everyone excited.

My stomach quivered at the thought of Julian in the limo, on his way to either Bailey or Leah. I was so nervous that I finished my bottle of water during the brief intermission and had to get another one to combat the constant dry mouth I was experiencing.

"You're shaking," Mya whispered as the lights started to dim. "Breathe."

I inhaled and exhaled noisily. I didn't even realize it was that loud until I noticed Nicole looking at me from the other side of the stage.

Mya put her hand over mine and squeezed.

Julian's face filled the enormous screen and the catcalls erupted from the crowd. I sucked in a sharp breath.

Julian Winters was truly breathtaking. The lines of his face were a work of art. His jawline was masculine and strong and lightly peppered with a sexy stubble that somehow made him look darker, more intense. His full lips, that looked as soft as they felt, parted to show off the hard work of some California orthodontist. His teeth were straight and white and gave him the most endearing smile. I used to think his smile was the best thing about him. But my favorite facial feature of Julian Winters was his piercing, grey eyes. It wasn't the fact that his eye color was unique and changed depending upon the weather or his mood. It was what he did with his eyes that reeled me in.

When Julian fixed his eyes on me, I felt it everywhere. I loved that he looked at me like he wanted to know me in every way possible. I loved that he could both turn me on and bring me to tears by just staring into my eyes. Julian looked at me and looked into my soul.

*And I'm scared I'm never going to experience that again.*

Julian started answering the questions asked of him as he sat in the back of the limo. The tinted windows didn't give anything away about his destination. But thanks to technology, all of us as spectators saw Leah standing in a vineyard in a beautiful gown and her light brown hair swept over one shoulder. We saw Bailey standing on a pier with her gown blowing in the wind and her hair slicked and pinned into a bun on the top of her head.

I felt sick with sharp pains in my heart. I wouldn't have been surprised if I was just as nervous as the two of them in that moment.

The screen flashed back to Julian as he ran his hand through his short black hair.

"Do you know who you're going to pick?" A male voice asked Julian in the limo.

Julian glanced at the camera and then back out of the window. "Yes."

"Do you have any doubts about your choice?"

He shook his head. "No, not at all."

"Do you have any regrets about this experience?"

"I have no regrets. I would've done a couple of things differently, though."

"Like what?"

Julian smiled. It was small and a little sad, but it was a smile. "I would use my time a little better. This process is hard. You gravitate toward people and then they're gone. You connect with people and then they're gone. It's an environment that makes you question the things you're feeling because everything seems to be on fast forward. So I would just use my time to really make the most of it."

"If you were able to say something to one of the contestants that didn't make it this far, what would you say?"

"You want me to single someone out? Right now?" Julian shook his head. "Come on, man."

"Before you make your decision and pick the one, is there one woman you'd like to say something to?"

Julian looked out the window. "The only person I'm thinking about right now is the woman who has my heart."

"Is this an exclusive? Are you saying you're in love?"

Julian smirked as he looked at the camera. "We're here."

My heart was in my throat and tears burned my eyes. I felt my blood run cold as I tried to think about anything that would keep me from bursting. The urge to cry had never been that strong.

*Well, there you have it. I took a chance. I took a risk. And the embarrassment will come, I'm sure. But I'm more concerned about the way my heart feels like it's crumbling into pieces.*

The split screen showed a black limo pulling up near the pier and although it was sad, I felt a little bit of relief. But then, a black limo pulled up at the vineyard and my anxiety peaked. Although I didn't have hope that Julian had some elaborate plan to pick Bailey and then drop her to ultimately be with me, I still preferred him to pick Bailey over Leah.

The suspense was killing me. I glanced around and every one of us had our necks craned to see which door opened. I figured a commercial break was being taken because of the length of time it was taking for us to see movement in either limo.

The live studio audience stood on their feet. Taking a page out of their book, Emma, Tiffany and Samantha stood as well. After thirty seconds, Tori, Ana, Mya, and Nicole also rose to their feet. Not wanting to be the only one seated; however, not wanting to fall flat on my face from shock if Julian picked Leah, I stood slowly, shakily. Bryce must have seen how unsteady I was because he helped me. Once I was standing with my back to everyone, including the cameras, I ran my fingertips underneath my eyes, careful not to smudge my makeup.

It was silent, yet the anticipation in the air was palpable. I could hear the buzz of curiosity as everyone stood on edge in front of the huge screen before us. I felt stifled. I felt like Julian's decision was a cloud of smoke that was suffocating me. I started having trouble breathing.

*Hold it together for ten more minutes and then you never have to do anything regarding this show again.*

As soon as the drivers of the limo eased out of the front seat, heading toward the back door, Bryce turned to the audience and yelled, "Let's get a clap going."

*Clap.*

*Clap.*

*Clap.*

Everyone slapped their hands together along with him except for me.

*I'm not clapping to support Julian choosing someone else. I'm not clapping to celebrate him picking someone over me. I'm not clapping to applaud my heartbreak.*

The hairs on the back of my neck stood up and a chill ran through me. I didn't know if it was the last-ditch Hail Mary of coming on the show and proclaiming my love or what, but a calm came over me. Butterflies unraveled the knot that had been in my stomach since I woke up knowing it was the day that Julian was going to make a decision. I put my hand to my belly just as the audience started screaming. All of us on stage searched the screen for movement confused before turning around to see what they were screaming about.

My heart stopped.

In a slate grey tuxedo with a black shirt and shoes, Julian Winters was standing at the bottom of the steps staring directly at me.

I let out small gasps as my mouth hung open. I was in shock and seeing him rendered me speechless.

"Zoe Jordan..." His voice trailed off after he addressed me. Everyone else in the room faded away.

*Oh my God.*

Unhurriedly, Julian's eyes slid up and down my body

before he met my gaze again. He took a step. "I've thought about you every hour of every day that you've been gone."

*Oh my God.*

He licked his lips. "Your beauty is undeniable, but I crave the feel of your skin against mine because I know the depths of your soul. The poet in me sees the poet in you and craves that connection."

He took another step. "I see you."

He took the next step. "I feel you."

He took the last step up onto the stage. "I love you."

*He loves me.*

My lip and then my body started trembling. The first of many pent up tears trickled down my cheek as he made his way across the stage toward me. I quickly swiped it away.

Stopping two or three feet away from me, Julian's grey eyes stormed over. His facial expression was somber and gave nothing away. But his eyes were so expressive and deep.

*This man literally takes my breath away,* I thought as my breath hitched.

It took me a minute to realize Julian was nervous. "I love you," he repeated. His voice was softer with a hint of agony in his tone.

I closed my eyes for just a second, basking in his words. When I let my lashes flutter open, I handed him my entire heart. "I love you, too."

As soon as the words were out of my mouth, Julian inhaled deeply. The distance between us made me dizzy. It was the intoxicating blend of being in his presence and the feeling of wanting something, someone so much and finally getting it. I was overwhelmed.

My stomach bottomed out and I felt like I was on a rollercoaster as I mentally wrestled with the desire to touch him. In reality, I stood shaking, relishing in the sexy sound of his voice when he said my name.

"Zoe Jordan..." He paused dramatically, his eyes rooting me where I stood. "You're 'The One.' There was never any doubt in my mind that you were the one for me. You are the one for me. You will always be the one for me. So will you make me the happiness man on Earth and accept this final charm?"

"Absolutely," I replied softly as the thunderous sound of people clapping and the loud, boisterous catcalls surrounded us.

His panty-melting smile was reward enough, but he reached out, his hand encircling my wrist, scorching my skin. With his other hand, he clasped a number one charm onto my sparsely filled bracelet. His fingers lingered on the inside of my wrist as he stared into my eyes.

Seconds ticked by and he didn't advance, he didn't kiss me, he didn't say anything. Our only contact was Julian's gentle grip on my wrist and the soft brush-like strokes of his thumb across my skin. The audience roars started to slow down as they waited for what was next. I was sure they were waiting for the big kiss. I know I was waiting for the big kiss. And the fact that it hadn't happened yet only heightened the angst in the room. But between the exclamations of coos and squeals of excitement, I felt a nervous trepidation.

My chest rose and fell in time with his as I felt us gravitating toward each other. I didn't remember us moving, but we went from being a couple of feet apart to a couple of inches apart. The cheers and claps had completely stopped and the air was thick and heavy with anticipation.

I took a breath...and then another. His body just barely touched mine and just when I thought he was going to lean in for a kiss, he didn't. Instead, he smirked and started reciting

Pablo Neruda's *Sonnet LXIX.*

*Oh my God.*

I put my hand to my chest. "Julian," I managed to choke out, my heart pounding.

*This is the most romantic, over-the-top, beautiful gesture. This is...*

My thoughts disintegrated as he started to move.

The audience screamed and shocked laughter rang out over the deafening applause that echoed around us as he dropped to one knee while still holding my right hand.

*Holy shit.*

The flurry of cameras readjusting and lights brightening to capture the unexpected moment was a whirlwind. But none of that compared to what was happening inside of me.

"Ladies and gentlemen, this has been a night of firsts here on *The One*!" Bryce exclaimed.

*Holy shit. Holy shit.*

I looked around to verify that it was actually happening. Everyone on stage with us seemed shocked, yet happy, with the exception of Tori whose arms were folded across her chest. I looked around at the audience on their feet and I squinted due to the glare of the lights. I took my free hand and wiped my eyes before I let my gaze meet his again.

Withdrawing a ring box out of his pocket, he popped it open and I gasped. He pulled out a ring with square cut diamonds encircling the small platinum band and placed the box on the carpeted stage. The ring was stunning.

I was speechless, not that I could be heard over the ear-piercing noise in the room anyway.

"Dude!" Bryce uttered in shock before he seemed to remember where he was and what he was doing. "Alright, alright! Ladies and gentleman, this is live folks! Please quiet down so we don't miss what's coming next!"

Even though everyone had quieted, an excited murmur traveled through the room as they waited for what Julian was going to say next.

Staring up at me from his kneeled position, Julian made my heart skip a beat. The love and adoration he felt for me was so apparent with just that look that another tear slipped from the corner of my eye. I swiped at it.

*God, I love him.*

I was so caught up in my emotions that I almost considered accepting a marriage proposal. Almost.

"Zoe," he whispered my name as he ran his thumb across my knuckles. "This ring represents a promise to you that I will never again make you feel like you're one of many when you are my one and only."

Holding my right hand steady, Julian slipped the ring on my finger. "So Zoe Jordan, will you...go on a real date with me?"

I stifled a laugh. "Absolutely."

He bit down on his bottom lip to keep from laughing. "This is not an engagement ring."

The diamonds on my right ring finger sparkled under the stage lighting. "Yes, I gathered that," I giggled.

"This ring is a proposal for a date."

The gleam in his eyes made me smile harder. "Just a date? Just one?"

"Woah, woah, woah, slow down...I'm not trying to rush into anything," he joked. "Once we get to one full month of knowing each other, I'll see about a second date. If that goes well, I was thinking we could go on a date every day for the rest of my life."

I threw my head back and laughed, pulling him to his feet. "I knew an engagement was the end game for you!"

Laughing, Julian's lips found mine sweetly as he wrapped

his arms around me, lifting me off of my feet. The kiss was short, but the effects were longer lasting.

"Ladies and gentleman, put your hands together for the newly...committed couple," Bryce announced with an uncertain laugh as he tried to explain what had just happened. He shrugged and turned his attention to the audience. "Those of you at home and in our studio audience, thank you for being here. Ladies, thank you for being here. We had a wild ride this season. So many twists and turns to bring us to this point. And after four weeks and out of thousands of women, Julian has made his decision. And Zoe Jordan, you are..."

"The One!" The crowd called back in unison, clapping and screaming.

# Chapter 21

After yelling 'cut,' a producer dispersed the crowd while another told all of us that our party bus would be leaving in thirty minutes. Most of the women on stage hugged both Julian and I before departing. Tori stormed off set, rolling her eyes and muttering under her breath without acknowledging us at all. Mya admitted to being a little jealous, but she said that it would pass and that she would call me in a few days. Nicole and Emma congratulated both of us and told Julian that he made the right choice. The rest politely said goodbye and left.

Hand-in-hand, Julian and I made our way off of the soundstage, thanking people as they passed on well wishes to us and our future. Stopping every few feet made the trip to the Green Room that much longer. Only Ana remained when we walked in.

"You better hurry," Ana warned, stuffing her makeup into a bag. "The bus is leaving in less than five minutes!"

"She's coming with me," Julian replied, slipping his hand

out of mine in order to put his arm around my shoulders. "I'm not letting her out of my sight." He kissed the top of my head.

I couldn't see my face, but my cheeks hurt from how hard I was smiling.

Ana rolled her eyes as she walked by us, heading toward the door. She turned, looking around the room once more. "Okay, looks like I have everything." She met our eyes and gave us a small smile. "Zoe, thanks for the advice. I think it went well. Julian, if you get tired of her, you know how to find me."

My eyes narrowed. "Ana!"

She gave me a wink. "Just putting it out there. See you guys around."

She walked out, closing the door behind her.

"I can't believe she just said that." I looked up at him and he was gazing down at me. I melted. "You can't keep looking at me like that."

"I can and I will." Julian turned me so that my body was flush against his. He ran his hands down my fully exposed back sending chills down my spine.

I pushed away from him gradually. "Well I need to talk to you and you know you make me swoon when you look at me like that."

He gave me a smoldering look, licking his lips excessively. "You mean like this."

My eyebrows came together and I frowned. I backed away from him dramatically. "Don't do that again."

He started laughing. Reaching out to grab me, he pulled me into him and kissed me. "Is this better?"

"I don't know. I think I need another."

He put his hands around my neck, using his thumbs to keep my head in place. His eyes bore into mine as his nose just barely touched mine. His lips were a mere inch away and

I could feel his minty breath tickling my skin.

"Thank you," he uttered softly.

"For what?" I sighed, getting lost in his eyes.

"For taking the risk," he whispered against my lips.

Capturing my mouth with his, Julian kissed me with a tenderness that caused me to feel faint. I gripped the front of his tuxedo as he took his time exploring my mouth with his own. The kiss was tender and worshipful. He deepened the kiss, causing me to moan lightly into his mouth.

I let go of his tux and moved my hands up until they were mussing his hair.

The sound of a man clearing his throat caused us to startle away from one another, ending the kiss abruptly. Our arms were still around each other as we shifted our bodies to see who had interrupted us.

Robert Brady closed the door behind him and looked between us. "Julian Winters and Zoe Jordan." He laughed, but it sounded off. "Well, I did not see that coming."

"Listen, Robert... I know you wanted it to be Leah, but—"

The older man lifted his hand and interrupted. "Yes, I did. I was very clear with you." He slowly started crossing the room. "The polls showed Leah being the crowd favorite, but Bailey kept inching on her. Leah was the mean one that was pretty enough to get away with it. Bailey was the dumb one that was pretty enough to get away with it. Both had such compelling storylines over the course of the show. But when Zoe left..."

Robert stopped in his tracks and shifted his gaze to me. He lifted his arms in the air. "When you left, the way you left...it was a ratings dream. You two had such chemistry and then— poof!—you up and leave. It had drama! It had suspense! It had romance! The final interview when you both were on the brink of tears and..." He scratched his head. "The ratings poured in."

"What's this about?" Julian asked, clearly annoyed.

"This is about me needing to know the direction that my own show is taking." He put his hands on his hips. "I worked around your demands. Viewers like sex. Sex sells. But you told me you weren't having sex with anyone so I let creative editing and angles tell the story. You barely wanted to kiss anyone, but when you had to sell it, you sold it."

"Robert, I've fulfilled my contract. I fully participated in the show. I kissed and dated the women you wanted me to be with and then when it was time for me to choose, I chose the woman I wanted to be with. I wasn't in breach of anything. I've had my lawyers go over the paperwork several times to ensure that when I came for my girl, there was nothing you could do about it," Julian replied evenly.

I looked up at him and I was almost positive my eyes bulged out of my skull in the shape of hearts. Since I was a child, my mother always told me that it is disrespectful to call a woman 'girl' unless you are being informal with friends. So being called 'girl' never failed to get under my skin. But hearing Julian call me his girl made my heart flutter.

When Julian's jaw clenched, I looked back at Robert who stared at Julian hard. He nodded slowly, licking his teeth. His face was pinched and he seemed to be holding something back. "You are very lucky that this turned out so well, ratings wise." He grimaced as he backed away. "I'll leave you lovebirds to it."

*He seems happy that the ratings were good, but mad because it wasn't a storyline he created.*

Robert was almost out of the door when he turned to look at us with a smirk. "Julian, you may want to take a look at your contract again. If you find love on the show, we still own the rights to the relationship for two years." He let out a hollow laugh. "I'll be in touch."

The door closed behind him and my eyebrows flew up. "He's an ass."

Julian gritted his teeth and let out a harsh breath. His eyes were focused on the closed door.

I turned into him and placed my hands on his face. "Hey." I tilted my head to the side. "That only applies if we were to get married. We are a newly not engaged couple. We don't have to worry about that."

"I know." His eyes met mine and he sighed. The tension rolled from his body as my fingertips skated over his jawline, down his neck, and across his chest. "It just pisses me off that he thinks he can control me. I haven't had a boss for a long time and I don't deal well with him trying to tell me what to do."

I smiled up at him. "I think he's just mad because you didn't do what he said and things turned out even better than he anticipated."

He raked his bottom lip between his teeth, analyzing my face. "How are you so calm about this? You hated being on this show."

"As long as we don't get married in two years, there's nothing to worry about."

He kissed my forehead. "My lawyers and I are still going to have a little talk with him."

"Are you going to try to renegotiate parts of your contract? Because you might not have to since he didn't do his due diligence by making sure I was contractually obligated to do anything outside of the show."

Julian's eyebrows came together in confusion. "What do you mean?"

"The paperwork I signed when I left the show only stipulated I had to appear on this reunion. I'm not required to do anything else."

Seeming to understanding, a slow smile crept onto his face.

I lifted up onto my toes, pressing my lips against his smiling mouth. "So when I tell you not to worry about it, don't worry about it."

He ran one of his hands down my spine. "Is that right?"

"Yes." I put my head on his chest, directly over his heart. Feeling the strong thumps comforted me and I wrapped my arms around him. "I missed you."

"I missed you, too. I meant it when I said I thought about you all the time. I even tried to get your phone number."

"We weren't allowed to have phones or computers...or a way out."

A chuckle rumbled from deep in his chest. "Did you have a TV?"

I pulled my head up so I could look at him. "Yeah," I said slowly. "And as much as I didn't want to, I watched the dates." I paused, waiting for him to fill in the blanks so I didn't have to ask.

He didn't.

"You and Leah looked pretty close," I started, pausing again.

"None of that was real."

"But those kisses were and the chemistry or whatever you had with her was apparent. There was something there. I just want to know..."

*What did I want to know? He chose me. He picked me.*

If I was honest with myself, I would've admitted that I worried that Julian would just change his mind arbitrarily. It wasn't that I didn't trust him. It wasn't even that I thought Julian was anything like Tate. But to have someone who claimed to love me so much that they wanted to marry me turn around and throw it all away because of the possibility of new ass messed with my mind. It occurred to me that I just wanted assurance; even though I knew nothing was ever guaranteed. Matters of the heart were risky.

"Come here." Julian took my hand into his and tugged me behind him as he went to the loveseat. Sitting down, he brought me down with him, into his lap. "I'll tell you anything you want to know. I don't want any of this between us."

I swallowed hard as one of his hands tickled my bare back. "When you kissed her, it looked like you were into it."

"It was easy to fake it with Leah because she reminded me a lot of Lillian. So my mind went into autopilot with her. It was hard to fake it with the other women because there was no automatic recall for me to try to attach it to, no person in my past for me try to fake a feeling with. I could go through the motions with Leah. But everyone else just reminded me of the show...and the show just reminded me of you...and thinking of you made it impossible for me to try with anyone else."

"And you didn't have sex with her or Bailey?"

"Not at all. The farthest it's ever gone was kissing. What you saw on camera was all there was to it. I just did what I needed to do in order to get the shots they wanted." Julian's eyes explored mine.

"I bet they tried."

"Leah, yes. Bailey and I had an agreement of sorts. She didn't try anything. She wasn't interested."

I smiled. *Thank you Bailey.*

"But it didn't matter what anyone else did or said. I didn't want to be with anyone, but you. I still don't want to be with anyone, but you." His fingers flexed on the outside of my thigh. "And it's not just because sex with you is insane or because you did that thing with your tongue."

336

My head fell to the side as I let out a short, unexpected giggle.

He watched me laugh with a smile as his fingers traced circles into the skin of my thigh. His gaze dropped, watching in apparent amazement that the pads of his fingertips created goosebumps in their wake.

*He has no idea how he affects me.*

As silence surrounded us, he appeared to be lost in thought. I kissed his temple.

He turned his head so that our foreheads touched and I was immediately drawn into his gaze. "Before I met you, I didn't know what I was looking for exactly. I knew I wanted someone I could be myself with, someone I could be better than myself with. And when I told my dad about coming on the show, he told me to just enjoy myself and don't worry too much about it because the moment I know I'm with the right one, everything changes."

His hand relocated to the back of my neck, bringing my lips closer to his as he continued. "I don't want anyone else because just being with you, in your presence, makes me a better man. I was mad that you left because I didn't want to be away from you, but just thinking about having to watch you kiss other men pissed me off, so I get it. But I want you to know that there was never any chance of anything happening with anyone after we met. Everything changed when I met you."

My belly quivered as something in his assurances resonated with me deeply. I believed him. I believed him in a way that was so absolute that I knew that I was all in.

Staring into his eyes, my heart had never felt so full. I took one shaky breath after another as I tried to slow the flood of emotions I felt. "I love you."

"I love you, too."

Pressing his lips against mine, Julian kissed me softly. His mouth moved over mine gently, luring me in before his tongue parted my lips and he kissed me possessively.

My body reacted to the sharp contrast of soft and hard, sweet and sexy, love and lust. I moaned into his kiss and twisted my fingers in his hair. The kiss ended in a series of lingering pecks.

"I want to take you home," Julian whispered between kisses.

"Let's go."

We had just stood up and were intertwining our fingers when the door opened and shut, pulling our attention away from one another. In a flurry of hair and limbs, we saw a man carrying a woman as they aggressively clawed at each other's clothes. The woman's ass was completely exposed to us.

"Well, this is awkward," I commented, slightly amused.

Koko and Bryce froze. She unwrapped her legs from around his waist and adjusted her dress before turning around.

"Bryce was...helping me find my makeup brushes," Koko offered in her hilarious way.

I bit my lip to keep from laughing. "Did you lose them at the same time you lost your panties?"

She made her way toward me, leaving Bryce looking shocked and embarrassed at the door. "Touché. From the way Julian's hair looks, I'd say you have no room to talk," Koko replied with a smirk.

I looked over at Julian who immediately started fixing his hair. I moved to meet her halfway. "I won't confirm or deny anything."

When we met in the middle, only three or four seconds were able to tick by before we both burst out laughing. I wrapped my arms around my best friend and she squeezed me tightly.

"You look happy," she remarked, touching my face.

"So do you," I returned.

"I'm glad you got your happy ending."

"I'm sorry we interrupted yours."

We both snickered.

"Okay, what's going on here?" Julian questioned, looking around suspiciously.

"Do you two know each other outside of the show?" Bryce asked, looking just as confused.

"Well..." Koko and I said in unison.

# Epilogue

"What's wrong?" Julian asked as I unlocked the front door of my apartment.

Tucking the stack of mail under my arm, I held the door open for him as he carried our bags inside. "Nothing. I'm just exhausted. That was exhausting."

Dropping the bags in the middle of the walkway that separated the kitchen from the living room, he turned around and smiled. "Yes, it was. It's been a long week. But we survived."

"Woo hoo!" I cheered playfully as I made my way into his open arms. "First big holiday as a couple."

"And the first time our families were able to all come together," Julian added, kissing the top of my head.

We spent Thanksgiving in Maryland because Julian's mom's mom, Grandma Pearl, couldn't travel due to a hip replacement. In order to really up the ante and test our relationship, Julian's parents flew with us to Virginia where we met my parents, my brother and his girlfriend and then drove to Grandma Pearl's Chesapeake Bay home for a big family dinner. Although I'd met his immediate family soon after the finale wrapped and he'd met mine a couple months after that, our families hadn't had the opportunity to all meet each other until Thanksgiving.

Even though Thanksgiving was traditionally known as the holiday where family came together to fight, our families got along really well.

*A little too well.*

Grandma Pearl did not have a filter, so she kept things interesting. The widowed hostess broke the ice and before the first course was served, everyone was getting along marvelously. Somewhere during the second course though the tide had turned and by the third course our families had decided to make us the butt of every joke. Allegedly it was all light-hearted fun, but by the time we left, a wedding date was set and countdown to Baby Jordan-Winters had started— both without our consent or encouragement.

"It went well. I think they all had a little more fun than we did. But it went well and Thanksgiving is officially over," I murmured, lifting my head off of his chest and smiling up at him.

He kissed my lips softly, sending a chill down my spine and lighting a fire everywhere else. "And we are no longer surrounded by family." He flicked my top lip with his tongue and then smirked.

"And we are finally all alone." I pushed his leather jacket off of his shoulders and it fell down his arms.

He pulled at my hair tie, letting the mass of curls fall wild and loose around my shoulders. "Let's get out of these clothes..." His fingertips massaged into my scalp and my head fell into his skillful motion. With my neck exposed, he trailed kisses from my collarbone to my ear. Biting down gently on my earlobe, he whispered, "And I can run you a bath..."

I moaned, twisting so our lips would meet again. I moved my body against his in a way that I'd wanted to all day.

"I can massage your exhaustion away," he groaned between kisses. His hands palmed my ass, pulling me into his growing erection.

Easing out of the kiss with a breathless giggle, I gazed up at him. "We may need to change the bath to a shower so we can take care of this," I breathed, running my hand between us, against the front of his pants. "I haven't seen him all day and he's been on my mind."

Julian's eyes were closed as he groaned, pressing his forehead against mine. I watched the way he raked his bottom lip between his teeth in response to my touch. My fingers flexed against his girth and I let my fingernails scrape against the material of his jeans. He sucked in a sharp breath and my heart raced.

"Zoe..." His voice was low, needy. "The things you do to me."

"Julian, I feel the exact same way."

He opened his eyes and when they locked with mine, it was as if all the air in the room had been sucked out. My stomach swirled and fluttered. The mail under my left arm slipped a little as my body relaxed.

"I love you."

"And I love you."

We kissed sweetly, the desire taking a backseat to the genuine love and affection that we felt for one another. With his recording schedule and my study schedule, our relationship wasn't always easy, but it was always worth it. Even if our schedules weren't, our love was the one thing that was consistent over the last nine months.

"I'll go put the bags away and get the water started." Julian dropped one more kiss against my lips before walking over to our luggage.

"I'm right behind you."

I pulled the mail from under my arm and thumbed through it out of habit. I was about to drop everything onto the coffee table so I could reconvene with my boyfriend in the shower when one of the last letters in the stack caught my eye.

"Julian!" I screamed before I realized words had left my mouth.

He was by my side in seconds as I stood surrounded in a sea of white and tan envelopes at my feet.

My hands shook slightly as I tried to get the one remaining envelope open.

"It's okay," Julian whispered gently, taking it out of my hand. He slid his finger under the flap and opened it seamlessly. "Here you go."

I looked at the envelope in his hand and then I looked back into those gorgeous, grey eyes. "I want you to read it to me."

*Good news or bad, he'll make it okay. And if it's bad news, he'll help me figure out how to fake my death so my parents will never find out.*

I smiled at my own joke and without any clue as to what I was thinking, Julian smiled right back at me as if he heard everything word for word and thought it was funny.

I fell more in love with him in that moment. It just highlighted how much peace Julian Winters brought to me and my life.

"Ready?" He asked as he pulled the tri-folded letter out.

I nodded with my eyes closed, gripping the front of his shirt.

"Congrat—"

Pushing myself up onto my toes, I crashed my lips against his.

He dropped the letter and cradled my head in his hands, his fingers tangling in my hair. I didn't resist as his lips moved over mine powerfully, emotively. I may have initiated the kiss, but he took complete control of it. If I kissed him in excitement and celebration, he kissed me back with pride and adoration. I felt simultaneously like the winner and the prize.

He pulled out of the kiss slowly, still hovering millimeters away. "I'm so proud of you," he whispered, our lips meeting again. "I love you." Another kiss. "Go call your mom."

I smiled dreamily as the butterflies danced in my belly. *This is perfection.*

With all of our flaws and annoying habits, through the arguments, the time apart, the stress, Julian and I together were perfection. I never knew perfection before him because I didn't know him.

"I love you. Thank you for believing in me."

He kissed me again before letting my face go and slapping me on my ass. "Now make the call."

I laughed as I scrambled to dig my phone out of my bag. I scrolled to my parents' number quickly.

After the first ring, I grew even more excited. "Pick up, pick up, pick up," I mumbled as I paced across the room. Out of the corner of my eye, I saw Julian picking up all of the mail scattered on the floor and pretending not to be watching my every move.

After the second ring, I grew anxious. *What if I have to wait to tell them the news? Ugh. That would suck.*

After the third ring, I grew disappointed. *Oh no! I really might have to wait to tell them the news! And I don't want to call one and the other not be available because then that one would feel slighted. They both—*

"Hello?" My mom's voice, slightly breathless, cut through my rambling thoughts.

"Mom!" I shouted as I stopped in my tracks. "Oh my God!"

"Zoe! Zoe, what is it? Are you okay? Did you and Julian make it back okay? Did something happen?"

Elise Jordan was ready to handle things at the first sign of trouble and I loved it.

Laughing, I apologized. "No, I'm sorry to scare you. I just didn't think you and Dad were home so when you answered, I got excited because I really want to tell you both something at the same time."

"Oh no, we're just on the deck. Your father is cooking on the grill because it's a beautiful seventy degrees today. The final few days of November and it's like summertime."

"Virginia weather," I replied with a shake of the head. "I don't miss that."

"One second, sweetheart. Zachary! Pick up the phone! The ribs will be fine." She laughed. "If they are overcooked in the time it takes you to pick up the cordless phone in the kitchen then they would've been overcooked anyway." She laughed again. "No and why would the lottery call you since you don't play? It's your daughter."

"You should've just said it was Zoe to begin with, Elise," Dad joked playfully in the background.

Just hearing their back and forth made my heart smile. I looked over at Julian and his eyes were fixated on me. Seated on the couch, he smiled as he tapped his pen against our notebook. Julian and I each had individual poetry notebooks, but we also had one that we shared. We'd write poetry to each other back and forth and pass the notebook every time we were leaving each other for more than twenty-four hours. Seeing our notebook made me a little sad because that reminded me of his upcoming trip to New York.

*I miss him already.*

"Zoe, you have us both and you have our undivided

attention," my dad's booming voice announced, interrupting my thoughts.

"Well, I just wanted you two to know that I officially passed the California State Bar Examination!"

"Congratulations!" My parents yelled in unison.

After fifteen minutes of rereading the entire letter to them twice and then going over how the test felt to me before, during, and after taking it, they were ready to let me off of the phone. My father hung up first after telling me how much he loved me and how proud he was of me. My mother waited until after Dad had hung up to say the same and then to add that she knew that I had nothing to worry about.

"I was scared that I wouldn't pass and I wouldn't live up to you and your legacy," I admitted, no longer feeling the weight of that burden on me.

"Zoe," Mom sighed. "The world doesn't need another Elise Jordan, Esquire. The world needs a Zoe Jordan, Esquire. Better yet, a Zoe Jordan-Winters, Esquire." She giggled as I stifled mine, trying not to feed into the lunacy. "I made you an original, sweetheart, not a copy of me. Now go out there and show the world who Zoe Jordan is."

My eyes watered as I thanked her. After an exchange of I love yous, I put the phone to my chest and blinked back tears.

I spent the months leading up to the February bar exam panicked because I thought I would fail at being Elise Jordan, who was the most amazing woman and lawyer ever. I allowed that pressure to cause me to freak out at the thought of not passing the bar and how that would reflect on my entire future and the life I planned for myself, the life my parents worked so hard to support. I allowed myself to freak out at the thought of passing the bar and still not measuring up to the woman or the lawyer that I called mom. More than that, I convinced myself that the disappointment and embarrassment my parents would feel when they realized that the straight-A, overachieving child they raised couldn't hack it as a woman in the real world. I allowed myself to react based off of scenarios my mind created that weren't even probable, seeing as how my parents never made me feel bad about anything I've attempted to achieve.

But that momentary lapse in judgement, that irrational freak out moment, that completely out of character quarter-life crisis, led to the best year of my life. My meltdown started a series of events that changed my life for the better in ways I didn't even know were possible.

I looked up at Julian as he made his way over to me.

"Everything okay?" He inquired, lifting his eyebrows.

"Everything is perfect."

# Julian's Journal Entry

### I Want To, a poem
((a poetic collaboration by Brittainy C. Cherry & Danielle Allen))

I want to make love to your soul.
All at once, I want in.
To start from your bottom lip and ease down to your neck,
To feel you curve your spine against my fingertips.
I
Want
You
To
release your fears through your hips.
I
Want
You
To
find forever against my lips.
Then I pause, and remember the truth:
You're missing me, just as I'm missing you.
But tonight
I
Want
You
To
release the doubt that distance creates
I
Want
You
To
find me in my dreams before we wake

to see that no miles, no time, no conscious state
can prevent our love from finding a way.

# Zoe's Journal Entry

Your love, my love

Your love...
It doesn't just set it.
It eases in slowly.
It slips through the cracks.
It burrows in deep.
It doesn't just set it.
It races in quickly.
It bursts through the cracks.
It scorches everything in its wake.
It doesn't just set it.
It burns.
It aches.
It hurts.
It infiltrates.
It overwhelms.
It doesn't just set in.
It takes over.
It takes over.
It takes...
Over.

# Unaired Finale Footage

Leah stood in the vineyard, her pink gown popping against the lush green bushes and land surrounding her. The sunlight made the honey undertone of her skin glow. Her wavy light brown hair was perfectly positioned over her shoulder as she gazed at the limo that pulled up almost ten minutes prior. Her nervousness was evident even though she seemed to be doing everything in her power to play it cool.

Leah looked directly at the camera and flashed a smile. Her eyes shifted slightly to the left and through clenched teeth, she asked, "What's happening? What's taking so long?"

"It's probably a long commercial break or maybe they cut to the women in the studio. Just be patient and smile," a man's voice could be heard off camera instructing her.

The camera zoomed in, highlighting the tension in her face.

"Would you like a glass of wine?" The same man's voice could be heard as he offered her a beverage.

Leah nodded and her hand shook slightly as she touched her hair. "Yes. Thank you. Your best white. Riesling." She fidgeted and her eyes darted in the direction of the limo again. "And not from California. It's too sweet and doesn't have enough acidity for balance."

Moments later, a woman with a clipboard and a headset rushed the glass to Leah.

"Thank you," she said, taking the stem of the glass between

shaky fingers. She sipped. "No, no." Pouring out her wine into the grass, she turned and looked at someone off camera. "This is too sweet. Way too sweet. Is this Moscato? Because I asked for Riesling. Do you even know the difference? I would think being at a winery you'd be able to get that simple task right."

"We're still rolling, Leah," the man reminded her as she handed the empty glass off.

Turning to face the camera, Leah's perfectly poised smile returned. She held her pose for only sixty seconds before it broke with relief and exuberance.

The front door of the limo opened and the driver stepped out. Wearing all black, he adjusted his hat and then made a show of walking over to Leah. Holding out his arm, he greeted her.

"Hello Leah. I'm Benny."

She beamed at him as she squealed, "Hi Benny!"

"Mr. Winters asked me to escort you to the limo. Is that alright with you, young lady?"

"It most certainly is!" She looked at the camera and winked. "I knew it."

Hooking her arm with the older man, the camera caught the shift in her demeanor from anxious to confident as she strutted across the vineyard. Leah allowed herself to be escorted to the back door of the limo.

"Wait, wait, wait," she hissed as Benny reached for the door handle. "How do I look?"

"Beautiful, young lady," he answered kindly.

"Obviously. But do I look worried? I want him to know that I was calm."

Benny didn't answer as he opened the door.

Leah peeked in and then stood up straight, looking around in confusion. "It's empty? Where is he?"

"Mr. Winters wanted you to know that he appreciated you

being on the show. You will be chauffeured back to the mansion with a token of Mr. Winters' appreciation and his warm regards." Benny pointed and the camera zoomed in on a basket of imported wines and cheeses that sat in the backseat.

Leah's face started turning a deep shade of crimson. "What?"

Benny took a couple of steps back. "Mr. Winters wanted—"

Leah looked at the camera and then beyond it. "Did you all know about this? You let me stand here like an idiot and get stood up. I am beautiful, cultured, worldly, and far more intelligent than any of the other women in the house. And he chose that imbecile over me! Over me?!"

She let out a scream that caused a few crew members to come into the frame to try to calm her down.

"Don't touch me!" She snapped angrily, ripping her arm out of a woman's grasp. "I want to get my shit and meet my family in Paris. I missed a gala at The Louvre to be runner up to someone who can't even spell Louvre."

Leah got into the limo and slammed the door shut.

One of the producers opened the door. "Leah, we need to debrief with you—"

"I'm not doing any interviews!" She interrupted, glaring at them and the camera. "I have nothing else to say. I could be a lot of things, but Julian wanted a dumb bitch and that's just something I'm not."

"Bailey isn't who he chose," someone off screen offered, causing the two producers on screen to shoot daggers from their eyes.

They glared for a solid ten seconds before turning back toward Leah.

"What? If you tell me he went back for that low budget bartender..."

Although the producers' backs were to the camera, the way they looked at her must have confirmed what she was asking.

"I'm done." Pulling the door shut with force, the producers jumped back.

One of them walked out of the camera range with his cell phone in hand.

Benny looked perplexed as he slowly made his way to the front of the vehicle and climbed in.

The last shot of the vineyard showed the limo pulling away as the gift basket was heaved out of the window. Before the screen went black, a low whistle could be heard in the background. "Wow."

Bailey walked down the pier with her blue gown blowing in the wind and her sleek bun pinned in place on the top of her head as she listened to the limo driver explain Julian's absence. The ocean provided her sun-kissed skin and bright blue eyes with the perfect backdrop. Although she was from the Mid-West, Bailey looked like the quintessential California girl.

"So, Peter, you're telling me that Julian went to the studio to get Zoe," Bailey inquired as the driver paused at the back door of the limo.

"Yes, but Mr. Winters sends his regards and his appreciation for you appearing on the show. He asked me to give this to you." Opening the door, Peter gestured inside. "He said that he hopes that your turn in the hot seat proves to be as successful as his."

The camera only caught a glimpse of what was in the limo before Bailey jumped into the old man's arms, hugging him tightly. "Peter! What else did he say?"

Letting out a jolly giggle, Peter said, "There should be a note under the flowers and balloons."

Scrambling into the limo, the camera zoomed in on Bailey as she read the note. She put the small square piece of paper to her chest and let her head fall back onto the leather seats.

"What does the note say Bailey?" A woman inquired from just outside the limo door.

Bailey flashed her million dollar smile and batted her big blue eyes. She held up the note as she read. "Bailey. Congratulations on your new show. You are a force to be reckoned with and your talent knows no bounds. Thanks for the advice. Let me know if you need an ally. I owe you one. We will be in touch." She laughed to herself before looking back up at the camera.

"What advice did you give him?"

"I told him to follow his heart."

"That obviously didn't work out well for you though."

Bailey shrugged. "Who wants a man who's in love with someone else when I can have twelve men all in love with me?"

A giggle was heard off screen. "Good point. Well you seem pleased with the parting gifts. Is there anything you'd like to say to Julian?"

Bailey looked directly into the camera. "Hi Julian!" She waved. "Congratulations! Thanks for everything. Looks like we all win."

"And what about Zoe?" The producer pressed. "Is there anything you'd like to say to Zoe?"

"Congratulations Zoe! I'm happy for you. Never forget that even when you don't see all of the parts, always trust the alliance. Three's a crowd unless everyone wins." She winked.

"I don't think I understand."

Bailey's smile split her face as she grinned at the camera like she had a secret no one knew but her.

"Okay..." She said slowly as if she didn't take Bailey seriously.

After a couple more questions, Bailey was waved off with fanfare as the on location production members clapped. The limo pulled off slowly and before it turned the corner, Bailey popped out of the sunroof.

"Now it's my turn! I'm ready to find 'The One'!"

The camera zoomed in on the limo as it faded away and then a long shot of the pier and the waves crashing against it. A female voice could be heard as the screen started to go dark. "Who told her to improvise that? Was that you? Tom? Sarah? Did she just do that on her own? Bailey is going to be a star. I can feel it."

The screen went black and the title card appeared in scrawling hot pink. *The One.*

# The One Playlist

Music inspires me. The artists mentioned below wrote songs and lyrics that I feel accurately depict the thoughts, feelings, and mood of Zoe and Julian as they navigated falling in love in a crazy environment in such a short amount of time. If you haven't had a chance to listen to any of these songs, do yourself a favor: purchase each song immediately and listen to them in order, on repeat.

| | |
|---|---|
| Fink | Clare Bowen & Sam Palladio |
| Foot In The Door | I Will Fall |
| | |
| Hoozier | Maroon 5 |
| Like Real People Do | Sweetest Goodbye |
| | |
| Tori Kelly ft Ed Sheeran | Drake |
| I Was Made For Loving You | Jungle |
| | |
| Tweet | Sza ft Kendrick Lamar |
| Addicted | Babylon |
| | |
| Outkast | Justin Timberlake |
| Prototype | Blue Ocean Floor |
| | |
| Busta Rhymes ft Janet Jackson | James Bay |
| What's It Gonna Be? | Need The Sun To Break |
| | |
| FKA twigs | Tink |
| Papi Pacify | Million |

# Danielle Allen

Work Song

Heartache (Heartache #1)

Heartfelt (Heartache #2)

Love Discovered In New York

Autumn and Summer

Back to Life (Back to Life #1)

Back to Reality (Back to Life #2)

# Acknowledgements

I am so incredibly blessed to have my family and friends surrounding me and supporting me through this writing journey. In two and a half years, I've written eight novels and I am so incredibly proud of the hard work that went into that. But I know that I wouldn't have been able to do that without the people I've had in my corner.

I wrote The One during the tail end of the most difficult time in my life. I used the story and the characters to bring me through a number of challenging situations and I am forever grateful for being able to lose myself in The One, in Zoe Jordan, in Julian Winters. I gave this story everything I had left because I had to and the end result was more than I could've bargained for. I love this story with everything in me because it brought me out of the darkness.

When things were falling apart, I had my family and friends to support me and I am blessed to have those people in my life. I love you all to the moon and back.

Kumiko—thank you for letting me steal your name and use it for Zoe's best friend. I appreciate your help, your feedback and your support. You are amazingly supportive and I appreciate you.

Summer, Olivia, Kendall—your friendship, your insight and your generosity has meant more to me than anything. Thank you.

Michelle and Mia—your friendship and your encouragement has been a source of inspiration and I thank you.

Brittainy—you are truly my soul sister and my kindred spirit. Thank you for your friendship and I can't wait for our island!

Script Easer Editing and Shawna Gavas—thank you for the awesome job making The One as error free as possible.

CP Smith—thank you for being you and for using your formatting magic on my finished product.

To everyone who has been there for me, thank you. Authors, bloggers, readers, your support means so much to me. I am honored to have so many people who have read my work. It's truly mind blowing to know that I have touched people with my words. From the bottom of my heart, thank you. I can't begin to explain how much it means to me to be able to write and publish my novels and to have you take the time to read them.

30287244R00203